PRAISE FOR WEINA DAI RANDEL

Night Angels

"*Schindler's List* takes an Eastern twist in *Night Angels*, the incredible true story of the Chinese diplomat who saved thousands of Jews in WWII Vienna. Quiet, scholarly Ho Fengshan has just been made consul general in Vienna, preoccupied with his troubled American wife, Grace, and disquieted by the new anti-Semitic laws sweeping Austria. Grace's friendship with Jewish musician Lola forces both Fengshan and his wife to the breaking point: How much can one sacrifice to save innocent lives? Weina Dai Randel pens an unforgettable tale of quiet heroism and blazing defiance in the face of evil."

—Kate Quinn, *New York Times* bestselling author of
The Diamond Eye

"Weina Dai Randel once again takes readers into a chapter of history we know too little about. *Night Angels* is a fascinating look at the bravery and foresight of real-life Chinese diplomat Dr. Ho Fengshan, who was stationed in Vienna in the years just before World War II began, as Hitler was already beginning to deport Jews from Germany and Austria . . . An illuminating look at a little-known, inspiring piece of history we should never forget."

—Kristin Harmel, *New York Times* bestselling author of
The Forest of Vanishing Stars

"Weina Dai Randel's *Night Angels* is a gorgeous WWII historical tale of daring diplomatic pursuits that had me turning the pages way past my bedtime. Based on the true heroic story of Dr. Ho Fengshan, Randel's prose is rich and powerfully layered. By day, Fengshan is a warrior for his country and a fighter for humanity while secretly issuing thousands of visas to Jews to Shanghai to escape Nazi persecution. It is a sweeping novel filled with love, loss, high stakes, sacrifice, and redemption that will break your heart and fuel your soul."

—Lisa Barr, *New York Times* bestselling author of *Woman on Fire*

The Last Rose of Shanghai

"Fans of sweeping, dramatic WWII epics that are rich in historical detail, such as Lisa See's *Shanghai Girls* or Paullina Simons's *The Bronze Horseman*, will be enthralled."

—*Booklist*

"Weina Dai Randel's novel deserves a place of distinction among WWII fiction."

—Historical Novel Society

"Weina Dai Randel skillfully shines a light on a little-known moment in history through the lens of two vividly drawn characters whose unique and unexpected relationship is one readers will never forget."

—Pam Jenoff, *New York Times* bestselling author of *The Woman with the Blue Star*

"Set in Japanese-occupied Shanghai, this is an unforgettable, page-turning tale of an impossible affair between lovers from two cultures."

—Janie Chang, bestselling author of *Dragon Springs Road* and *The Library of Legends*

"Weina Dai Randel's poignant, sweeping love story paints a vibrant portrait of a little-known slice of World War II history. Not to be missed!"

—Kate Quinn, *New York Times* bestselling author of *The Rose Code* and *The Huntress*

"*The Last Rose of Shanghai* is a must-read for historical fiction lovers. Filled with page-turning suspense and a poignant and unforgettable love story, Weina Dai Randel wholly immerses the reader in this richly detailed and powerfully drawn story."

—Chanel Cleeton, *New York Times* and *USA Today* bestselling author

"Set against a panorama so vivid you can almost hear the jazz in Aiyi Shao's nightclub, Weina Dai Randel brings to life fascinating WWII history new to me and, I imagine, countless other readers."

—Sally Koslow, author of *Another Side of Paradise*

"*The Last Rose of Shanghai* is a riveting story of love, heartbreak, and redemption. Weina Dai Randel is a skilled artist, giving the reader well-drawn characters of great depth, complexity, and heart. In the WWII genre, within the genre of historical fiction, *The Last Rose of Shanghai* stands out for its boldness and originality."

—Erika Robuck, bestselling author of *The Invisible Woman*

The Moon in the Palace

"This eloquent first novel follows the life of a young girl during China's Tang dynasty (618–907). . . . This story of a woman who made her own destiny and has been often vilified is a must for historical fiction fans, especially those fascinated by China's glorious past."

—*Library Journal* (starred review)

"Like fragile yet strong silk threads, Randel's beautifully composed debut ensnares readers in the dynamic story of the young girl who would become Empress of Bright Moon."

—RT Book Reviews (Top Pick, 4½ stars)

"The intrigue and machinations of the imperial court come to life under her hand, a vast and dangerous engine with each piece moving for its own reasons."

—*Shelf Awareness* (starred review)

"A very successful and transporting novel that beautifully captures the sounds, smells, and social mores of seventh-century China."

—*Historical Novels Review* (Editor's Choice)

"Mei gives life to this richly detailed novel. She is adventuresome, intelligent, hardworking, and a risk taker."

—*The Dallas Morning News*

"The real triumph of *The Moon in the Palace* is how Randel succeeds in showing court politics exclusively through female eyes, and how every decision and subsequent action, success, and failure are skillfully plotted like a chess match by the palace women . . . Magical."

—Washington Independent Book Review of Books

"An astonishing debut! Weina Dai Randel spins a silken web of lethal intrigue, transporting us into the fascinating, seductive world of ancient China, where one rebellious, astute girl embarks on a dangerous quest for power."

—C.W. Gortner, bestselling author of *The Queen's Vow*

The Empress of Bright Moon

"The author's talent for dramatic, well-timed dialogue and portrayal of women's friendships and emotions—especially dislikes, jealousy, and fear—intensifies the reader's understanding of palace intrigue. . . . A full immersion, compulsively readable tale that rivals both Anchee Min's *Empress Orchid*, about the Dowager Empress Cixi, and the multilayered biographical novel *Empress* by Sa Shan, which also features Empress Wu."

—*Booklist* (starred review)

"A must-read for fans of historical fiction set in ancient China, this novel offers a compelling look at a woman's unprecedented rise to power."

—*Library Journal* (starred review)

"Randel (*The Moon in the Palace*) offers a rich conclusion to her historical fiction duology about the woman who would become China's only ruling empress, in this work filled with sorrow and pain. . . . Randel has done much to breathe life into the life of Empress Wu."

—*Publishers Weekly*

"Once again, Randel's gift for evoking the atmosphere of the palace shines. Readers are immersed in a world where vengeance is a way of life. Though accurate, the reality and brutality of some incidents may disturb gentle readers. Truly a fascinating read!"

—RT Book Reviews (4 stars)

"A fascinating vision of ancient China concludes far too soon in this suspenseful, romantic finale."

—Shelf Awareness

"Along with its predecessor, *The Empress of Bright Moon* is one of the most beautifully written, impeccably researched, and well-constructed historical fiction novels released this year."

—Book Reporter

NIGHT ANGELS

ALSO BY WEINA DAI RANDEL

NIGHT ANGELS

— A NOVEL —

WEINA DAI RANDEL

LAKE UNION
PUBLISHING

Text copyright © 2023 by Weina Dai Randel
All rights reserved.

Published by Lake Union Publishing, Seattle

www.apub.com

Amazon, the Amazon logo, and Lake Union Publishing are trademarks of Amazon.com, Inc., or its affiliates.

ISBN-13: 9781542038003 (paperback)
ISBN-13: 9781542037990 (digital)

Cover design by Faceout Studio, Tim Green
Cover image: ©Ilina Simeonova / ArcAngel; ©kentaylordesign / Shutterstock; ©Jon Bilous / Alamy Stock Photo / Alamy

Printed in the United States of America

*This book is dedicated to
Dr. Ho Fengshan,
his family,
and all the angels in Vienna and beyond*

May 1938, Vienna

The rich and the powerful were arrested, the prominent and the talented were harassed, and the skilled and the hardworking were attacked. Men fled, their shoes thundering in the hallway; men shuddered, their backs jabbed by rifles; men groaned, their skulls cracking on the cobblestones.

In the dead of night, hundreds of thousands of people, the disillusioned, the dehumanized, the despairing, sought passage out of Vienna.

CHAPTER 1

GRACE

When I met Lola for the first time, it wasn't entirely my choice, for if it had been up to me, I wouldn't have taken a chance on her. But many things were not up to me, such as the official dinners that lasted for five hours, or the extravagant parties hosted by the royal Hapsburg family, or the dances in the grand ballrooms overflowing with high-ranking officials in gold-trimmed uniforms and duchesses in diamond tiaras, or even Vienna.

It was late May, another long afternoon: the desultory rays of pale sunlight writhed on the vast stretch of the Ringstrasse; a cloud of dust, silent like shadows, descended on the rusty lampposts and islands of Baroque buildings; nearby, a crust of cobwebs clung tightly to the swollen buds of the lindens, branches bending low in a sudden shift of the wind.

In my conservative attire suitable for a diplomat's wife—a silk jacket over a blouse with a lace jabot, an ankle-length skirt, a pair of blue gloves, and a wide-brimmed hat with a ribbon in the same shade of blue—I came to the entrance to the Stadtpark. Near a bust of a stern composer with an elusive name, I sat on a bench outside the park. Lola arrived a moment later, took her seat, and introduced herself.

I did my best, nodding politely and listening patiently. She sounded all right; her English was gently accented, and she was a Viennese, a student from the University of Music and Performing Arts in Vienna, or something like that. She appeared eager to teach me German and assured me she'd help me with some phrases that would be useful at official dinners where I whiled away the hours by gazing at the crystals.

Lola was twenty years old, five years younger than me, if I remembered correctly, but I never remembered things correctly. Her appearance gave me the impression that she was younger, and maybe it had something to do with her sense of fashion, which was minimal at best—her green dirndl showed some signs of wear, and her double-breasted black jacket was out of style. But she was striking in a raw, energetic, and genuine way, with green eyes, plump cheeks, and smooth skin imbued with a sheen of youth. An enviable young woman, not yet dented by the stress of marriage, parenting, or other worldly shackles and shames.

Anyway, I had little to say to her—it was too windy, too dusty—and I felt dizzy, my thoughts flying like discarded pamphlets, scattering in the wind, and her voice, warm as it was, hazy like fog. I mumbled along, nodding now and then, until a torrent of heat ran through me, and I wrung the strap of my handbag, spinning the twines of uneasiness and regret—those knotty German verbs and complicated consonants with sounds that might as well come from someone with allergies. Learning German would be a daunting task for me and likely fruitless, for if there was one thing I knew well about myself, it was that I had little talent in foreign languages.

"Miss Lee?" she asked.

"Yes?"

"Are you all right?" Those green eyes were like the eyes of a Russian doll in a department store, intimate and inscrutable.

"Oh yes. I'm all right. I was just . . . What were we saying again?"

"You said to meet here next Thursday."

"Oh, right. Here. Yes . . . Do you mind? Here at the park it'll be great. You see, I live inside a consulate, and it's not convenient for me to have German lessons there. It's just . . . too many people . . . But we can meet somewhere else if . . ."

"The park is fine. I'll be here, Miss Lee."

"Great . . . That's great. See you next time." Clutching my handbag, I stood up. I had spoken more words in a few minutes than in an entire month.

"May I ask you a question, Miss Lee? How long have you been in Vienna?" She smiled—a friendly smile, easy, golden, like the patch of sunlight pressed against her forehead.

"Hmm . . . about a year . . ." Now came a predicament. Should I stay, or should I leave? The protocol for a diplomat's wife that I had recently learned did not include interaction with a tutor, but if I bolted, it would reflect poorly on my manners. So I sat back on the bench, set the handbag on my lap, and fixed my gaze on several German words etched on the back of the bench near her arm. Such a strange city, Vienna, words everywhere. On the walls and benches.

"Did you have a German tutor before?"

"No."

The dreadful silence.

Maybe I should explain. Fengshan had introduced to me at least a dozen tutors over the past few months, but I managed to avoid them. She was the first I'd met, having run out of excuses. But my pulse raced faster, and it was as though I was at a dinner table again, under the scrutiny of those ostentatious diplomats and their sophisticated wives specializing in polite drivel and critical gazes. I would have made an excuse and hidden in the private bathroom if I could, but there was no private bathroom nearby where I could escape.

"I heard you were a diplomat's wife, Miss Lee."

Lola's tone sounded as though she had doubts about that, and so did I. Every day, I woke up hoping this wasn't true.

"May I ask which country your husband represents?"

The look in her eyes. She couldn't be twenty; she had to be older than that, even older than me. "He . . . is Chinese."

It occurred to me I had not told Fengshan that I'd meet Lola today, but then things like this couldn't possibly attract his attention, so busy was he.

"Oh, you're Chinese." She looked curious, a different reaction from all the harsh and judgmental stares I had received.

"I'm . . . from the United States." I picked up my handbag.

"American. No wonder your English is so good. Do you like Vienna, Miss Lee?"

I held tight to my handbag. *Miss . . .* I had forgotten her last name. "It's a fine city."

"You don't like Vienna?"

I pulled down my hat, then pushed it up and pulled it down again. I had hurt her feelings; now I couldn't leave.

"Vienna is special. Have you heard of this: 'The streets of Vienna are paved with culture, the streets of other cities with asphalt'?" she asked.

"I'm sorry . . ."

Her hand swept in a dramatic and almost indignant way, gesturing at the Baroque buildings facing us across the street. "Everyone loves Vienna. We have magnificent architecture and many palaces in Vienna. The Hofburg, for instance. It has the Imperial Apartments, the collections of Empress Sisi, and the Imperial Treasury, with relics that date to the Holy Roman Empire. And Schloss Schönbrunn. Have you visited it? It's not that far. You'll also adore the Marble Hall in Belvedere Palace, and of course, you know every Austrian enjoys the operas and ballets in the Wiener Staatsoper."

All those foreign names. Who could remember them all? I had been to a party in the Hofburg, or maybe it was the apartment of Empress Sisi or Empress Maria Theresa. Same thing. "Miss—" I wrung my hands. Her last name finally jumped to my mind. "Miss Schnitzel, I'm afraid—"

"Schnitzler. Schnitzel is a type of food."

"Oh."

"No relation to the well-known author."

My face heated up. Now that I was growing embarrassed, I couldn't stop. "Of course . . . Miss Schnitzel—Schnitzler . . . I'm terribly sorry. It's hard to remember German names . . . And you know it's difficult to get around if you don't understand the language. The names of the shops are unpronounceable, and so are the streets. I can't read anything. This. This here. Look. What does it mean?" I pointed at the Germanic scribble etched on the back of the bench.

She fixed her gaze on the words. A light flashed in her green eyes, and then she jutted her chin up. "It means it's for Aryans."

"Pardon?"

"We're not allowed to sit on this bench."

"It's a public bench. Everyone can sit here."

Her head turned to the benches across the street. They were also inscribed in German, not the word for *Aryan* but one starting with *J.* "As it should be."

"Yes, of course. I agree . . . But pardon me. Did you say we are not allowed to sit on this bench?" I had sat here before she arrived, and I had not paid attention to the inscription, unable to comprehend it.

"It's the new law in Vienna, Miss Lee." She was quiet, staring at a giant tram squeaking past us, its windows flanked by flags with a swastika, making a clack-clack noise. I couldn't recall if I'd seen these flags when I arrived in Vienna last year, but lately, they were everywhere. It was politics, Fengshan had said about the flags, barely lifting his gaze from the German newspaper he was reading.

Of course, these days, Vienna was only about politics. At the last party in an empress's apartment, the diplomats with thick mustaches, their wives in sequined gowns and feathered Tyrolean hats, and even those footmen in white wigs and jabots with layers of white lace whispered about the Führer. A welter of apprehensive faces, a noisy tableau of glee and gloom. And I sat at the end of the table, smiled and nodded, unable to understand their words, couldn't care less. This city had nothing to do with me; it had no need of me, a stranger, an outsider.

Not so for Fengshan, the diplomat with an impossible mission to save his country. Oh well.

"I don't quite understand, Miss . . . Schnitzler."

"It's hard to believe, I know." Her gaze traced a green squad car—a police car; it had to be, with the logo *Polizei*, and inside were two men wearing beige trench coats and swastika armbands. The car was driving along, following the tram, passing us, when one of them turned to me and cast me a long, piercing look. That was just the way they were, policemen, stiff and humorless; they often stood guard in ballrooms with dead eyes, but they held Fengshan in high regard, like many Viennese professionals.

Suddenly, from the ocean of dust, there came a squeal of brakes, loud and startling, and in a blur of sensation, among the rush of horse carriages and pedestrians, the car with the unremarkable policemen screeched to a stop right in front of me.

The two men jumped out, all menacing poses and harsh, angry voices, and I stared, frantic, speechless, wringing my handbag's strap, which seemed to enrage them even more. The awkward moment must have lasted for an eternity, and I had nearly torn the strap off my handbag in nervousness when Lola, the girl with a fresh face, the girl who wouldn't stop asking me questions, stood up and delivered a long speech in German.

Nothing she said made sense to me, but I was relieved, and I could tell German was a perfect language for her. And it was quite admirable to see her speak in that clear voice, with dignity, without wringing her hands. She appeared to be fully capable of sorting things out on her own. She could have been one of those confident diplomats' wives I met in the ballrooms.

But I must have been daydreaming again, for there was a splutter of German and Lola's pained cry, and next, I saw a convulsion of arms and beige coats, the ruffling of Lola's skirt, and then her twisted frame huddled inside the police car, her head against the seat.

Startled, I stood up. The streaks of sunlight blurred my vision, and the gust that had whipped the lindens was picking up once more. Somehow a sharp pain stabbed my back, and I pitched forward, nearly tripping. What was happening, I wondered, and turned around—the dark barrel of a pistol was aimed at me.

I gasped, tumbling into the car, my feet tangled in my long dress, my head crashing against my unfortunate tutor's shoulder.

"Are you all right, Miss Lee?" She held me steady. She had lost her hat, and so had I.

My mind was blank. Hard as I tried, not a single word came out of my mouth. But really. Nothing would make me talk again, not the overpowering smell of cigarettes and sweat, not the growling policemen in front of me, not even my verbose tutor.

And my ears hurt—there was another ear-shattering screech, followed by the angry revving of the car, sputtering, and then, without warning, all the stately Baroque buildings, the prancing equestrian statues, and the pointed spires of Gothic churches rapidly receded. The bench where Lola and I had sat was diminishing, then out of sight.

It was then I realized the unthinkable. "Where are we going?"

The girl who promised to teach me German lowered her head and held two pendants, a six-pointed gold star pendant and a cross, which I had not noticed before, to her chest. Then she turned to me, her green eyes flooded with guilt. "I don't know, Miss Lee."

My entire body trembled. I had gotten myself arrested. Now, this would undoubtedly get Fengshan's attention. How could I explain myself?

CHAPTER 2

FENGSHAN

Dr. Ho Fengshan put down the phone, his heart pounding. For once, he was not pondering the conversation with his superior, or his country's devastating defeats by the Japanese, or his speaking event at a German club. With steady steps that revealed not a trace of his anxiety, he walked out of his office, passed through the hallway graced with paintings of Austrian royalty, nodded at the few staff at the gilded desks in the lobby, and headed toward the elevator, which led to the bedroom he shared with his wife on the third floor.

He was thirty-six years old, with a broad forehead, wide, intelligent eyes, faint eyebrows, and a posture straight like a pen. Clad in a three-piece suit, a tie, and a pair of black wing-tip shoes, he looked modern, Western from head to toe. Fluent in three foreign languages, German, English, and Spanish, well versed in Western civilization, and thoroughly educated in Chinese culture, Dr. Ho Fengshan was a distinctive fixture among the gruff Russians, the bulky Germans, the aloof American officials, and the fastidious English diplomats who were more inclined to conversing with him on topics of philosophy than to listening to the dire need of his country.

He approached the waiting area near the elevator, raised his hand at several Chinese men seated on a row of golden upholstered Baroque-style chairs, and greeted them in Chinese. He knew them well: the peddlers who had been caught selling food on the street without a license, the leather-purse makers who had illegally arrived in Austria by climbing over the mountains in Hungary, and the two students in gray robes who studied at a university in Vienna. They had all come here to apply for new passports that were required by the Austrian authorities. A motley crew, they appeared, incongruous on the large, ornate armchairs, but they were his people, whose needs were his job, and the consulate under his leadership was their protector.

In front of the elevator, Fengshan pressed the button to go up; the voice of *Hauptsturmführer* Heine, a captain of the police force in the first district in Vienna, echoed in his mind. On the phone, the captain had said his wife had been arrested and detained in the Hotel Metropole, the Nazi Headquarters. She had been charged with breaking the law—sitting on a park bench designated for Aryans.

Fengshan's first reaction had been disbelief—this must be a mistake. His American wife, Grace Lee, a delicate woman with a soft voice and a shy smile, was frustratingly introverted, forgetful, and, admittedly, growing increasingly erratic and withdrawn with their every move. At twenty-five, she was petite, with the small hands of a child, wearing size five shoes, still a dreamer, still the immature girl she had been when he had first met her four years ago. But she was hardly a meddlesome woman who would get herself arrested.

The timing of Grace's arrest, if it were true, couldn't be worse. Since Austria had lost its statehood due to the Anschluss, Fengshan had found himself suddenly straddling unexpected political trenches. The Chinese legation's diplomatic status was dissolved, the chargé d'affaires of the legation was reassigned, and Fengshan was ordered to take the position as the consul general and establish the consulate of the Republic of China in Austria, now known as Ostmark, a province in Greater Germany.

A similar fate had befallen all other foreign legations in Vienna, which were now forced to operate as consulates, and their ambassadors as consul generals. Several legations were also abolished. The ever-powerful British had closed the doors of their embassy at Metternichgasse 6, and the French, following suit, were busy packing and shipping the expensive silverware back to Paris.

The diplomatic relationships in the new German province had taken a sharp and sinister turn, fraught with tension. The animosity that had hidden under a thin fabric of diplomacy was ripped open by the aggressive, newly empowered Third Reich, who relentlessly prosecuted their political dissidents, the conservatives, the Social Democrats, and the Communists. Only yesterday, the first secretary of the Soviet legation, which was about to be abolished, had secretly pleaded with him to issue a Chinese passport to their Austrian nurse, a Communist, fleeing from the Nazis' dragnet. Fengshan had no choice but to turn down the request, given the woman's red hair and blue eyes, obviously non-Chinese features.

His direct superior, Ambassador Chen in Berlin, to whom he reported regularly, had advised him to remain discreet in the face of the Germans' domestic policies. It was vital, the ambassador said, to maintain a cordial, functional diplomatic tie with Germany's new regime, even though the Führer's policies had strained the two countries' relations. Fengshan concurred. It was confidential information, known only to him and several key officials, that China was relying on Germany to help them fight their enemy, the Japanese who had invaded his beloved homeland. To defeat them, his government needed to upgrade their antiquated weapons, purchase sophisticated fighters, train their pilots, and feed their soldiers, which required financial support from the international community, a loan of five million dollars. Ambassador Chen had already requested the loan from the League of Nations, composed of representatives from Great Britain, France, and Italy, among others. It was currently in process, and Fengshan's mission was to assist the ambassador and follow his orders. It was Fengshan's hope that once the loan was approved, they would be able to purchase weapons from Germany, who had promised to sell them the desperately needed sophisticated weaponry. The last thing Fengshan expected, at this crucial moment, was to see his wife, who represented him, arrested by the *Geheime Staatspolizei*, tarnishing his country's image. And worse, if she angered the new regime, the weapons deal would fall apart, and his government would plunge into an unimaginable political maelstrom.

Fengshan entered the elevator, and when it stopped on the third floor, he stepped out. At the end of the hallway, he knocked on their bedroom door.

Grace, preferring her solitary time, had been puttering in their bedroom for months. Friendless in a new country whose language she could not understand, she had retreated to her Emily Dickinson, gramophone, and outdated American magazines. He had repeatedly encouraged her to hire a German tutor to learn German, as he had encouraged her to learn Chinese while they had been in China, and French in Istanbul. Still, his dear wife had shown absolutely no interest or talent in foreign languages. Since their arrival in Vienna, she would pick up laundry or go to the park and stores, but after nearly losing her way on Kärntnerstrasse while shopping for a hat, she rarely left the consulate. To his great disappointment, she had even forgotten to walk to school with Monto, his son from his first marriage.

No one answered his knock.

He unlocked the door. The bedroom was empty.

He went downstairs, his mind reeling. With the increasing presence of the German policemen and the Brownshirts on the street, many Chinese citizens had wisely retreated indoors and stayed out of trouble. It was beyond his comprehension why and how Grace would be embroiled with the *Geheime Staatspolizei*, but if she had been indeed detained, the most urgent matter was to seek her release and ensure her safety. He put on his bowler hat and called for his manservant.

⌘

The drive to the Hotel Metropole, located on Morzinplatz near the Danube River, took longer than he expected. It was late in the afternoon. On the distant horizon where the Vienna Woods loomed, darkness was visible, ready to descend on the streets, and the light from the magnificent St. Stephen's Cathedral flickered, a waning compass.

His car finally stopped in front of the hotel, a fashionable four-story building famous for its opulent dining hall, spotless white silk napkins, and splendid inner court. Fengshan had not had a chance to visit, but he could see the famed hotel was no longer a welcoming place for the rich and the famous. There were no well-dressed guests in hats and suits, no servants carrying luggage, no bellboys pulling carts. The building looked ominous. Near the elaborate stone caryatids were thick metal rods, beneath the meticulously spaced atlantes were dark rooms with drawn curtains, and in front of every window, red flags with the black swastika were planted.

He asked Rudolf, the consulate's manservant, to park the car by the curb and walked to the hotel. Several men in brown shirts, toting rifles, watched him, and some young women holding cameras studied him coldly. He held his head high, past the impressive Corinthian columns, the motorcycles, the squad cars, and the members of the *Geheime Staatspolizei* in black uniforms and caps emblazoned with disturbing *Totenköpfe*. He was not a superstitious man, but the skull and crossbones seemed macabre to him, and these policemen reminded him of the new man in power, Hitler, the Führer, at the routine meeting he'd attended a month ago. It had been a disheartening event—the man was a hysterical martinet, and the foreign diplomats had left the meeting with low spirits and elevated anxiety. Fengshan had a dreadful feeling that his request for his wife's freedom would be denied, even with his diplomatic status.

He grasped the brim of his bowler hat, gave it a push, and entered the hotel. In the lobby's corner, near a potted palm stood two guards holding rifles; under a brilliant chandelier, several women with manila folders passed by, bidding each other *auf Wiedersehen*—it was after office hours. At the counter where a concierge or receptionist would have sat was a man in the black uniform and the appalling cap.

"Entschuldigen Sie die Störung." Fengshan walked to him.

The man looked up. Surprise leaped in his gray eyes, and he rose and strode toward Fengshan. "Herr Consul General? How are you? It's an honor to see you at the Headquarters. How may I be of assistance?"

The man was a low-ranking officer, an *Untersturmführer*, likely, judging by the medal on his uniform. His German was formal, and he looked to be in his early thirties, tall, with narrow shoulders and lush hair. His face appeared long, thin, his gray eyes piercing, and his smile oily, with a detectable quality of sleaziness. This was a man eager to climb the social ladder, Fengshan could tell. But the man had recognized him, which was a surprise. Perhaps his appearances at clubs, cultural events, and banquets had helped increase his visibility.

"Sir, my apologies for visiting without formal notice beforehand. I haven't been here before. The Hotel Metropole is quite lovely. I hate to trouble you after the work hour. I am here for my wife. It seems there was a mix-up, and my wife was taken here. May I request, humbly, for her release?" Fengshan spoke in fluent German.

"Your wife, Herr Consul General?" The man smiled, almost obsequiously.

"Ah, she's one of the few Asian women in this city, I reckon, but she was born in America. Would it be too much trouble to have you look into the matter?"

"No trouble at all, Herr Consul General. May I offer my apology? This mix-up is most unfortunate. I shall take care of this right away. May I have her name?" He went back to the counter.

"Grace Lee." Grace had kept her family name after their marriage.

"I see. The file says she broke the law, sitting on a bench that was designated for Aryans."

He was not aware of that law. "Is that so? My wife can't read German."

"An honest mistake then. My apologies again, Herr Consul General. I shall have her released right away." The officer presented him with another oily smile, turned on his heels, and picked up a phone on a counter behind him.

A huge weight lifted off Fengshan's shoulders. His concerns about his country's reputation being tarnished by the arrest seemed to be overblown. Once he rescued Grace, they would leave the building as quietly as possible, and few people would hear of this incident. He turned to admire the lobby. The Nazis had chosen a good hotel for their headquarters. Working here was like taking a vacation in a resort, with the grand chandelier, the expensive paintings, the mosaic marble floor, and notes of piano music tinkling in the air.

A thud came from somewhere, reverberating in the lobby. It sounded as if something heavy had crashed against the walls, and a faint groan echoed. Fengshan frowned.

The rumor about the brutal methods that the Nazis used at the Headquarters might be true. Confined in the opulent rooms must be some of the government's dissidents, the Communists, Schuschnigg's supporters, outspoken union leaders, or perhaps some Zionist leaders. Fengshan remembered what he had read in the newspapers. Grace, he prayed, was not subject to any torture.

Fengshan turned to the officer. "Sir, which room is she in, if you don't mind my asking?"

"Well, I have made proper arrangements for your wife's release, Herr Consul General. She should be here momentarily."

Fengshan frowned. The man had not answered his question.

"I assure you she's well, Herr Consul General. The officers will never do any harm to your wife. We Germans value the friendship between our countries. We've met, Herr Consul General. Do you remember me? I gave you a list of friends in Vienna who might be of interest to you."

Fengshan studied him carefully. Since his arrival in Vienna last year, he had attended clubs, socialized with people at banquets, and organized many cultural events, including the ones in the Vienna Police Academy before it was absorbed into the *Geheime Staatspolizei*. He never forgot people's names or faces. His exceptional memory was a source of his pride. "You must forgive me. Your name has slipped my mind."

"I'm Adolf Eichmann. I came to Vienna a few months ago. I was working in Berlin."

The name didn't ring a bell. "Berlin?"

"I was transferred here to solve the Jewish problem."

Adolf Eichmann.

"Hotel Sacher Wien, Herr Consul General. We had a cocktail together, and we had a great conversation regarding your country's superb aircraft."

Fengshan felt the heat rising in his face. In a country where Asian men were a pitiful minority, it was easy to be misidentified. But still, it was a nightmare to be mistaken for the diplomat of an enemy country that had invaded China and murdered thousands of his countrymen. There was no mild rebuff to this oversight. Fengshan raised his voice a notch. "I hope those fighters will be destroyed soon, Herr Eichmann. The merciless Japanese have murdered enough innocent people in China. I am Dr. Ho Fengshan, the consul general of the consulate of the Republic of China."

A flicker of surprise passed through Eichmann's eyes, and then his face changed. It was a concerning change, for the sheen of his sleaziness slid off, laying bare the skin of distaste underneath. Fengshan was alarmed—this was a lizard of a man who was skillful at changing his color and adapting to scruples as he wished.

"Of course. My poor memory. You're Dr. Ho, the Chinese consul general. Forgive me. Delighted to meet you, Herr Consul General. Look, here comes your wife."

Fengshan turned around. In the red-carpeted hallway, next to a guard, the small figure of Grace appeared, faltering. Her eyes were wide, alert, and her face was bloodless, lips swollen, a smear of redness on her chin. There was a peculiar expression on her face—something akin to happiness, it seemed. He rushed to her and put his arms around her to support her entire body, which was almost weightless.

"I've got you. I've got you. Let's go home." He wiped off the blood on her chin and murmured in English. Out of courtesy, he gave Eichmann a nonchalant nod, even though he was burning with fury. How could it be legal to arrest a woman for sitting on a public bench? And what kind of regime would torment a defenseless woman who weighed less than one hundred pounds? The Germans—the Nazis—couldn't be trusted.

Outside, he passed the Brownshirts and the policemen in black uniforms and settled Grace in the car. He rubbed her back, comforting her. If they had had privacy, he would have let go of the Chinese custom and kissed her.

"Let's go home, Grace." He asked Rudolf to start the engine. The sooner they left here, the better.

"Wait, my dear." Grace's voice was a whisper, but she looked rather poised, not devastated, fearful, or tearful, as he had thought.

"What's the matter?"

"Lola Schnitzel, my dear. She's still in the dungeon. Could you please ask for her release as well?"

Grace had a habit of addressing him in her American way. But he, a conservative Chinese man adhering to Confucian teaching, didn't consider it appropriate to address his wife in endearments. "Who's Lola Schnitzel?"

"The tutor you recommended."

He remembered all the tutors he had urged his wife to hire. Lola Schnitzel—or was it Schnitzler?—was a student. "Did you interview her?"

She nodded. "I just met her today. We were sitting on a bench outside a park when the policemen came for us."

So that was how it happened. The tutor, he recalled, was an Austrian. Rescuing his wife from the Nazis was his duty, but asking for the release of an Austrian was crossing the professional line he had set for himself.

"Please, my dear. She didn't do anything wrong."

He glanced back at the policemen, the squad cars, and motorcycles. "Grace, I think we should just leave."

She gripped his hand with surprising strength. "She's a lovely girl, very young and brave. We were brought here together and placed in a dungeon in the basement. I can't just leave her alone. Please get her out. Please do me a favor."

He sighed. His wife. He would do it for her. He pushed open the car's door, entered the hotel, and went to the counter in the lobby. One of the guards approached him, but Eichmann gestured him away.

"Herr Consul General, it is my pleasure to see you again. How may I help you?" The man straightened his cap with the skull and crossbones. The skin around his mouth sprang to form a smile, but his gray eyes flashed coldness.

"Herr Eichmann, pardon me, I heard my wife's tutor—Fräulein Schnitzel—was also detained. May I request your kindness in granting her release?"

He prayed that the tutor was not a supporter of Schuschnigg or a Communist, like the Austrian at the Soviet legation whose passport he'd been asked to provide. If she were, then his effort in rescuing her would be not only in vain but also messy.

"By any chance, does Herr Consul General mean Lola Schnitzler?"

Fengshan gave an affirmative nod. It was Schnitzler after all. "She's my wife's tutor."

"Herr Consul General, perhaps it is not known to you that she's a Jewess." A note of warning had crept into Eichmann's voice.

A Jewess. Not as serious as a supporter of Schuschnigg or a Communist, but still a point of concern. For about a year, he had read about the absurd rhetoric of racial purification in Nazi propaganda; since the Anschluss, however, instances of harassment and discrimination against the Viennese Jews had been unfortunately legitimized. Fengshan had deep misgivings about the race theory. In the course of China's two-thousand-year history, the Chinese had conquered other races and had also been conquered by other races, and who could say which was superior? And Confucianism and Taoism, of course, always gave sage instructions of tolerance and coexistence. If there was one thing definitive about the argument of race, it was that it derived from the imbalance of power; in the world of *Ruo Rou Qiang Shi*—the strong devoured the meat of the weak—the weak were doomed to be vulnerable.

The ambassador hadn't explicitly mentioned to stay out of the Jewish business, only that of the dissidents and the Communists, and Grace was waiting in the car. He didn't have the heart to disappoint her after the ordeal she had gone through. "Is she? I didn't know. I hope it's not too much trouble."

The look in Eichmann's eyes grew intense—the man was calculating. It seemed to be of great interest to him that a foreign diplomat would care to meddle in his country's domestic affairs, or maybe he was assessing the pros and cons of granting a diplomat's request, and it was even possible that he was considering reporting him to his Japanese counterpart with whom the Nazi had rubbed shoulders. Then

Eichmann shrugged with aloofness and callousness—it was only a Jewess, and the city was full of them. "No trouble at all, Herr Consul General."

Fengshan let out his breath, and out of politeness, he smiled to express his gratitude. But he was warier than ever—Adolf Eichmann was not only sleazy but also callous. *Ich bin Ihnen dankbar.* I'll wait in the car."

He went out to his car and sat next to Grace, nodding at her, willing her tutor to come out as soon as possible. It occurred to him that the Jewish business was also part of the Führer's domestic policy. He had made a careless request that might have inadvertently conflicted with his superior's order; he prayed he wouldn't regret this.

It was growing dark when finally a figure staggered out of the hotel—a young woman in a dirndl and a black jacket. Stumbling, she didn't see the car parked by the curb and hurriedly passed it. Grace bolted upright and called out, and the woman turned around, shielding her eyes with her hand against the bright headlights. Her face, Fengshan could see, was thrashed with red lines like whips, and there was a bruise on her forehead. With a gasp, she came to Grace, held her shoulders, and gave her a tight embrace, and Grace, his introverted wife who preferred to sit quietly on a chaise in the corner of a ballroom and who could only utter a few perfunctory German phrases, didn't let the young woman go. They had just met, Grace had said, but he would have believed they had known each other for years. What had happened to these two in the dungeon?

After Grace's tutor waved to leave, Fengshan told Rudolf to drive. His car started to roll, and he caught a figure in the rear mirror—Adolf Eichmann, a lizard of a man, lurking behind his car. There, in the stark light, turning up on his face was a smile, crooked, like a hook.

CHAPTER 3

GRACE

I turned around in the car and craned my neck to trace Lola's figure weaving through the opaque haze of streetlights, diminishing as the distance between us grew and finally sliding into the dark velvet of the night. It occurred to me that I should have asked where she lived and how she could find a taxi or a coach at this hour. It was late, and it would be dangerous for a single woman to walk on the streets.

When we arrived at the hotel, we had been forced down a winding metal staircase to a claustrophobic dungeon in the basement with a bare light bulb. The air was musty, stifling, thick like leather; coils of shadows clustered in the corners. There was no chair or bench. Lola sat on the ground; I stood some distance away, feeling the strength drain from my legs, paralyzed by waves of regret and fear. I shouldn't have come out today; I should have put off hiring a tutor for another year. And now, a simple mistake of sitting on a bench had gotten me arrested. What if Fengshan found me here? What if Fengshan couldn't find me here?

"You should sit, Miss Lee."

"I can't." The floor was certainly not an appropriate spot for a diplomat's wife.

"You can't stand there all night."

"All night?"

Lola pulled her legs together and rested her head on her knees. "You were right. Vienna is strange these days. We have new laws devised every day. They are baked and rolled out faster than *Apfelstrudel*. But don't worry. It's temporary. Vienna is a lawful and sophisticated city. This will pass."

Maybe it was the sincerity of her tone—no one in Vienna, or Istanbul, or China, had spoken to me this way—or maybe it was that she spoke in English, my mother tongue, the only language I knew. She sounded like a friend I hadn't had in so long.

"I'm sorry I got you arrested." Her voice was gentle, swelling to fill the room.

I looked down at my hands—my silk gloves were smudged. "It wasn't your fault. I chose that bench. I couldn't read German."

"It wasn't you." She played with the two pendants on her necklace again, a cross and a star. "They don't like me. I'm a *Mischling*."

"I don't know what that means."

"Oh. It means a half-breed."

I had met one of my kind. Here, in Vienna, of all places. That was unexpected. I wondered if she grew up like me, alone and lonely, with no companions other than a book of poetry; I wondered if her mother slapped her for calling her *Mother* in front of others.

The light bulb was flickering. I stepped closer to Lola, nearly touching her shadow. Somehow, despite this injustice, this captivity, for the first time in four years since I'd left America, I thought I was close to someone.

Later, two policemen in black uniforms interrogated us. Each time I tried to say something, they shouted impatiently; each time I leaned on the wall for support, they whipped my shoulders with a stack of newspapers. Lola suffered more. They slapped her when she answered; they smacked her when she refused to answer. And I turned to her, catching her gaze whenever she stopped to breathe. They had beaten us to break us, yet each blow, each groan had tied us together.

"Grace?"

Fengshan's voice brought me back to the car. I straightened, wanting to look at him but facing ahead instead. It was almost pitch-black, save for a few cars flashing white beams in the distance and pricks of light emitting from shadowy coaches in front of towering buildings. My chin was burning, and my arms were sore. I'd rather lie down and sleep a little. "How did you know I was there, my love?"

"Captain Heine called me."

He sounded calm and didn't appear angry at me for disgracing him and his country. Or did he? His mood had once been easy to understand, clear as a mirror; not so these days. I could imagine his shock, him holding the phone and hearing I was arrested. And indeed, paying more attention, I could hear a trace of his anger, his disapproval, above the rumble of the engine. I said weakly, "I didn't do anything wrong; neither did Lola. It doesn't make sense."

"This is, sadly, the Austrian crisis. I'm afraid it won't make sense to many people."

The pale gaslights flickered by the side of the street. "I'd like to take German lessons from her, my love."

"When we get home, we should discuss this."

I looked down at my handbag. "I thought you wanted me to learn German."

"She's a Jewess, Grace."

Something about politics, no doubt. For once, I wished he could forget about it and think of me. But Fengshan was a traditional Chinese man through and through, firmly believing that a man's will must prevail over a woman's. When he talked about marriage, it was always *Fu Chang Fu Sui*—the husband sings, and the wife accompanies. These days sitting in my bedroom I had some occasional qualms about that, but that attitude of his, perhaps, was how he'd captivated me when we met in the noodle shop in Chicago where I toiled. Growing up fatherless, I had found it reassuring to see a man radiate confidence. So when we married, I gladly embarked on a nomadic life with him, from Chicago to his remote hometown in China, where English speakers were rare. When he joined the Chinese legation, I had followed him to Istanbul and lived a restrictive lifestyle—a step out of the door required a male escort. Then with his promotion, we relocated again to Vienna.

Life in Vienna might have appeared splendid to some people, with banquets in glorious Baroque buildings and dinners at stately ballrooms, but it was just another Istanbul, another China, where I had no friends, no work to do, no one to talk to. Inside the ballrooms, the snooty diplomats' wives would sprinkle a few words of English and then rattle off in German. Outside the consulate, operas, plays, and movies were all in German.

Fengshan was the only one I could talk to—he was my sun, my rainbow, my golden trellis to lean on—yet he was busy, busy with socializing, public speaking, lectures, debates, opinion pieces, busy cultivating his career, and protecting his country. He was always on the phone, always in meetings, always speaking German.

The car turned onto a dark and narrow street, Beethovenplatz, and arrived in front of a Baroque-style three-story building, the Chinese consulate, our residence since last year. It was late, so the staff had left, sparing me from a most mortifying moment. Imagine. The consul general's wife had returned from the dungeon. The gossip, the questions, and the prying gazes.

The manservant, Rudolf, opened the car door for me. I heaved out, passed the newly installed black plaque inscribed with the Chinese characters for *Consulate of the Republic of China*, which I couldn't read, and entered the building. The lobby was dimly lit by a lamp. On a desk were stacked newspapers, mail, invitations in elegant script, and visiting cards with gilt edges in German, which I couldn't read either.

I took the elevator to our bedroom as Fengshan bade good night to Rudolf. Fengshan would join me later, after locking the door and checking on Monto, his son, sleeping in the adjacent room, as he did every evening.

But once I stepped into the bedroom, I didn't know what to do. A gilded enclosure of luxury, this bedroom, with crown-molding high ceilings, golden brocade drapery, a shining ormolu clock and candelabras, and an old-fashioned flowery Persian carpet, courtesy of the generous landlord who leased this building to the consulate. I felt as if I were drowning again, inhaling the same musty air, listening to the same silence, sitting in the same room I had left this afternoon.

At least my Dickinson poetry book was near my pillow, just where I had left it. I held it to my breasts. My poor recluse poet. I had turned her into a wanderer. But without her, what would I be then? Finally, I placed my poetry book back near my pillow and began to undress, removing my jacket, gloves, skirt, boots, and stockings. Then I put on a red nightgown and got in bed.

Sometime later, I heard Fengshan's murmur in my ear; in the fog of sleepiness, I threaded my arms around his neck, pulling him close to me. I could smell the familiar scent of his cologne, his favorite cigar, and I wanted him to make love to me. I craved him, his undivided attention and his open, uncurbed affection, an affirmation that I was not useless and that he still loved me, still needed me.

Make love to me.

". . . ordeal . . . at the Headquarters . . . go to see the doctor tomorrow?"

Doctor?

"Grace?"

"You said . . . Why?"

"You had blood on your chin."

That must have been Lola's. "I'm fine. I'm not injured." I sat up and unbuttoned his shirt.

". . . Learning German is a good idea, Grace. I've given it some thought. I shall find you an American tutor."

I dropped my arms. There was no need to find another tutor. I would like to have Lola, only Lola. But this was Fengshan's polite way of telling me to distance myself from her in order to avoid potential trouble; his country, after all, was always his priority. I wished I could say to him that his career was important to me too, and I would never intentionally harm him in any way. Politics was his career, but he was my life. "My love . . ."

"I'm concerned about your safety, Grace. The political situation in Vienna is precarious and worrisome."

I couldn't insist on it—confrontation, even the thought of it, would trigger the memory of Mother's chokehold on my neck. So I lay back down and pulled the coverlet over my head. "That's fine, my love. I won't see the Viennese again."

CHAPTER 4

FENGSHAN

At the sixth sound of the church bell, Fengshan rose from the bed. Grace was still sleeping, a frown on her face. Those beautiful eyes that had captivated him years ago were shut. She had agreed not to stay in touch with the Viennese tutor, conceding as he had suggested, willingly, in her docile manner. He had mixed feelings about this. He had hoped that Grace would enunciate at least some of her thoughts and then they would engage in an open discussion, but this kind of frank communication had remained elusive. When he first met her, he had taken her meekness as the tenderness of youth and believed she would grow stronger in the test of life. But he was wrong. Grace's meekness had been an intractable retreat, a helpless grief, an infinite prison in which she volunteered to sit.

Recently she seemed to be drifting away. She appeared to care little about Monto and complained of a headache whenever he asked her to attend the clubs, and he had resigned himself to it. But Grace had other qualities as well, her ethereal beauty, her loyalty, and her innocence, and she was making an effort—hiring a tutor to learn German. He should take her to dinner, or the opera house, to spend time together to cheer her up. Since their arrival in Vienna, he had been busy lecturing, going to clubs, and building connections, and predictably, Grace was lonely.

He got out of bed and put on a white shirt, a double-breasted three-piece suit, a black silk tie with silver stripes, and a black felt bowler hat. Proper attire that exuded modernity and sophistication was essential to represent his country. He had his friend Mr. Rosenburg to thank, for he had recommended the famed bespoke tailor in Vienna who served the local nobility.

Fengshan went down to the dining room on the second floor and ate a typical Viennese breakfast: a slice of semmel with apricot jam, a boiled egg, and ham. With a meal like this, he missed China with all his heart—how he wished for a bowl of hot rice porridge with shredded pork and some pickle. His mind could switch effortlessly between four languages, but his stomach remained Chinese.

At seven o'clock, he went to the lobby. The consulate was empty; the few staff would appear two hours later. He was always the first one at work.

The Chinese consulate in Austria, or Ostmark, as it was known by the Third Reich after the Anschluss, was small, with Vice Consul Zhou and two hired local help: Frau Maxa, a typist, and the manservant, Rudolf. The legation before the Anschluss had been more prominent, sufficiently staffed, and better funded, even though its influence was limited compared to that of the other members of the League of Nations. That was partially due to the fact that the Republic of China, led by its democratic government, the Nationalists, was a newcomer to the world's political stage. Only as recently as ten years ago was the legitimacy of the Nationalist regime recognized by the United States, the first nation that had granted his government full tariff autonomy.

Fengshan checked his watch. One hour before Ambassador Chen's phone call. He unlocked the consulate's door, picked up the stack of German newspapers on the ground, and walked to his office at the end of the hallway. Before the dissolution of the legation, he had been involved with many responsibilities, and now his duties had been reduced to reporting to his superior, protecting Chinese citizens, and simple consular actions such as visa issuance.

Each day he read the news, assessed current events' importance and implications, and relayed a summary to his superior, Ambassador Chen, in Berlin. The ambassador relied on his knowledge; his predecessor in the legation, who could only speak French and read French newspapers, had fallen behind with the updates and frustrated the vice minister of the Ministry of Foreign Affairs at home.

Fengshan skimmed the headlines for any mention of Grace's arrest or the consulate. It still angered him that she had been mistreated by the German policemen, but if the incident made it to the news, it would cause gossip and potential damage. To his relief, there was no mention of Grace, only news of suicides of the Communists who'd attempted to escape arrests and more stringent laws about the Viennese Jews.

The phone rang.

It was his friend Mr. Rosenburg, a prominent lawyer in Vienna. A supportive friend with a genuine interest in Chinese culture, he was likely calling to confirm his attendance at Fengshan's upcoming speaking event at the German Club. But Mr. Rosenburg's grave tone made Fengshan sit upright. "Is everything all right, Mr. Rosenburg?"

"Dr. Ho, Vienna is descending into hell, and it has an elevator—"

The phone lost the connection.

He dialed Mr. Rosenburg's office number; the busy signal rang in his ears.

He frowned. The Viennese considered etiquette and manners an important part of character. His friend would never hang up the phone in the middle of a conversation. Fengshan planned to seek Mr. Rosenburg out at today's event to learn more. His friend's comment, though, reminded him of Grace's arrest and his unpleasant encounter with Eichmann.

The phone rang again.

"Fengshan?" It was Ambassador Chen.

"Zao shang hao, Chen da shi," Fengshan greeted in Chinese.

Ambassador Chen was from Beijing, the capital of several dynasties in China, which meant he considered himself a highly refined man and Fengshan a lesser man, since he came from Hunan, an economically disadvantaged province. Fengshan's German was as good as the ambassador's, but that didn't elevate his status in his superior's eyes. Ambassador Chen, a son of a renowned general, had been groomed to be a powerful politician since birth, well connected, with a direct line to Mr. Sun Ke, the president of the Legislative Yuan, the son of the Nationalists' founding father, Sun Zhongshan. Thus Ambassador Chen was guaranteed to have a secure, stable political career, which was something Fengshan could aspire to but might be well out of reach.

There was also this fundamental distinction between Fengshan and his superior, of which he was acutely aware. Ambassador Chen was a seasoned veteran who was attuned to the nuances of internal and international affairs, whereas Fengshan, having worked as the first secretary in Istanbul, was on his second post in Vienna, still a neophyte charting the meandering waters in diplomacy.

After a curt greeting from his superior, Fengshan gave a brief report of the consulate's finances and the news he had gathered—the rumor of Chancellor Schuschnigg's house arrest, the exile of many Communists and Schuschnigg supporters, the clandestine visit of the first secretary of the Soviet legation and his request. Fengshan concluded his report with Grace's arrest—not to ask for sympathy, naturally, only revealing in the spirit of transparency.

"Did it make it to the news?"

His superior had had the same concern as he. "I don't believe so."

"Good." The ambassador's voice sounded unfazed. "Fengshan, I'm calling to inform you that the German secretary of foreign affairs has declined to meet me."

Fengshan was shocked. This was devastating news. The relationship between Germany and China had reached a new low indeed. Germany had given the ambassador the cold shoulder last year, purposefully postponing the confirmation of his credentials by seven months. When Hitler had declared his recognition of the Manzhouguo years ago, the illegitimate government that the Japanese had set up in the northern area of China they had conquered, the German ambassador to China had tried to ease the tension. But just about a year ago, Germany shocked them again by signing the Anti-Comintern Pact with Japan. Ostensibly, the goal was to contain the Soviet Union's power, but the pact was a raw reminder that Germany's diplomatic direction had shifted decisively.

It was worth noting that before Hitler, China had enjoyed a solid relationship with Germany for years. Their diplomatic ties had gone back to the early 1920s, when Germany, a defeated country, was stripped of resources and lost consular jurisdiction in China, in accordance with the Treaty of Versailles. But his government had been gracious and cultivated a close partnership with Germany, providing them with raw materials to help them recover. In return, China received military modernization from Germany. Many elite Chinese politicians sent their sons to Berlin for military training, including his party's president, Chiang Kai-shek.

Fengshan rubbed his forehead. He thought of Adolf Eichmann, who had mistaken him for the Japanese consul general. All signs pointed to a strengthening bond between Japan and Germany and a deteriorating future for China and Germany. This was a new reality that they must face: the age of China as Germany's partner was ending. "Ambassador Chen, what's your order?"

"Do not let your emotion interfere with your judgment, Fengshan. The incident with your wife is unfortunate, yet for our country's best interest, I suggest forgetting it. Our relationship with Germany is tenuous, but to lose an ally when our country is under attack is a risk we can't afford. We need Germany's sophisticated weapons to fight the

Japanese. Without the weapons, we cannot win the war. Germany is the only country that can help us."

This was true. The British and the French had turned a deaf ear to them, and the Americans had the Neutrality Act in place, effectively prohibiting them from selling weaponry to any country at war. If Ambassador Chen's plan to win the funds from the League of Nations succeeded, then the ambassador would use his resources to purchase rifles, bullets, tanks, and a squadron of Luftwaffe, armaments his government desperately needed.

The situation in China was dire. His government was bankrupt, and the Nationalists' antiquated tanks and guns were no match for the sophisticated weaponry the Japanese possessed. In the past nine months, Japan had attacked many important cities on China's east coast, such as Qingdao and Shanghai, slaughtered countless people in the capital, Nanjing, and captured the city. The entire Nationalist government had retreated to Wuhan, with the Japanese bombers and tanks and cavalries chasing closely behind, threatening to annihilate them all.

"Ambassador Chen, how may I assist you?"

"Fengshan, you're aware I have submitted a request for a loan from the League of Nations; I was notified that to grant the funds, the League must first convene a meeting. But the British and the French have repeatedly ignored me. I'm looking at other channels, the Americans, for instance. They wield a huge amount of influence over the diplomats, and I'm hoping they'd help put in a good word for us in front of the League. I have an important mission for you."

Created after the Great War, the League of Nations had deemed war a crime to humanity. To prevent future conflicts, it passed twenty-six articles restricting armaments, threatening offenders with a punishment of economic sanction, arbitration, and even joint military actions by all members. When Japan, a council member, failed to uphold the principle of the League by attacking China's Manchuria during the first Sino-Japanese War, the League deemed it a violation, and Japan left the

League. Consequently, the League was unable to take further actions to penalize Japan.

"Anything, Ambassador Chen."

"Are you on good terms with the American consul general in Vienna?"

"I believe so." Fengshan had met Mr. Wiley, the previous chargé d'affaires of the American legation, now the consul general of the American consulate, at a party and discussed China's critical situation with him. The consul had listened. A man in his forties, he had the unruffled manner of a well-trained diplomat and exuded a certain amicable air.

"Good. Will you ask the consul general to help arrange a meeting between me and his superior, Ambassador Wilson, in Berlin? The American ambassador has just presented his credentials, and I was told that his schedule is full for the next six months. But if his consul general speaks on our behalf, the ambassador might agree to a meeting. Once I gain an audience, I'll reason with him and persuade him to propose to the League to hold a meeting about the loan."

"I'll call him right away."

"The meeting with Ambassador Wilson must happen expeditiously, Fengshan. In a month, the Japanese could decimate the entire population in South China. We need the loan from the League desperately." The ambassador hung up the phone.

Fengshan looked at his watch. It was about nine. The American consulate might have opened. He dialed the number. The secretary indicated Consul General Wiley was not in the office yet.

When Fengshan put down the phone, it rang again.

Captain Heine's smooth voice came through the receiver, asking him whether Grace had returned safely home.

Fengshan thanked him profusely, despite his reserved opinion of the captain. They had not exactly been friends, unlike him and Mr. Rosenburg. The captain was a fastidious man and a policeman who appeared to retain traditional Viennese pride and values. But he had turned in his baton that had been used to curb the Nazi violence and put on the armband with the swastika after the Anschluss, like much of the Viennese police force who had once sworn their oath to protect an independent Austria. Now that Austria was part of Germany, Captain Heine had become a member of the *Geheime Staatspolizei*, the Gestapo.

But had it not been for the captain, Fengshan would never have known Grace was detained or where to look for her.

"Don't mention it, Herr Consul General. I look forward to your speech at the club."

The captain's interest in his event was yet another surprise—as far as he knew, the captain was only attached to two things: wine and women. Nonetheless, Fengshan thanked him again, hung up the phone, and looked at his watch. Four hours to the event. He had time. He rubbed his forehead, formulating his plans. His day was just beginning, and he already had his hands full. Opera tickets for Grace, Mr. Rosenburg's phone call, Mr. Wiley, and the event. He would tend to them all, meticulously, in the order of urgency, gravity, and practicality.

The doorbell of the consulate buzzed. He went into the lobby, opened the heavy oak door, and greeted his staff in fluent German and Chinese.

It still amazed him that he was the consul general, working in Vienna, a city resplendent with stately fountains, palatial theaters, vast squares, and towering statues. A son of impoverished peasants, Fengshan had grown up fatherless, raised by an illiterate mother who couldn't read or write her name and had wept at their empty hovel without a kitchen, unable to keep him fed. Barefoot and hungry, he had resolved to walk for miles each morning to a school hosted by Norwegian Lutheran missionaries with blue eyes and golden hair. They offered him free education and bowls of rice, and he sat on the bench listening raptly to the story of Jesus's sacrifice and recited, *"Mens sana in corpore sano."*

After he graduated from the missionary school, he entered college and took it as his responsibility to provide for his mother and sister by teaching at a high school during his free time. He wanted to build a secure future for his family, and he understood this acutely: as a man of humble birth, he must work diligently, with blood, sweat, intelligence, and fortitude, in order to achieve success. By chance, he heard the government was sponsoring two students for advanced education in Munich, Germany, a rare opportunity to study abroad, and the qualified students would be chosen from a state exam. Aware that the selection was highly competitive and that he must compete with five thousand well-off students nationwide, Fengshan came home from work, lit the late candles and studied until three o'clock in the morning for six months. He clinched the number one spot on the exam and became one of only two students from all of China to attend the University of Munich, where he received his PhD in political economics.

With his doctorate, Fengshan had been glad to offer his service as a secretary to the governor of Hunan province in China. But it broke his heart to see his country besieged by foreign powers and blighted with war indemnity and economic poverty. Resolved to fight for China's survival, he took a gamble to join the foreign ministry, quit his secure secretary's job, and worked tirelessly in Istanbul to establish a place for his government in the world of diplomacy.

His current position as the consul general in Vienna was a high point in his diplomatic career and a vital opportunity to fight for his country's future. It was imperative that he do all he could to assist his superior and secure a meeting for the ambassador. Fengshan looked at his watch again.

CHAPTER 5

LOLA

I was expelled today.

And I was not the only one. A routine morning practice of Mahler's Ninth Symphony turned out to be a trial, a contest of spit and slander, and in the end, there was nothing else to do other than pick up my case, join the miserable concertmaster and fellow string musicians, and march out of the room like I didn't care.

But I did care. Was this expulsion temporary? Was this a stunning crush of my musical career? For months, rumors had been bouncing in the chamber that Jewish musicians had been banned from the conservatories in Berlin, and that many Jewish professionals and musicians in Germany had lost their jobs without cause. But we were Viennese. We had Chancellor Schuschnigg, and religion had not divided us. We, Jews and Christians, had marched on the street to support Schuschnigg's policies when he defeated the Nazi Party and restored order; we had worn crosses and the Star of David to show our pledge to a Socialist regime; we had linked our arms, shouted for freedom and justice for all. It had only been four years ago.

Carrying my violin case, passing the Vienna Staatsoper on the Ringstrasse, I saw a group of actors in costumes stumbling out of an arch of the stately building while some youths in brown shirts were taunting them, shouting. One Brownshirt shoved a woman holding a bag. Startled, the poor actress tripped, dropped her bag, and spilled colorful dresses, combs, and necklaces on the pavement. Still, the Brownshirt was relentless, spitting on her, kicking her. Someone near me whispered that she was the actress Frau Weiss, the perennial draw at the Burgtheater, and that she had been dismissed. Another said the distinguished professors at the University of Vienna were removed as well, like Frau Weiss and all of us.

I felt like getting a beer. But none of my friends wanted to come, so I held tight to my case and resolved to go to a tavern by myself. The glorious tunes of Strauss's *An Alpine Symphony* cascaded from a nearby building, lifting my spirits. Summer was approaching, and soon we'd dance to the lively accordion music, drink *Sturm* in the *Heurigen*, and forget about all these absurdities.

I turned onto a cobblestone street and passed a banner bearing the enormous black-and-white face of the man who swallowed Austria. Near it, a butcher with a face like a burnt pastry tossed his head toward me, scowled, and spat out some vicious epithet. I broke off my walk, tucked the two pendants into my blouse, and turned around.

At home, I had no choice but to tell Mutter that my school attendance was no longer required.

"Did you leave the house with your left foot out first, Lola?" she asked, looking anxious.

"No."

It was easier to fill up the Danube Valley than to convince Mutter that the theory of luck in relation to the order of footsteps was flawed. But Mutter couldn't be persuaded; she belonged to the old generation.

"What are you going to do, Lola?"

I shrugged. But I knew it would be harder to support my family now. Since Vater's passing, Mutter had been managing the household with the little income from the fabric shop left by Vater, and my sister, Sara, had been diligently helping her with the sewing and needlework. But business had been dismal for the past few years, and we had trouble making ends meet. For some months, I was able to earn some schillings to cover the living expenses in the house, but since the Anschluss, the taverns and bars had banned me from performing. My older brother, Josef, promised to provide for us and often brought us cheese, loaves of bread, and fruit. I took them without complaint, but all the same, I wished I were the one looking after everyone. And Josef was being Josef. He tended to act like an older brother who knew best and believed that because he had a pharmacy degree, a decent job, and a fiancée, he was the only one who could help the family.

In two years, I'd graduate from school. With my glowing résumé filled with successful recitals and excellent recommendations, it had been my dream to join the orchestra of the Vienna Staatsoper and ultimately to become a member of the Vienna Philharmonic Orchestra, an honor that would have made Vater proud. After this expulsion, though, a future in the Vienna Philharmonic would be up in the air.

But Mutter worried too much these days. When she saw the bruises on my face yesterday, she was almost in tears. Upon her insistence, I had to tell her briefly of Frau Lee and the arrest.

Frau Lee was an introvert, I could see, but a diplomat's wife. I had never met someone like her before, and I'd like to know more about her. There were few people I could socialize with lately. All my friends with a drop of Jewish blood were now pariahs, afraid of going to bars and clubs, and talking about leaving Vienna. My non-Jewish Viennese friends avoided me, afraid my Jewish breath would set them on fire even though they had been perfectly safe around me only months ago.

I had enjoyed meeting Frau Lee, although I had to bear the blame for getting us arrested. Had I taken this law more seriously, warned her, or left the bench, we would have avoided the policemen. But it was infuriating. So many restrictions had been forced on us: no more swimming pools, public libraries, music halls, or hotels. And now, no more conservatory.

Working as a tutor would be a refreshing job for me, and I would be able to support my family. I hoped to see Frau Lee again.

CHAPTER 6

GRACE

The bell tolled. Outside the window, the spire of the St. Stephen Cathedral sat in the pale air like a steely crown; the wind brushed by, rustling, like the sweeping hem of a dress. I lay on my bed and didn't want to get up. A night's rest had done little to restore my strength. My bones ached, and the skin of my shoulders and legs was bruised, reminding me of my arrest, Lola, and my promise to Fengshan. And I asked myself—what if I had insisted on keeping Lola as my tutor? What if I hadn't been in such haste to promise anything?

I turned around. The clock on the nightstand said it was eleven. The bed was empty. Fengshan, an early riser who kept a strict schedule, was likely working at his desk downstairs. I was glad—at least we wouldn't talk about the arrest. Or anything, really.

Groaning, I sat up. It would be another day in the consulate, another day of me as a mute diplomat's wife, another day of holding my poet's book and reading about the ribbons of sunrise in Amherst, sinking in the imaginary bower with my wandering thoughts, spreading like a canopy of vines, daring to ask myself—is this my life from now on, to be seen but not noticed, to be heard but not known, to only feel but not to be touched? My poet never answered me.

I had bled again. A small flow. Which had already happened a week ago and shouldn't have appeared for another month. An erratic show, sinister, a chart of endless grief and the haunting fear that despite my dream, despite years of trying, my body was not made for pregnancy, and motherhood, the distant shores of joy and reverie, was forever out of my reach.

Fengshan always said Monto was enough for him, but Monto wasn't enough for me. I would like to have a child of my own. If I had conceived and given birth to a child—our child—would he spend more time with me?

I cleaned myself in the bathroom and took out a pair of underwear from the dresser drawer to change. In the Baroque mirror, I studied myself, my father's eyes and my mother's complexion. The last time I saw her was four years ago. I had told her I was leaving for China with Fengshan. She said I was making a mistake, slammed the door in my face, and swore she'd have nothing more to do with me. I supposed she had had her wish now.

I missed her, even though I didn't want to; I missed Boston, too, my hometown, and even those lonely days in childhood. My Chinese father, a martial artist, had died while I was four, leaving me to my Irish mother, who ordered me to stay outside by the road while she worked in someone's house as a maid, slapped me if I tried to hold her hand in public, and instructed me to address her as Miss O'Connor in front of other people.

Those years, a time of flames and wind, how lonely I was—always a few steps behind my mother—burning with the desire to be with her but chilled with the fear of being near her; those years, a time of ice and thunder, how confused I was—longing for somewhere but belonging nowhere—sitting by the road, daydreaming, holding Dickinson, the book she gave me to keep me company—*I'm Nobody! Who are you?* I was my father's daughter, my mother's child, but I was a nobody.

Mother had her reasons. None of the Americans around her liked Asian faces or Asian children. If the woman of the house saw me and realized she had a half-Chinese child, Mother would lose her job; if she acknowledged me in front of her newly made friends, she would lose her lodging. Then how would she shelter me and feed me? Hadn't she gotten excommunicated because of Father?

I took the can of Tiger Balm from the medicine cabinet and dabbed some on my neck. A soothing sensation seeped into my skin, and I inhaled the comforting scent of menthol. Mother had mentioned this was Father's favorite choice to treat ailments. So when I found cans of Tiger Balm on a shelf in Chinatown in Chicago, I bought a few. The traditional Chinese pain reliever made of menthol and camphor was the only token that linked me to my father. I had kept it in my handbag, like a piece of advice from a father I couldn't remember.

I put the can back in the cabinet. I should get dressed, check on Monto, eat breakfast, and look up my schedule as a diplomat's wife, but I didn't feel like it. The nightgown was loose on me, my collarbones protruding. A pitiful, fragile thing I had turned into. How had it happened? In Chicago, before I met Fengshan, I had been content working in the noodle shop, relieved to escape from Mother, and I had read Dickinson and dreamed of poetry. But now, after four years of here and there, playing the role of a diplomat's wife and a stepmother, I had even forgotten how to dream.

Monto was not in his bedroom, so I went to the dining room, where the scents of sweet cream and fried dough wafted. For my breakfast, the manservant had brought in some fresh Austrian pastries that I couldn't name, some strudels with cabbage filling, some fried fritters shaped like dumplings. I ate alone—I was always alone.

On the table sat a stack of German newspapers left by Fengshan. I peered at it with no desire to touch it. Now I really wished to speak to Lola. She could tell me about the pastries and the news in English. And I still wanted to know—had she returned home safely?

"You can't read German!" Monto came in. He was eleven years old, a skinny boy with intelligent eyes like Fengshan's, his young face plump with baby fat. He wore the black trousers and blue plaid shirt with suspenders I had folded on his nightstand. His short hair stuck up on the side. It needed a good brush, but he wouldn't let me touch it.

I glanced away. My mother was right, after all: I was weak. I was twenty-five, but when Monto talked to me like this, full of justification and indignation, I couldn't defend myself. Really, I didn't know what to do with this little person. He had mocked me repeatedly about my German, which had finally prompted me to reach out to Lola.

"Where have you been? I was looking for you. Shouldn't you be in school?"

"You'll never know how to speak German, Grace." He reached for a stack of cards with people's signatures on the table and stuffed them into his school bag.

Lately, he had been walking around asking the staff in the consulate for signatures. He claimed that he could foretell people's futures by studying their handwriting. When the Austrian prime minister resigned and the German soldiers poured into the city, Monto had studied the signatures of Schuschnigg and Hitler and made a bold prediction that Schuschnigg would live a long life and Hitler would commit suicide.

"Monto, are you asking for people's signatures at school? I don't think it's a good idea."

"None of your business."

Fengshan would have warned Monto to be respectful, had he seen his son behave in this petulant manner, but Monto only acted this way in front of me.

"How's school, Monto?" He had started third grade, or fourth. I couldn't remember. He loved school, and unlike me, he had no trouble adapting to his new life in Vienna.

"Fine." He opened the refrigerator.

Monto never called me *Mother*, for a good reason. "Did you make any friends yet?"

He shrugged.

"Now, what are you doing with the refrigerator, Monto?"

"Packing my lunch."

"I made you a peanut-butter-and-jelly sandwich." The recipe was decades old, originating in Boston, I was told, and I grew up eating that.

"I hate the American sandwich." He stuffed some strudels into his bag.

"But your father said not to eat apple strudels for lunch."

"I can pack my own lunch!" He stormed out.

I might call Monto my son, but, sadly, he would never be mine.

In the lobby, the staff were working at their desks: a Chinese man, Vice Consul Zhou, and an Austrian woman, Frau Maxa, who had been working for the Chinese legation. In the sitting area near the elevator idled some passport applicants. Since my arrival in Vienna, I had only seen a few Chinese men in that area. Most of the time, it remained empty.

Vice Consul Zhou looked up from his desk as I passed him. Fengshan often said that the Austrians were uptight and proud, but Chinese men were no different. Rarely smiling, Vice Consul Zhou was a severe and peculiar man with long nails on his pinkies. Each of those nails was at least an inch long, and he used them as a head-scratcher and a line pacer when he read newspapers and documents. His gaze was friendly and respectful, but I had the nagging feeling that he talked about me behind my back. *She's the wife of a Chinese consul general, but she can barely speak Chinese!* My inability to speak German had made me an outsider in Fengshan's circle, and my limited vocabulary of Chinese had made me a stranger to the staff in the consulate.

"Good morning, Mrs. Consul General." The Austrian woman in her fifties, Frau Maxa, was organizing a stack of manila folders. She was a typist, a woman with a dour face; she spoke English with a German accent, like Lola, but heavier.

I was glad she didn't ask any questions. I stopped at the main desk and picked up thick envelopes and gilded cards so Fengshan could go through them later and inform me of my obligation. There really wasn't much for me to do, useless as I was, but as Fengshan's wife, I was expected to attend luncheons and banquets. Looking at the mail, I wished that the consulate had enough financial support to hire me an assistant who could help translate. Someone like Lola.

Mail in hand, I walked into Fengshan's office. He was on the phone, speaking English, looking distressed. It seemed that he was trying to get ahold of Mr. Wiley, the American consul general, but was deterred.

When Fengshan finally put down the phone, he collapsed in his seat, rubbing his forehead. "I'm at my wit's end. I have a few urgent matters in desperate need of consultation with the consul general, but he's been in a meeting all morning and is not available to answer my calls."

I put the mail near the cigar humidor on his desk—so enormous, the box, it was large enough to hold ten volumes of Dickinson and heavy, a challenge for me to lift with two hands. Masterfully hand-crafted, made of Spanish cedar with fine grain patterns, it was one of many gifts Fengshan had received—he might be a diplomat from a country with little influence, but he was beloved by many professionals in Vienna.

"Does Mr. Wiley know I was arrested by the Nazis?"

He looked at me. "I hope not. Your arrest is an embarrassment. For the sake of the consulate's image, it needs to stay private."

"Well . . . You're right . . . Maybe it's best he won't know . . ." I had met the consul general twice and had talked to his wife at a party. I had been eager to make friends with her, but she wasn't American, as it turned out, but a Polish woman who spoke a few languages, at least ten years older than me and an established sculptor. We had nothing in common, and it was a disaster. I rambled on about the solitary life in the city, and she stared at me like I was a child and told me to get a hobby.

"If only I could find an excuse to reach Mr. Wiley. A good excuse to pique his interest. What's the matter, Grace?"

"Nothing . . . Never mind." Fengshan rarely discussed politics or asked for my opinion, and that was fine with me.

"Grace, what is it?"

"Well, I was thinking, my love, I'm an American citizen, so if you tell Mr. Wiley of my arrest, he might be concerned."

His face lit up. "Grace, that is an excellent excuse indeed. Mr. Wiley needs to know about your arrest. He has a responsibility to protect you."

Fengshan dialed the American consulate's phone number again, identified himself, and asked to speak to the secretary of Mr. Wiley. Then he explained that I had been detained at the Headquarters last night and asked to speak personally to the consul general. For a long moment, he held the phone and listened; when he hung up, he smiled broadly. "Grace. I have an appointment with Mr. Wiley. He cares about your safety and would like to meet me."

"That's good news."

"Excellent news indeed."

"When will you meet him?"

"Tomorrow. You came in the nick of time and gave me an excellent suggestion, Grace. I had been calling the American consulate for hours in vain." He was in a good mood.

I threaded my arms around his neck. "Well, I have something to ask you. The Viennese girl . . . Lola . . . I promised I wouldn't hire her as a tutor. It's just . . . It was late at night, and she was alone. She might have lost her way or gotten arrested again. Anything could happen to her. I want to know if she's safe. Would you object if I call her?"

"The Viennese girl?" He looked at his watch, picked up his leather briefcase from the shelf, and reached for his bowler hat from the coatrack near the door.

"Just a phone call to make sure she's safe. Where are you going?" I took his hat from his hand and put it on my head, and then I pulled the hat down to cover my face. Playing with his things, putting on his tie or his pajamas—my spontaneity and girlish impulsiveness, as he said—had amused him when we were in Chicago, and he would laugh, but not in Istanbul or here in Vienna.

"I have an event." The corners of his lips tilted upward, fortunately—no frowns or fuss.

I gave the hat back to him. "I thought your meeting with Mr. Wiley was tomorrow."

"I'm going to an event in a German club."

"Right. Well, you must go."

He put his hat on, hesitating. "Do you really need to call the Viennese girl?"

"She was beaten, my love. And alone at night. Aren't you worried as well?"

"Fine. Just a phone call. I need to go."

"What time is your event?"

"In an hour."

"So you have plenty of time. When will you have time for me? I got up and you were gone. Won't you stay in bed with me in the mornings?"

"Grace."

I whispered in his ear, "Well, do whatever you need to do; I'm not going anywhere. You know where to find me."

I called Lola the moment after Fengshan left. Her voice, when it came through, was as fine as the music the orchestra ensemble played in the ballrooms, and yes, she had arrived home safely. "And would you like to have some coffee?" she asked.

No one had invited me for coffee, or tea. Not in Chicago, or China, or Istanbul.

"Oh yes," I said.

She suggested that we meet at Café Caché near the Stadtpark, as though understanding perfectly well my limits—Café Caché was the only coffeehouse I knew. *See you tomorrow, Grace.*

I put down the receiver, smiling. I had not forgotten Fengshan's disapproval, his warning of the danger in the city, and the humiliation of my arrest. But we would meet in a coffeehouse; it would be safe.

CHAPTER 7

FENGSHAN

The crowd at the club was smaller than he expected—a pitiful group of five, two women with gray hair and three elderly Viennese men in brown coats and fur muffs that appeared incompatible with the warm weather, a sorry sight compared to the rapt audience of two hundred at the National Assembly Hall, where he had lectured last year. There were no familiar faces of bespectacled university professors, or well-dressed businessmen keen to learn the ancient Chinese Four Great Inventions, or his friend Mr. Rosenburg. This almost never happened.

For a good forty minutes, in his fluent German, Fengshan excoriated the Japanese for their invasion of China and for violating the laws of the League of Nations. He also revealed the Japanese ambition of conquering the world that he'd found in a secret memo from Tanaka Giichi to Emperor Hirohito, their savage destruction of his homeland, and the devastating losses of human lives. China would defend herself, he vowed. But frustratingly, his lecture was met with silence and bewilderment. When he opened for questions, the few people in the audience asked irrelevant, ignorant questions: Did all women in China have bound feet? Did women in China wear pants like men? The latter was uttered with some disdain, since it was customary for Austrian women to don skirts.

Vienna today was not the Vienna of last year.

A man came to his lectern at the end of the lecture, clad in a black uniform and the cap with *Totenkopf*. Captain Heine appeared to be the doppelgänger of the SS man, Eichmann, at first glance. Both were tall, sophisticated, exuding severity with their uniforms, though with one distinction: Eichmann's eyes were cold gray, and Captain Heine's were strikingly blue. It was likely paranoia, but the captain's intense interest in him, after Grace's arrest, could not be completely a whim.

"You're a commendable orator, Herr Consul General. Your speech has, once again, enlightened us." Captain Heine raised a glass of cognac in his hand—the captain always knew where to find cognac.

Fengshan had known the captain for about a year. He was a powerful man, well acquainted with the nobles, the magistrates, the department-store owners, the Rothschilds, as well as the international diplomats. He was also a regular patron of popular haunts in the city, German clubs, jazz bars, and cabarets. Rumor said the captain was a fastidious man, had his barber come every morning for a fine trim of his hair on the sides and back and a warm toweling around his neck. Although he was a married man, he made no effort to hide his attentions to young, attractive women, often claiming that it was fashionable for officers to have lovers.

Fengshan collected his materials and tucked them in his folder, willing the captain to leave him alone. It was not his intention to become entangled with a Gestapo officer, but for the sake of his country, in desperate need of a hefty loan and international assistance, he must remain friendly to marshal any potential allies. "I am pleased to see you, Captain Heine."

"How's Frau Consul General faring?" The captain didn't seem to be in a hurry to leave.

Fengshan felt his throat tighten. It was not entirely out of the question that Captain Heine and Eichmann were well acquainted. "She's well. I'm indebted to you, Captain Heine."

"Do not mention it, Herr Consul General. It was my pleasure. Are you ready to leave? Well, I must say I expected a bigger crowd. A pity. The Viennese are missing an important opportunity. Where are your admirers?" The captain gave a smirk that must have been practiced on many attractive women, or maybe on the poor dissidents or even Jews these days.

Fengshan smiled warily at the captain.

"I'm serious. Where are your admirers, Herr Consul General? Everyone in Vienna loves your lectures."

"Mr. Rosenburg said he'd attend."

Heine knew well of his friend, an influential attorney. Vienna was a small city, after all; all the rich and the powerful knew each other.

"Of course, Mr. Rosenburg. I was thinking about him. Is he ill? What would make him miss your lecture?" The captain swirled the liquid in his glass in his irritatingly smooth manner as though he were flirting with a woman. Another reason Fengshan would rather stay away from him.

"I'm sure he's fine."

The captain had a gulp of his cognac. "Do you have plans after the event, Herr Consul General? Would you like to have some coffee at Café Central?"

"I would be delighted, but regretfully, I have another meeting to attend." He put on his bowler and stepped out of the room, into the hallway.

"Perhaps tomorrow, Herr Consul General?" The captain followed him.

"I'm afraid I have a full schedule tomorrow."

Two policemen in uniforms strutted toward them, shouting, "*Heil* Hitler," and Captain Heine saluted back. Fengshan's steps slowed. Suddenly, the space felt crowded.

51

"Next week, Herr Consul General?"

"That would be splendid. But allow me to look at my calendar and get back to you. My apologies. I must take my leave."

Outside the club, Fengshan passed a couple holding tennis rackets on the circular stairs and took out his handkerchief to dab at his face. In his haste, he had forgotten to shake hands with the attendees, a regretful oversight that must have shed a negative light on his country's image.

He tucked his handkerchief in his pocket, went down a cobblestone path lined with lindens, and turned onto a street with white stone buildings, the traffic and shouts from the Ringstrasse growing louder with each step. He thought to stop at the Staatsoper to purchase opera tickets for Grace as he had planned. She was lonely; she needed attention. And he was quite pleased with her in helping to make making the appointment with Mr. Wiley.

Fengshan, a loyal man, valued every friendship. Three years after he had been posted outside China, he still remembered the birthdays of his friends at home and regularly sent them postcards printed with beautiful images of Vienna, the Ferris wheel of the Prater, the lilacs of Votive Park, Schönbrunn Palace, and St. Stephen's Cathedral.

Mr. Rosenburg never missed his events, and he had not called back this morning. This was an unusual lapse of etiquette on his friend's part. Fengshan wondered what happened. Mr. Rosenburg was a wealthy Jew who had made a fortune by overseeing one of the Austrian royal family's properties; he owned a mansion near Votive Church, an apartment complex in Vienna, and two chalets in Salzburg. Fengshan had met him at a lecture about Chinese culture he'd given. It had struck a chord with the Viennese man, who appeared to be immensely interested in Chinese calligraphy. He was a good friend, a generous man, and he had invited him to many dinners and parties. With his help, Fengshan befriended renowned Viennese professors and Czechoslovakian men with diplomatic status and wealthy German businessmen. Mr. Rosenburg was also the go-to source whenever Fengshan needed help—he had recommended the bespoke tailor and several Viennese tutors for Grace, including the new tutor, Fräulein Schnitzler.

Fengshan thought to pay his friend a visit. His office suite, a complex with twelve rooms, was located on the Ringstrasse. It was within walking distance.

⁓

At an intersection across from the stately Hofburg palace, Fengshan stopped abruptly, gripping his leather briefcase. Near a fountain in the plaza, a uniformed *Sturmabteilung* was striking a hatless man with a baton, shouting offensive racial slurs.

Since when had the streets of Vienna, part of the mighty Austro-Hungarian Empire, the center of culture and civilization, become a site of fear and violence? Fengshan switched his bag to his left hand and crossed the street. As soon as he arrived in front of the grand building complex that contained Mr. Rosenburg's business suite, he came upon two columns of Brownshirts carrying rifles, their polished black handles glaring in the afternoon sun. Hesitating, Fengshan was heading toward the portico with colossal columns when a man called him from behind. Fengshan turned around. The man, clad in a blue Savile Row suit, was sitting on the pavement near a bench designated for Aryans, a pile of papers scattered around, and his right eye was bruised, but Fengshan recognized him instantly.

"Good God, Mr. Rosenburg, what happened to you? Why are you sitting on the ground?"

His friend gave a terrible laugh, but his bearing was still aristocratic after spending his entire life addressing the nobles in the country. "My apologies, Dr. Ho, I'm afraid I can't offer you a seat. They've taken my firm, the money in my bank accounts, my license, my desk, my collectibles, and my chalets in Salzburg. There's nothing I could salvage. I simply needed a rest after all those visits to the banks."

"But you're a lawyer—would you like to sit on the bench for a moment?"

"They gave me a good beating for sitting on that bench. I fear my old bones cannot take it anymore."

Fengshan glanced at the file of Brownshirts. The metal handle of his briefcase, cold, was cutting his hand. Grace, and now Mr. Rosenburg. "I was only made aware of the change of the law recently, Mr. Rosenburg."

"There are so many laws that target Jews. It's understandable that the foreign diplomats are not privy to this legislation." His friend sighed; in his grave voice, he recounted the recent happenings in the city. Since the Anschluss, all Jewish attorneys and judges had been removed from the city's court. All cases against Jews were dismissed without a trial, and the Jews were incriminated simply because of who they were. A few days ago, he was told some of his friends were visited by two SS men who had demanded they "donate" their savings in bank accounts to the government. Today, he'd been paid a visit by these men, who made the same demands. He refused, stating his accounts were protected by the Austrian court. They held him at gunpoint, escorted him to the court, and had the judge, a former friend of his, sign to grant the SS men access to his bank accounts. So in this way, they legally robbed his money.

Fengshan was at a loss as to how to reply. In China, a homogeneous country, racial tension was hardly an issue, but he was familiar with suffering and strife stemming from politics. The rise of one party always meant the bloodshed of the innocent. During one of the conflicts between the Nationalists and the Communists at home, one of his friends had been tried by a mob and murdered at their demand, and Fengshan himself had nearly died at the hands of the gang who demanded his death.

Mr. Rosenburg gazed at the grand building guarded by the Brownshirts. "Yesterday, I was still a wealthy man, and today I'm out of a job, poor. My career in Vienna is over, and even my own survival, my family's survival, is in question."

Devastated, Fengshan had an urge to have a cigar. What could he do for his friend? He was a diplomat of another country; he couldn't give back his friend his job or assets, or protection, or justice. "Do you need a place to stay, Mr. Rosenburg?"

"I'm staying at my in-laws' apartment with my family, Dr. Ho. But I'm afraid it's temporary. They have also accused me of actively destroying Austria throughout my career, forced me to sign a confession, and ordered me to disappear."

"Disappear?"

"To permanently leave Vienna. Under the order of Adolf Eichmann, the Devil's Deputy."

The lizard man at the Headquarters. He had mentioned he was assigned to the city to take care of the Jewish problem, Fengshan recalled.

"The man ordered me to emigrate, or he'd send me to the Dachau camp if I continue to stay in Vienna."

"Dachau camp?"

"A labor camp for prisoners. I'm afraid you won't read it in the newspaper."

Never in his wildest dreams had he imagined this would happen to his dear friend: robbed of all his wealth and properties and threatened with forced labor. "You can't go to a prison camp. Where would you like to immigrate to?"

"Palestine, England, or America. I'm planning on applying for visas in these countries' consulates tomorrow."

There had been many embassies in Vienna, but the prominent countries, such as Great Britain and France, had closed them after the Anschluss. Palestine was a natural choice for Jews, and America was a desirable destination. Fengshan had not received any visa applications in his consulate, other than the clandestine request from the first secretary of the Soviet legation. But that was to be expected. China, a country on the far side of the world, a country with poor commerce and ravaged by war, was hardly an ideal home for the wealthy Viennese.

Besides, China didn't have an immigration policy. Even if the Viennese applied to immigrate to China, Fengshan would need approval from his superior. But Ambassador Chen, in the midst of securing a loan from the League of Nations, would not be distracted to consider such an impractical policy, and as a subordinate, he was bound to obey the ambassador's order.

"I'd better start working, Dr. Ho. The Devil's Deputy gave me two months to find visas." Mr. Rosenburg struggled to hoist himself up but faltered.

Fengshan extended his hand and held his friend firmly—the least he could do.

Two months, or his friend would be sent to the Dachau camp.

CHAPTER 8

GRACE

The next day, I talked to Fengshan briefly—he seemed preoccupied, contemplative, smoking his cigar, but asked whether I'd like to join him in the meeting with Mr. Wiley. I shook my head and slipped out of the consulate, glad he didn't ask where I was going.

Walking down the quiet Beethovenplatz, I reached the Stadtpark, then turned left, heading toward Café Caché, a coffeehouse sandwiched between a tailor shop flaunting a row of tall mannequins clad in mauve, lilac, and turquoise gowns and a boutique watch store with wall-to-wall clocks: pocket watches with gold chains, wristwatches with duo-dial formats, watches in silver cases and golden boxes. I had never dreamed of these luxuries, growing up happy with a torn piece of warm bread Mother slipped in my hands. A diplomat's wife now, for the sake of Fengshan's country's image, I routinely put on a pearl necklace or a tailored evening gown or a Rolex Oyster steel watch, yet I would have gladly traded all the pastel colors of summer and all the finery of Vienna for the warm smile of a friend.

In the coffeehouse, Lola was already waiting, wearing the same full-length green dirndl dress and a pair of leather pumps with low heels, sitting by the window. Her eyes had the glow that she had in the dungeon, warm and compassionate, and her face, lightly powdered to cover the bruising, was friendly, a face to talk to, to ask directions on the street, and to sip coffee with.

I wove through the round tables covered with white cloth and two red velvet couches—a cluster of men in brown shirts and armbands with swastikas were sitting there, their gazes penetrating. I averted my eyes.

"*Grüß Gott*, Miss Lee." Lola stood as I approached.

"Ah . . . *grüß* . . . I thought it was *guten* . . . *Tag*?" I stammered, sitting across from her. When I came to the coffeehouse last time, I had stood at the counter, panicking, trying to decipher a long list of drinks written on a board. Who would know the great city that prided itself on its coffee had a menu as long as my stocking but did not contain a single word that looked like *coffee*? In the end, I pointed at the shortest German word on the board and received a black drink that tasted like whiskey.

"That's a German tradition. We Austrians say *grüß Gott*."

"Ah. I didn't know that."

"You'll know, given time."

I smiled but was unsure what to say next. Should I bring up tutoring and let her know that I couldn't hire her? Should I say good morning? But I'd already said that.

"I'm so glad to see you again, Miss Lee. I wish to tell you how thankful I am that you helped release me from the Headquarters."

She leaned toward me, her green eyes the shade of spring in the Stadtpark, and her dark hair a lush braid. Her manner was smooth, like cream pouring into the coffee. How did she cultivate such a manner, I wondered. But perhaps finesse had nothing to do with the practice. Some people were born with it.

"It wasn't me; it was my husband, Fräulein Schnitzel."

"Please convey my deepest gratitude to your husband. And it's Schnitzler."

"Oh, right. You said you were related to an author."

She laughed. "You're funny, Miss Lee. But please, call me Lola. I'll be honored if you consider me your friend."

A friend, after all these years. "Will you call me Grace, then?"

"It'll be my pleasure, Grace. Thank you for coming to meet me. Did you have trouble finding this place?"

A man's harsh voice screeched beside me just as I was about to answer. I glanced around, surprised. I rarely saw Austrian men behave poorly in public, but these Brownshirts could use some etiquette lessons from a footman. They were young, or maybe they weren't—I could never tell the age of the Austrian men, camouflaged with beards and mustaches.

I focused back on our conversation. "I've been here before. I was almost lost on the street."

"If you get lost again, take a taxi to your consulate."

"I don't know how to speak German."

She turned to the newspaper rack behind her, tore a piece, and jotted down something. "Here. The consulate's address in German. When you take a taxi, you give this to the driver."

Lola was helpful. I thanked her and tucked the slip into my handbag. But the men around me were growing rowdy; some had their gazes fixated on Lola—those were not friendly gazes.

"Ignore them. The times are strange, but as we Austrians often say, the situation is helpless but not entirely serious." Lola held a menu, ready to order coffee.

"Well . . ."

"Our country has gone through some violent times, Grace. When Chancellor Dollfuss was assassinated four years ago, many of us feared the National Socialists would take over the government, but the party's leaders were executed, and Schuschnigg was elected. Now he's been arrested, and the National Socialists have seized power. But they won't be in charge forever. Vienna will always be Vienna."

The ease, the confidence in her tone. There was no reason not to trust her. "They have thick beards." So thick they could hide an entire brood of birds from Dickinson's household.

"Don't be intimidated by those beards. It's a Viennese thing. The Austrian men have a love affair with music and facial hair."

I laughed. I hadn't laughed like that since I left Chicago. And it felt good. I was thinking about what to say when suddenly the window near me exploded. A loud crash burst in my ears; instinctively, I slipped below the round table. A shower of cold shards rained on my head and neck. I shrieked.

"Grace, Grace? Are you hurt?" Lola's voice came a moment later.

I pulled myself up, my knees weak. "I'm fine . . . What's going on? What happened, Lola? Oh my God. What happened to you?"

Blood gushed on Lola's face; a shard had cut deep in her cheek, just below her left eye. Half an inch higher, it would have pierced her eye. "Someone hit me with a coffee cup. It struck the window."

I turned around. The Brownshirts were pointing at me, blustering in German. My brain froze.

"Let's get out of here, Grace."

I tried to walk but bumped into a table. A cup fell, splashing my wrist with black coffee. Lola turned around, grabbed my arm, and prodded me along. When we finally made it out of the door, all I could see were the cars driving by and the pedestrians with curious looks. I should have listened to Fengshan. First, the arrest in a park and now an assault in the coffeehouse. Was it me? Or Lola? Or Vienna?

I heard Lola say something but could barely understand her. Then suddenly, Lola's face seemed to explode. Thick blood streamed down her chin, to her pendants, to the front of her dirndl—she had drawn out the shard.

"You're bleeding! Oh no. Oh no." I fumbled in my handbag—lipstick, bills, the slip of newspaper, Tiger Balm, and finally, my monogrammed silk handkerchief. "Here, take this. Do you want to take this?

It's mine. You can use it. You need to go to the hospital. Do you know any hospitals, Lola?"

She pressed my handkerchief onto her face; in an instant, red bloomed on the silk. "Vienna General Hospital is nearby."

"Oh good. Let's go there. Wait. Let's take a taxi. Do you want to take a taxi?" And then, because she didn't speak and I didn't know what else to do, I hailed a taxi.

The ride was excruciatingly slow, passing the grand opera house, the Hofburg palace, and the equestrian statues in the Heroes' Square. By the time we reached the hospital, my handkerchief was soaked, and the front of Lola's dirndl dress had turned black, but the blood continued to ooze endlessly, and she had to borrow my glove. When we entered the hospital's lobby, a stout man wearing glasses greeted us. He looked at me and then Lola and said something in German. One hand on her face, Lola dug into her wallet with the other, perhaps searching for an identification card, and fired away some German phrases rapidly. The pain must have been unbearable; her words were slurred. But the man nodded in understanding. I was relieved. Fengshan had admired Viennese hospitals greatly, praising their advanced equipment, well-trained physicians, and good care.

But something was not right. The man should have gotten Lola a seat or taken a look at her wound—the bleeding had fortunately just been stanched, and her entire face was swollen. But he, and the white-gowned nurses milling around the lobby, did nothing other than talk. In the end, Lola turned around. "We need to go to another place, Grace."

"What's wrong?"

"It's a new law. The hospital is prohibited from accepting Jewish patients."

"What? Are you sure? It's a hospital. It's supposed to treat all patients. And you need stitches and some morphine."

She was trembling. "Let's go to a Jewish doctor's office."

Had I been an eloquent diplomat's wife, I would have questioned the staff in the hospital about the law and pleaded with them to make an exception to treat Lola. Instead, I bit my tongue and hailed another taxi—Lola needed stitches.

Soon we arrived at a clinic in an apartment on a narrow cobblestone street. Lola looked relieved. I held her arm—she was growing pale, her face a ruined orb of swollen purple, and her hands were as cold as ice.

Inside the Jewish clinic, two men in tall black hats spoke to her. Again, Lola showed her identification card, and again, a rapid exchange in German ensued. The men looked at each other, then called out, and a doctor in a white gown stepped into the room.

Finally.

The conversation between the doctor and Lola sounded promising; this was a Jewish clinic, after all, and the doctor looked sympathetic, his tone soothing, soft, but then Lola turned around. "Let's go, Grace."

"Wait. Are they going to give you stitches?"

"They can't." She stumbled outside and nearly crashed into a pot of red geraniums at the door. She steadied herself, leaning against the wall. The narrow street was quiet, without the sun.

"Why?"

"They are not allowed to accept half-Jewish patients. It's another law."

"What?"

Tears welled in her eyes, exhausted and bloodshot, and in an instant, they were tinged with the blood near her brow, but she looked up, and those tears didn't fall, and her voice, even though intelligible, was the same, fearless and forceful. "I'm a *Mischling*."

I actually remembered what that meant—she was like me, a woman of mixed blood. So a woman of mixed blood, Lola, was declined at a Christian hospital for being Jewish and declined at a Jewish clinic for being only half-Jewish.

I wrung, and wrung, the strap of my handbag. "This is unexpected . . . What are you going to do, Lola? You need stitches. What can you do, Lola?"

"Let's try another clinic."

"Yes, yes." I held Lola's arm and walked by her side. She was different from me, a weeper, and how many times had Mother shaken me, her hands on my neck, screaming, trying to instill in me some steeliness that she believed would do me good—*Have some grit, Grace. Learn from your father, Grace.* Yet I was never my father, a hero, a man who had the backbone to save her from five gangsters.

We left the narrow lane and came to a broad street with traffic lights. Nearby, a group of women, picking at flowers in a florist's cart filled with white tulips and red carnations, frowned at us, and in front of a news kiosk, three men in double-breasted summer suits turned to watch us and mumbled something in German.

Lola's steps slowed and then stopped. "Grace, do you know how to return to the consulate from here?"

"I'll take a taxi with the slip you wrote for me. Let's go to the clinic. Where is the clinic?"

"You should go home, Grace, and I think I should go home too. I'm sorry about this unexpected disruption. I was hoping we would have a good time drinking coffee."

What made her change her mind, I wondered. "But you said to go to another clinic. You need to get stitches . . ."

"Don't worry about me. I hope I'll see you again, Grace." She handed me back my glove, and the gash on her face bared itself, a raw, scarlet groove. Then she staggered toward a tram that had just stopped, held on to the door, and climbed in.

The tram clattered away, fluttering with those disturbing swastika flags, passing the men with their newspapers and the prim women holding the flowers. In the air played a thundering, fast-spinning Hungarian folk song. I looked at the glove in my hands, a bespoke silk glove, small, fitting my hand, now damp, sticky, soaked with Lola's blood. And now my hands were sticky, bloody as well. But I understood why Lola had changed her mind, and it dawned on me. No matter how many clinics we were going to visit, Lola would not be able to receive treatment.

I returned to the consulate later. In my bathroom, I washed my handkerchief and glove in the sink, watching Lola's blood splash in the porcelain bowl, thinking about the apathetic looks of the nurses in the hospital and the cold stares of the prim women and the newspaper-carrying men. I burst into tears. Lola had been right—they didn't like her, and Fengshan was right too—Vienna was no longer safe. If Lola and I continued to go to places, another park or another coffeehouse, we would likely face more unexpected encounters that were now part of Vienna. For the sake of my husband and the consulate, it would be best to stay in the bedroom and read my poetry.

Yet I would have followed Lola to another clinic or another ten clinics, and I wished with all my heart that there were something I could do.

CHAPTER 9

FENGSHAN

Before noon, he left the consulate.

He had lost some sleep over the meeting with Mr. Wiley. Whether his country could receive the desperately needed loan depended on how it went, and he'd like to probe Mr. Wiley about the current state of Vienna as well, for the image of his friend with a bruised eye sitting on the street in his Savile Row suit wavered in his mind. Two months, he had said.

Fengshan arrived at the Blaue Bar inside the Hotel Sacher precisely at one o'clock and dove into the bar, a dark burrow with bright vines of lights crawling on its walls. He held his bowler hat in hand, his steps cautious, while his vision adjusted. Now and then, a wave of translucent light swept over a few faces, and a roar of laughter and music rushed to his ears. Modern, poorly lit bars like this rarely appealed to him, and he would have preferred a bright coffeehouse with an open fire or a view of the grand theater or a calming garden. Mr. Wiley, a man of unruffled manner, didn't seem an edgy type, but he had requested to meet here.

Fengshan spotted the diplomat sitting in a corner near a tree made of blue lights. "Good afternoon, Mr. Wiley," Fengshan greeted him in English.

"Dr. Ho." The American diplomat looked stoic with a pair of glasses. He was in his forties, wearing a gray tie and a black suit and a smile that at times appeared to be almost friendly. His background, like Ambassador Chen's, was nothing short of illustrious, coming from a prominent family, his father being an American consul in France. Mr. Wiley had served as the consul general in Moscow and then in Antwerp and was appointed the ambassador of the American legation in Austria before it was demoted to a consulate.

Fengshan had little direct contact with the American diplomat. When he came across Mr. Wiley and his wife at balls, they conversed briefly. The American Foreign Service Officers, Fengshan had learned, were not outspoken or empathetic people. They appeared cultivated, unflappable, and perfectly institutionalized, with a mindset of conformity and veneration of their superiors.

"Sit, sit." Mr. Wiley looked at his watch, streaks of blue lights brushing his face. "Dr. Ho, I'd love to offer you a drink under normal circumstances, but I must offer my most sincere apologies. My presence is needed at another location, and I regret I don't have much time."

An ominous prelude. Fengshan braced himself. "I'm grateful for your time, Mr. Wiley. Grace sends you her regards."

China's diplomatic relations with the United States had been fraught with doubt, if not mistrust. The seed was perhaps planted decades ago by President Wilson, who urged China to join the fight against Germany during the Great War, promising that China would retrieve the German concessions in Shandong province. Eager to regain full control of its mainland territory, China abandoned its neutrality and shipped thousands of laborers to Britain, France, and Russia to help dig trenches, repair tanks, and man factories. But when the war was won, Wilson signed the Treaty of Versailles with Japan, France, and Britain and gave the German territory to Japan, whose grip on China had tightened ever since.

"How is Mrs. Ho? It was brought to my attention that she had an awkward encounter with the German authority. Is that so?"

Fengshan gave a brief account of Grace's arrest and how he had been notified and secured her release. "She's doing well, although she prefers to forget the unpleasant stay."

"It must have been quite an ordeal. Dr. Ho, if anything happens to her again, please do inform the consulate. We're here for our people, and we care about every American citizen. Vienna poses great challenges for Americans, I understand. The language and customs are an obstacle. Many are homesick. Irena talks about how much her friends miss American soda and Thanksgiving dinners. Now, forgive me, Dr. Ho, for my haste. An Austrian, a renowned founder of psychoanalysis theory, has been under the protection of my consulate, but I just heard that he was harassed again. The man is in his eighties, and I fear the old gentleman, frail as he is, won't take such nonsense any longer. I must attend to the matter promptly."

"Of course," Fengshan said. "Mr. Wiley, I'm honored to meet you here today. May I congratulate Ambassador Wilson, on behalf of my superior Ambassador Chen, for his new position in Berlin? My superior is looking forward to meeting him in person. Could this possibly be arranged with your attention?" He went on to describe briefly the aggression of the Japanese, who had ravaged his country for years, and his country's desperate need for a loan.

Mr. Wiley squinted at his watch again. "I shall be glad to relay the plight of your country to my superior in Berlin. However, with the most profound regret, Ambassador Wilson has a full schedule for the next six months. As for the loan from the League, I'm certain that you're aware that the procedure requires the input of some key council members. However, I'm afraid such a meeting is not on the League's agenda, due to the escalating political situation in Europe. As you know, the French and the English are focused on their matters at home."

Fengshan let out a sigh. Ambassador Chen would be disappointed. "It's a shame that the League that has been a spokesperson for world peace is too beset by its own woes to carry out its mission."

"I couldn't agree more, Dr. Ho. I'm sorry I don't have good news."

He couldn't allow the American to leave yet. "May I ask, Mr. Wiley, who's the prominent Austrian figure your consulate is protecting?"

"Dr. Freud. I'm sure you've heard of him."

"Why is he being harassed?"

"The reason many people are living in fear."

Fengshan hadn't known Dr. Freud was also a Jew. He sighed and recounted the story of Mr. Rosenburg, a prominent lawyer being forced to leave the country. "Mr. Wiley, forgive me, I hate to take more of your time, but the situation in Vienna is most disconcerting. As you're aware, Anschluss has caught many of us by surprise, and some of the uncivil incidents are most disheartening and cause much grief for many Viennese. What are your thoughts regarding the future of the Viennese Jews in Greater Germany?"

Mr. Wiley sighed. "I won't mince my words. I am quite alarmed. I have received multiple petitions regarding the treatment of Jews born and raised here. Some petitions come from Quakers, who have expressed similar concerns like yours. I assure you that I've made my country aware of the situation, and President Roosevelt has decided to take action."

"This is most heartwarming to hear. Would you care to elaborate?"

"The news will soon be made public, Dr. Ho, but I am pleased to inform you now that our president has made an urgent call summoning thirty-two nations of the world to convene in Évian-les-Bains, France, to discuss options to assist the Jewish people in Greater Germany who need humanitarian assistance."

Thirty-two countries. If this were not an ultimate demonstration of a country in power, he didn't know what was. Ambassador Chen was still unable to meet the key members of the League after a month's request, but the president of the United States made a phone call, and the representatives from thirty-two countries cleared their schedules for a meeting. Fengshan dared to dream that one day China would follow America's footsteps and prosper and wield great power and influence in the world.

His feelings aside, it was apparent to him that the United States, once a nascent power on the world stage, now played an increasingly important role. If the president of the United States called for action, there was good reason to believe some positive outcome would be reached.

"Mr. Wiley, may I venture to ask if there will be sanctions on the German government?"

"It wouldn't be unexpected, given the atrocities we have heard of."

"Perhaps there's an agenda of a new immigration law, provided that the Viennese Jews are willing to leave the country?"

"With thirty-two countries attending the conference, I would daresay some of them, if not all, will welcome the talented, wealthy, intellectual immigrants to their country."

Fengshan concurred. What countries wouldn't open their arms to educated people with skills and wealth? Had China not been embroiled in war, it would be glad to accept these Viennese as well. Mr. Rosenburg would be relieved to hear this news. He would have several countries, not just the US, to immigrate to, if he decided to do so. Or he might be able to stay in Vienna and regain his properties and savings.

"I can assure you, Dr. Ho, the United States is the guardian of humanity, the advocate of world peace and freedom. Who will we be if we fail to protect the vulnerable? With Congress's approval, we will see to it that democracy, freedom, and equality will be achieved for everyone."

It was typical grandiose American discourse, yet it sounded comforting and strangely uplifting, and Fengshan dreamed of the day when he would make a similar claim on behalf of his country and instill his countrymen with the same aspirations. "When is the meeting?"

"July sixth." Mr. Wiley stood.

In about six weeks. "It's a long wait for those harassed."

The American patted his shoulder. "Dr. Ho, it is admirable that you have such compassion, but I'm sure you understand that it is recommended to diplomats that we maintain a certain distance among the political upheaval."

Fengshan laughed. "I beg your pardon, Mr. Wiley, but didn't you mention Dr. Freud was under your consulate's protection?"

Mr. Wiley chuckled and left.

They were diplomats, bound by their duty to their countries and by their ambition for their careers, not necessarily to each other. But Mr. Wiley had left him with important hints and intelligence to reflect on.

"How did the meeting go, Fengshan? Was it successful?" The ambassador's voice came through at the first ring.

Fengshan dove into his report, expressing the regrets of Mr. Wiley. As he had imagined, Ambassador Chen sounded deeply disappointed that the prospects of meeting his American counterpart were dim and the desperately needed loan remained unobtainable.

Fengshan cleared his throat. "With much respect, Ambassador Chen, before you go, may I share with you an observation?" When he'd conversed with Mr. Wiley, something else, another perspective about America and the League of Nations, had sparked in his mind. "Ambassador Chen, what are your thoughts on the League? How often do the council members meet?"

"It's irregular and slow-paced, with prolific correspondence and predictable bureaucracy, as we all know. What are you trying to say, Fengshan?"

He ventured, "Mr. Wiley seems to have an uncomplimentary opinion of the League. I can't help but observe that on short notice, the president of the United States succeeded in gathering thirty-two nations for a conference, but the League hasn't had a functional meeting of council members for a long period of time. I wonder if a new direction in seeking the loan is warranted."

"What are you suggesting?"

"Would you agree that it's more favorable to obtain a loan when we speak directly to the US via diplomatic channels rather than relying on the League? What would be your thoughts if we contact Mr. Henry Morgenthau, the secretary of the treasury in the United States?"

"This certainly is not something within my consideration, and it is unfortunate that the new ambassador to the US, Mr. Hu Shi, hasn't presented his credentials yet."

"Perhaps the Ministry of Foreign Affairs will be involved and offer their valuable help."

There was a noncommittal cough.

Fengshan persisted. "Allow me to share another thought with you, Ambassador Chen. It seems that Mr. Wiley believes his president has great concerns about the suffering of the Jews under German rule. The US has called for a conference of thirty-two countries to look into the treatment of the Viennese Jews. Mr. Wiley predicted that they would spearhead a refugee policy around the world. I wonder if the Ministry of Foreign Affairs has taken similar steps on the same subject."

"Why would the Ministry take an interest in accepting refugees?"

Fengshan cringed.

"Our country is under attack. We're struggling to survive. We need a loan, and we need sophisticated weapons to defeat the Japanese. The last thing we want is an influx of foreign refugees to feed. Let the Americans devise their strategies, and you remember my instruction. We must not interfere with the domestic controversies in Greater

Germany, or the Third Reich will find an excuse to decline the weapons sales, and our relationship will be doomed. Is that clear?"

"Of course."

Ambassador Chen ended their conversation with another grave piece of news. The Japanese artillery led by General Hata was in relentless pursuit of the Nationalists sheltered in Wuhan, their temporary capital. To defend the city, President Chiang Kai-shek had withdrawn one million troops from the country's Fifth and Ninth War Zones. A fierce battle to safeguard the temporary capital was imminent.

Fengshan put down the phone. If he had not been tied to responsibilities and duties to the consulate, he would have packed up and plunged in to protect his country and countrymen.

He took a cigar from his cigar box and began to smoke. The ambassador's indifference to the Viennese Jews and his disinterest in the conference that the American president had summoned, disappointing as it was, was to be expected. But Mr. Rosenburg would be overjoyed about the Évian Conference, and he would be delighted to know. Fengshan stubbed his cigar in a crystal ashtray and wrote a note, informing him of the wonderful news of the conference and potential rescue from the countries around the world. Then he ordered the vice consul to deliver the note to Mr. Rosenburg's in-laws' apartment.

Once the vice consul left, Fengshan sat down in his chair and sifted through the stack of newspapers in German and English. There were many pages headlined with the slogan of *One Country, One Führer*, articles that demanded the departure of the Viennese Jews and the closure of their businesses and shops, warnings of their insatiable appetite to dominate the world, and caricatures that ridiculed their appearance.

He put down the newspapers. The Jewish Viennese were left defenseless; it was of paramount importance that the international community unite to assist them.

"My love?"

He looked up, shocked. Grace, in her delicate purple dress, the dress bought in Shanghai, stood in front of him. She looked utterly distressed, her face pale, her eyes misty; she wasn't wearing her gloves or hat. What was happening to his wife? She had been arrested by the SS, thrown into a dungeon at the Headquarters, and now she looked about to collapse. "Grace! Are you all right?"

She waved her hand weakly. "I've been waiting for you in the bedroom, but I thought to come down to speak with you." Then, her voice quavering, she recounted the incident in the coffeehouse and how a hospital and a clinic refused Lola treatment.

She had said she was only making a phone call. "This is devastating. But I wish you had told me you were going to meet her." Mr. Rosenburg, and now Grace's tutor. Waves of atrocity kept coming.

"Well, I meant to, but I forgot. It's just . . . I'm a half-breed too. Does it mean they'd refuse my treatment in a hospital?" She paced, biting her nails.

"I doubt that. You're an American. Not Jewish. Hitler's policy seems to aim at the Jews only."

"It doesn't make sense . . ."

He put his hand on her shoulder. "Austria is like China, Grace. Both countries were ruled by dynasties and transformed into nascent republics with hopes and hustles. Now China struggles under the invasion of a foreign power, and Austria faces a demon of its own. It is an unsettling time for the people. Your friend—I hope she'll get the treatment she needs."

Grace nodded, then shook her head, but she didn't speak.

"Have you seen Monto? Did he come back from school yet?"

She didn't seem to hear him; on her face was that distracted look, as if she were drawn to something distant. Then she blinked, her eyes gazing at a row of gifts he'd received—a statue of St. Catherine carved in walnut, a limewood figurine of an angel, and a Bible—and then a set of boxes containing clay soldiers he had brought from China.

"Grace?"

She turned to him, and on her face emerged an expression that he had never seen before. "Do you know Lola's address, my love?"

"Frau Maxa should have it. She has the list of all the tutors Mr. Rosenburg recommended to you. Why do you wish to know?"

"I would like to visit Lola."

"Are you saying that she invited you?"

"No."

"Dropping into people's homes without an invitation is quite improper. You know well the etiquette in this country, Grace. Austrians observe the custom of appointments before visits."

"Are you talking about—what is that thing called? Part of the etiquette, I remember. Like a note." She gestured, thinking, trying to unearth the part of memory that she often seemed to have trouble with.

"A visiting card?"

"That's it. You have some, don't you? Can I borrow yours?"

He frowned. "My card has my title and the consulate's address. It's unsuitable for your social call."

"All right. I'll buy a blank note for myself. Could you write the message for me? In German?"

He seldom had the need to plead with Grace and remind her to be sensible. The memory of the Headquarters should still be fresh in her mind. "Grace. The situation in Vienna is delicate, let me reiterate. You must stay safe."

She bit her nails, looking as though she was going to cry, and he was sure she would give in, slip into her meek prison.

"I'll write it myself," she said.

CHAPTER 10

LOLA

It was only a cut, but deeper and wider than I had thought, and the pain and humiliation were unbearable. It could have been worse. It could have struck Grace.

On the tram, ignoring the glares of the Brownshirts by the window, I turned my face away, thinking about where to find help. Finally, I decided to go to the family nurse who had known me since I was born—she was not a Jew. I got off the tram and knocked on her door. She looked startled and told me to go to the back of the house, so her neighbors wouldn't see me. When she stitched up the gash, I thanked her profusely and left promptly. There was the law now that Jews were not allowed to be in physical contact with the non-Jews; shaking hands and hugs were prohibited.

Onkel Goethe, an avaricious man, the sly cousin of Vater, was in the family room again, a stout, domineering man standing in front of poor Mutter, Sara, and little Eva, her daughter. He stopped amid his diatribe and frowned and puffed as I stumbled through the door. Mutter looked worried to death.

"Lola, you're covered with blood. Your face! What happened to you?"

Mutter was wiping my face, but it hurt! I swiped her hand away and did my best to explain what had happened. Now Mutter would be convinced that with a scar on my face, I would end up a spinster like her tante.

"You deserve this." Onkel Goethe pointed at me. "The law is the law. They have the right to decline your treatment."

I gritted my teeth, for I couldn't open my mouth widely without tearing the stitches. And my face. It was hot, burning. But since when did being a *Mischling* mean falling through the cracks? Since when was having Jewish blood a crime? I wore my pendants, but it was not as if we paraded our Jewishness or went to Stadttempel Synagogue every week. In fact, we had never made an effort to observe the High Holidays or other Jewish traditions, and we ate schnitzel and pork; we drank beer on the Sabbath. We were certainly not like our neighbors, the devout Jews who wore kippahs and prayed in separate sections for men and women, but we were all Jews, and we were also Viennese.

"The law is stupid!" I was glad I was not born with a tied tongue. Sara was too modest to utter her opinions, and Josef was too righteous and polite to confront the elders—where was he now? Always at work or with his fiancée. He knew well that Onkel Goethe wielded his seniority like a weapon. Years ago, while Vater was alive, Onkel Goethe had put on an act, but for the past few years, he had bared himself, unleashing all his ugly nature. After the Anschluss, he had seen a perfect opportunity to rob us of what little we had—the fabric shop. This was his fifth trip.

"You should go to jail for contempt! The Führer is doing what is best for us. He cares about us. He is a true Austrian and loves Austria, and he understands we are fighting for our lives because of people like you. He's looking out for us. Look what he did to Austria! He has pulled Austria out of bankruptcy, and children are eating meat again!"

Dogs always followed those holding out bones.

"Lola. Let me take a look at your face."

"I'm fine. It's stitched up. Not a big deal—"

"He loves Austria! He has done more for Austria than Emperor Franz!"

"Cousin, could you—" Mutter said.

He jabbed his fingers at Mutter, forcing her to stagger backward. "I've been patient with you, but time is running out. The fabric shop is mine. I need the key to the shop."

"That's my vater's shop!" I shouted.

"I've warned you before, I can bring the police!"

"You . . ." My head felt like a violin with all strings vibrating and screeching at once, and the room was flooded with twisty silhouettes. And Mutter, Sara, little Eva, and even ugly Onkel Goethe were engulfed in a black curtain.

"Lola!"

The last thing I heard was Onkel Goethe's sharp voice, quoting those despicable headlines from the newspapers that were sold everywhere. "Jews must leave, and leave in droves, and leave all their wealth behind!"

CHAPTER 11

GRACE

I learned that Lola lived on a street called Berggasse, in the ninth district, north of the Innere Stadt. A few days after I mailed the visiting card, I asked Frau Maxa about the location, the tram route, and the landmarks in that area. Then I took a map, bought a bunch of lilacs from a flower cart on the street, and got on the tram. This was an adventure I had never imagined I was capable of. Fengshan's warning kept hovering in my mind, but I was not asking for his consent this time—or maybe I was. Still, Lola had been assaulted, and I needed to know whether she was all right.

I was the only woman on the tram, which made me nervous. I averted my eyes from the Brownshirts looking at me askance and fixated my gaze on my shoes, a practice I'd perfected since childhood. I thought of the men who had caused Lola's injury; they would likely have threatened her had she been on the bus.

When the scenery began to change outside, I was possessed with fear again—I had never ventured this far in Vienna on my own. Would I get lost again?

At Votive Park, I got off. Lola's house was a few blocks away. With the map and lilacs in hand, I passed the park blooming with spring flowers, streets with signs written in cryptic Germanic lettering, and stately Baroque and classical architecture buildings. The area seemed busy with taverns, wine stores, and shops selling furs and dresses, but several buildings were graffitied in German in black paint, the windows smashed.

I was walking down the neat pavement when I heard some shouts from the park on the other side of the street. In the distance, a group of adults, holding bats, and some children in dark shirts were gathered. At first, I thought they were playing baseball, but then I realized those people were not holding bats but rather horsewhips, and the small figures were not children but older men with gray beards and some women, crouching on all fours on the grass. Cruelly, the men holding horsewhips lashed them, and the crouched older men and women dipped their heads, tore off the lawn's grass with their teeth, and munched. My pace slowed. Who were these people, and why were they eating grass? But there was no question about who the men holding horsewhips were—they wore the same black uniforms as the police at the Headquarters.

When I arrived at Lola's apartment, a young woman in a plaid dirndl dress opened the door. She had Lola's eyes, and her right hand was deformed. *"Grüß Gott,"* she said.

Lola's greeting. My face grew hot; I stammered in English, "Oh yes, *grüß Gott*. I'm her friend, Grace Lee. So sorry to bother you. I sent a card a few days ago. I'm here to see Lola. May I see her?"

She hesitated, didn't seem to understand me or what to do with me. Fengshan was right; it was taboo to visit a Viennese without an invitation. I gave her the lilacs and turned to leave, but then, on second thought, I repeated, "I'm here to see Lola, Lola Schnitzel, Schnitzler."

She looked relieved and wiped her good hand on her apron—her other hand was twisted awkwardly. She had just ushered me into the parlor when from inside, a stout man with too much facial hair but none on his head stomped out, blasting something in German. Upon seeing me, he stopped and switched to heavily accented English. "You've invited a foreigner to your house! A foreigner! This is the plague Austria is facing! All the Socialists, Communists, and foreigners are polluting the Austrian custom and traditions."

The man pushed me aside and left the apartment.

I froze in the parlor. Leave or stay?

"Are you Miss Lee? Welcome, Miss Lee. Welcome. Come. Come. Lola talked about you. I'm Lola's mother." An older woman with gray hair came to me. "That was my cousin. I apologize on his behalf. Please don't be offended by him. He had an argument with Lola a few days ago and he wanted to sort it out . . . It's . . . Well, he's dogged, but he's harmless."

Mrs. Schnitzler's English was heavily accented as well, but her manner was amicable. I hastily introduced myself again, wringing my hands. This was the hard part, talking to strangers.

"How kind of you to visit. Sara is fetching Lola in her room. She should come out in a minute." Mrs. Schnitzler took me to a sofa near the window and offered me a cup of water poured from a silver pitcher, apologizing for the lack of tea and biscuits. The store had turned her away, she explained, and she had not gone grocery shopping for three weeks. I could have misunderstood, but it sounded as if she was banned from grocery shopping.

Lola's home looked like an apartment ready for rent. It had few pieces of furniture, only a tall seven-drawer Biedermeier chest, and a faded blue rug. The walls were painted in cream, bare, without the ubiquitous paintings I had seen everywhere in Vienna.

"Grace, I can't believe it's you." Lola, in a long flowery dress, appeared, holding a violin. She looked groggy, her eyes rimmed with red threads. On her plump face were uneven stitches in black thread—a jagged scar, a swollen caterpillar of malice.

I apologized for visiting without an invitation, but Lola waved her hand and sat on the sofa next to me, her violin on her lap. She looked happy to see me, waiting for me to speak. It was as though we were in the coffeehouse again, chatting about the Viennese men and their facial hair.

"You got stitches. I'm so glad. How many stitches did you get, Lola?"

"Twelve."

"Where did you go?"

"An old friend. She used to be a nurse."

"She could have done a better job," I said without thinking.

Lola looked like she was going to smile but held her face.

"It hurts, doesn't it? How long will it take you to heal?" Months, probably, and with the scar so wide and deep, she would never look the same again.

"I won't worry about it, Grace."

I took out the can of Tiger Balm in my handbag. "This might help, or might not. I don't really know. It's not medicine, but its scents will soothe you. I hope you'll like it."

"Smells good." She dabbed it on her forehead.

"No, no, not on your forehead. Let me." I smoothed a tiny bit of the pale-yellow ointment on her wrist. Lola sniffed at it; she seemed to like it.

Sara, who was Lola's sister, and Mrs. Schnitzler leaned over. Lola smeared some Tiger Balm on their hands. They smiled, sniffing the aroma, murmuring in German. Lola and her mother were tied by a strong bond of affection, I could tell, unlike my mother and me.

A girl in a pink ruffled dress whom I hadn't noticed earlier appeared by Sara and said something in German. She had curly hair, expressive, large green eyes like Lola's, and looked younger than Monto. Sara pulled her aside and covered her mouth with her good left hand, looking mortified. I looked at Lola.

"This is Eva, my niece. She needs to learn her manners. Eva, go to your room," Lola said.

"Let her stay. What did she say?" I asked.

"Eva was asking if you ate foie gras every day."

"Why would I eat foie gras every day?"

Eva studied me, my oatmeal-colored cloche hat, my pearl necklace, and my sage-green dress of chiffon and lace. "I see." I told them about my awkward life as a diplomat's wife in Vienna. I had once sat on a sofa at a ball attended by the Hapsburg royal family members and diplomats and their wives. To my puzzlement, the wives gasped and stared at me strangely. Seconds later, an official in a uniform with many golden buttons evicted me from the sofa. I was mortified; I had not known that according to the protocol, a sofa was reserved for a duchess only.

Eva burst out with more German.

"Eva!" Sara looked at me apologetically.

"What did she say?"

"She said you were very small. Why wouldn't she share?"

I laughed. A little dynamite of a girl, who barely knew me, was defending me; if only Monto could do that.

Later, when it was time for me to leave, Lola saw me out to the door. I wrung the strap of my handbag and asked whether I could come to visit again.

"Of course, Grace, but you might not know this: non-Jewish Austrians are not allowed to visit us."

The arrest in the park, the attack in the coffeehouse, the people in the park. I understood what her life was now. "But I'm a foreigner."

"It'll be dangerous for you."

"We're friends, aren't we?"

Her green eyes glittered—the look she'd had outside the clinic when she looked up to stop tears from rolling out—and then she smiled. I stepped forth and hugged her.

I went to Lola's apartment again a few days later, bringing a box of Swiss milk chocolates in colorful wrappers, another bunch of fresh lilacs, and roses. But soon, I realized they needed something other than flowers—they had run out of flour, cream, cans of fruit, and yeast because of the shopping ban. So for my following trip, I brought groceries, a loaf of bread, a bag of raisins, some baked strudels with meat and potato, more chocolates, and crackers from the shop where I had bought Monto pencils and candies. It now had a sign that said *No Jews Allowed.*

Lola's family accepted my gifts with genuine happiness; they sat in a circle, passing the crackers, the raisins, and the chocolates. They appeared to be appreciative of anything I brought, including Tiger Balm. Mrs. Schnitzler claimed the fragrance of menthol did wonders to calm her nerves. Eva was sorry that it didn't contain real tiger bones. All tried to speak English so I would be able to join their conversation.

The scar on Lola's face was healing slowly, turning into a glistening red mound of skin. In her cheerful way, Lola taught me German, one word at a time. I repeated after her. *Die Sonne, der Mond, die Blumen, die Lebensmittel, die Freundinnen.* Foreign words, words with gusto, words like portals. I ate them up, filled my lungs with them, and felt larger with them, but I forgot them as soon as they were released into the air. In turn, I introduced Lola to Dickinson, whom she had never heard of. She had not read much poetry, she said, but she was fond of Nietzsche.

Mrs. Schnitzler, unlike my alcoholic mother, was a superstitious woman—I was told flowers must be given in odd numbers, for an even number of flowers indicated funerals. When Lola sneezed, Mrs. Schnitzler tugged Lola's ear lest an evil spirit hear and latch on to her. To keep the evil spirits away, I was also told to step out of a house with the right foot first. There was a painful history behind this, she said, that went back to Spain's Edict of Expulsion in 1492; during that time, many Jews left their homes with their left foot out first, and they were all either persecuted or forced to leave the country. Mrs. Schnitzler believed that this was a critical survival lesson for Jews and that their life depended on the order of the foot stepping out of the home.

Lola's sister, Sara, was always busy doing housework, despite her deformed hand. She collected the dishes, picked up the chocolate wrappers, and wiped the banisters or rubbed the rug's stains. She could knit with her feet—she was too modest to demonstrate but obliged at Lola's insistence. Her toes clutched the thick sticks, in and out, in and out, making magic with the threads. She was a widow; her husband died of pneumonia a few years ago and left her with Eva.

Eva, a nine-year-old, was very different from Monto. She was curious, full of energy, and loved to dance and sing. She had a favorite toy, a music box with a ballerina that played Beethoven's *Moonlight Sonata*. She wanted to be a dancer when she grew up.

I also met Lola's brother, Josef, a typical Austrian, uptight, formal, enjoying operas and following the traffic rules. He wore the Austrian men's trademark beard in the shape of a crescent curve, peered at me through his thick glasses, and always paused before he spoke. He had a reserved manner, rarely smiled, and smelled of pills. He was twenty-three years old, born in Vienna, and worked at a pharmacy that was said to be associated with Dr. Freud. He reminded me of a stuffy British diplomat I once met at a dinner table.

"Dr. Freud, is he a witch?" I couldn't remember where I heard it.

"Oh, people have called him worse: a madman, an idiot, a psychopath, but as far as I can tell, he's a doctor who treats your mind by looking into your dreams," Josef said, his finger pushing his round glasses with silver frames.

Looking into your dreams. It sounded as though dreams were handkerchiefs that could be held in one's hands. A novel concept I had never heard of before.

Sometimes Lola played "The Lark Ascending" on her violin. She had been scheduled to attend an audition a few weeks ago, but it had been canceled. She loved this piece, I could tell, and she explained how the composer created the serene melodies to evoke the image of a chirping lark, and indeed, when she drew her bow, the elegant melody resembled a divine trill of lively tunes of birds, leaping and diving. She had good skills; she should perform for the public.

Listening to Lola play the violin, I thought of my childhood. When Mother told me to go away, I would sometimes climb on a giant elm near the house she cleaned. At the nook of branches on the top of the tree, above the ground, I could see beneath me the grassy land, the barns scattered like old toys, the loop of a winding dirt path, and the pearly horizon like spilled milk. Often, I would sit on the branch for hours, reading Dickinson, watching the arrows of sunlight glint through the leaves, the chipmunks' ballet-like pirouettes, the brown beetles with wings flaring like cupped hands. Creatures came to visit, sitting close to me, the woodpeckers, the cardinals, the goldfinches, the red-breasted robins, the blue jays, like fussy aunts and amiable uncles that I never knew.

In Lola's sparsely decorated family room, sitting with her family, listening to her music, watching her red scar, a broken chord, a ridge before the storm in Amherst, I felt I was back to the tree of my sanctuary again.

But always, the shadows of danger loomed. There were Sara's nervous whispers in German the moment I stepped into their family room, Josef's careful and distressing account of harassment at work, the visits of the uncle who had taken over the Schnitzlers' fabric shop at last and now demanded the key to their apartment, and the disturbing news in the newspaper—the new restrictions, recent riots, and heartbreaking property destruction, which I made Lola translate for me. Then it was ordered that the Schnitzlers report their bank accounts and donate all valuables over five thousand reichsmarks to the government. Lola was furious. They had barely gotten by, and now they must surrender the last of their valuables her father had left for them.

Anxious, Josef mentioned leaving Vienna—he believed the rising hostility was detrimental to his career. Palestine, the United States, and Britain were ideal destinations, he mentioned. I had never paid attention to visa applications in the consulate before, but, concerned, I asked Fengshan about the process. China didn't have an immigration policy, Fengshan said casually.

Anyway, Lola didn't want to leave Vienna. She was a Viennese, she said. Her music career and her life belonged here; she had no plan to go.

Then one afternoon in June, when I arrived at their apartment, Lola pulled me inside. Her usually calm face looked strained and tearstained.

"What's wrong, Lola?"

"It's Josef."

A group of policemen had raided his pharmacy that morning, searching for Josef's boss's daughter, whom they accused of engaging in an illegal sexual relationship with an heiress of a jewelry company in the United States—somehow, they had seized the letters sent by the heiress. Josef's boss and his daughter had left on an overseas trip a few weeks ago, so the police arrested Josef and the rest of the pharmacy staff, accusing them of aiding a homosexual. They were taken to the Hotel Metropole, the Nazi Headquarters.

CHAPTER 12

LOLA

Sara pedaled on the sewing machine in the family room, frantically feeding the needle a long strip of cloth with her good hand. Working was a way for her to relieve fear and stress, but she was sobbing. Little Eva looked frightened, her eyes lowered, winding her music box with the mini ballerina figurine. Mutter locked herself in her room. Now and then, she murmured, "He must have left the house with his left foot first."

I opened the door and closed it behind me. It was up to me to save my brother.

I asked for advice from Josef's fiancée, his friends, my musician friends, and the neighbors who still dared to speak to me. They said I needed to gather any valid documents to prove Josef was a good citizen, documents from non-Jews who could vouch for his good character, and that the best case to prove that was a letter of recommendation from a Nazi Party member. As far as I could tell, Josef had few non-Jew friends. But after hours of thinking and querying, I finally thought of one of his clients who was German, a Nazi, working in the Rathaus.

I put on my wide-brimmed straw hat and applied my lipstick in the mirror. The scar on my face looked crimson, hostile, so I smoothed on a thick coat of powder to cover it up. Then I went to the man's office in the Rathaus, and, swallowing my pride, I begged him to write a letter to confirm Josef's good character. "Josef is a good brother, a capable employee, and a good fiancé. He is going to get married next year."

"Miss Schnitzler, if you can wait, I'll have the letter ready for you in an hour." The man—thank God—still had a conscience.

I wanted to kiss him when he handed the letter to me, despite his uniform and the swastika armband.

Then I went to the War Ministry to request my father's war record, which would prove Josef was the son of a war hero, and then I lined up outside the tax office to receive a tax record that would show how diligently my brother had paid taxes. It took me two weeks to finally receive both. With the letter confirming my brother's good character, the certificate demonstrating his good breeding, and the tax record verifying that he was a dutiful citizen, I went to the dreadful Headquarters where Grace and I had been confined, waited outside for three hours, presented the documents, and was told I should come back the next day.

The next day, when I arrived, I was told my brother couldn't be released due to insufficient documents.

"Insufficient? What else do you need?"

Apparently, they had lost the letter that indicated Josef's good character.

I had never run on the street—in Vienna, only desperate people ran—but I was desperate now. I raced back to the Rathaus as fast as I could and pleaded with Josef's client to write another letter. The man took a sip of his coffee, asked me if it was hot outside, and then picked up his pen. He wrote this out of pity, I could see, but for my brother's freedom, I didn't care.

The new letter in hand, I went to the Headquarters again, waiting outside the majestic building in the rising heat of summer, sweat dripping from my forehead and pooling on my neck. I waited from morning to evening. No one bothered to take my documents; every Nazi official was busy in and out of the Headquarters. June went by, and then came July. Then finally a man with a blond goatee took my letter and certificates. After a quick glance, he said these were all rubbish.

"Please, what else do you need?" I felt my eyes moisten, but no. I could beg but must not cry.

"Your brother is an enabler of a homosexual, a traitor to this country, and a Jew. He must vow to leave the country and never come back. Show us proof of his intention to depart; then he'll be released." The Blond Goatee threw me back the stack of papers I'd prepared.

The Nazis could have told me weeks ago while I begged and waited outside in the suffocating heat. They were toying with my brother's life.

A visa, then. A visa for my brother's freedom. As if we still had the illusion of having a decent life in Vienna!

CHAPTER 13

FENGSHAN

"May I talk to you, my love?" Grace's voice came.

He folded up the newspaper he was reading. The Évian Conference had convened yesterday, and an effusive wave of jubilation and relief was printed across the few liberal newspapers that still reported the plight of Jews. It was time for humanitarian intervention from the world, they cheered. But the local weekly newspaper, *Der Stürmer*, which appeared to be propaganda for the Nazi government, published a scathing article mocking and criticizing the overreach of the United States, Britain, and France.

It had been a long wait for the thirty-two countries to convene. If Mr. Wiley was right and the United States would take the lead, then the Évian Conference would provide justice and establish a safe future for all the Jewish people in Vienna. Mr. Rosenburg would welcome this news. It had been nearly seven weeks since he last saw his friend. Fengshan had mailed him a note and gone to his in-laws' apartment but was unable to meet his friend, who had been away. Mr. Rosenburg must have received his visa to Palestine by now.

"Yes?" Fengshan put down the newspaper. They had just finished lunch, and Monto was doing his homework at the table. Grace, dressed in a pink gown with lace, looked very attractive. Her cheeks, which used to be pale, seemed to have filled out, and her expressive black eyes sparkled with light. It occurred to him she had been busy in and out of the consulate, and he hadn't seen her in his office lately. "What have you been up to, Grace?"

She glanced at Monto and sat across from him. "What do you mean?"

He touched her face. Grace looked different. The sleepiness, the distraction that had veiled her, had slipped off. "Are you all right? What pills are you taking, Grace?"

"I'm not taking any pills."

"You look good, Grace."

"Well, my love, I'd like to talk to you about Lola's brother."

Lola. Not Miss Schnitzler. "You said she was attacked. How's she doing?"

"That was more than a month ago. She received twelve stitches on her face, and I visited her a few times."

That explained why he hadn't seen her lately. He had mixed feelings about the visits. But his wife was a grown woman.

"My love, this is about her brother, a pharmacist and an honest Viennese. He was arrested and imprisoned at the Headquarters. Lola has been working hard for his freedom, and she was told that for them to release her brother, he needed a visa to prove he intended to leave the country."

More harassment. The Évian Conference was the only hope for the Viennese Jews. The world's leading nations must hold the Third Reich accountable by pressuring or imposing sanctions; alternatively, the thirty-two nations must provide humanitarian support by allowing Jews' mass migration out of Vienna.

"Who's arrested?" Monto asked, pencil in his mouth.

"Do your homework, Monto. I'm not sure what I can do, Grace."

"Could you issue him a visa?"

"Grace, you asked that before, and I reiterate, China doesn't have an immigration policy."

"Could you talk to the policemen at the Headquarters and ask for his release?"

He sighed. "I wish I could. The ambassador instructs me to stay away from Vienna's domestic controversies. It is not my intention to conflict with his order."

"Please. You released Lola and me."

"Were you arrested, Grace? When?" Monto asked.

"Do your homework, Monto," Grace said.

"That's different. Besides, have you read this? The Évian Conference is in session. Thirty-two countries of the world will discuss the possibility of sanctions against Germany and extending a refugee program to the Viennese Jews. They'll receive support and assistance from thirty-two countries, Grace."

She picked up the newspaper, even though she couldn't read it. "When will the conference conclude?"

"In a week."

"And what will they propose to the Viennese like Lola?"

"Visas to other countries, property protections, humanitarian support—anything is possible. Have you checked Monto's homework?"

"I can do it myself, Father." Monto glanced at him and then Grace.

"He can do it himself, my love." She dashed out with the newspaper in her hand, and before he could ask where she was going, she was gone.

CHAPTER 14

GRACE

A piece of good news. I couldn't wait to share it with Lola. The German newspaper in my handbag, I went to Lola's apartment. I trusted Fengshan. If he said thirty-two countries were discussing strategies to protect Jews, then there was no reason for doubt.

Monto had appeared curious enough, polite even. I wished I had remembered to ask him about his friends at school or the signatures he collected. Monto and I had not started off well. His mother, Fengshan's first wife, had died when he was a toddler, years before I met Fengshan. When I arrived in Fengshan's hometown from Chicago, Monto was shocked to see that his father had left China as a widower and returned as a newlywed. At our celebration dinner, he, a seven-year-old, had cried during the entire meal.

I thought he was grieving—I must be a poor replacement for his mother, so I tried to do my best, but Monto only spoke the Hunan dialect, and I only English. At twenty-one years old, as someone who still had nightmares of being choked by an alcoholic mother, I didn't know how to play the role of a parent, and resources were limited in the inland town—no strollers, no swing sets, no playgrounds. I let Monto feed himself with chopsticks, I walked with him, and when he had a nightmare and crawled into our bed, I told him to sleep in his room.

Fengshan's relatives clucked their tongues at me for doing it all wrong. A good parent, I was told, would hold a boy in their arms at all times and feed him with a spoon, and under no circumstance should I kick a boy having nightmares out of my bed.

In Istanbul, without the relatives' pointing fingers and prying eyes, I found it easier to talk to Monto, and Monto, who shunned his old Turkish nanny, found me to be a rather acceptable alternative. His English also improved with a tutor, so our conversation was no longer riddled with guesses. But in Vienna, where Monto started German, he was perfectly capable of doing things on his own.

In Lola's apartment, stifling with summer heat, I spread the newspaper in front of them. Lola leaned over, frowning, beads of sweat on her forehead, her lips tightly pursed. She looked exhausted. The month of begging for favors, facing the SS men, and worrying about her brother had drained her energy.

"Would you read it, Lola? What does it say? Fengshan said the international community would unite and provide protection to the Viennese. A discussion about immigration policy is on the agenda. Can you read it?"

Lola held the newspaper with two hands as if it were sacred scripture. "I haven't read a newspaper for weeks. I never thought there would be good news. Yes, it does mention a proposal about the refugee program."

"This is good news! Great news! You can immigrate to another country!"

"If that's the only option."

"You would leave Vienna, then, Lola?"

She put down the newspaper. For a moment, she didn't speak, but the scar under her eye twitched, and then she looked at me. "If Josef leaves, we'll all leave, Grace. And he's right. We'll never get the old Vienna back. If I can, I'll apply for visas for all of us."

"When will the conference announce their decision, Lola?" Mrs. Schnitzler asked.

"In one week, Mutter."

I put my hand on Lola's arm. "One week, Lola. Tell your brother. How is he?"

"They won't allow me to see him. They're torturing him!"

Mrs. Schnitzler, in tears, turned her head away; near the sewing machine, Eva was watching us with her mother.

I squeezed out a smile. "Thirty-two countries! The world won't watch people suffer and do nothing, Lola."

"I just want Josef back."

"He'll come home, Lola."

She rolled up the newspaper; for the first time in a month, she smiled, and Mrs. Schnitzler prayed, "God is not silent." The light of relief radiated from their eyes to their lips to their toes.

CHAPTER 15

FENGSHAN

In his office, Fengshan spread his hands on the desk and dropped his head. He could hardly believe what he had read in the newspaper. Each word appeared dark, smoked, like burnt skin.

The meeting of thirty-two countries had finally concluded.

The representatives from the US, the leader that had organized the conference and voiced its concerns about Germany's treatment of the Jews, argued that its quota, set in 1924, was already full this year. They declined to amend the quota on the grounds of the US Johnson-Reed Act; they expounded that the US had just suffered the Great Depression, and the American citizens didn't want competition from the immigrants who would take away their jobs.

The British assumed the same stance and added that their country was too crowded to accept immigrants. With these two leading countries refusing to take action, other countries echoed similar concerns. Australia closed its doors to immigrants; Canada expressed their regrets, and other nations maintained that accepting refugees would create a burden for their citizens and hardships for their economies.

There was no motion to sanction the German government that viciously attacked their own citizens and illegally terminated thousands of people's jobs and robbed their wealth.

There was no proposal to protect the Jews who were left homeless, destitute, and with a bleak future. No protection, no justice, no shelter for his friend and people who were like him.

Thirty-two countries, including the USA, Britain, and France, had failed in their humanitarian mission.

Fengshan lit a cigar and smoked furiously. Mr. Wiley had appeared so righteous and confident regarding the conference, but his promise proved empty. And if the countries in the League reneged on their pledges and showed little concern for Jews, the famous and the wealthy, the intrinsic part of Europe, why would they care for the fate of China, a distant, poor, disadvantaged country in Asia? The Nazis couldn't be trusted, and neither could leaders such as Chamberlain, Daladier, or even Roosevelt. It was a dangerous dream for China to rely on those countries to end the war in his homeland.

Fengshan thought of Mr. Rosenburg, who must have heard the news by now. It was likely he had received his visa and prepared to depart, but still, he would like to check on his friend.

As his car drove down Beethovenplatz, Fengshan looked out the window. Summer was blooming. Vibrant flowers in florists' carts adorned the cobblestone streets, shafts of light shone on the ivory buildings, and pedestrians in pink straw hats and gray summer suits strolled by the statues of Beethoven and Mozart. The classic buildings, the artful decorations, the lush foliage, and colorful flowers exuded a sense of privilege and sophistication, a saturated feeling of a city brimming with luxury, yet it was also evident that the beguiling beauty belied the control and discipline that was typical of Vienna.

There was an accident on the Ringstrasse, blocking traffic; Rudolf decided to take a detour.

Near the intersection, his car stopped again. Fengshan rolled down the window. Ahead of his vehicle, a long line had formed, extending from the street's corner to the avenue that led to the American consulate a few blocks away. Many people in line were holding bags; beneath their hats, their faces were sweaty, anxious. It was obvious why these people came to the American consulate, but he had not imagined there would be so many Viennese applying for visas.

"Dr. Ho, Dr. Ho!" a voice called out.

"Mr. Rosenburg! How are you doing? What are you doing here? I thought you already received your visa." He got out of his car and went to his friend in the line.

His friend was still wearing his blue Savile Row suit, now rumpled and stained. He tucked his bag under his arm and drooped his head. "I'm afraid this has been a long quest, Dr. Ho. I've been applying for visas since we talked in May. I went to the Palestinian consulate, but I was told the British mandate restricts immigration to Palestine, and to apply for that visa, I must receive written approval from the British embassy. But the embassy in Vienna had been closed, so I traveled to the British embassy in Berlin, only to discover that the embassy processed visas every Tuesday for a few hours. I was there for three weeks. Then I had to leave empty-handed. There were many people ahead of me. I would never get my turn."

"I didn't realize it would be so challenging to apply for a visa to Palestine."

"Neither did I. And it's been a long wait here too. Look at all these people! That man over there, Mr. Bahndorf. He's a world-renowned surgeon, and now we are paupers who desperately need to leave Vienna. With some luck, the Americans might accept our applications."

Fengshan took a deep breath. "How long have you been here?"

"Since dawn. I've waited here for four days, but I can't even get my foot in the door. Now I'm running out of time. I have seven days to get a visa, or I'll be sent to the Dachau camp."

Seven days! "Let me see what I can do for you, Mr. Rosenburg. I'll have a word with the American consul general. Maybe he can help. Why don't you go home? You look exhausted."

His friend rubbed his red-rimmed eyes and sighed.

"I'll let you know what happens, Mr. Rosenburg. You go home and rest."

Finally, his exhausted friend shambled away. Fengshan told Rudolf to park the car and passed the long line to get inside the consulate. Even though it was most inappropriate and he didn't have an appointment, he was resolved to speak to the consul general. They had had an amicable meeting about the conference, so he felt emboldened.

To his surprise, Mr. Wiley was in the lobby.

"Dr. Ho! Good to see you. I was on my way out." Mr. Wiley beckoned him to a quiet area in the hallway, away from the visa applicants.

"This is rather impetuous of me, but I assume you've heard the news about the conference, Mr. Wiley. It's a sad day for the Viennese, a sad day for the world. I am astounded."

The American took off his glasses and pinched the bridge of his nose. "I confess I'm equally disappointed. This outcome is beyond my imagination."

"Mr. Wiley, I hate to bother you; however, would you mind my asking some questions regarding visas to the United States? It's for a friend."

"Dr. Ho, my country has a strict law regarding visas. I regret to inform you that as a Foreign Service Officer, I can't give favors. However, perhaps granting visas is something your consulate would consider?"

He sighed. "I have orders from my superior to stay clear of Germany's domestic affairs."

"As do many consulates."

He persisted. "Mr. Wiley, on behalf of my consulate, may I express my deepest admiration; your heroic protection of Dr. Freud shall remain an inspiration to all of us."

"I must be frank, Dr. Ho—Dr. Freud and his family requested to travel to the US, but unfortunately, they were unable to receive visas. I certainly hope some of our British friends will help him settle in England. As a Foreign Service Officer, I have my obligations to my country. I hope you'll understand."

It was shocking to hear that the American consulate had declined even Dr. Freud a visa. "Mr. Wiley, if it's not too much trouble, would you enlighten me on the status of your country's immigration quota? So I may relay the information to my friend?"

A grimace appeared on the American's face. "This is not a state secret, and it's within my authority to discuss this with you, as a fellow diplomat. The American quota for Greater Germany, including Austria, was 27,370 for the year 1938. This quota was allocated to four consulates in the country. The Viennese likely received about five thousand visas."

"But there are many Jews in Vienna!"

"There are about one hundred eighty thousand Jews."

The quota was only a small fraction of the population. "And has your consulate met the quota this year?"

"All five thousand of them."

Just like that, the US had closed its doors to about 175,000 Viennese.

"Regretfully, Dr. Ho, there's nothing I can do. If I were you, I would urge your friend to apply now. Provided that he has the documents and the affidavit and sponsorship ready at this moment, he'll be able to receive the visa next spring."

"Next spring!" Mr. Rosenburg only had seven days!

"My apologies, Dr. Ho."

Fengshan thanked Mr. Wiley and left the American consulate. On the street, he took a good look around him. All these visa seekers. Mistreated. Harassed. Forced to leave the city. But where would they go now that thirty-two countries had shut their doors? He was not an emotional man, but he could feel their desperation, their fears.

One hundred eighty thousand Jews in Vienna. No visas were available until next spring.

Later that day, in their bedroom, he informed Grace of the announcement the conference had released. With a heavy sigh, he added that people had flooded the American consulate, but the country's immigration quota for this year had been filled.

"But I told Lola there would be a protection plan and an immigration policy from the thirty-two countries. You said so." Grace looked stunned.

He could recall every word in the newspaper—a humanitarian disaster.

"What about Lola, my dear? Her brother is still at the Headquarters! She needs visas!"

CHAPTER 16
LOLA

I went to the British embassy on Metternichgasse; it was closed. I went to the French embassy; it was shuttered. Outside the American consulate, I joined the Viennese dentists, professors, singers, and actors, applying for my brother's freedom and my family's future. But the consulate gave no answers about when the visas would be issued and also required a long list of documents, including police certificates, health records, sponsorship, and an affidavit from relatives in the US. My family didn't have American relatives.

I went to the Netherlands consulate, then the Canadian consulate, then the Greek consulate; I was told a limited number of applications had been accepted, and the official application period had ended. Switzerland had declared it would close its border with Austria in August.

In front of a newspaper kiosk, I lost all my strength to walk—those devastating headlines highlighting the disastrous decision of thirty-two countries at the Évian Conference. Grace had been hopeful, but she couldn't have known. Who would have known?

We were willing to abandon our home, to flee to the end of the world, but none of the countries wanted us.

In the far distance, a low rumble echoed. Above the domes and steeples, a fleet of aircraft, which had dominated the sky on the day Hitler's Wehrmacht swarmed the streets, loomed over Vienna.

CHAPTER 17

GRACE

With a heavy heart, I went to Lola's apartment the next day, again with the newspapers, but Lola had already read the news. *What are you going to do?* I wanted to ask her. Without a visa, her brother remained in prison; without a visa, her family remained stuck in Vienna.

In my bedroom, I put on my favorite nightgown and my lipstick and waited for Fengshan. I decided to talk to him about visas again. He could change his mind when we were alone, when the timing was right. A diplomat with a suit and a tie, he was also my husband, a compliant negotiator who made easy concessions in our bed.

By the light on the nightstand, I read Dickinson, the poetry book that had attracted Fengshan when we first met. I had been a twenty-one-year-old, working in a noodle shop near the campus of the University of Chicago, full of fear of my mother. Fengshan was thirty-two, a secretary to a governor in his hometown, and part of a Chinese delegation attending the World's Fair in the US. He had noticed the book in my hand and asked what my favorite verses were when I took his order. I felt awkward, didn't know what to answer, vacillating between "I felt a Funeral, in my Brain" and "I felt my life with both my hands," but in the end, gazing at his infectious smile, I said, "'Hope' is the thing with feathers—that perches in the soul." He was charismatic, empathetic, and had a hearty laugh that made people believe everything would be all right. Like many people, upon first meeting him, I was awestruck. Later, he returned to the noodle shop, but not always for the noodles. When the fair ended and he was scheduled to return home, he asked me to marry him. Flattered and eager to escape from Mother, I agreed.

When I arrived in his hometown, it had never crossed my mind that domestic life would be a challenge, having worked in a noodle shop and kept house while Mother passed out in her rocker. But in China, water needed to be boiled, laundry was rinsed in the river, vegetables for salad must not be raw, and cooking chicken involved a life-and-death battle with a hen that could fly over the table and run along the windowsill. To eat chicken, duck, rabbit, fish, or shrimp, I played the role of executioner and butcher and cleaner.

Fengshan commented and appeared proud—his American wife possessed skills essential to Chinese living. I wondered if he knew I put on a brave face while holding a cleaver with my small hands. And sometimes I'd rather not do it. Once, Monto wanted to eat a chicken for his birthday, a rare treat for the birthday boy—there was no cake in Fengshan's hometown. I chased after the bird with a cleaver in hand, and finally had it grasped firm between my legs. It was the most beautiful bird I had ever seen, with a sleek neck and snow-white feathers, and it was energetic and full of life. I couldn't do it. "Tomorrow, Snow White, I will kill you," I whispered. So that evening, Monto had rice and cooked cabbage for his eighth birthday, no chicken. The next day, I still couldn't slay Snow White. After spending all day with her, I had grown to admire her, her beauty, her spunk, and her queenly walk across the kitchen counter. Snow White lived a long life, to Monto's disgust.

That was perhaps why Monto could never be close to me.

I put down my book and turned to the clock. Nine o'clock. This was late. I wondered where Fengshan had gone. It was quiet in the bedroom. Some music would be lovely, but turning on the gramophone would wake Monto, whose bedroom was on the same floor.

I walked to the small row of terra-cotta soldiers on the shelf near the sofa. Each wrapped in a red cloth sachet, these soldiers were Fengshan's favorite gifts, which he often presented to foreign diplomats and professionals in Vienna. To their intrigued faces, he would explain the centuries-old northern Chinese tradition of creating figurines out of terra-cotta. He would then dive into a story that went back to two thousand years ago, before the birth of Jesus Christ, to the first emperor of China, the emperor of the Qin Kingdom, who had conquered the other six rival kingdoms to create one country, known as China today. Legend said that the emperor, believing in immortality, had ordered the creation of thousands of terra-cotta soldiers, cavalries, horsemen, horses, and chariots to guard him in his tomb. Until this day, his tomb remained undiscovered.

Fengshan was proud of the terra-cotta figurines, their craft, their symbolism of unyielding loyalty to the emperor, and their eternal purpose, in humble clay.

When I heard him tell the story, I had a feeling that he was explaining himself, a man of clay, born in an unremarkable family in a rural region, transforming himself into a man of gold, a warrior for his country. Would such a man be owned by me? That was too good to be true. I tried to love him with all my heart; I tried to keep him all to me, but he was a man molded by his own will and led his own battle. Still, I followed him, rooted beside him, danced with him. I wouldn't say I was entirely happy, but I wasn't entirely unhappy either. My love was like a shadow, waxing and waning, and I didn't know what was wrong with me.

"Grace, you're staying up late." Fengshan's voice came to me.

I turned around. "Where have you been?"

His arms threaded around my neck, his breath warming my ear. He smelled of cigars, wine, and the warm summer air. I slid my hand under his shirt. He was athletic, with muscles and great strength.

"Some church friends were troubled by the news in the newspaper and invited me for some coffee. Then we went to a bar."

I kissed him. Of all his facial features, I loved his lips the most—supple, sumptuous, with a clearly defined curve. "What news? The news released by the Évian Conference?"

"Yes. There are reports that many in Greater Germany cheered the result and urged more forceful actions to remove the Jews. It's really unfortunate."

I untied my gown. He lowered his head to kiss me; it was so pleasurable I groaned.

"My dear, do you love me?"

"What's going on now, Grace?"

"Lola is having a difficult time finding visas. She's still unable to free her brother. Could you issue her family visas?"

He stopped kissing me.

"I know you must follow the ambassador's orders, but it's only a few visas. It won't damage the country's relations with Germany."

"Grace, it's complicated."

"Will you bend the rule for your wife?"

He sighed.

My husband. He would decline my request at an intimate moment. I pulled away and tied up my nightgown. "I'm going to the bathroom."

CHAPTER 18

FENGSHAN

All night, he tossed and turned, thinking about Grace's request and Mr. Rosenburg's visa quest. In his heart, he would have gladly issued visas to Grace's friend's family, but as consul general, he was bound to his superior's order.

Before dawn, he rose, ate breakfast, and went to the quiet lobby. Outside the consulate, he picked up the newspapers and went to his office. On the desk were his letters to his friends in China, which still needed to be posted, and in a few hours, he would report to Ambassador Chen again. He picked up the newspaper and began to read.

A new office, the Central Office for Jewish Emigration in Vienna, would open in August, led by none other than the reptilian SS man he had met at the Headquarters, Adolf Eichmann. The sole purpose of its establishment was to expedite the departure of the Jews, because in the newly created Office, the Jews would be able to gather all the necessary certificates, passports, and other documents in order to receive their exit permits. The Office would also ensure that prior to the application for exit permits, the Jews would surrender all their properties, assets, jewelry, furs, and valuables and relinquish their citizenship.

It was evident that once the Viennese Jews were allowed to leave the country, they would be penniless, homeless, and stateless.

A wave of rage rose in Fengshan's stomach. Clearly, the emigration center was a response to the Évian Conference, which had evaded its responsibility and given the Nazis a free pass. Knowing the thirty-two countries in the world would turn a blind eye, the Third Reich was emboldened.

The phone rang.

Captain Heine's smooth voice came through. "Good morning, Herr Consul General."

"Good morning." Fengshan's stomach clenched tight. Captain Heine always seemed to follow in Eichmann's shadow.

"I was in a friend's Adler parked on the street the other day, and I saw Mr. Rosenburg climbing on a ladder with a pail of water to clean his former office's window with a toothbrush. The water spilled, and he slipped. It was a miracle he didn't fall to his death. Do you know how he's doing in the hospital?"

"Hospital?"

"After his near-death fall, he went home. I believe several SS men paid him a visit and ordered him to pack for the Dachau camp in two days since he had no visas. He collapsed, had a heart attack."

Fengshan's heart chilled. His friend was unable to receive a visa, and now he was on his deathbed. "Which hospital?"

᠅

Thirty minutes later, Fengshan arrived at a four-story art deco building, a Jewish hospital across from the Danube. The neighborhood, shrouded in early-morning haze mixed with heat, caught him off guard—despicable slogans written in black paint had defaced the pristine limestone of shops and even the hospital. When he entered the hospital building, the lobby was filled with pallets occupied by men, families huddling, and people crying for morphine. Fengshan found out Mr. Rosenburg's room number from a nurse hurrying by and went upstairs. In the hallway, he passed one room where an older man seemed to be having a nervous breakdown, another where two men were screaming about their fractured ribs, and yet another where a family consoled a man with a bleeding face.

He saw the familiar figure of Mrs. Rosenburg, a lace shawl around her shoulders, conversing in a corner with a man wearing a kippah. "Mrs. Rosenburg! Pardon me. How's your husband doing?"

She looked pleased to see him. Her face, however, bore signs of crying. "Herr Consul General, it's good to see you. My husband was hoping to speak to you about visas to China. Perhaps there is a chance that your consulate would issue visas? He needs them by the end of the day tomorrow. He's running out of time."

Fengshan felt a lump in his throat. "May I visit him?"

In her quiet voice, she said the SS men were watching her husband and wouldn't allow visitors. When Fengshan asked why, she said the SS men were trying to extract the contact information of Mr. Rosenburg's wealthy clients from him, but Mr. Rosenburg, determined to protect his clients, had declined.

Standing in the hallway, halfway to a man carrying a rifle, Fengshan caught a glimpse of his friend. Once an eloquent man who defended the properties of the nobles—who made heartwarming toasts at dinner as his guests shouted *"Prost!"*—Mr. Rosenburg lay on a narrow bed, sedated, as the minutes of his life slipped by.

In his office, Fengshan stood by the window, smoking his cigar. In this corner of Vienna, outside his window, there were no bleeding faces, no brutal batons ramming into people's eyes, no tormented men lying in beds. The bay windows were clear, the stones pristine, the fanlights and brass signs gleaming. Near the street, the hedges were pruned, the excess leaves trimmed, and the twigs chopped. All the undesirable branches had been discreetly removed.

There must be something he could do. All his friend needed were visas to avoid the fate of the Dachau camp, visas for him and his family to leave Vienna. He was the consul general of a consulate, familiar with the process and types of visas. If he ordered Vice Consul Zhou to start the visa process for his friend, it was unlikely the vice consul would object.

But would he risk defying the order of his superior, Ambassador Chen?

Fengshan expelled the smoke from his chest, the gray jet shooting in the air, hitting an invisible wall, and then dissolving.

When he turned away from the window, he saw Grace was sitting on a high-backed chair, her gloved hand pressed to her chin. She looked absolutely still, like a model for a painting.

"Grace, is everything all right?"

"I told you he was an honorable man."

She had just returned from Lola's apartment, she said. There had been a round of interrogations at the Headquarters last night. Josef, who had refused to make a confession that would incriminate his employer, had taken a handful of veronal, sleeping pills that he had hidden in the hem of his pants, and died.

CHAPTER 19

LOLA

I had come to the Headquarters hoping to speak to my brother and give him a word of hope and comfort, carrying with me a change of clothes, laundered and ironed by Sara, but I had returned with his possessions: a pair of glasses, a pair of trousers and a shirt, and a set of keys to his pharmacy. His clothes were torn near the shoulders, stained with blood, and those smudged lenses were the same glasses that he wore when he played chess with me, the same glasses that he took off his nose, pretending to clean, when he lost.

They wouldn't tell me where he was.

I sobbed on the tram, burying my face in my arms; I held Josef's possessions close as though they were him. His glasses slipped out of my hands, and I hastened to pick them up. But a shoe stepped on them; a string of vile slurs exploded around me. I didn't want to listen. Josef had heard too much of them; they had driven him to die.

On the street, everything was strange. The shops, the gardens, the buildings appeared warped, glazed in a sea of waxy light. In the park, women sat for picnics; men read newspapers; children savored wiener sausages; musicians played accordions. An ordinary summer day, yet the chilliest winter of my life.

When I arrived at my apartment, I stopped short—there was Onkel Goethe's face and his yelling again. I trembled, and hard as I tried, I couldn't find a word to counter him.

I gave Mutter Josef's belongings. "Mutter . . ." I couldn't continue.

What could I say? What could I do? I had failed to find a visa for my brother, and now he was gone.

CHAPTER 20

FENGSHAN

All that evening, Fengshan couldn't focus on the newspapers. A suicide, and Mr. Rosenburg was fighting for his life in the hospital, facing the dreadful prospect of a labor camp if he couldn't receive a visa by the end of the day tomorrow.

Visas were lives.

Would he stand by, do nothing, and watch a man perish?

He knew the answer, and that left him with only one choice.

The next morning, Fengshan sat by the phone, waiting for Ambassador Chen's phone call. His report had been prepared meticulously, but for the first time in his career, his mind was somewhere else. Ambassador Chen was not a superior who liked to be questioned, but he had to try.

"Fengshan?" The ambassador's voice came through the phone. "I have good news, as per your suggestion to contact the secretary of the treasury in the United States. I relayed your idea to our foreign secretary, and Mr. Sun Ke, the president of the Legislative Yuan, has expressed great interest. He believed it was worth trying and ordered the ambassador to the United States to request a meeting with the secretary. I received a surprise telegram yesterday. It seems the American secretary of the treasury is rather sympathetic to our country's plight. He recommended President Roosevelt extend the credit to us to improve our weaponry and purchase supplies. The amount the secretary offered is approximately twenty-five million American dollars."

"This is wonderful news!"

Twenty-five million dollars would provide a massive boost of morale. With the credit, the ambassador could move forward with the arms deal with Germany. The army could replenish and train the pilots and they could defeat the Japanese in China.

"Good work, Fengshan."

This was rare recognition from his superior. He was pleased. "I assume the meeting regarding the aircraft purchase will be arranged soon."

"I'm not optimistic, but we should hope our effort will not be in vain."

Fengshan cleared his throat. "Ambassador Chen, respectfully, I must report to you that after the devastating result of the Évian Conference, I have heard some tragic news of the Viennese who wished to leave the country but were unable to receive visas. I'm aware I have inquired about the subject before, but I wonder if I could urge you to reconsider. Will it be of interest to you to modify the no-immigration-visa policy and extend visas to the Viennese?"

"Fengshan, as I've stated, our goal is to maintain a friendly relationship with the Third Reich. Do not forget that. Even Chamberlain and Daladier have made their intention clear that they prefer nonaggressive, peaceful relations with Hitler."

Fengshan persisted. "Indeed, peace with Germany is imperative. The Americans are dedicated to keeping peace in Vienna as well, but it seems to me that they also value the Viennese highly. They have taken measures to place a few prominent scholars under their protection." He mentioned Dr. Freud and Mr. Wiley's attempt to help him with visas to England.

There was silence.

"A few visas won't pose a direct threat to our relationship with Germany," Fengshan explained, Grace's voice in his mind.

There was a sigh. "Fengshan, you have put me in the good graces of Mr. Sun Ke because of the credit from the Americans. I will speak to Mr. Xu Shumo, the vice minister of the Ministry of Foreign Affairs, regarding the immigration policy for the Jews. But here's a word of advice: immigration policy is not our priority, and it will never be our country's priority."

"I understand perfectly well. Again, I'm only suggesting a small number of entry visas, and I shall vouch that they would be issued under the strict requirement of your guidelines."

"In this case, you have my permission, and these visas must be issued in a small, acceptable number."

Fengshan's heart sang. He put down the phone and strode to the lobby. Near a wall of file cabinets, Vice Consul Zhou was yawning, a stack of paperwork in front of him. Fengshan asked him to come into his office. From the elevator appeared Grace, who had looked miserable since yesterday. "Come with me, Grace. I have good news about the visa issue."

Her face lit up; she sprang toward his office and sat as he asked Vice Consul Zhou to explain the current visa-application situation.

The consulate of the Republic of China had only received a few applications for visas over the past year, the vice consul said, scratching his head with his long nail. China, after all, was not a popular destination for foreigners.

The category of immigration visa didn't exist, since China was not an immigrant country. Tourist visas and student visas were also rare, given China's slow economic development and the ongoing war. Visas related to marriage, which Grace had received, were similarly rare. Once in a while, the consulate approved visas for foreign missionaries, government officials, and businessmen who conducted business in China, but that activity had also ceased due to the war.

As consul general, Fengshan's responsibility was generally related to the final step of the visa process: filling out the official certificate in both German and Chinese, writing down the visa numbers, signing his signature, and stamping it with the consulate seal. The lengthy pre-visa process of inspecting forms, collecting fees, and conducting interviews fell on the shoulders of Vice Consul Zhou, his subordinate.

Ambassador Chen had made it clear that the visas must not be related to immigration so he must not categorize them as immigration visas. But as consul general, Fengshan had the freedom to overlook the reason for visa application and issue the visa as a special entry visa, which would also give him the opportunity to waive the requirements such as sponsorship, to expedite the process.

But he would need to declare a port of entry in China to issue these visas.

This was a problem.

"My love?" Grace asked, unable to understand their Chinese.

He explained. China, after years of war with Japan, was no longer entirely controlled by his government. Northern China bordering Russia, a land called Manchuria, had been occupied by the Japanese. Beijing had been bombed and captured, and the ports on the northeast coast, which had been German territory before World War I, had been allocated to the Japanese after the betrayal of the Treaty of Versailles. Hong Kong in the south was a British colony, and Hainan Island, the French's. He had no authority to send people to any of those points of entry; if he risked it, it would be a violation of international law that would cause an uproar. It would also jeopardize the safety of the visa holders, who would be interrogated, turned away, or imprisoned before they got through customs.

"A port," she said. "Is Shanghai a port? We stopped there on the way to your hometown. I bought this dress there." It had been nearly four years since they landed at the wharf in Shanghai. Grace had been delighted to see the cluster of European-style buildings near the Huangpu River, a lively area with jazz clubs and luxury hotels.

"Shanghai is now under the occupation of the Japanese."

"That's too bad. It looked like part of Europe."

But it was not Europe; it was the International Settlement in Shanghai, leased to the foreign countries and controlled chiefly by the British and the Americans.

"Grace!" He did his best to suppress his excitement. Even though the Japanese had conquered Shanghai proper, the International Settlement remained unviolated by the Japanese, since it was administered by the British and the Americans, whom the Japanese did not wish to offend. But the Settlement was still on Chinese soil, an essential part of the Chinese territory. Which meant it was in his power to designate the city as a port of entry on a visa.

Fengshan picked up a stack of application forms. "Grace, tell your friend to come to our consulate to apply for visas. They can go to China if they wish."

"I will, my love. Wait, where are you going?"

He slid the application forms into a large envelope. "To the Jewish hospital."

Fengshan was perspiring when he arrived at the crowded hospital. Feeling like a spy, he preferred not to be seen, questioned, or identified by the guards in case anyone recognized him. Perhaps he should have asked the vice consul to deliver the forms, but the matter was too important. He wouldn't trust anyone else to hand them over.

In the hallway, Mrs. Rosenburg, who looked like she might have been spending nights on the floor, caught sight of him. She motioned him to stay, pulled her shawl around her shoulders, and went into Mr. Rosenburg's room. Soon, she came out with the SS guard, heading toward the stairway—she had created a diversion.

Fengshan slipped into the room. His friend, he was glad to see, had regained consciousness.

"Dr. Ho," Mr. Rosenburg said. "What a surprise. How are you?"

Aware that the SS man could return any minute, Fengshan exchanged brief pleasantries and presented him with the application forms. He explained that with China's limited resources, immigration was impossible, but this was the best he could do. "For all intents and purposes, it's a visa that will allow you to leave this country, not heading to the camp. Once you arrive in China, you can apply to the USA, the Philippines, or Argentina. I understand your family will also leave the country with you, is that correct? To expedite the process, I've waived the requirements, such as affidavit and sponsorship. With these application forms, you can apply for visas for yourself and your family."

Mr. Rosenburg closed his eyes.

Fengshan waited, uncertain how his friend felt. China was not his choice, and he wished he could have done better.

When Mr. Rosenburg opened his eyes, tears ran down his cheeks. "It will be my honor to go to China. You've saved my life and my family's lives, Dr. Ho."

"Mr. Rosenburg, I must be candid with you. The only port in China that I can send you to is the International Settlement in Shanghai. The Settlement is protected by the British and American governments but still is on Chinese soil, so it falls in my authority. To the best of my knowledge, there is no staff at customs to inspect passports, entry visas, medical records, or police certificates. You'll be admitted without trouble, but you must be warned that China is at war with Japan, and the country is ravaged. Life in Shanghai will be harsh."

"But there will be freedom. There won't be labor camps; there won't be the Nazis threatening to kill me." His friend's voice cracked.

Fengshan gave Mr. Rosenburg a pat on his shoulder. How the world turned. Once a wealthy man, now a pariah. He was not a diplomat bound by the strict code that Mr. Wiley adhered to, nor was he a sentimental man. But looking at his friend's dry lips and face etched with grief, he felt a surge of emotion run through him. His eyes moistened.

Rosenburg gripped his hand. "Dr. Ho, may I bring to your attention that there are many people whose lives are intertwined with mine? I have friends, wealthy clients, and prominent people who have access to enormous funds. The SS men are interrogating me. They want to know their names and financial status so they can confiscate their fortunes as well." He fumbled beneath his pillow. "Here. I'm giving you their names in case they need any help. I won't be able to keep the list anymore. They're search—"

Mr. Rosenburg froze, his eyes filled with terror, looking behind him.

Fengshan couldn't see, but he could feel a sudden rush of air behind him. He took a silver cup from the bedside table. "It is a pleasure to see you're doing well, Mr. Rosenburg. Your visas will be approved today. Please have a sip."

Mr. Rosenburg's hands were trembling as he reached out to touch the cup and surreptitiously passed the list to him. Fengshan slipped the paper inside his sleeve.

"Stop! What are you doing here? What's in your hand?" The SS man lunged toward him.

Fengshan held up the cup. "This? I only intended to remind my friend to have a sip. I came to deliver the wonderful news to my friend that his family's visas have been approved, and they should come to receive the visas in a few hours. Now that my business is done, please excuse me."

His back straight, his steps steady, he went into the hallway crowded with men with bleeding heads and dislodged shoulders. Outside the hospital, Fengshan felt dizzy, his hand clutching the paper that Mr. Rosenburg had risked his life to deliver to him. Carefully, he unfurled it. It was a list of names, as his friend had said, who appeared to be leaders of Jewish communities, Zionist organizations, and relief organizations based in Germany and Switzerland. If this list fell into the SS men's hands, these people would lose their wealth and probably their lives.

He folded the paper and carefully tucked it into his pocket.

An hour later, Mrs. Rosenburg came to the consulate with the application forms she had filled out. Vice Consul Zhou examined them and had a brief interview with her. Then he brought the documents to Fengshan in his office. Fengshan took out visa forms from his drawer. And with the black fountain pen, he wrote down the visa number on each form, signed his name, and stamped it with the consulate's seal. After he finished, he put all the signed documents in Mrs. Rosenburg's hands.

With these visas, his friend would be spared from the Dachau camp, and he and his family would be able to leave Vienna.

CHAPTER 21

GRACE

Immediately after Fengshan left to see his friend in the hospital, I took a taxi to Lola's apartment and told her the good news.

Lola shook her head, bursting into tears. She explained that she had heard visa applications required police certificates, but she had broken the bench law and had been arrested. Her criminal record would prevent her from receiving the police certificate needed by consulates.

I went back to the consulate, but to my frustration, Fengshan had not returned from visiting his friend. When he finally stepped into the office, I sprang to my feet and told him the problem.

"Please tell them the consulate of the Republic of China will waive the police-record requirement."

I went to Lola's apartment again and brought her to the consulate. In Fengshan's office, I sat with her and introduced her to my husband. With a serious look on his face, Fengshan explained the nature of the visa, expressed his willingness to help, and asked if she had any questions.

Lola didn't have questions. She looked elated, but tired, wearing a threadbare black dirndl dress and a straw hat tied with a white ribbon; the loss of her brother had taken a toll on her. The freshness and easy charm I had once admired were gone, and she looked like an embittered widow, alone, on the verge of an emotional breakdown.

"Mr. Consul General, we've met before. I went to a lecture of yours at the University of Vienna. You demonstrated calligraphy with a brush and ink. It was awe-inspiring," Lola said in English.

"You were there?" Fengshan's gaze, full of sympathy, was fixed on her scar.

"I was playing the violin next door. My classmates were talking about your art, so I went out to see it. It was last year, I believe. I'm sorry, I thought you were the Japanese ambassador."

"You were not the only one."

"I would love to learn the art of calligraphy someday."

Fengshan smiled. He appreciated it when people mentioned their interest in Chinese art. Often he would volunteer to teach them. Had he not been a diplomat, he would have been a scholar. "Do you speak Chinese?"

Lola shook her head. "I've always wanted to learn Chinese."

"I should have the visas for you and your family in a few hours, Miss Schnitzler. Grace, would you mind giving her the application forms? I believe you can find them in the lobby."

He liked her, I could tell.

❧

In the lobby, Lola filled out the forms, her hands shaking. She wrote down her mother's name in the blank space, then that of her sister and Eva, and herself. She must have been thinking of her brother, too, because she broke down, sobbing, and dropped the fountain pen.

I picked it up for her.

When she finished, I counted the forms to ensure I hadn't forgotten any necessary pieces. Then I pored over the lines: *der Name, die Adresse, das Alter.* I just needed to make sure. There could be no errors.

All the stringent documents that barred many Jewish people from obtaining a visa were waived by Fengshan. No requirement for tax returns, financial statements, sponsors, notarized affidavits of support, or police records.

I went to Vice Consul Zhou's desk with the documents while Lola waited. The vice consul looked surprised to see me, and appeared annoyed when I continued to stand next to him. "I'll give these forms to the consul general, Mrs. Consul General."

"I'll take the papers to Fengshan when you're ready," I said.

He shrugged, and with a pen in his mouth, he began to examine the documents with his nail as a pacer. It took him a long time, the visa forms, the passports, the birth certificates, his long fingernails sliding from one page to another, and then, as if testing my patience, he chatted with Frau Maxa. Then he put down the forms and went to use the restroom on the other side of the building. Then, holding the documents, he yawned, refocused, and yawned again while I waited, while Lola sat and watched expectantly, her family's lives in her hands. I would have paid him if it would make him stop yawning and expedite his inspection.

Finally, he handed over the documents, and I went to Fengshan's office. He was listening to the radio in German, clad in his black suit and a red tie, his eyes intense. Nodding at me, he turned off the radio and took the forms.

"Lola is waiting outside. Would you issue her the visas now?" I stressed *now*.

"It won't take long. I'm glad you got the passports."

I stood beside him as he opened the drawer of his mahogany desk and took out a yellow sheet the size of a greeting card. On the sheet were printed some Chinese characters, the visa of the consulate of the Republic of China in Austria, I figured. I gave him his favorite fountain pen and watched as he wrote down the visa number, the destination—Shanghai—the date, and finally, in Chinese, in his fine calligraphy script, his Chinese name, Ho Fengshan.

He wrote carefully, each stroke a sweep of elegance, each line firm like conviction. Once, he had told me every Chinese character had a meaning, and his meant Phoenix Mountain. It came from a legend, he had explained. It was said that phoenixes, the mythical creatures that brought fortune and good luck, only resided on a mountain near Penglai Island. The sacred mountain was a healing home for the phoenixes to restore their energy and a resting place where they came to die and be reborn.

It was fitting that a man with such a name would give life and opportunity to the people who were hunted and persecuted.

I watched him, his faint eyebrows, his black eyes, and his pursed lips. In silence, with the summer wind tapping against the windows, I thought I could hear his worry, and I could feel our thoughts flow and converge, a bridge to walk on. When we made love, I believed I controlled the deepest part of him, his desire, weakness, and strength, but this quiet unity was different. It was as if, after four years of marriage, we were finally spiritually united.

He was still the same man, the man made of clay, the man who turned himself into gold, the man with intelligence, astuteness, and a deep sense of loyalty, and he was mine.

"Are you finished?" I asked.

"Not yet."

His pen moved to the German section below the Chinese, where he repeated the same information with the visa number, the destination, and the date in German.

"May I have the visas?"

"Patience, Grace." He took out the consulate's seal from his drawer and stamped the visa. When his hand lifted, a round black circle was printed on the sheet. It had Chinese characters, which I had grown to recognize, valid for six months, and it was wet, shining, a coin of freedom.

⚶

In the lobby, near the usual small group of passport applicants, Lola held the four sheets of visas, her fingers hovering above Fengshan's signature and the consulate's seal. She made an odd noise, like a groan or sob, and her eyes brightened with tears.

Fengshan came out of his office to the hallway. He stood there, a cigar in his mouth; obscuring his face was a phoenix of smoke, a tail of luminescence, of light, climbing in the air. When it dissipated, I saw his face glowing with perspiration, and he raised his hand to wipe his brow.

"Thank you." I went to him.

He took a drag of his cigar and then expelled the air. "This is the right thing to do."

CHAPTER 22

FENGSHAN

In his office, he opened the drawer and took out the carefully folded paper Mr. Rosenburg had given him. He studied them: Gunther, Schultzman, Bussbang. He picked out a name, Dr. Joseph Löwenherz, the director of the *Kultusgemeinde*, the Jewish Community Center in Vienna, and dialed the phone number. The phone wasn't answered.

The next day, Fengshan dialed again. The phone was answered by a gruff man's voice. Fengshan sat upright and introduced himself.

"Herr Consul General!" The man's voice was full of joy. "I've been trying to get in touch with you since I talked to Mr. Rosenburg yesterday. I have many desperate people who seek their way out of Vienna. What are your requirements for visas?"

"Dr. Löwenherz, the consulate of the Republic of China is open to accepting applications. We waive the police records and other certificates, and we only accept a small fee for the application."

"I'll be there right away."

Dr. Löwenherz arrived at the consulate about ten minutes later. He was a heavily built man with a thick mustache. He stood in a stance akin to a boxer's—his back arched, his arms held by his chest, ready to accept blows. He didn't come alone, accompanied by eight men in three-piece business suits who all requested visas for their families.

Fengshan led them to Vice Consul Zhou, who had just arrived at his desk. Eleven o'clock! Two hours late. For the sake of the Viennese, Fengshan held his tongue. "I'd like to see the application forms on my desk as soon as possible, Vice Consul Zhou," he said politely, though his subordinate deserved a good admonishment.

One hour later, he went to check on the vice consul to make sure he had not spent his time scratching his scalp with his long nails. In the lobby, Dr. Löwenherz and his friends were waiting patiently; near them were the peddlers from Qingtian County in China who had received their passports a month ago.

Fengshan asked the traders if there was anything he could help them with. They appeared grateful, saying that they had been caught by the police for unlawfully selling their wares on the street, who had confiscated their passports and expelled them to Hungary. But they had successfully climbed over the mountains to Austria so now they'd need new passports. Fengshan promised to issue them passports as soon as possible.

"Herr Consul General, Mr. Wiley's office just called. The American consul general would like to have a word with you. He's waiting outside the consulate." Frau Maxa stomped close to him. A tall, strongly built woman, she often announced herself with her heavy footfalls.

"Mr. Wiley?" Mr. Wiley had rarely visited him in his consulate, and he almost never came unannounced.

"His office said it was urgent."

Outside the consulate, a black sedan was parked at the curb. The window rolled down to reveal Mr. Wiley's face.

"Good afternoon, Dr. Ho."

"Well, Mr. Wiley. What a surprise to see you. Would you like to come in for some tea?"

"I'd be delighted, Dr. Ho. But I'm afraid I have to pass. I've been appointed the minister to Estonia and Latvia. I'm scheduled to depart tomorrow, so I thought to stop by to say goodbye."

Fengshan was shocked. The two countries, Estonia and Latvia, were nations of little diplomatic significance to the US. And the position of minister sounded vague, hinting at a possible demotion of the American diplomat.

"Congratulations, Mr. Wiley. This is a profound change in your diplomatic career. I wish you all the best. If you don't mind my asking, why were you reassigned?"

"The Department of State makes its decision. It is not up to me to make a judgment."

"You'll be missed, Mr. Wiley. You have remained an inspiration to many of us. Your consulate has provided life-saving visas for many people in Vienna. Did you mention that Dr. Freud was waiting to depart Vienna?"

"He has left for London, thank God. Since you asked, you might as well know: I'm now known as the Diplomat Who Sticks His Neck Out for Dr. Freud. Take care, Dr. Ho."

That was it. Had Mr. Wiley decided to leave Dr. Freud to the Nazis, he might still be the consul general of the American consulate in Vienna. Those were perhaps the unsaid words from his peer, from one diplomat to another, that for them, the consequences of taking sides were immediate.

Fengshan returned to his office and sat at his desk. He had grown fond of the American diplomat, his mild manner and adherence to principle. It was to be expected that another American official would soon be appointed to replace Mr. Wiley, someone who would be less likely to stand up for the Viennese Jews and more likely to follow the orders. This was politics, after all.

An envelope on his desk caught his attention. It had an elegant German script, addressed to both him and Grace—*Herr Consul General of the Republic of China and Frau Consul General of the Republic of China.* He opened the envelope. It was an invitation to the occasion commemorating the grand establishment of the Central Office for Jewish Emigration in Vienna, an event to be held in late August.

But the party's host sent a chill down Fengshan's spine—Adolf Eichmann, now the chief officer of the center. What was Eichmann's intention with this invitation? To celebrate his promotion? To test Fengshan's country's commitment to Germany?

Fengshan went to his phone, picked up the receiver, hesitated, and then dialed Captain Heine's phone number. "Captain Heine! Pardon me. Perhaps you'll have time for coffee at Café Central?"

An hour later, Fengshan wove through round tables covered with white cloths in the coffeehouse. There were a few familiar faces in the corner, people who went to his church Lutherische Stadtkirche, Lutheran City Church, in the Innere Stadt. He greeted them; they politely nodded back.

Captain Heine, clad in his uniform, was seated in the center of the café, right beneath a golden chandelier. His handsome face was like a magnet to the women smoking cigarettes around him, and the captain looked as though he relished the attention, grinning, raising his glass in a toast.

Fengshan's steps slowed. Meeting the captain was a bold move by any measure, for he had yet to fathom what kind of man he was. He had started to have interactions with him last year when Heine, a graduate of the Police Academy in Vienna, had invited him to speak there. Fengshan had elaborated on religion, Confucianism, Taoism, and Buddhism, the key aspects of Chinese culture in his lecture, and Heine seemed to enjoy it. If he could ever convince a policeman to be on his side, it would be the captain.

But Heine's flirtatious manner with women was an irritant. As a man raised with Confucius's beliefs, Fengshan held dear the five virtues, *Ren*, *Yi*, *Li*, *Zhi*, and *Xin*—benevolence, righteousness, decorum, wisdom, and trustworthiness—just as he believed in the importance of the auxiliary role of the wife in a marriage and a man's devotion to his family. To form a friendship with the captain expressing an unmasked interest in adulterous affairs was easier said than done.

"Herr Consul General, what may I offer you, coffee or cognac?" Captain Heine pulled a Bohemian bentwood chair beside him, and Fengshan sat down.

"Kleiner Brauner," Fengshan said to the waiter in an immaculate suit with a bow tie. *Kleiner Brauner* was a small black coffee with some milk, and by all means a fine drink, although Fengshan, having grown up in China, still preferred his green tea.

Heine opted for *Fiaker*, coffee with rum and whipped cream. "Allow me to say this, Herr Consul General: I was delighted to hear from you. How's Mr. Rosenburg doing?"

It occurred to him that the captain always asked about Mr. Rosenburg. "I've issued him and his family visas so they can depart Germany."

"I certainly didn't expect that Mr. Rosenburg would immigrate to China."

"It was the last resort."

Heine raised his glass of cognac in a gesture that could only be seen as one of celebration. "Vienna has failed him. This is the time for clowns and cretins, unfortunately."

Fengshan observed the captain's face. If he could be optimistic, this would be a positive conversation. "Captain, I know you're a police officer, it's your duty to follow orders, and you certainly do not need to defend your loyalty, but it seems the veil of politics has blinded many people. I can hardly recognize the lovely Vienna before the Anschluss, and it's disheartening to see the Viennese torment other Viennese. Would you care to enlighten me?"

"All I can say is, Herr Consul General, there's so much about the Viennese that you don't know." The captain smiled his charming smile, his hand brushing over his impeccably groomed hair.

"Please accept my sincerest apologies."

"There are three types of men in the Federal Gendarmerie. People who are like me, people on the administrative side, and criminals, yes. Would you believe it, one of the men I had put in prison for a felony is now under my command."

Captain Heine came from a family of military men in Austria, Fengshan remembered. His father had been an *Obersturmmann* of the cavalry, and his grandfather had been another military figure in the Austro-Hungarian Empire. Captain Heine had exuded a good sense of discipline, fairness, and tradition—the Viennese concepts of "quiet, order, and security"—before the Anschluss, anyway.

The waiter set a tray with two glasses of water, two cups of coffee, a saucer with sugar cubes, and two spoons on their table. Fengshan picked up his coffee cup. "How are you getting along with them?"

The captain laughed, turning to the side, winking at one of the women looking in his direction.

He almost spilled his coffee. The man was a lost cause!

"Captain?"

"Well, yesterday, two high-ranking gendarmes from the Federal Gendarmerie were detained for disciplinary reasons. One was ordered for forced labor in Styria. He was a war veteran, twice wounded." Heine downed his glass of cognac.

Fengshan watched him intently. "In China, we have a phrase, *'Shu Da Zhao Feng.'* Big trees attract gusts."

132

The captain was shaking his head. "Good cognac. You should try it."

Fengshan suppressed the urge to sigh. He had intended to ask the captain about Adolf Eichmann and his celebratory party; this conversation seemed to be going nowhere. "It has been a pleasure meeting you. I regret I must take my leave."

"But, Herr Consul General, why in such a hurry? I have some information I thought you might be interested in. It's about Adolf Eichmann."

Fengshan sat upright. "Eichmann?"

"He mentioned you in a club and made some comments about you and China."

This didn't bode well. If Ambassador Chen heard that a German officer, even one of low rank, had vilified his country because of him, his opinion about him would change. "What kind of comments?"

"I shall not repeat his words here, but it seems he included you on a blacklist of some sort, citing your request of release for a Jewess at the Headquarters."

"Well, it's rather complicated. Back in May, when Grace was arrested, her tutor, a Jewess, was arrested as well."

"And then you've provided visas to Mr. Rosenburg's family."

"It was only a handful of visas," he protested.

"You've stopped issuing visas to the Viennese since then?"

He smiled. He didn't intend to explain the visas he had issued to Dr. Löwenherz's friends. Now that Ambassador Chen had relented, there was no reason not to open the door of his consulate wide.

"Eichmann is now the *Obersturmführer,* the chief of the Central Office for Jewish Emigration. All Jews with visas who leave Vienna must seek his approval and receive exit permits from him. He has ascended to be the Czar of the Jews."

"Is this a genuine title?"

"It might be someday, considering the circumstances. I confess that Eichmann's ascendance has taken everyone by surprise. He claimed he could oust a great number of Jews with this new agency, and he would expedite their expulsion. The Central Office was his idea. He'll notice every visa approved by your consulate." The captain leaned over the news rack behind him. There was the daily newspaper *Völkischer Beobachter*; near it was the popular political and entertainment magazine for women, *Das Kleine Frauenblatt*, and the sickening *Der Stürmer*, which the patrons inside the café were reading. The liberal newspapers, such as *Wiener Zeitung* and *Neue Freie Presse*, had disappeared from the shelves. Captain Heine pulled out a stack and placed it on the table. A black-and-white portrait of Adolf Eichmann, with a thin face and a sleazy smile, stared back at him.

The coffee felt terrible in Fengshan's stomach. "I have his invitation to attend his celebration party."

The captain's smooth smile disappeared. "The party should be nothing short of a spectacle, but whatever happens, I will be there. Now please excuse me; I have other matters to attend to. But, Herr Consul General, you might wish to learn more about the man's background."

This was indeed a positive conversation—at least he was able to make the distinction between a friend and a foe. "What can you tell me?"

"Perhaps you might wish to speak to the family of Adolf Böhm, a learned man, an author of two volumes that describe the history of the Zionist movement."

"What happened to Böhm?"

"He's under psychiatric care."

"Do you mean Böhm had a nervous breakdown?"

"What I mean is it's not an honor to be on Eichmann's blacklist."

"But, Captain Heine, here's the conundrum: the chief officer of the Central Office for Jewish Emigration wants the Viennese Jews out of the country, and my country's visas provide exactly an outlet they need. Why would the officer antagonize the consulate when we're assisting him in his goal?"

"This, I reckon, is complicated."

"I don't mean to be ungrateful for your explanation, Captain Heine, but I doubt the chief officer of an emigration center wields influence over the foreign diplomats."

"I'm afraid the American consul general should be the one to answer your questions."

"Mr. Wiley?"

"As we all know, the Third Reich has many friends overseas. I bid you a good day, Herr Consul General." He left some cash on the table—he even paid for both coffees. He was a good tipper.

For a long moment, Fengshan sat, stunned. Then he finally picked up the newspaper the captain had left. The headline lauded the inventive idea of speedily expelling the Viennese Jews, and there was a paragraph on Eichmann.

He was a salesman for an oil company before he joined the Sicherheitsdienst in Berlin, where he demonstrated a cunning ability to conduct incognito interrogations while donning plain clothes. With his exceptional literary acumen, he devoured Jewish literature to impress scholars in the Jewish community and befriend leaders of Zionist organizations. His knowledge of Judaism and his insight into the Jewish organizations are invaluable assets in helping solve the Jewish situation in Germany.

Fengshan could see why Captain Heine would warn him about Eichmann—when a man's powers grew, the blade of his hostility sharpened. Was he ready to face Eichmann's sharp edge? Would he end up like Mr. Wiley?

CHAPTER 23

GRACE

I learned later that the visa Fengshan issued to Lola was only the first step needed for her departure. For her family to leave the country, she would need to receive exit permits, and she must collect many related documents in an emigration center to demonstrate her family's eligibility: proof that her family didn't possess foreign bank accounts, proof that they no longer owned any assets—their apartment would be handed over to the uncle after all—certificates of tax forms that showed her family didn't owe the government money, tickets for an ocean liner with a departure date, and others.

For weeks Lola was busy gathering documents and purchasing boat tickets, and I was unable to see her. Then one day, when I stopped by, Lola was finally in her apartment. She invited me for a walk in her neighborhood. She appeared sober, reserved, lacking the vivacity that had captivated me when we met. Her long black dirndl dress looked as if it hadn't been laundered for days, and the scar twitched on her face like the red needle of a silent radio.

It was late August; the leaves were turning golden; a gust of wind blew toward us, sweeping the fallen leaves on the pavement. A few feet away, a family, carrying suitcases, was moving into the apartment next door.

I asked if she had gathered all the documents, and Lola nodded. It had been hard work, especially purchasing the boat tickets, which required a train ride from Vienna to a port in Italy. But she had secured an appointment for the exit permits at the Office, she said, and the exit permits were the last documents she needed to obtain.

"When is the appointment?" I asked.

"In October. We'll be able to stay in this apartment until we leave."

The apartment, I realized, belonged to her uncle now, who had allowed them to stay until their departure.

"Where is the Office?"

"It's located inside the former Palais Rothschild on Prinz-Eugen-Strasse, a few blocks from your consulate."

"I'll pick you up." I jotted down the date and time, so I wouldn't forget. I wanted to accompany her to the appointment. October would be here before I knew it, and that might be the last time I saw her.

"Thank you, Grace," she said, facing me, and smiled.

"I'll pick you up," I said again.

We began to walk again, passing the windswept streets, the closed windows, and the empty portico. Nearby, the trees, oaks and lindens, bent in the wind as if to say goodbye.

In the consulate, I went to Fengshan's office. But he was not inside. I sat in a high-backed chair, feeling depressed. So I turned on the radio; it was playing a French song. The lyrics were a mystery to me, but the mood hit home. Seeing Lola and knowing she was leaving had made me feel melancholy. I already missed her. What would I do after she left? She was my only friend in Vienna.

Just like that, Mother slipped into my mind. I should stop her but couldn't—her alcohol-scented skin and her rich red hair like a sunset. She was an arresting-looking woman with lovely brown eyes. A few years after Father died, she had finally given up raising me alone and remarried. Then she began to drink heavily, especially on Sunday mornings, to mark her own Eucharist. In her singsong voice, soaked in dreams and alcohol, she would mention Father, who had saved her from harassment, how they fell in love, and how his horrific death—beaten to death by a crowd—spelled the disaster for her life. She would look at me then, scold me because I was so mellow, so weak, and she would clamp her hands around my neck and scream, "Have some grit! Can you learn from your father? Say something, Grace—are you a mute?" while I was rolling my eyes, gasping for breath.

She always apologized later, hugged me, cried, and promised she would never hurt me again, but then she would drink more. She got divorced, relocated us to Chicago, and remarried again. When I told her about marrying Fengshan, she said I was foolish and warned me of a miserable life like hers. Since I left the US, I had dreamed of her, missed her even, but each time I spent too much time thinking about her, I would have nightmares—she would be scolding me for calling her *Mother*, she would be drinking again, yelling at me to speak louder, the house would smell like a cellar, and she would clasp her hands around my neck. I would swear never to think of her again, and then I would miss her.

Mother was like a precious bracelet I wanted to have close to my skin but was afraid to wear. But it didn't have to be this way. She loved me; she loved me. It had to be so, and I wanted to believe that.

"There you are, Grace."

Fengshan came in and went to the bookcases full of encyclopedias, chronicles, and books about world relationships. He looked like he was searching for something, scrutinizing. He shook his head and studied the other bookcase where leather-bound books were carefully arranged:

geography, religion, history, and culture; near them were manila folders and envelopes, all were sorted in alphabetic order. Stacks of newspapers, in which he immersed himself on Saturday afternoons, were set on a cart near the door.

I turned off the radio. Fengshan was different from Mother; he was constant and forgiving and determined. He was a genius with a photographic memory, and his mind was like a book with clear-cut edges and pages of erudition. He had picked me out and given me his hand, even though I was ordinary, my mind a river of random thoughts without border or clarity.

He turned away from the bookcases and rummaged for something in the drawer. "Have you eaten your lunch, Grace?"

How Chinese he was! Always asking if I had eaten, a common greeting in his hometown, where people often went an entire day without food and many were starving because of poverty. So asking about eating was not only a courtesy but also a show of care. I had been embarrassed at first, and he had said I was too American.

"I think so."

He took out an envelope inscribed in German. "Are you going to get dressed, Grace? We have an hour before the party."

"Where are we going?"

"Adolf Eichmann's celebration party. I thought I had told you a few weeks ago. He's now the chief of the Central Office for Jewish Emigration."

"Who?"

"The officer who released you at the Headquarters in May."

"I can't remember. I have a headache."

He put the envelope back in the drawer. "That might be for the best. Your presence shouldn't be required. Eichmann will recognize you."

He looked rather stressed, apprehensive. I changed my mind and threaded my arms around him. "It looks like you have to go. Then I'll go with you."

CHAPTER 24

FENGSHAN

The party was held on the fifth floor in a mansion near the Burggarten. Fengshan, with Grace in the nook of his arm, walked into the building, decorated with many swastika standards. He had not forgotten the sly nature of Eichmann since their first encounter, and now that Captain Heine had revealed Eichmann's sadistic reputation and influence over Mr. Wiley's departure, he was even warier. But he was a diplomat; playing by the rules of courtesy was part of his job. In no circumstances would he act out of line to decline the invitation and endanger his country's image or his career. With Mr. Wiley's departure, however, he had occasionally entertained the thought that perhaps it would be wise to take a step back and assess the situation before diving into further visa issuance.

Out of the elevator, he went to the table, where many cards, boxes of gifts, roses, irises, and wines were set, and put down his gift, a terra-cotta statue wrapped in red silk. On a stand near the table were articles about Eichmann published in *Der Stürmer*, duplicated and arranged in a framed collage to show the man's rising fame.

The ballroom was crowded with old gentlemen holding meerschaum pipes, middle-aged men in uniforms, and young fellows in suits decorated with pins and medals. A full orchestra played in a chamber nearby, and waiters in bow ties and tuxedos flowed around, carrying trays of drinks. This would be another typical Viennese party, marked by decadence, and the expense for the evening's food and drink could easily reach thousands of reichsmarks, enough to feed an entire village in China for six months. He felt guilty, dining on the fine foods and drinking champagne while his countrymen lived in hunger and hid from bombs. If he were not concerned about protocol, he would leave early. This would be a long evening.

He searched for Eichmann among the mass of people—German officials, Czechoslovakian diplomats, Hungarian men, influential industrialists, traditional Austrian noblemen in Tyrolean hats and feathers, and even a few faces with dark complexions who appeared to be from South America or some far-off islands.

"Don't leave me alone. I don't want to be here all by myself," Grace whispered.

Fengshan took two champagne flutes from a waiter and gave one to her. "Did you see Captain Heine?"

"No. Are you expecting him?" She was wearing a pair of satin gloves and a shimmering evening gown, which showed her slender figure and complemented her feminine curves. Her hair was piled up, a small pillbox teased on the top, and her earrings glittered. She looked elegant, like a portrait by Joseph Wright of Derby. He was fortunate to have her as his wife.

"Well, he said he'd attend."

"Maybe he'll show up soon. Well, maybe I should try to socialize on my own. You go ahead and talk to your friends."

"Are you sure?" When Grace was alone at a social engagement, her favorite destination at any venue was the bathroom.

"I'll be fine. I'll let you know when I see Captain Heine." The champagne flute in her hand, she turned around, still with a shy, uncomfortable look on her face, despite her brave words.

This was good for her, getting out of her shell. Fengshan was head-
~~ing to speak with the~~ Czech consul general when Eichmann, conversing
with a Wehrmacht official in an ornamented piped uniform fastened
with a belt of silver stripes, turned to him. He stuck his long arm
straight out like a stick. "*Heil* Hitler!"

Fengshan took a sip of the champagne. "Herr Eichmann, I'm glad
to see you're doing well. Congratulations on your promotion."

Eichmann, in his black uniform and cap, was grinning. "Thank
you, my dear friend. Is that Frau Consul General? She looks splendid.
I'm pleased you've come to celebrate the creation of our country's most
important agency. You and all the luminaries of Vienna have accepted
my invitation and come to see me! I'm flattered. The publisher of *Der
Stürmer* also dropped by to congratulate me, and *Sturmbannführer*
Hagen expressed his full trust in me. Have you read the article about
me in the Reich's most important newspaper? The reporters expressed
their absolute faith in my talent and insisted on addressing me as the
Czar of the Jews. I gave them the statistics and the numbers of Jews
who should emigrate over the next six months, and I reminded them
at this rate, very soon, our country will be *judenfrei*! They have never
heard anything like that!"

It seemed the man could go on and on with his nonsense. His thin
face looked puckered with the salt of perspiration under the glare of
the light.

Fengshan decided to ask, "Herr Eichmann, in your opinion, how
would a man stay safe at his own home, presuming he's completely
innocent?"

"Are you talking about Jews? Jews are not innocent."

"Well—"

"You see, I have proposed a perfect plan to leaders of Jewish organizations. They must show me their willingness to cooperate and
present their proof of departure in order to leave the city. But how
many can leave is limited, as they must first surrender their wealth.

You understand, Herr Consul General, I'm not called a genius for no reason!"

So it appeared that the Office would force deportation on those who were unwilling to leave and strip off their wealth as they departed the country, and that those who wished to leave must pay to receive their permission. Either way, the Office kept their wealth.

"Pardon me, I'm going to switch to another drink. This champagne doesn't agree with me." Fengshan turned around, blinking, feeling sick at heart. Nearby, Grace was speaking with a couple—a man wearing a white shirt and a yellow and green waistcoat and red sash, and a woman with an orange head wrap and a pineapple-colored dress with trim. They appeared to be islanders. Fengshan raised his flute and gave Grace a smile. When he went to switch his drink, he saw Captain Heine appearing in the hallway with a young woman. Fengshan nodded at him, put his champagne flute on a waiter's tray, and made a beeline for him.

The woman, hooked on the captain's arm, still bothered Fengshan, but he had warmed up to the captain since their latest meeting at the coffeehouse.

"Dr. Ho!" The Czech consul, Mr. Beran, came up to him before he got closer to the captain. Mr. Beran was an immense, thickset man with a long beard who always reminded Fengshan of one of the revolutionary bandits from the classic Chinese novel *The Tale of Life at the Water's Edge*. He had a rough face like shriveled ginger, and he loved snacking on herring.

"Good evening, Mr. Beran," Fengshan greeted in German.

Captain Heine shook his head, gave a brilliant smile that made women in the ballroom turn their heads, and walked away with his companion. He was not on good terms with the Czech consul. There appeared to be a feud between them.

"Do not trust that man, Dr. Ho," Mr. Beran mumbled. "He's devious, malicious. He has many faces."

"Would you fancy a cigar?" Fengshan walked to a cigar box on a nearby small table. Eichmann's party, not surprisingly, had the best cigars, the slim, long Habanos.

"This city is doomed, Dr. Ho! Doomed! Everyone has left, even our American friend," Beran said in his heavily Bohemian-accented German.

Beran was well acquainted with Mr. Wiley, Fengshan understood, and the Czech, whose country bordered Germany, had expressed deep unease since the Anschluss. Fengshan understood his trepidation. When the British closed their embassy and withdrew diplomats from Austria, the English-speaking voices in the ballrooms had receded considerably, and now, with Mr. Wiley's departure, the ballroom rumbled in German, French, Bohemian, Slavic, Spanish, and Italian. "He's going to be missed."

Mr. Beran sighed. "The British are asking us to hold a meeting again. Are you aware that Hitler is now demanding that we give him the Sudetenland, the frontier where our thirty divisions and the Škoda arms works are stationed? Czechoslovakia is the keystone of inner Europe; if we give it away, then all hell breaks loose!"

"The British?"

"Chamberlain and Daladier!"

Unfortunately, a weak country had no right to claim its own land—just like China's loss of the Shandong peninsula, the hometown of Confucius, when Britain and France gave it to the Japanese at the Paris Peace Conference. Would history repeat itself, with Chamberlain presenting Hitler a gift at the expense of Czechoslovakia? It had seemed unthinkable months ago.

"My love." Grace tugged him, her face pale.

"Grace. What happened?"

"I don't really know. This waiter was talking to me in German . . . I couldn't understand what he said . . . I think he was asking whether

I'd like to have another drink. Eichmann grew angry and yanked him away. Look."

He turned around. In a corner on the other side of the ballroom, Eichmann had seized the front of the waiter in a tuxedo from whom he had taken a champagne flute. A groan reverberated in the ballroom just as the orchestra paused, and Eichmann's violent voice exploded in the ballroom. "How dare you harass an honorable guest! She's a diplomat's wife! Where's your armband? Where's your pin?"

The guests stopped chatting; there was a wave of murmurs of disgust. Fengshan quietly translated what Eichmann said to Grace. Grace looked mortified; she shook her head, her voice a whisper. Fengshan gave her arm a reassuring squeeze. He had no doubt that Grace was speaking the truth, but why did Eichmann fabricate something as vile as harassment to defame his wife and humiliate an innocent waiter? This was a serious accusation—harassment of a foreign diplomat's wife in a ballroom. Fengshan studied the accused offender. He was a young man with blue eyes, and he staggered back to the wall, blood trickling out of his nose.

Fengshan crossed the ballroom to Eichmann. "Sir, please forgive me. Allow me to clarify. There was no harassment of any sort; my wife was merely speaking to him about a drink. This has to be some misunderstanding. I give you my deepest apology."

Eichmann glanced at him, Grace, and the waiter. For good measure, Fengshan took Grace's hand and kissed her. And as he observed, the expression on Eichmann's face began to change: there were signs of anger, hesitation, threat, and menace. Then the man smiled.

"Herr Consul General, I'm ever grateful for your clarification. There is no need for an apology at all. This indeed is an unfortunate misunderstanding." He loosed his grip on the waiter, who hurried to pick up his tray and left the ballroom.

Around him, the guests still looked indignant. Some glared at the departing waiter with suspicion; some gave Eichmann a nod, praising his action. Fengshan walked away in utter bewilderment. It was beyond his comprehension that Eichmann would concoct a case of harassment and make such a scene with the waiter, but to his relief, the music restarted: a waltz. People took each other's hands, flooding the parqueted floor. Ump-pa-pa, ump-pa-pa. The Viennese, having entertained themselves with Schumann and Mozart for ages, always knew how to enjoy a party.

At last he took Grace to the floor. He was a superb dancer, and so was Grace. His feet slid, his shoulders swayed, turning left and then right, but he bumped into an older couple. Murmuring an apology, he led Grace to the other side of the ballroom and searched: the waiter had not returned.

"I don't like this. Can we leave now?" Grace whispered to him.

"That would reflect poorly on our manners."

Eichmann, his face intense, was speaking to a man in a uniform by a bouquet of flowers, who nodded and left. Repulsed, Fengshan whirled away and caught Captain Heine's handsome face a few steps away, his eyebrows raised in question. Fengshan gave the captain a nod of assurance, his mind slowly at ease. The music was helpful, too, rising to a joyous crescendo, flooding the ballroom.

Suddenly a shriek pierced the waltz, followed by a loud thud outside. The music stopped; Eichmann's figure flitted across the ballroom, disappeared, and swiftly returned. "Ladies and gentlemen, I regret to inform you that there has been an unfortunate incident that involved the waiter. The man, ashamed of his depravity, just jumped off the balcony. I have dispatched people to look into the matter. Meanwhile, let's dance!"

Some people sighed; some looked shocked. But a string of violin notes poured in the air—a torrid Hungarian dance, and instantly, people, young and old, in uniforms and in dresses, turned around, and their feet began to shuffle.

Fengshan's body, which had been throbbing with warmth from dancing, grew cold. He went to Eichmann. "But Herr Eichmann, the man was innocent. Why did he take his own life? Have you called the hospital?"

"There is no need, I assure you. This is the fifth floor."

The callousness in his voice would have made people turn their heads had they heard him. Fengshan felt sick to his stomach. He took Grace's arm. "I must beg your forgiveness, Herr Eichmann; I feel unwell. If you don't mind, I'd like to take my leave with my wife."

On the man's face was that sly smile. "Herr Consul General, this is regrettable. We're only halfway into the party. I have enjoyed chatting with you. You're a man of admirable character. But I suppose you haven't been in Vienna for long. May I give you a word of advice—where are the journalists who have been begging me for a word of advice? Well, this should be in the newspaper, don't you agree: we all need friends in Vienna."

A chill ran down his spine. "Have a good evening, Herr Eichmann."

Fengshan rushed to the elevator, Grace on his arm. This was the fifth floor, but perhaps there was a chance the waiter had survived. He could use the building's phone on the ground floor to call the ambulance.

"Herr Consul General. Are you leaving?" A Polish consul was sitting in a chair near the elevator, attacking a piece of Sacher torte. The layers were perfectly moistened, the whipped cream inviting, the rich chocolate fragrant. It was his favorite dessert, an indulgence.

"Did you hear what Eichmann said? A man just jumped from the balcony. Someone needs to call the hospital!"

"The waiter?"

"So you heard what he said. The waiter was innocent. He didn't harass my wife."

"I saw him."

"Pardon?"

"Eichmann's man pushed him off the balcony."

"Pardon?"

"He was a Jew. Obviously, we all know that. Eichmann wouldn't tolerate a Jew working at his celebration party."

"How . . ." Fengshan swallowed. "If he was a Jew, why would he be allowed to work here?"

"They have their ways of blending in, but Eichmann must have found out." The Polish consul put a chunk of cake in his mouth. "You have to agree that the Austrians make the best chocolate cake! Have you tried it?"

The elevator door opened; Fengshan entered it without answering the consul's question. Then the elevator descended, squeaking and groaning, slow as a horse carriage, and Grace's whispers rang in his ears like something from another world. His head pounded, a strange pain thundering in his brain. When he reached the ground floor, he stumbled outside.

In the dimness lit by the streetlamps, he couldn't see anything on the ground. Then he heard voices speaking roughly in German and curses—"Such a mess." He reached out for Grace's arm but missed. His stomach wrenched, and a sourness surged in his mouth. He retched, trying to empty the few drops of champagne he had drunk.

In the car, he told Grace he would like to go to his church. It was closed, but he didn't mind. He just wanted to see it, to remember the solidity of the cross that he had clutched in his hands when he was a hungry child, the strength that it had instilled in him, and the vision that it had revealed to him. When they arrived, he sat on a bench outside the church, his hat on his knees, gazing at the building, steady like a mountain, the streetlights casting a pale glow on the fanlights and the giant wooden doors. Across the street, the neon light on a cabaret flashed, and several youths wearing red robes and skirts were playing a game with daggers; near him, his Grace was soaked in silence.

He had arrived at the party with careful steps and sensible pragmatism, hoping to preserve the diplomatic relationship with Germany, yet that had only been wishful thinking. Eichmann had deliberately fabricated a scandal to defame his wife, to warn him, and to threaten him for helping the Viennese. And mercilessly, he had ordered the man to be thrown off a balcony, a man he was too glad to murder, disguising it as a suicide. Yet, some of his guests danced while the others ate their cake.

And this waiter, this nameless victim, was only one of the thousands of men in the city, hounded, unprotected, turned away by thirty-two countries. And there were still more on the streets, in their own homes, in the ballrooms, facing the danger of being beaten, slandered, arrested, or murdered.

Staring at the cross in front of him, he swore then that just as he would fight for his country's survival, he would now fight for the survival of the defenseless, the unprotected. He resolved to stop the inhumanity from happening in front of his eyes, and he would do everything he could to save lives.

CHAPTER 25

GRACE

My husband worked in his office late that evening, making phone calls to his church friends, Jewish organizations, and even Frau Maxa. Let the word spread that the Chinese consulate was open to accepting visa applications, he said.

The next day, the lobby was full of people. Sitting in the large Baroque armchairs that had been occupied by the Chinese peddlers and students were people speaking German. They wore tall hats, long beards, and black caftans. Their manners were sophisticated, and their voices were soft. Vice Consul Zhou was busy, his face pink, stuttering in German, interviewing a man applying for visas for his twenty family members. Frau Maxa was handing out forms to a group of people who had just entered; then, speaking rapid German, she rushed to her desk to collect cash and write receipts.

Once people received their visas, they could apply for exit permits at the emigration center, like Lola, I realized. I wished I could help, but, unable to understand German, I stood in a corner. Soon I grew uncomfortable, with the applicants glancing at me curiously, so I decided to go upstairs.

As I passed through the lobby, I heard Monto asking Frau Maxa something. They were speaking German, and Frau Maxa responded with a swipe at his head—Austrian women seemed to know how to handle children.

"Excuse me?" I asked. Frau Maxa explained that Monto had been pestering her for a signature to predict her future. She was too busy, she said, with all these applicants waiting.

"Do you want my signature?" I asked Monto. A button was missing on his shirt, and there was a tear on his sleeve. He must have ripped his shirt playing on the playground. Or he had gotten in a fight at school. I could ask, but Monto's mind was like a radio with a broken switch that I had no idea how to turn on.

He shrugged. "No one wants your signature, Grace."

"Why are you not playing with your friend?" *What is his friend's name?* He had mentioned him in the summer. *Wallace? Wilson? Bobby? Willi!*

"Not your business, Grace!"

I could feel the entire lobby looking at me—the insensitive, crude stepmother who didn't know how to talk to her stepson. This felt worse than the humiliation last night when people had gawked at me after Eichmann claimed I was harassed. I lowered my head. I should go to the bathroom.

"What's going on here?" Fengshan showed up.

"Nothing," I said. Monto had skipped to the applicants near the elevator now. A strong-willed boy. I would never have had the courage to speak to Mother like that.

"Grace, let's go to the park for a walk."

"You have time for a walk? Yes, I'd love to." I looped my arm through his, heading toward the consulate's entrance. "Let's go get some fresh air. It's a good day today. How many visas have you issued?"

"Forty-eight people applied. I'll have the visas ready tomorrow."

He didn't sound pleased. "What's wrong?"

"These people have no idea what Shanghai is like. It was bombed for four months, and the city is nothing but rubble. They will live under the shadow of Japanese fighter planes and gangsters' gunfire. They won't be able to survive there."

"Where else could they go? They are not allowed to live here," I reminded him.

It was a beautiful day in the park. The sunlight shone like a mirror, the pavement sparkled, and the chestnut trees locked their limbs with one another and swayed. A flock of birds rushed above a fountain and flitted to stand on a statue's head. In the air played an Italian overture, a familiar melody that I had heard in a chamber.

Fengshan sat on a bench, pensive, the bright sunlight on his shoulder. "I wish there were a protected area for them, a special place where they wouldn't need to worry about the assault of the Japanese, like an island."

"There's already an island for them."

He turned to me. "What did you say?"

"Well . . . Wait, let me think. A couple at Eichmann's party mentioned that to me. Their country offered visas to the Jews. What was the country called? Let me think . . . I remember . . . Dominic, no, the Dominican Republic."

"Are you sure?"

"I am. I meant to tell you, but with Eichmann, it slipped my mind. The Dominican Republic. Yes. That's the country. The couple didn't quite fit in at the party, so they were delighted to speak to me. They spoke good English. The lady wore a pineapple-colored dress. I didn't know where the country was. They said it was an island in the Caribbean."

"An island country."

"The couple said Mr. Wiley approached them a few months ago. He offered a large sum to the ambassador of the Dominican Republic in exchange for a path for Jews to immigrate to their country. The

Dominican Republic happened to need help for their agriculture, so a deal was made. Did Mr. Wiley tell you when you met him?"

"He had no reason to, but if it's true, it's extraordinary. I didn't know the American government would provide a large sum for the refugees."

"Oh, it wasn't the government. It was from the Quakers; do you know Quakers? And some Jewish organizations in the US."

"I've heard some church friends talk about Quakers. What was the sum Mr. Wiley offered?"

"I don't know. I didn't ask."

"How many refugees will the Dominican Republic accept?"

"I heard ten thousand."

"That's ten thousand lives!"

"I think so. But I can be wrong. My love?"

He shot up to his feet. "Well done, Grace, well done indeed! Let's go back to the consulate. Quick. We need to go. I have an important rescue plan that I need to write."

CHAPTER 26

FENGSHAN

China had many islands, too, small, like those in the Caribbean, and China had many vast lands, underdeveloped in the southwest. With some strategic planning, those islands or the uncultivated lands could be home to the desperate Viennese.

It might have been inconceivable before, but this was an opportunity for China to rise on the world stage by solving the Jewish situation. What a windfall it would be if China could receive international acclaim and financial support like the Dominican Republic!

Preoccupied, he didn't talk to Grace or answer her questions and went straight to his office, passing the visa applicants in the lobby. He had to hold on to his thoughts, fearing the brilliant plan would escape if he spoke. Once at his desk, he spread out sheets of paper and grabbed his fountain pen. A rescue plan, a perfect plan, throbbed in his head. Feverish, he drafted his proposal.

❧

On his report day, Fengshan first asked about the defense that Wuhan had been putting up for the past two months. Ambassador Chen didn't seem to be anxious about the Japanese attack on Wuhan, which boded well. If the Nationalist army succeeded in defending Wuhan, there would be hope for them to recoup, gather strength and train the army with the funds they would receive from the Americans.

Then Fengshan articulated his rescue plan to his superior as calmly as he could. "If China implements a broad, lenient policy regarding the Jews and accepts them, it will elevate the country's reputation and win the admiration of countries such as Britain and France and many others in the world. China will also gain many allies and support of willing lenders among the powerful organizations in the United States."

Fengshan heard a loud groan from Ambassador Chen, but he had prepared, and he pleaded for the ambassador's patience. "Many Jews are talented, and they will be grateful for the rescue. Some of them are powerful bankers as you might have heard." He couldn't verify this yet, but he knew this would be very persuasive to Ambassador Chen.

"You've made a good case, Fengshan, but I've reminded you repeatedly that we're at war with the Japanese. Cities have been lost, looted, and burned. You're talking about sending Jews to fire. Is a good death in China better than a bad living in Germany?"

"Ambassador Chen, if you can bear with me. We have many islands—Taiwan, Hainan Island, and a few small islands in the Pacific Ocean, all remote, unoccupied by the Japanese, and sparsely populated. They could be a safe sanctuary."

"The plan sounds far-fetched. It's not feasible."

"May I be so bold as to say this: if the islands sound unfeasible, perhaps a designated land in the southwest is another consideration. Those acreages are mostly farmland, unpopulated, but once people immigrate there, with their intelligence and resources, they'll become valuable human resources to help our country prosper."

Ambassador Chen made a noise, but he didn't sound testy.

"With all due respect, Ambassador Chen, this is a bold plan. I have drawn up the proposal for your perusal, and perhaps you'll discuss this with Mr. Sun Ke. Have we heard any good news from Ambassador Hu?"

"The twenty-five million dollars are in process, Fengshan. The Americans' word was good." There was a sigh. "How many refugees are you proposing?"

"Ten thousand."

"Ten thousand!"

"A small island such as the Dominican Republic can accept this number. Why not us?"

Silence again.

"It's worth considering, Ambassador Chen."

"Mail me the proposal, Fengshan, and I shall bring this to Mr. Sun Ke's attention."

Fengshan put down the phone, exhilarated. He had pleaded for ten thousand lives! He picked up the proposal he'd written, scrutinizing every sentence for ambiguity or potential misinterpretations. When Frau Maxa came to work, he would ask her to put aside anything she had in hand and rush to the post office.

"Grace! Grace! You have to hear this!" He burst into their bedroom. She had inspired him; this was her success as well.

Grace, in her long purple nightgown, was standing at the window, pulling aside the curtains, as a waterfall of golden sunlight poured through.

CHAPTER 27

GRACE

A few weeks after Fengshan's proposal, another phone call from the ambassador came. Fengshan, exuberant, beckoned me over. They were speaking Chinese, so I paid attention to every twinkle in Fengshan's eyes. When he hung up, he held me and twirled in his office, an almost scandalous move for someone like him.

The ambassador had good news, he said. The Roosevelt administration had finalized the credit for twenty-five million dollars to the Nationalists, which had lifted the morale of many officers and soldiers. Mr. Sun Ke, after a lengthy phone conversation with Ambassador Chen, had expressed interest in the rescue plan of the ten thousand Jews he had proposed. The Ministry would discuss the proposal with the committee in the coming weeks.

"Ten thousand lives, Grace!" Fengshan said.

"What type of visas will they receive?"

"Immigration visas. An exclusive island in China would be designated for their home. Ambassador Chen mentioned Hainan Island. Separately, the Ministry of Foreign Affairs has agreed to a lenient visa policy regarding the Jews."

He had done it—extending a hand to ten thousand lives and successfully establishing a lenient policy for the Viennese Jews. Many people, like Lola, could go to China if they wanted to.

❧

October came.

The day for Lola's interview at the Central Office for Jewish Emigration arrived. I asked for Fengshan's permission to use the consulate's car to pick up Lola and her family.

When we arrived at the Office, it began to rain, but the entire street in front of the building was crowded with men holding briefcases and bags. Lola, Mrs. Schnitzler, Sara, and Eva joined the queue in the back. Without an umbrella, Lola tucked the documents under her jacket to keep them dry.

I went back to the consulate to fetch two umbrellas and returned to the palatial building. Mrs. Schnitzler, Sara, and Eva kept one, and Lola stayed with me.

"It's going to take a while, Grace. We haven't moved much. Maybe you can come back later," Lola said. She looked different. The desperation and flame of anger had left her green eyes, replaced by a different expression, expectant and determined.

"I'll wait."

It was pouring; many were shivering without umbrellas, craning their necks at the grand limestone entrance. Most exiting the building looked jubilant, waving their documents. But there were also some people who looked as though they had walked out of a boxing ring, their faces swollen, bruises on their foreheads, their steps unsteady.

A man with a thick accent I couldn't identify asked for shelter from the rain. He looked to be in his twenties, with blue eyes and thick eyebrows. A good-looking man. Lola spoke to him in German for a while; then the man nodded and left.

"Who's that, Lola?"

"A Polish Jew. His passport was declared invalid at the emigration office."

I had met several Polish diplomats before. They were friendly, demonstrated great culinary knowledge, but their facial features and even their dress code appeared very Austrian to me. "That's unfortunate."

It was pouring now. My dress stuck to my back, and my shoes were soaked. Waves of water rushed up to my ankles.

"You're shivering. Go back to the consulate, Grace. Don't wait in the rain," Lola insisted.

Finally, I obliged.

When I returned a few hours later, the queue had moved. Among the many people holding umbrellas, there was no Lola or her family. They must have entered the building.

CHAPTER 28

LOLA

Sitting at a wide desk in the center of the grand hall that had once been the Rothschilds' ballroom, Eichmann, that cold man with icy eyes, was lashing out at a couple for a misspelling on a form. He threw the paperwork on the floor, and the couple scrambled to gather it up, their sobs echoing in the grand hall. It was not as though they were responsible for the misspelling—the forms were filled out by the officials in the Office—but all the same, the couple must wait in line, reapply, and repeat the process they had gone through months ago. Was there anything else that could possibly be more defeating, more hopeless than this?

It was no wonder people in the line whispered of gloom, of depression, of suicides. Since Josef's death, I had often wondered why he took his life. I had thought because the torture was unbearable, because he wanted to protect his employer, but now I knew he took his life because he saw the city that had been our home had become a city of crimes and was no longer worth living for. This was what the Nazis were doing to us—to make us drown in our despair, to lose the will to live, and to perish.

"Schnitzler!" a voice barked, echoing in the enormous hall.

I went first, holding Mutter's arm; behind me followed Sara and Eva. On the long table where Eichmann sat, I spread out the documents, the visas, the passports, the certificates, and the boat tickets I had purchased in Italy.

The man scanned the documents; his eyes turned colder, and he mumbled something.

"Pardon?" I said, but a punch smacked my jaw. It came from a guard nearby.

"The head of the household presents the documents. Are you the head of the household?" Eichmann said without looking up.

Mutter held me; her voice was weak. "I'm the head of the household." She pushed the documents closer to that stony man.

"Shanghai again." This time those steel-gray eyes were fixated on me, then on the scar on my face, and then on Mutter, Sara, and Eva.

"Schnitzler," he said slowly.

I bit my tongue. He had defiled Vater's name.

"How's that yellow man? Of course I won't forget him."

To my shame, I couldn't defend the righteous consul who'd issued my family visas. Eichmann held the fate of my family; a hint of anger from me would jeopardize our passage out of Vienna.

"It's just as well, mongrels and Jews coupling together."

Finally, the man waved us aside to the desk next to him, where we were to sign a stack of papers for three purposes: to surrender our movable and immovable property to the government, to denounce our Austrian citizenship, and to vow that we'd never set foot in Vienna for as long as we lived.

When I walked out of the building, it seemed a part of me had been peeled off. I had been born here, grown up here, and with one signature, I was a woman without a country. I put my arms around Mutter, pulling Sara and Eva close. They were all I had now.

"Lola, come over here!" Grace was holding an umbrella, waiting in the rain across the street. "Did you receive the exit permits?"

"Grace! Yes! I told you not to wait here. It's cold."

"Thank God! Now you can leave Vienna."

It was as if her words held enormous power, and I suddenly felt a great weight lifted off my shoulders. It was true. Now we would leave, leave the hateful Eichmann, leave all the misery, hatred, and death behind. Shanghai would be a new beginning, and I could play the violin again.

"Come here, you're all wet." Grace pulled me under her umbrella, but a gust of wind swept over us. Her umbrella bent and the handle slipped from her grip. A torrent of rain poured down, drenching me. I shivered, but I laughed.

"I love the storm, the torrential rain. Do you like it, Grace?" Thunder and rain. A heavenly symphony, my favorite orchestra. I had played that before, the rage of *Die Walküre*, the fiery squall of the string music. It was a chilling tempest, a prelude to another life.

"Well—"

"Shall we dance in the rain?" I grabbed her hand as she reached for the umbrella. "A waltz? Come on. Come on. A waltz!" And I danced with her, twirling, splashing water between us.

"Oh, I didn't know you could dance."

"Every Viennese can dance."

"Lola." Mutter was calling me.

I gave Grace another twirl and picked up the umbrella. The rush of euphoria vanished, as suddenly as it had come, and I could feel the chill of the rain on my face, plunging down my neckline.

"That was nice, cold but nice. But Lola, now that you've received the exit permits, when will you leave for Shanghai?" A trickle of rain ran down Grace's face.

"November ninth."

How fast time went by. It was already October. Soon it would be November, the month that would start the opera season that heralded many performances and recitals that the Viennese enjoyed, that I had lived for. But I hadn't played the violin in public for months; all my friends had scattered since May. Who would perform at the operas and concerts of the Vienna Philharmonic and the Vienna Symphony this year? They would not be the same as before, with so many Jewish musicians and actors dismissed and detained, so many enthusiastic Jewish patrons confined in prison, departing, or struggling on the brink of survival.

A lightning bolt, stark, severed the dark sky; all the buildings seemed to be melting; a flood of water surged toward me, splashing my shoes.

"I'll come to see you off, Lola. November ninth. I won't forget."

Grace was soaked, her hair sticking to her lovely face; her eyes glimmered with the indulgence and admiration that always made me feel special. And I wanted to ask if she liked Shanghai, ask her stories about her time in China and Istanbul. I swore I'd never look back on Vienna again, but I would remember her, her face, her stories, and how she'd danced with me in the treacherous storm.

It was pouring.

CHAPTER 29

FENGSHAN

In mid-October, he still had not received the green light for the immigration of the ten thousand Viennese. It concerned him. To confirm the lenient policy regarding visas for Jews, he telegraphed the Ministry, requesting a written statement to be sent to the consulate. When the telegram of the message arrived a few days later, Fengshan carefully filed it in a manila folder with other important letters from the ambassador and the Ministry.

One day, while Fengshan was listening to the radio, an exhilarated voice declared that the British and the French had agreed to hand the Sudetenland in Czechoslovakia over to Germany, the outcome that the Czech consul had feared. It sickened Fengshan to hear that these two countries had sold out their ally Czechoslovakia, the country they had sworn to protect, laying bare their cowardice and duplicity.

Ambassador Chen didn't appear to be concerned about the annexation of the Sudetenland. The European crisis was irrelevant to his primary goal to forge a solid relationship with Germany, he said, as he was in talks with Germany about aircraft. He had yet to secure a meeting with his German counterpart, but he was optimistic.

News about the Nationalist armies' struggles was scant. When Fengshan managed to get ahold of his friends in China, reports of devastating losses and casualties kept him up all night. He prayed his tenacious countrymen would hold on. China would defend itself; China would prevail.

November arrived. One morning he awoke to snow, piling on the consulate's marble triangular pediment, and the wintry storm whipped the chiseled face of Beethoven holding his score and tugged at the standards bearing swastikas and the banners that advertised operas and concerts at the Vienna State Opera.

A German newspaper printed a large headshot of Adolf Eichmann on the second page. It was reported that since the establishment of the Central Office for Jewish Emigration, approximately thirty thousand Jews had legally departed Vienna after they had compliantly surrendered their properties and assets. Thirty thousand people ousted in three months.

It occurred to Fengshan that Eichmann must have a clear picture of how many visas he had issued. Since the dreadful evening when Eichmann ordered the death of the waiter, Fengshan had not come across him, but he was aware he would run into that man again—Vienna was a small city, after all.

One evening, he took Grace to the opera, something he had planned five months ago.

"Lola is leaving in three days," she said, walking down the dimly lit aisle. "I love this theater."

These days Grace was moody and melancholy, like the French songs she listened to on the radio, constantly talking about her friend's departure. She was conflicted. On the one hand, she understood Lola must leave; on the other hand, she hadn't quite figured out what to do without a friend.

Mr. Rosenburg, who had loved the opera, would leave, too, in three days. The end of the year, 1938, it appeared, would be the end of an era.

❧

The phone rang.

"Good afternoon, Captain Heine."

Fengshan looked at his watch. It was almost two o'clock. He had planned to meet the captain at Café Central. A few weeks ago, the captain had mentioned briefly that the police had caught some Viennese crossing the border to Switzerland with Chinese visas. They must be the friends of Dr. Löwenherz, Fengshan realized, and defended himself and his consulate—he had no control over how the visa holders chose their route to China. The captain, to his surprise, had agreed and further revealed that those Viennese had been permitted entry to Switzerland and that no one in the police force was told of the escapade. Fengshan had been glad—Heine had not wholly lost his conscience. A genuine friendship had sprouted between them, despite his irritation at the captain's fallibility with women.

"I'm afraid we must cancel today's meeting. There is a national emergency."

"What's going on?"

"You will hear it from the radio soon." Captain Heine's smooth voice was careful. "A seventeen-year-old Polish Jew walked into the German embassy in Paris and shot a German diplomat, Third Secretary Ernst vom Rath."

The gravity of the event made Fengshan's hair stand up. This would have an explosive effect. "How did this happen? Who is the foolish young man?"

"We do not yet know the perpetrator's name; we are only told he's a Polish Jew."

It occurred to him that the crisis had been brewing for a while. The newspaper had mentioned that the Nazi government had expelled all Polish Jews in the country last month, forcing them to migrate to Poland; however, the Polish government had revoked the citizenship of the Poles who had lived outside Poland for more than five years. So hundreds of Poles were stranded at the border, stuck at a refugee camp at a border town called Zbaszyn, unable to return to Germany or enter Poland.

"It appears that the man was frustrated that his parents were trapped in a camp in Zbaszyn at the border of Poland. He acted alone and was arrested on the spot. The third secretary is currently in critical condition. All the police forces in Greater Germany are ordered to stand by."

"Why would the police forces in Greater Germany be on standby? It was a reckless act by a lone young man, as you said."

There was a long pause, and when the captain's voice came through, it had lost the flirtatious tone he often had. "I have the order to take action, should it turn out that the wound the third secretary suffered is fatal."

Action? "I assume there will be a trial."

There was another pause. "It's not within my authority to make any prediction, but, Herr Consul General, for safety, I advise you and your family to cancel all activities and stay in the consulate for the next few days."

Fengshan hung up the phone, went out to the lobby, and watched the men in black overcoats and homburgs waiting for their visas. None of them had heard the news of the attempted assassination yet.

CHAPTER 30

GRACE

On the day I'd see Lola off, I put on a mauve velvet dress, stockings, and a black wool coat. While I was getting dressed, Fengshan came up a few times. He was keeping a close eye on the news of the wounded diplomat and feared an impending catastrophe in the city. I thought he was overly anxious, and I couldn't decide what to wear. The black wool outfit looked grave for the occasion. So I took it off and put on an astrakhan coat Fengshan had bought for me last year—but it was too big. I removed the astrakhan coat and put the wool outfit back on. In the mirror, I practiced how to smile—today was a happy day for Lola; she had waited for so long.

At six o'clock, two hours before Lola's scheduled departure at the train station, I stepped out of the elevator. The visa applicants in the lobby were trickling out, and Frau Maxa, staying late for work, told me Fengshan had asked to see me in his office.

"Grace, I'm sorry, but you might consider staying in the consulate tonight," Fengshan said the moment I walked in.

"Why?"

Third Secretary vom Rath had unfortunately died, Fengshan said. And Hitler, furious, had ordered the Gestapo to conduct door-to-door searches for any suspects or conspirators. Jews were ordered to remain at home or risk being shot if they stepped outside.

"Lola's train leaves at eight, honey. Will she be able to go to the train station?"

"Not if the home-arrest order is in effect." Fengshan was pacing, frowning.

"But I promised I'd see them off."

"Mr. Rosenburg and his family were scheduled to leave later this evening as well. I was going to visit him too. But I have been warned by Captain Heine."

"We're foreign nationals. Are we restricted from traveling as well?"

"It's only for the Jews."

"Then I want to go to Lola's home."

"Grace."

"I'll be fine. Tonight will be the last time I see her."

Fengshan sighed. "I suppose I'll go with you, if you've made up your mind."

Outside the consulate, the Ringstrasse, lit up by the gaslights, appeared normal, with a thin layer of snow, cars, and the uniformed police. But as we drove toward the area where Lola lived, the streets seemed eerily quiet. All the flower shops and news kiosks and retail shops were closed; no one was milling about.

When we turned onto the street to her neighborhood, a cacophony thundered in the distance, growing louder and louder. It made me uneasy.

I pressed my face to the window, but it was too dark to see anything outside, and then a fleet of motorcycles roared past. I jumped; my husband gripped my hand. Finally, when we were a few blocks away from Lola's house, I saw some wooden blockades and the Gestapo officers, pistols pinned on their belts, holding cudgels and flashlights, searching house by house. A few police cars shrieked past, their back seats filled with men with their coats unbuttoned and their hands behind their heads.

One more block to Lola's apartment. Finally. The car slowed and stopped at a blockade near a pile of snow. I could see Lola's apartment building in bright headlights, the staircase leading to her apartment—and then the doors, which I had knocked on many times, were flung open. From inside came two Gestapo officers, heading toward a car, between them a woman with an apron.

"That's Sara! They arrested Sara!" I shouted. Why had they arrested Sara? She had a visa! She couldn't be a conspirator of the assassin! "We have to stop them. My dear, stop them!"

"Mr. Rudolf," Fengshan said. "Could we go around the blockade?"

"Yes, Herr Consul General." The car reversed, and at that precise moment, I cried out—Lola and Mrs. Schnitzler were stumbling from their apartment to the staircase that led to the street.

"Sara! Sara!" Mrs. Schnitzler shouted.

"Stay inside! That's an order! Stay inside!" Through the window, I could see the detestable Gestapo whip out his revolver and point it at Lola and Mrs. Schnitzler.

Oh, Lola, my dear friend, so far from me, appearing motionless, her face blurred in the darkness; then, just as I hoped, she held her mother's arms and pulled her back toward the apartment as the car that had taken Sara rumbled, sped, wove past the blockade, and exploded past us.

Rudolf swerved our car, narrowly missing the police vehicle, but then he was having trouble turning around again, and I lost sight of Lola and Mrs. Schnitzler. I could only hear her heartbreaking wail. "Sara! My Sara!"

It took forever for Rudolf to turn around, and when I looked out again, my heart chilled. Ahead of us, Mrs. Schnitzler had somehow slipped from Lola's grip and stumbled onto the street, while the fleet of motorcycles that had been circling the neighborhood appeared in the opposite direction. They revved forward, racing toward Mrs. Schnitzler. They didn't slow down.

"Jesus Christ!" Fengshan shouted.

A cloudburst of silver rushed over the windshield, a thunderous rumbling shook the street, the floor beneath me rattled, and the discordance, deafening, pierced my ears. The unnatural clatter of tires, of bones, of groans didn't stop; it went on and on.

As if nothing had happened, the fleet of motorcycles blasted past us.

Then the world stopped. There was no more clash, no more shooting silvers, no more voices. I wanted to get out of the car, but my knees trembled. Fengshan leaped out instead and shouted something, his voice drifting above the street like an echo of a moan, and there was Lola's howl, too, trailing behind the thumping of the Gestapo's boots from somewhere.

Somehow I rolled out of the car, but I couldn't walk—a map of blood had spread near my feet, glistening in the car's cold light. There was no way to avoid it. It was everywhere; Mrs. Schnitzler was everywhere. *Right foot first, Grace,* she had said. But which one was right?

She was still on the ground, Fengshan kneeling next to her, murmuring something, his voice gentle, and then he stood up and carried her up the stairs to the apartment, where Lola had collapsed at the doorstep.

"Grace, let's go inside," he said.

"What—"

"Get inside."

I went in obediently, a mute again, full of fear again, and I fidgeted, fingering my pearl necklace. I couldn't ask; I must not ask. I couldn't see, either, and I was afraid to see.

"Miss Schnitzler," Fengshan said to Lola, and put Mrs. Schnitzler down near a suitcase in the family room. He took off his overcoat and covered her up.

Lola jerked, her face cleft by the light from outside. Then she scrambled to her mother and threw herself onto her. "Mutter! Mutter!"

I leaned on Fengshan, unable to push back my tears. Mrs. Schnitzler shouldn't have stepped onto the street, but then Sara shouldn't have been arrested, but then they shouldn't have been on this street at all.

Fengshan was saying something, looking anxious. *Mr. Rosenburg, Mr. Rosenburg.* It dawned on me that he was worried about his friend, and he wanted to make sure of his safety. But I couldn't go. I wanted to be with my poor friend. In a matter of months, she had lost her brother, her mother, and perhaps her sister as well.

"Fine, Grace, you stay here. I'll be back. I'll pick you up. Don't go anywhere." He closed the door behind him.

My head hurt, and I could hardly breathe. I opened my purse, took out the tin can, and inhaled the Tiger Balm. Just one whiff to make my headache go away. Then I crawled to Mrs. Schnitzler and placed the tin can, the last I had, on her chest. It was her favorite.

Then I realized something else. Eva. The little girl. Where was Eva? Was she out on the street? Had she been taken with Sara? I wanted to go search for her, but I couldn't leave Lola.

"Lola?"

She could hardly hear me, her face covered with tears and blood, her body limp against the wall. Then suddenly she let out a scream, long, deep, and full of grief.

"Hush, hush." I moved to lock the door, turned off the lights, and pulled the curtains. Then I slid next to Lola and put my hand on her arm; I listened to every sob of hers, felt every shudder of hers, as the room grew darker and then was split open by the daggers of light thrust through the curtains, as the cries rose and then shattered like glass, as the cars' wheels ground the pavement, as the shrill curses swallowed the gay music, as peals of sinister chuckles eclipsed the darkness.

CHAPTER 31

FENGSHAN

The neighborhood of the Rosenburgs, like Miss Schnitzler's, was chaotic. His car passed many frantic shadows trying to run away from the thugs holding rifles, and finally, it stopped in front of Mr. Rosenburg's in-laws' apartment. Fengshan straightened his tie and ducked out of the car.

Mrs. Rosenburg, in her shawl and a long black dress, opened the door.

"Good evening, Mrs. Rosenburg. I told your husband that I'd come to see you off. This is early, but I was just in the neighborhood, so I thought to stop by. I believe your train departs at ten. Is that right? Is he around?" The apartment appeared quiet.

"I'm sorry, Herr Consul General. My husband was taken by the Gestapo," Mrs. Rosenburg said.

His heart dropped. He was too late. "When?"

"An hour ago."

"Where was he taken?"

Mrs. Rosenburg wrapped her shawl tighter around her. "The police station. The man who took my husband is a former employee. He said it was a routine interrogation. My husband showed them the visas and exit permits. We're hoping he'll be freed before our train departs."

Fengshan turned around. A few Gestapo had just appeared under the streetlights, heading toward the Rosenburgs' apartment. What had happened to Mrs. Schnitzler must not happen to his friend's family. "It's been a weird day. Would you mind my waiting here for him?"

"Of course, Herr Consul General."

He went into their living room and sat on a couch, smoking his cigarette, listening to the heavy footfalls outside the door. He had not devised a plan to protect his friend's family yet; he only knew one thing—he must protect them.

The violent pounding on the door came. Mrs. Rosenburg opened the door; the Gestapo demanded to search the apartment.

"We were already searched twice," Mrs. Rosenburg said.

"You'll be searched again!"

There were two of them, wearing black uniforms, their caps emblazoned with the skull and crossbones. They stomped through the narrow hallway to the living room and the two bedrooms in the back. They yanked open the cabinets, searched the wardrobes, and threw the chairs across the room as if the ghosts of criminals of all sorts indeed existed in this house.

When they found nothing, the Gestapo officers looked visibly frustrated. They ordered Mrs. Rosenburg to come with them; she dropped her shawl, staggering back.

Fengshan stood up, and in his fluent German he said, "Sir, excuse me, but as you see, there are no conspirators in this house. There is no need to arrest her."

The two thugs tramped over to him. "Who are you?"

Fengshan took a drag of his cigarette. In their eyes, he was an irrelevant, wealthy, well-dressed Asian with a tie. Perhaps they regarded him as Japanese, but they knew he was not German or Jewish. He thought about how to divert their attention to leave Mrs. Rosenburg alone. "I'm a friend of Mr. Rosenburg. He is supposed to be on his way to the train station, and I've come to bid farewell. I hear he's already been taken for interrogation."

The man in front of him said, "Our Führer is right. The foreigners are a scourge! Our country is polluted by them. Where's your identification card?"

"I shall be happy to show you, but by protocol, you must show me yours first."

The man's face was distorted with malice, his eyes wild—a bully, a small man. "Show me your identification card! Tell me your name!"

Fengshan took another drag of his cigarette; he remained calm.

The other Gestapo, shorter, grabbed his silver revolver from his holster and pointed it at him. "Speak! Who are you?"

The cigarette smoke burned in his throat. He was unarmed, alone, and the Gestapo—brutes, murderers who threatened and intimidated innocent people—could shoot him. But Fengshan spoke, in his voice that was accustomed to addressing an audience, firm and full of authority. "I've already told you, I'm a friend of Mr. Rosenburg. I'm here waiting to say farewell to my friend. If you wish to know who I am, by protocol, you must identify yourself first."

It must have had something to do with what he said, or the way he carried himself. The despicable man in front of him leaned over to the other Gestapo and murmured something into his ear. The two hesitated, scrutinizing his face and suit. Finally, they kicked a side table near the couch and left the living room, and Mrs. Rosenburg hurried to close the door behind them.

"Who is that Asian man?" he heard one of their voices asking from the doorway. There came Mrs. Rosenburg's reply, followed by an angry voice. "Why didn't you tell me earlier!"

When Mrs. Rosenburg returned, Fengshan collapsed on the couch behind him. "May I take a seat, Mrs. Rosenburg?"

He stayed for hours while the chaotic clamor of crashing and screaming continued outside, a rising frenzy that didn't seem to end. Sometime around midnight, Mr. Rosenburg finally returned home, the top buttons of his shirt missing, his face pale.

"Thank God you're home. But you've missed the train," Fengshan said. "When will you leave now?"

"Tomorrow, I hope, Dr. Ho. I shall call you when I have the new train tickets. The ocean liner is set to depart from Italy in four days. We can still make it."

Fengshan was relieved, and he promised to see them off at the train station tomorrow, ensuring their safe departure.

"You have done enough for me, Dr. Ho. For your safety, you must go. This is going to be a long night," Mr. Rosenburg said.

A long night, he agreed. For his friend and his family, for Miss Schnitzler and her family, and for many others in Vienna.

Fengshan gave his friend a pat and left. Outside, the streets were ablaze with flames, torches, and glaring lights from the apartments' broken windows and doors. The neighborhood was deafening with ambulances and police cars screaming past, looters shouting and carrying bags and paintings, and Brownshirts hollering and brandishing torches. Rudolf seemed to have trouble discerning directions, swerving, stopping, and inching forward. A few times, Fengshan lurched forward as the car went over something lumpy, nearly unseating him.

Finally, Rudolf turned onto a broad avenue lined with shops, and there, the car stopped abruptly. Fengshan was about to ask why they had stopped, when the sound of glass crashing burst ahead of him. He looked up.

In his car's headlights, in stark whiteness, men holding clubs were walking from shop to shop, smashing the windows, hollering and cheering as the glass crashed. Near them, a mob holding torches was striking two elderly men with thick clubs; another Brownshirt was hammering a youth trying to flee. And Fengshan saw a man, hatless, lying motionless near a pile of shattered glass, his face smashed beyond recognition.

Fengshan closed his eyes, shaken. Memories of another mob welled in his mind. But this was Vienna, not China. He was alive, and he was not twenty years old.

He opened his eyes, forcing himself to be the witness to the evil of the night, to remember the heinous crimes, to etch in his brain the faces of the mob that belonged to the human race.

People. So many people. Their faces twisted with menace, their legs spread wide, their arms flung high, their mouths dark caverns of depravity. They were shrieking with delight, their laughter roaring above the exploding windows, above the sound of clothes ripping, above the heart-wrenching pleading and screaming, and God help him—he was inside the safety of his car, but he could smell the choking fumes mixed with the acrid odor of burnt fur and leather and the sickening scents of torched hair and flesh.

"They set the shul on fire! The shul!" A woman's voice, shrill, unbearable.

And he saw it. Amid the darkness, the sickening smoke, the cloud of detritus and dust, a blaze, red, blistering, shot out of a building with a single arch, above which quavered a star, the star his friend Rosenburg had worn around his neck and kissed and prayed to.

When a house of God was set on fire, what else could not be destroyed?

Tears flowed down his cheeks.

CHAPTER 32

GRACE

Near dawn, Fengshan came to fetch me.

Lola was dozing off, frowning, her head on my shoulder. For the entire night, she had fallen into a trance, barely said a word, only stared. Her wine-red dirndl dress was stained with blood, her hair disheveled. Her feet were bare, the toes pale like rain-soaked pebbles.

Whenever a car drove by outside and the sound of its wheels grinding the pavement rolled in the air, she jolted. "Mutter!"

I held her; I held her tight. The mundane sound would torment her for the rest of her life. Each time the grinding wheels rang in her ears, she would relive the horror of losing her mother.

Sometime after midnight, I discovered Eva hidden inside a suitcase behind a curtain. She had hid there when the Gestapo came to search the apartment. While her mother was taken—I understood, from Lola's murmur, that Sara's deformed hand, a mark of imperfection, had made her a victim—and Mrs. Schnitzler was killed, Eva had stayed in a suitcase the whole time, and refused to leave the space. *"Ich will nicht nach draußen,* Tante Grace,*"* she said.

When I opened the door for Fengshan, I had to lean on him—I could barely stand, and my legs were numb. Outside, there was the blood-splattered street, the strewn hats and scarves and shoes, the other apartments' open doors and smashed windows.

As the car slowly drove down the street, I heard the wailing sirens of police cars and fire trucks. Nearby, a building was still ablaze; through thick fumes and smoke, I could see the fire brigade and police cars parked on the street. Batons in hand, they were blocking anyone who held buckets of water, ensuring the fire would consume the entire building.

In my bedroom, I dropped onto my bed. I had never realized my stuffy bedroom where I had wept and slept, which I had thought was a corner of exile, was such a lovely place. How laughable I had been—wallowing in boredom. This bedroom, with its golden tapestry and ornate Baroque bed and couch, its quiet solitude, and its familiar scent of Fengshan's cigar and cologne, was a sanctuary, a bower of solace. If only Lola had the same luxury.

She must leave Vienna. And she must leave as soon as possible and take Eva with her. Since her train tickets had expired, she would need to purchase new tickets. But I couldn't remember when her ocean liner would sail from Italy to Shanghai.

I was about to fall asleep when I heard a loud trickling in the bathroom. But, tired as I was, I had trouble getting up from bed. "My love?"

No reply.

I turned around. Through the gap of the bathroom's open doors, Fengshan was standing by the sink, his back straight, a towel pressed onto his face, his shoulders shaking violently. And then he released a low howl that I had never heard from him before. My stoic diplomat husband; for the entire evening, he had remained unflappable, swift and resolute, and now he was wailing like a child.

⁓⁂⁓

When I awoke, it was late afternoon. I changed my clothes, put on my gloves and scarf, and rushed downstairs. The lobby was quiet, empty, with no visa applicants, only Frau Maxa and the vice consul at their desks. The order of house arrest had been rescinded, and Fengshan, who had received word that Mr. Rosenburg was able to take the train, had gone to see him off at the train station, Frau Maxa said. Without the consulate's car, I would need to take a tram to Lola's apartment. I walked quickly down the street, holding the scarf to my nose to keep out the heavy smoke. At the tram station, I was disappointed to see a sign saying there were no taxis or trams in service today.

In the consulate, I took a selection of newspapers and the mail and went to the dining room. Monto was eating alone, looking at a stack of papers with signatures.

"Monto, could you read these for me?" I set the newspapers in front of him.

"Read them yourself."

"You know I can't."

He cleared his throat, and in his innocent, childish voice, he read, "'Justice is served! Six thousand Jewish men were rightly apprehended and sent to Mauthausen. The owners whose shops were damaged must repair them at their own cost. All their insurance compensations will be justly transferred to the Third Reich. Have no fear! Ongoing arrests of the Jewish criminals and' . . . I don't know this word . . . 'are underway to ensure the safety of the German people!'"

I leaned forward; on the newspaper were images of shops with broken windows. There was no mention of Mrs. Schnitzler or Sara or the brutal beatings and murders by the SS I had witnessed on the street. I covered the newspaper with my hand. "You can stop reading now."

"Why did the newspaper say the Germans must protect themselves from the Jews? Are they dangerous?"

"They're not dangerous." I gathered up the newspapers. Perhaps it was a bad idea to have Monto translate the horrible reality.

"At school, the teachers ordered me not to talk to them."

"Are they your friends?"

"No, but Willi is."

"If he's your friend, you should talk to him."

He studied me. The flicker of petulance he aimed at me seemed to have vanished, replaced by something like worry. "Something bad is going to happen to Willi."

"How do you know?"

"I read his signature."

Near dusk, I went to Fengshan's office. He had returned, and he was speaking to someone on the phone in his office. When he put down his phone, he said Mr. Rosenburg and his family had safely left Vienna. They would reach Italy by dawn, wait for their luggage and then board the ocean liner that would sail to Shanghai.

"Who were you talking to on the phone?" I asked.

"I was warning the Chinese citizens in Vienna. With the violence on the streets, they need to stay at home to be safe."

"That's a good idea." I went to his desk and set down a pile of mail that I had collected. Looking pensive, he didn't pick it up right away. Then he sat at his desk, took out a sheet of paper, and began to write in Chinese.

"What are you writing?"

"A letter to the Ministry of Foreign Affairs at home. The rescue plan must go through as soon as possible. The Viennese Jews must leave or they'll perish. And I would do anything in my power to help them escape Vienna."

"Will your proposal get approved?"

"I hope so. How's your friend?"

"I couldn't see her. You took the car, and the tram stopped running."

He put down his pen and turned to me. "May I urge you to wait for a few days before you visit your friend? I fear you'll get caught in the crossfire."

Slowly, I nodded.

"Thank you. What happened to your friend's family is a great tragedy."

I could feel tears threatening to roll out of my eyes, thinking of Mrs. Schnitzler, Sara, and Lola. "So many are suffering in Vienna."

"You're a good wife, Grace."

My reserved husband, averse to shows of affection, uncomfortable with terms of endearment, had expressed explicitly what he had never said before.

I kissed him. "Go back to work. I'm going to bed."

CHAPTER 33

FENGSHAN

In twenty minutes, he finished writing his letter. Carefully, he sealed it and set it aside. On the desk was the mail Grace had brought. He picked them up and examined them one by one. There was a telegram from China; it was sent two weeks ago, delayed due to the turmoil in Vienna. His hands trembling, he tore open the telegram.

武汉失城。蒋公命令立退重庆。犹太拯救计划暂停

"Wuhan is lost. Stop. President Chiang orders the government to retreat to Chongqing. Stop. Jewish rescue plan suspended indefinitely. Stop."

Nanjing, Shanghai, and now Wuhan. All had fallen. Thousands of his countrymen had given their lives to protect the capital, and now the city was lost. His Nationalist government, once again, faced a devastating retreat into a city surrounded by mountains, with the Japanese fighters and tanks charging behind. The survival of China was hanging on a thread.

And after all these months of planning and expectations, the rescue plan was jettisoned—at the moment when the world saw the bowels of the Nazis' dark regime.

The ambassador was not available to answer his call.

Fengshan paced in his office. He imagined, with pain, his countrymen, at that exact moment, toiling on the rocky mountain roads, running for their lives, and his colleagues, his friends, the leaders of the Nationalists, sitting in straw huts and shelters in caves in the landlocked city of Chongqing. He had never visited there; he could only imagine how they climbed the cliff, clad in leather shoes and suits, fearing for their lives.

With all his devotion, loyalty, and beliefs, he couldn't save China from the Japanese.

Despite all his effort and the best of his intentions, China couldn't be a home for the Jews.

At the crack of dawn, Fengshan got out of bed, dressed, had a simple breakfast of cheese and milk, and went downstairs. When he opened the consulate's door to retrieve newspapers, the low howl of the wind growled in his ears and a flurry of snow poured in. He stood up, then froze—standing next to the consulate's black plaque, facing him, were many men, noses red, sniffling, layers of snow on their shoulders.

How long had they been waiting in the cold? There appeared to be at least two hundred of them waiting to be admitted; it was three hours before the consulate would open.

Fengshan gripped the newspaper. The violence he had witnessed the other evening had been reported all over the world in heartbreaking detail in print and by radio. The international communities responded with a show of sympathy. Daladier and Chamberlain condemned the violence and murders, and the Roosevelt administration, which had made some confusing moves, had recalled the American ambassador to Germany. But still, there was no sign of the leading countries mobilizing to mitigate the sufferings of the defenseless Viennese.

"Come in." Fengshan pulled the door wider. "Come in, come in. It's cold out."

They looked at him with an expression with which he was familiar—they didn't know what to make of him, an Asian man in a well-tailored coat, with folds of a navy-blue handkerchief visible in his breast pocket. It would not cross their mind that the consul general of the consulate would open the door for them.

In the lobby, they formed a line, their faces anxious. There were mostly men, but there were also a few women of various ages. When Fengshan asked how they had survived the horrible night, they broke into tears. Some had lost their fathers, some their siblings, and all had barely any possessions left. They were local Viennese who had lived here for generations, bakers, fishermen, fabric manufacturers, fur sellers, cabinet makers, meerschaum-pipe carvers, and store owners. Their businesses had been forced to go through Aryanization—sold at a fraction of their value or handed over to non-Jewish Germans.

The Viennese women, dressed in their long gowns and coats, broke down as they spoke. Their husbands, sons, or brothers had been arrested and sent to Dachau or Mauthausen camps, and the only way to regain their freedom was a visa that proved their intention to leave the country.

Mauthausen camp, Fengshan had heard from Captain Heine, was located in a market town in Upper Austria near Linz. Because Hitler had boasted about a transformation of the country that included many construction projects, such as apartments and military complexes, many building complexes had been built and the German industry had encountered dramatic shortages of materials. Mauthausen, rich with granite quarries, provided the much-needed resources, and the prisoners were sent there to excavate granite, often facing deplorable conditions, without proper tools or sufficient food.

Fengshan choked up. How many people would be imprisoned in the labor camps, and how many needed the visas for their freedom? He passed the vice consul's desk, already piled with application forms, and opened the drawers in Frau Maxa's desk. He took out a pile of blank application forms and handed them to the people in the lobby. When the vice consul arrived later, he would remind him to expedite the process.

In his office, taking out his seal and his fountain pen, Fengshan began to complete the visa forms that required his attention, starting with the visa number, then the destination, the date, and the applicant's name, in Chinese and then in German, and finally, the consulate's seal. He went out to check on the vice consul's progress a few times, took a brief break at noon to replenish, and wolfed down a sandwich that Grace had prepared. At the end of the day, at eight o'clock, he put down his fountain pen.

In two days, he issued one thousand visas.

Flexing his fingers and massaging his wrist, he estimated that he could save twenty-five hundred people in five days, five thousand in ten days, which, regrettably, might not be sustainable.

But he would try. Even though he was unable to save China from the Japanese, he could keep the Viennese from the Nazis. And so long as he was the consul general of the consulate of the Republic of China, he would do all he could to save lives, one visa at a time.

CHAPTER 34

LOLA

I opened the door. The sunlight was sharp like a shard, plunging into my eyes. It was another day in a city of hate. In fact, I hated everything: the Baroque buildings, the shops, the people, the music dripping out of a window—the repulsive Bach Cello Suite No. 1 in G major—and the greasy, malodorous smell of fried wiener sausages. Nietzsche was right. God is dead. God remains dead.

On the street, the tram had stopped running; taxis had disappeared; the newspaper kiosks and flower shops and coffeehouses were closed. A chilly winter gust hurtled toward the prancing statues and lunged toward the aloof pedestrians, their faces buried in their coat collars.

I kept walking, looking for a coachman, but the roaring of cars reverberated, and I felt the cobblestones quake beneath my feet. My heart trembled. Mutter! Mutter! What if I were struck by a motorcycle? But I couldn't die; I must not die. They had crushed Mutter; they couldn't crush me.

A coachman, whose bowler was pulled down to cover his face, agreed to carry Mutter to the graveyard on the outskirts of the city. Eva wouldn't come, still hiding in the sanctuary of the suitcase, so I left her alone. In the graveyard, I passed the defaced tombstones and trampled flowers. I took off the pendants with the star and the cross, laid them beside Mutter, and buried her in my family's grave next to Vater. I spoke the Mourner's Kaddish.

Then I went to the Headquarters to deliver clothes and toiletries to Sara, just as I had looked after Josef, but I was turned away. Sara couldn't be located; she was missing, I was told. She had been arrested a few days ago, and she had a deformed hand, I kept saying. Where else could she be?

So exhausted. And cold. My skirt was laden with snow and ice—when had it snowed? I leaned against a streetlamp pole, shivering, trying to sort out my thoughts. Mutter was gone, Sara was out of reach, but I still had Eva. I would take her to Shanghai, to safety, as we had planned. But my train tickets had expired, and the ocean liner had left yesterday. I needed to buy new ones.

The game of patience. Train tickets. Boat tickets. I could do this.

Pulling my coat tight, I walked to a travel agency to purchase the tickets to the ocean liner, holding the last few bills Sara had sewn in my coat—oh, Sara, Sara. Sara with the dexterous hand, Sara who pedaled her sewing machine like a magician. Where was she? After waiting for one hour in line at the counter, I was told that the ocean liners scheduled to sail in January, February, and March were sold out, and the tickets for the ships sailing in April must be purchased in person in Italy.

I laughed until tears spilled out of me. April, then. It would come eventually. Anywhere was better than Vienna.

Eva refused to leave her suitcase.

"*Mein Schatz*, you're going to have cramps. You've been there for days." I sat across from her and leaned against the wall. The room was dark, but I was too tired to turn on the light. If Eva asked when we'd leave Vienna, I would tell her next week. She needed that—hope—and she needed me.

"I'm fine."

I picked up a piece of bread Grace had left for us. It was hard and smelled, but that was all we had. It had been a few days since Grace visited. "Are you hungry? Come out for a minute and eat."

Eva pushed up the suitcase flap, hesitated, climbed out, and grabbed the bread.

She was ravenous; she hadn't had food for days. I was hungry, too, but couldn't eat. I wrapped a blanket around me and closed my eyes. Somehow I began to dream: the Gestapo snapping in harsh German, Mutter crying out for Sara, cars roaring, and banging on the door. Heavy, loud. Bang. Bang. Bang. Louder and louder.

I awoke with a start. It was not a dream—someone was banging on the door. Onkel Goethe, and there were strident voices pummeling the entire apartment. *By order of the Central Office for Jewish Emigration, all Jews in this building must evacuate and relocate to the second district.*

Second district? Second district! The slums in Leopoldstadt.

I lunged toward Eva, thrust her back inside the suitcase, and pulled the curtain over to cover her.

The pounding continued, each a thunderclap; the walls threatened to crack; the floor trembled; the air, porous, a hive of stolen breath and pulses. I held my knees and played in my head my music, my fugues, my sonatas, my lark of serenity and freedom. They couldn't force Eva and me to go to the slum. I would take Eva to Shanghai, not the slum. They would go away; they would go away.

The door burst open.

CHAPTER 35

GRACE

The billows of smoke from the burning buildings cleared a few days later, and finally Fengshan agreed it was safe for me to visit Lola. I took the consulate's car, my mind preoccupied with Lola's departure details. She must leave Vienna with Eva as soon as possible, and perhaps I could assist her with purchasing train tickets and boat tickets. There was so much to discuss.

When I reached her neighborhood, some men in brown trench coats were riding up and down on motorcycles. It made me nervous, and I saw there was a gathering, with many groups of people heading in one direction. Rudolf, unable to go through the throngs and vehicles, had to park his car a block away from Lola's apartment, and I went out. It was a chilly day. I had put on my heavy astrakhan coat—it was still several sizes too large, but my wool coat had been stained with blood.

The street where Mrs. Schnitzler had died looked chaotic. So many people. Men in overcoats and hats, women in long plaid dresses and black shawls, all squeezed between the police cars and the SS men's sedans. At the far end, near a black SS car, a woman in a green dirndl was turning her head from left to right frantically—Lola. The scar on her face twisted; the plumpness of her face, the youthfulness that had been part of her, the charm that would have disarmed Fengshan, were gone, replaced by something I had never expected to see—fear. Our gazes met. She froze, was knocked over by a force behind her, lost her balance, and turned to me again.

My heart dropped. Where were they taking Lola? She had her visa and exit permit. She should be allowed to leave!

For a moment, I lost sight of her among the coats and hats. I grew frantic but couldn't call out—there were the Brownshirts and the SS men.

Lola's green dirndl appeared again, and once she saw me, she thrust her head toward the apartment. Her mouth opened and closed, opened and closed. But I couldn't hear her. Then I realized she was shouting like a character in a silent movie, pleading dramatically but without sound. *Eva, Eva,* she said.

They hadn't found Eva!

I lowered my head and scurried past a crowd of people with suitcases, a family of four, and then two brothers with identical faces, one with blood on his nose. When I reached Lola's apartment, the door was wide open. I dashed inside the bedroom, toward the suitcase.

It was left ajar, unzipped, and inside, curled up, her knees pressing to her chin, was Eva, just as I had seen her last time.

"Eva, you have to get out of the suitcase and come with me. Would you come with me?"

She shook her head. *"Ich will nicht nach draußen, Tante Grace. Ich will nicht nach draußen."*

"Quiet, quiet, Eva. You must be quiet. They'll hear you."

She pulled the flap of the suitcase down.

I was not good with children; I didn't know what to do with children. *Lola, Lola. Help me. Tell me what to do. How can I talk Eva into coming with me? She can't understand English very well. She won't come out.*

I rushed to the window, lifted a corner of the curtain, and peered out. Facing me, just on the right, a group of boys wearing swastika armbands were throwing rocks at a family who had been driven out of their apartments. Some distance away, near an art deco building, two tall blond boys with ruddy faces were tormenting a girl in a yellow dress, pulling her hair, tripping her. Two Gestapo in black uniforms, holding batons in their hands, were searching door by door across the street.

"Eva, Eva! They're coming! We must go!"

"Ich will nicht nach draußen!"

She was afraid, and so was I. If they found her, they'd take her, maybe even me. What should I do?

I begged. "Please, Eva. Please come with me. Here, Eva, come with me, and I promise no one will see you. You'll be safe. Here"—I unbuttoned my astrakhan coat, the coat that was too big for me—"you can hide under my coat; it'll cover you up. Hold on to me and I'll carry you, all right? No one will see you."

Eva sat up finally, and I flapped my coat open, crouching for her to hitch onto me, gesturing, encouraging her as she looped her slender arms around my neck, her legs around my waist. I straightened—she was not heavy at all. As I buttoned up my coat, my fingers kept missing the holes—the German voices sounded louder now. When Eva's shape became a small bump under my coat, I let my scarf drape loosely around my neck to hide her, picked up the suitcase, and rushed out of the apartment.

The sky was frighteningly vast and chilly, under which swarmed uniformed men and motorcycles, sedans, and trucks. My knees grew weak. If I were caught, it would be a disaster—a diplomat's wife carrying a Jewish child. Would the SS men shoot me?

"Don't be afraid," I said to Eva, and myself. "Don't be afraid."

My right hand grasping the suitcase, my left hand on my coat over Eva, I sidled along the buildings, past the Brownshirts holding rifles, the SS men with hard looks, and the trucks loaded with people like Lola, locking my gaze on the consulate's car at the intersection about a block away. I felt Eva's heart thumping against mine, the warmth of her breath against my skin, and her sweaty hands around my neck. I was wrong. Eva was heavier than I'd thought, and she was slipping. Oh, God. She was slipping.

A man in a beige uniform came out of a door near my right and barked at me in German. Did he detect Eva under my coat? I dropped the suitcase and fled. I didn't look back, didn't stop until I reached the car. Once inside, I told Rudolf to drive, took off my scarf with my shaking hands, unbuttoned the top of my coat, and the child's face, pink, perspiring, rose to greet me.

In the consulate, I had to button up Eva under my coat again to avoid attention from the visa applicants and the consulate staff. Once I reached my bedroom, I helped Eva settle down on the couch, gave her my poetry book to read, and made her a peanut-butter-and-jelly sandwich.

Later, when Fengshan stood in front of Eva in the bedroom, he looked pensive; before he asked, I said, "I know how this looks, my love. But it's temporary. Lola will come to fetch her."

"Where is she?" Fengshan asked.

I explained what I had witnessed and looked at Eva; she murmured something in German.

"So Miss Schnitzler was taken to Leopoldstadt," Fengshan said.

"Where is that?"

"Across the Danube River."

It was not the Headquarters. I breathed out. "She'll come back. Right?"

Fengshan sighed and left without answering me.

CHAPTER 36

FENGSHAN

He went downstairs, thinking about Grace's question, to which he didn't have an answer. It had only been a few days since the violent night, and now the Nazis had rounded up a large number of innocent people, dislocated them, and separated a family. He hoped he was wrong, but he feared there were more miseries and calamities that awaited the Viennese Jews.

When he went into his office, through the windows he could see people shivering in the cold, their gloved hands holding bags, their hats pressed low to fend off the chill. They were forced to wait outside since the lobby was too crowded—the number of applicants had increased tenfold.

He took his pen and began to work.

In December, a few weeks after Grace took in the Jewish child, the ambassador called. "How many visas did you issue in November, Fengshan?"

His superior rarely started the phone call with a preamble, but he had not bothered to talk about the government's retreat to Chongqing this time. That was rather concerning. Fengshan rubbed his eyes, glancing at the mound of visa forms that he had just approved. He had been signing ten hours a day, five days a week for three weeks, but he didn't keep track of the number of visas he issued. The total was easy to calculate, however, given that each had a visa number. But Fengshan said carefully, "Ambassador Chen, my apologies. I must look up the numbers to give you an accurate count. Have you heard the devastating reports of crimes in Vienna? It's—"

"This is why I asked, Fengshan. I hear there's a surge of visa seekers in many foreign consulates all across Greater Germany. It came to my attention that many have flocked to our consulate in Vienna. Now, I recall I gave permission to issue a small number of visas, Fengshan, a small number, but I've heard a rumor saying that almost four thousand visas were issued by your consulate. Is that true?"

He was caught off guard. He hadn't been aware the ambassador was watching him closely. "Ambassador Chen—"

"This is unacceptable, Fengshan. We discussed the Jewish rescue plan, which was aborted due to our country's situation. It is regrettable, but the plan was doomed to fail from the very beginning, if I must say. Now I would like you to halt the visa issuance to Jews."

Fengshan's mouth went dry. Ambassador Chen's view on Jewish immigration had been unfavorable since the Anschluss, yet to hear his reiteration, as the entire Jewish population in Vienna descended into chaos after the deadly evening in November, was confounding. Every fiber of his being resisted. "With all due respect, Ambassador Chen, surely you're aware of the atrocities the Brownshirts and Gestapo have committed—"

"It is most unfortunate, Fengshan, yet we must have China's best interest in mind. Germany's former ambassador to China has privately confided in me his concern that the relationship between Germany and China is facing a test because we accepted a great number of Jews, who are Germany's enemies. If we continue to offer help to Germany's enemies, how could we ask for allegiance from the Third Reich and persuade them to sell us weapons?"

The weapons, especially the aircraft, were essential to fighting the Japanese. But as much as Fengshan respected his superior and hoped for the success of the weapons purchase, he couldn't help questioning why it was in his country's best interest to pursue a relationship with a government that relentlessly persecuted its own people and drove them to despair. Besides, the Third Reich's commitment to the weapons sale had yet to be affirmed—the meeting that the ambassador longed for remained elusive, and Hitler had deliberately ignored China, favoring their enemy, Japan, instead. If he could speak candidly to his superior, he would dare say that seeking a diplomatic relation with Germany might no longer bear fruit for the long-term goal of his country's security and prosperity. The weapons must be obtained from another country.

"Respectfully, Ambassador Chen, we have remained Germany's stalwart partner for years, but their goodwill remains to be seen. Have they agreed to a meeting for the weapons sale yet?"

"It's not finalized, but I have verbal consent. The meeting will happen sometime in February next year. Halt the visa issuance until my further notice. This is my order."

Fengshan searched his mind desperately for some powerful logic, reasoning, or excuse. Suddenly it occurred to him: the telegram he'd received from the Ministry. "Ambassador Chen, may I be allowed to bring this to your attention—the Ministry of Foreign Affairs approved a lenient policy regarding the Jews in October. They sent me a telegram, ordering the consulate to enact a policy of leniency and tolerance toward this very minority."

There was silence on the other side of the phone. "The Ministry of Foreign Affairs is sheltered in a hut on a cliff with Japanese fighters circling above their heads. Their decision is outdated, and now they have lost communication with people beyond the foothill of the mountain. Pay no heed to the telegram from the Ministry, Fengshan. Follow my order."

Ambassador Chen, his direct superior, oversaw his job performance and reported his merits and demerits to the Ministry of Foreign Affairs at home. His approval and assessment determined his career. Any objections Fengshan raised would be considered impertinence to his superior. "Yes, Ambassador Chen."

Fengshan put down the phone. As a follower of Confucianism, he knew well the essential social order—*Jun jun, Cheng cheng, Fu fu, Zi zi*: a ruler rules; a minister ministers; a father acts as a father; a son behaves as a son. He, a subordinate, had considered it his duty to obey his superior's order, and the word *disobey* had never crossed his mind.

He picked a cigar from the cigar box, lit it, and went to the hallway.

In the crowded lobby, many men wore heavy overcoats and scarves. They spoke German with accents from Upper Austria and Lower Austria; they came from Munich and even Berlin; they all looked weary, worn out. Could he tell them to go home, which was nowhere?

He took a drag of his cigar and returned to his office. Disobeying his superior's order would be a betrayal of his duty, but obeying his superior's mandate and declining the wish of thousands of people on the brink of death would be a betrayal of his heart.

CHAPTER 37

GRACE

There was a call for me, I was told. I went down to the lobby, past the crowd of people waiting for visas, and went to the vice consul's desk to answer the phone. As I hoped, it was Lola.

"Where are you, Lola?" It was challenging to hear her over the background of human voices from the lobby, low and vibrating; I had to cover one ear to listen to her.

She gave me an address in German, but I couldn't remember it. "Could you repeat it? Can you spell it in English?"

"Did you find Eva, Grace?" she asked instead.

"I did." For about two weeks, she had slept on a bed I made in a storage room that held files and newspapers. Out of an abundance of caution, Fengshan and I had decided to keep Eva from Monto—a child, his behavior might inadvertently reveal her presence.

I had also purchased some basic clothes for her: two dresses, stockings, underwear, a sweater, some socks, a beanie hat, a pair of black doll shoes, and a coat. She was only two years younger than Monto, but with a completely different temperament, sensitive, agreeable, easy to please.

"Are you coming? When will you come to get her, Lola?"

"I don't know."

"She needs you."

From the phone came a sound like a sob.

"You'll come, right, Lola?" This was a consulate, after all, not a home for a child.

"Listen, Grace." Her voice sounded raspy and old. "I'm in a slum. It's horrible, and they're watching me. I fear the worst. I don't want Eva to live here like this. I begged my uncle for help, but he absolutely didn't want to have anything to do with us. I've called Jewish organizations and charity groups, but they have been banned from operating. Help her, Grace, find her a good family to protect her."

How could I find a good family for Eva? I didn't know anyone in Vienna, and I was a diplomat's wife without many options. "Lola . . ."

"Only you can help me, Grace."

"But . . ."

The line went dead.

I took the elevator upstairs. In the storage room that I had arranged for Eva, she was sitting on a cushion, reading the Dickinson book I'd given her. For a moment, I thought she looked like my childhood self, alone, immersed in the wilderness of a poet's whims.

"She's my favorite. Do you like her poetry?" I sat by her. I had used poetry to teach her English. Eva was a fast learner; her English improved quickly. "Look at this: 'I'll tell you how the Sun rose—A Ribbon at a time—'"

"It's pretty."

"It is." I had dreamed of becoming a poet, too; instead, I became a diplomat's wife.

"Is she famous?"

"Not really."

"Is she beautiful?"

"I imagine so."

"You're beautiful, Tante Grace."

I didn't know what to say. When I was her age, people called me "a strange-looking child," and Mother, of course, never said I was beautiful. I was surprised when Fengshan praised my beauty, my Asian eyes, and my delicate facial features. Now this, from a child. I had an urge to smooth her hair and touch her cheek. She didn't know, of course, that she was, absolutely, the most beautiful angel I had ever laid my eyes on.

Lola was right. I could protect her; I must.

CHAPTER 38

FENGSHAN

Grace paced his office and asked if he could help. He wished he had an answer for her. But Lola was Eva's blood relative, her only guardian. The only option for them was to go to Shanghai together. The ocean liners would return next year, and more tickets would be available. But he was also aware that, with so many people desperate to leave, boat tickets would be a challenge to obtain.

"There must be something you can do, my love."

"We'll see, Grace." He carefully set the visa he had just signed on top of the stack of completed documents. The matter about Eva was most urgent, he could see. The child couldn't stay in the consulate for long. He could find Eva a new home, a family who could take her.

He dialed Dr. Löwenherz's phone number. Since he received visas for his own family, Dr. Löwenherz had brought more people to the consulate for visas. The phone rang, but it was never picked up.

❦

He called Dr. Löwenherz again two days later, and the doctor answered in a deep, gruff, tired voice. When Fengshan explained the reason for his call, Dr. Löwenherz sighed. His organization was under unprecedented duress, as many members faced death threats, and many more were beaten, arrested after the *Kristallnacht*. Some had fled for their lives. The organization had no resources or staffing to shelter the young; besides, he was scheduled to depart the country himself tomorrow.

When Fengshan asked what other charities and organizations he could recommend trying, the doctor replied that the international charities and Zionist organizations in Austria and Germany had been prohibited from operating months ago. All the groups had been disbanded; his organization, the *Israelitische Kultusgemeinde Wien*, was the only one permitted to run in Vienna.

A few days later, Fengshan, at his wit's end, asked Captain Heine about how to find protection for Lola's niece when they met in the coffeehouse in the Hotel Sacher.

"You won't have luck with any organizations, Herr Consul General. As you know, since the Anschluss, all Jewish organizations have been prohibited from operating. Even the American Jewish Joint Distribution Committee, which tried to assist Jews, was ordered to cease functioning." Captain Heine sat on a red velvet cushion, a glass of cognac in hand.

Fengshan had a sip of his bitter black ersatz coffee.

"Cheer up, Herr Consul General. It's the holiday season."

The coffeehouse, decorated with festive holiday lights, was filled with people, non-Jewish, Fengshan believed. Several wore black uniforms, and Brahms's "Wiegenlied" was in the air. He gave a dramatic sweep of his arm. "Isn't it ironic that this is a season of joy? What was your order on November ninth?"

Captain Heine looked away. "It wasn't the proudest day of my life. It was an order. And I can't stop thinking about it. I've begun to wonder, what if my father had not been a military man? I would not be a policeman. I don't even like being a policeman. I only like three things: cognac, women, and cards."

Fengshan leaned closer. "Then help me, Captain Heine."

He downed his glass of cognac. "Have you tried to contact the German Quakers?"

He was aware of the Quakers in the US, as Grace had once mentioned them, but not German Quakers. "Enlighten me."

"Well, the Quakers provided generous aid to the Germans after the Great War; as a result, they've made many friends in this country. Some are officials among the Nazis. You might have luck asking them." He'd had too much to drink; his voice was slurred, and his eyes were searching among the patrons for pretty women. At last, his gaze fell on a woman wearing a red cap.

"Captain Heine?"

The captain pulled his gaze back to Fengshan. "Pardon me."

Fengshan sighed. "Do you have the Quaker organization's name?"

"I believe it's called the German Emergency Committee."

"Was that shut down too?"

"Now that you mention it, I think it disbanded in June."

Fengshan sighed again.

"You can try to speak to the former secretary and see if she can help. It's worth a try. I met her at a charity ball, a British woman teaching in Berlin. I had a drink with her, a typical British woman, uptight, but rather good at drinking."

"You never forget a woman's name."

The captain gave a roguish smile. "Bertha, Bertha Bracey."

For the first time, Fengshan was glad of Captain Heine's obsession. "How may I find her?"

"Herr Consul General," a voice, familiar, said beside him.

Fengshan raised his head. Just as he had thought. He'd run into him again. But this was the worst timing. Had he heard their conversation? "Herr Eichmann."

He was now an *Obersturmführer*, first lieutenant, judging from the medal on his uniform.

"*Hauptsturmführer* Heine." The man—the murderer—looked to be in high spirits, surrounded by a group of policemen wearing high leather boots and trench coats. He gave Heine, a man of a superior rank, a "*Heil* Hitler" salute, and Heine returned the salute.

"How astounding to see you here, *Hauptsturmführer* Heine. This is quite a meeting place, the best place in Vienna, to host a foreign diplomat."

Captain Heine had lost his flirtatious smile. "Herr Consul General is a good friend of mine."

Fengshan could sense a moment of antipathy wedged between Heine and Eichmann. Eichmann, the chief officer of the Central Office for Jewish Emigration, was an upstart of the SS on the rise, and Heine, a captain of the Viennese police in the first district, came from a military family and held on to some traditional Austrian values. It didn't seem that Heine would subjugate himself to Eichmann, but the SS men were the ones giving orders these days.

"That's good to know, *Hauptsturmführer* Heine. And what a coincidence, Herr Consul General; I heard through the grapevine that your consulate has been issuing visas to the Jews, who use them to apply for exit permits. Well done!"

He couldn't have heard through the grapevine, being the man in charge of the exit permits. The man's slyness knew no limits. "That's the least I could do."

"May I express my gratitude, Herr Consul General. Thanks to you, thousands of Jews have departed Vienna. Your help is enormous, and you've done a great service to the good German people. I believe I speak for many of my colleagues, who are genuinely grateful that you're lending a hand to get rid of the Jews. At least now they won't leave their filthy bodies in the ditches of Vienna."

Fengshan had not become a diplomat without knowing the merit of remaining equanimous, but the heat of fury shot through his head, and he had the impulse to punch the man in front of him. He said sharply, "Such is the great tragedy of humanity—may I be frank, Herr Eichmann? So much destruction, so many deaths and needless losses."

"Needless losses? Herr Consul General, I assure you, this won't go on much longer. Soon they'll all be gone."

Captain Heine stood before Fengshan had a chance to retort. "If you don't mind, *Obersturmführer* Eichmann, I must take my leave. Herr Consul General, may I have a word with you?"

Fengshan picked up his hat, gave Eichmann a perfunctory nod, and walked out. In the brightly lit lobby, the Nazi officials and their female companions looked at him quizzically. He put on his hat and looked away. Had the captain not interrupted him and led him out, he would have broken into an argument with the sly man. He needed to work on his temper. He was the consul general, for God's sake. Fengshan cleared his throat. "May I say that Brahms's 'Wiegenlied' is not the best of his work."

The captain looked absolutely at ease, a faint smile on his lips. "Coffee or cognac? We can stop at the Blaue Bar."

"I'll pass. What did he mean, they'll all be gone?"

Captain Heine shrugged and took out a bottle of cognac from his coat pocket.

Fengshan was stunned. "I hope I'm mistaken, my friend, but do I get the impression that you are not aware of your government's agenda?"

"All I can say is that Eichmann is a new member of the elite. His model of expelling the Jews launched him into fame. He has the ears of many top officials, including Göring and Goebbels. It's rumored that he'll set up another office of Jewish Emigration in Berlin under his command. Proceed with caution, Herr Consul General. I hope he didn't overhear about the Quakers."

Fengshan took a deep breath. "I don't think so."

Captain Heine looked around the lobby. "Anyway, I'll speak to Miss Bracey instead of you. But I'd strongly advise you, Herr Consul General, that you not be involved personally."

CHAPTER 39

GRACE

Finally, a few days later, Fengshan said he heard good news from his friend regarding Eva.

"Captain Heine got in touch with a British woman, Miss Bracey, Grace. And Miss Bracey disclosed to him that recently the British government has agreed to a policy that accepts a limited number of Jewish children under seventeen in Europe. These children will be transported to Britain by train. The first train departed from Berlin a few days ago, and the train from Vienna will leave on December tenth."

"Will the children go with their parents?" I asked.

"No, they are not allowed to be accompanied by any family adults. Miss Bracey and her group will be the escorts on the train. Captain Heine said the transportation must remain secret for the children's safety. There will be exclusive carriages for the children with windows sealed so no one outside the train can see through, and it is unknown where they'll be bound when they arrive in Britain. But I think this is still an option for your tutor's niece."

I shook my head. "No, Lola won't agree to this." Eva was only nine. She couldn't travel to a foreign country alone and live there without family.

"This is a drastic measure, I concur. However, given the circumstances that the charity groups have disbanded and Miss Schnitzler has no other family member who offers to look after the child, she might wish to consider it. Could you call her?"

I couldn't. Lola was in a slum, and I had forgotten the unpronounceable German address.

"Captain Heine said many parents have signed their children up. As I mentioned earlier, only a limited number of children are accepted to enter Britain. You must make a decision as soon as possible."

But I couldn't decide. Then, two days later, on the day the train was scheduled to leave, Lola called me, and when she heard about the transport, she instantly agreed to have Eva sent to Britain. Hurriedly, Fengshan made the last-minute arrangement for Eva to join the group on the train, and Lola promised to do all she could to slip out of the slum to see her niece off.

I said, "Lola, if you wait, the ocean liners will return from China in a few months. I'll help get you tickets, and you can sail to Shanghai with her."

"Who knows what will happen in a few months, Grace? Eva has a chance to escape. She must take it."

Part of me agreed with Lola, and part of me resisted. Had Eva been my daughter, would I have chosen to send her away, or would I keep her by my side, no matter what would happen?

Still, I packed all the new clothing I'd bought for Eva, gave her my suitcase, and told her she was going on a trip that Lola had arranged, and then we waited for Lola.

Half an hour before the train was to leave, Lola still hadn't shown up.

❦

I had no choice but to take Eva to the train station myself. At the entrance of the consulate, Eva stepped back, shaking her head. Who would say that she was the only one afraid of the outside world? I picked her up and carried her to the car.

When we reached the train station, it was ten minutes before eight o'clock. The train was ready for departure. Children, some looking to be Eva's age, some older than Monto, were boarding two carriages, numbered *14a* and *14b*. The parents were weeping, dabbing their eyes, giving their children goodbyes and last advice.

I got out of the car and nearly flew to the platform with Eva in my arms. Near a post with a gaslight, I was greeted by Miss Bracey, a woman in a plaid skirt and a black coat, standing next to a uniformed officer who was jotting down something at a desk. In her polite manner, she asked for the transportation fee and Eva's name and birthday, which Fengshan had filled out earlier; then an officer gave me a placard with a three-digit number attached to a string—Eva's seat number, also her identification number. The train was ready to depart; most children had already boarded.

"I guess it's time to go, Eva," I said, trying to stay cheerful. Lola had decided to send her niece away, and she couldn't even come to say goodbye to her. And really, this was thoughtless, sending her niece to a foreign country. Would Eva have food to eat on the train? Would she be able to sleep? And what if the train was stopped by the Gestapo? Who would look after her in England? I wished Lola had given it more thought.

"Is Tante Lola coming?" Eva asked.

"She got caught up with something, I think."

Eva's lips trembled; she glanced at the children boarding the train, their suitcases, and the parents crying and kissing their children. "Do I have to go?"

I knelt in front of Eva and straightened her coat collar. "Tante Lola arranged this trip, Eva. She wants you to be safe."

"I want my music box." Which we had left behind in her apartment.

"In England, you might be able to find another music box."

The last child had boarded the train; Miss Bracey looked at her watch.

"Is Tante Lola going to meet me in England?"

It was cruel to lie to a child, but it was even crueler to tell her the truth. "Oh yes."

"I'd rather stay here with you."

Just like that, I wanted to hold her and tell her she didn't need to go. I wanted to keep her, for I had grown attached to her, her small body, her German accent, her trusting eyes. But how unfair this world was—even though I wanted to be hers, she could not be mine.

Miss Bracey was walking toward us; the officer was holding the door. "You have to go now, Eva."

Eva lifted her suitcase with both hands and shuffled to the carriage. She looked so small, delicate, carrying the suitcase half her size, the only thing she had, a nine-year-old with a splintered family, without a friend, without a country.

The door shut behind her; the steel-toned light from the station's bare bulbs grazed the shuttered windows. A chain of squeaks rattled in the air. The train chugged forward, diving through the icy shards, into the ridge of darkness.

The wind barreled down the track from the opposite direction and swept over me. Never had I felt this cold. Would I see her again? Would Lola see her again?

The train wavered, plunging into the distant horizon; the tracks shuddered. Before me, a gibbous moon, ragged with streaks of red, floated in the distance, so close, yet so far away, and the heart of winter was black, full of ice.

CHAPTER 40

FENGSHAN

Near Christmas, all consulates in Vienna and embassies in Berlin were closed for the holidays and would remain closed for three weeks until after the new year. What did 1939 have in store for China? Fengshan refrained from speculation and held on to some hope that the ambassador would not take notice of the additional visas he issued.

It was indeed the holiday season, as Captain Heine had said. The streets of Vienna, where many Gestapo and Brownshirts and Hitler Youths roamed, sparkled with strings of blue, red, purple, and white lights. People flocked to the opera houses, concert halls, theaters, and movie theaters. The opera of Empress Sisi, the perennially popular Hapsburg empress, was in demand daily, lighthearted comedies featuring a duo of controlling mother and innocent daughter were popular in movie theaters, and the music of Strauss and Mozart waltzed in ballrooms and concerts. Children frolicked on the snowy slopes with their toboggans and skis; families packed the giant Ferris wheel cars in the Prater. *Hausfrauen* strolled the Christmas markets selling many household items, crystal candle holders, fur coats, woolen jackets, and even extravagant Gobelins tapestries. Many had been used in and likely removed from opulent mansions to be sold at jaw-dropping prices.

Sadly, for the Jews waiting in Fengshan's consulate, the concerts, markets, theaters, ballrooms, and hotels were prohibited. They had no entertainment, no joy, no dancing, no shopping; their only dream was a safe existence or an exit from Vienna.

As part of his duty as consul general, Fengshan attended several balls and parties organized by the government. It was awkward—the grandiose Hofburg palace that had been decorated with the coat of arms now fluttered with swastika flags. In the ballrooms, the Hapsburg royalty wearing the Order of the Golden Fleece, the officials clad in their full Tyrolean uniforms who had stood arm in arm with their wives in pillbox hats, and the aristocrats in suits with gold-trimmed waistcoats and gleaming cuff links were gone. They were replaced by flamboyant arms dealers, whose factories were rumored to be building a thousand bombs a day, accompanied by opera actresses clad in the latest clothes, and high-ranking Gestapo in their black uniforms.

Eichmann, Captain Heine had said, had attended the balls hosted by the film industry in Vienna. Fengshan was glad he had not come across him again. Overall, the Germans at the parties were friendly enough, but when he danced with several fashionable women, he was warned not to partner with them again because it was suspected they had Jewish blood. He smiled politely, though disgusted, commenting that he was a gentleman of etiquette, and it was not his intention to ignore anyone, a Jewess or not.

He was still mistaken for the Japanese consul occasionally, and once an obtuse officer included him in the gang of the Aryans. He discovered with dismay that Hitler, who had showered lavish praise on the Japanese's superb military power, had granted them the status of Honorary Aryans. Fengshan nearly choked on his champagne. The sincerity of the Third Reich's commitment to his country had long remained in question, but to hear that Hitler had taken drastic measures to please his country's enemy by elevating them to the race they approved was most disturbing. He had a sense of foreboding that the upcoming weapons purchase his superior had scheduled would not go well.

Grace came to the balls with him as he requested. Grace, who had been petrified of social situations, was still uneasy among the Viennese, though she no longer had to hold back her tears or spend long hours hiding in the bathroom. Since her return from the train station, she had appeared sad and talked about Eva and Lola often. She was still soft-spoken, but more assured, with a glow of confidence. Sometimes she talked about Emily Dickinson and mused aloud whether the poet's seclusion had been a nurturing shelter or the inevitable dissolution of her creativity, which he thought was an insightful topic yet to be discussed.

A few times, he came across Mr. Lord, the consul from the American consulate, who always donned a Foreign Service Officer's white suit at parties. They had become friends since the departure of Mr. Wiley. Mr. Lord introduced him to his new consul general, Mr. Morris, and mentioned that the consulate's activities had been greatly reduced since the American ambassador in Berlin was recalled. Fengshan also conversed with Mr. Beran, the consul of Czechoslovakia, who looked visibly shaken since the Sudetenland, the area that he'd boasted was the keystone of his country, had been ceded to Germany at the Munich Conference. Fengshan had also heard a rumor that Hitler had demanded that Czechoslovakia disband the Communist Party in their country and dismiss all Jewish teachers in ethnic German schools in Prague.

"Is this true?" Fengshan asked.

The Czech laughed hollowly. "We have already given in and banned the Jews from holding government jobs in the Czech provinces of Bohemia and Moravia, effectively excluding them from our economic circle. And their jobs went to the ethnic Germans in those provinces. If we can starve the Jews, we already did that! But our demanding neighbor continues to allege that the Germans in my country are facing racial discrimination and death threats. I'm not sure what more Czechoslovakia can do!"

Fengshan exchanged a glance with Mr. Lord, aware that after the Munich Conference, Hitler had promised that the Sudetenland was his last demand. But from what Mr. Beran said, it seemed that Hitler wouldn't stop at the Sudetenland, and very soon, Prague, Bohemia, and Moravia would be another Vienna.

Two days before the new year, Fengshan received a message about the war in China. The Japanese were bombing Chongqing, the new capital, systematically. In two months, they had attacked the city twenty times, and the Japanese Imperial Army had flooded the cities near the region with their cavalries and tanks.

If the Nationalist government failed to hold Chongqing, and China capitulated, the consulate in Vienna would cease to exist, and he would not be able to issue visas to the desperate Viennese.

CHAPTER 41

GRACE

I greeted the year 1939 from behind the frosted windows festooned with sparkles and splendors of a ballroom; my thoughts, however, couldn't be farther away. All the entertainment, the live music, the invigorating waltzes, and the abundant food, the caviar, the roasted venison, the crispy-skinned capons, the steamed fish astride a bed of asparagus, reminded me of Eva—once she had asked me whether the diplomats only dined on foie gras—and the lush orchestral music reminded me of Lola; she would have enjoyed playing her violin. Would she be able to play her violin in the slum?

Lola had not called me again. I didn't know why she had failed to see off Eva, and, unable to recall the German address, I didn't know how to find her. Pacing inside the ballroom, I wondered how long she would remain in the slum, and when she would be able to go to Shanghai.

Outside the ballroom, the wind screamed; the air, once vibrant with overtures and operas, was now pierced by shrieks and trucks and gunshots. In the morning, rays of sunlight shuddered on the snowy rooftops; in the early afternoon, the streets descended into a crevasse of gloom, the parks paved with a scattering of broken ice, and the city bleak with deserted buildings.

I was bleeding again but had none of the spells of dizziness and headaches that used to debilitate me. In fact, I felt healthier. When I walked in the snow, I didn't tire quickly. I began to dream of being a mother again—I was still young, just twenty-six.

Monto turned twelve after the new year, grew taller, and appeared melancholy. With the consulate closed, he couldn't pester Frau Maxa and the vice consul with signatures and predict their futures. He had stopped playing with his toy soldiers.

One morning while eating breakfast, he asked me, "Where is Mauthausen, Grace?"

"What house?"

"Mauthausen. Ugh. Your German is so bad."

"I don't know. Somewhere close by, maybe."

"Do kids go to school there?"

"They might."

Monto looked down at the plate of sausages that he hadn't touched.

"What's wrong?" I said.

"I want to go to Mauthausen."

"Why?"

He wouldn't say.

One day when I was cleaning Monto's room, I found a few envelopes that contained his transcripts of grades in his desk's drawer. It seemed he had collected them all over the past few months. I rarely checked his grades; that had been Fengshan's job—Fengshan was a strict father, holding a high academic bar for Monto. He had said, jokingly, that ninety-nine was an A for a Chinese boy, while ninety was a German A and a Chinese B. It was a high standard to keep, but Monto had never received anything below ninety. I opened an envelope. There were many absences, and the grades were not nineties; they were sixties.

I wondered if Fengshan was aware of Monto's grades; maybe not, with him so busy with the consulate. But something was happening with Monto.

Still no phone call from Lola.

ぷ

February was a heartless month in Vienna. The snow fell incessantly, like a swarm of trapped birds, coating the streets, skeletal trees, and benches. The lukewarm daylight skirted around the windows and the consulate's front entrance for a few hours during the day and then hastily made way for the night. By four o'clock in the afternoon, the sconces and lamps in the consulate lobby were turned on; their golden glow brushed the cheeks of Empress Joséphine on the wall but failed to warm up the crowd of applicants, who shivered in the chill.

To my delight, Lola finally called me. I jotted down her address and rode in the consulate's car to see her, since the tram was no longer safe. I had many questions in mind—why did she fail to see Eva off? How could she leave the slum?

The vehicle passed the opera house, veered north to the roundabout at das Tegetthoff-Denkmal, then crossed the canal. The giant Ferris wheel in the amusement park was immobile. The park, which had been crowded with festivalgoers, sausage vendors, and frolicking children, was blanketed in snow and ice. When we approached a tower, a gunshot sounded, and two Nazi guards in uniforms asked us to stop the car—this was why Lola couldn't leave, I realized. Entry and departure of the area were restricted.

I couldn't understand what Rudolf told the guards, but he kept pointing at the Chinese flag Fengshan had placed near the car's rearview mirror. We were finally let through.

When I came to the building Lola had told me about, I was shocked. A slum, she had said, but I had not expected it'd look like this.

The buildings looked to be part of a factory, and there was also a sour smell of rotten meat permeating the air. Many adjacent buildings were graffitied with black paint, the windows smashed, and guards carrying rifles seemed to pop out when least expected. I was glad that Lola was outside a building, drinking a bottle of beer.

She wore a black beanie, a long thick black woolen shawl, a long dirndl, and boots. A cloud of cold air puffed around her, her hair unkempt. She had aged, her eyes stagnant, her scar a long, curved claw. She looked like a homeless woman, and then I realized with sadness that indeed she was.

She was glad to see me, but for my safety, she said, I shouldn't stay here for too long.

I didn't know what to say. "There are guards outside the slums, Lola."

She nodded. "They come every four hours."

The way she said it, it was as though she were talking about neighbors visiting. "Are you a prisoner here?"

"More or less."

"How could you leave this place?"

"An ocean-liner ticket that proves my intention of departure. Everyone is talking about the boats to Shanghai, but no one knows if the boats are sailing."

I could look into that. "What happened last year? Why couldn't you see Eva off?"

"The guards in the slums demanded a concert because it was the holiday season, and they wanted to have some festivity. The orchestra played for the entire evening. I couldn't slip out. I never got to say goodbye to her, Grace."

"I took her to the train station. She's safe now, like you said. She's in England." I hoped; I really didn't know.

Perhaps it was my tone. Lola broke down, crying. "Will I see her again?"

She'd said it herself: Who knew what would happen in the future? "Of course you will."

"I wish she could stay. But there's no future for her here in Vienna, Grace. She's banned from school; her movements are restricted. I had to send her away. I have to fight for her life." She wiped her tears.

I had wanted her to stay too, and I had doubted Lola's decision. But I understood now that she was right. She had to let Eva go. "Oh, Lola."

"Do you believe in God, Grace?"

I had to think about this. I didn't know anything about God. Mother had vowed not to speak about her religion after she was excommunicated. I didn't understand it as a kid then, but now I knew that after Father's death, she had mourned him deeply and saw the world through a haze of sadness and rage. She had laughed at those hypocrites who preached to love your neighbor, mocked people who said *God bless you*, and warned that I would be better off staying away from the church. I had never stepped inside a church in Boston or Chicago.

But when Mother drank too much alcohol, she would let her feelings out, her self-pity for what could have been an honorable life. She never admitted it, but I thought that the excommunication, being disavowed by her own people and denied her right to worship, together with the loss of Father, was the source of her alcoholism. Had she been loved and accepted, she would not have been the mother of shadow and light, the mother who choked me and then begged for my forgiveness.

Fengshan was a devout Christian, regularly attending his Lutheran City Church and firmly believing in God. He once said, "What would we be without beliefs? Nothing but rag dolls with empty hearts and empty souls."

"I believe in angels, Lola. Angels of poetry, angels of friendship."

She gave me a wan smile and drank her beer.

"Did they give you the beer?"

"This? No. An old friend gave it to me. I came across him in the slum. Try it."

It was cold and bitter. "What's this?"

"Styrian beer."

"I've never had that before. I didn't know you were a drinker."

"Every Austrian drinks beer. Before the Anschluss, anyway." She turned to the building, where families huddled near bags and suitcases. "You won't believe it. I've heard so many heartbreaking stories from them. That man, can you see? With a long beard like a winter bush? In the corner? He can recite Kafka's *Die Verwandlung* from beginning to end. He's a well-known physician in Vienna and was locked in a dungeon at the Headquarters for six months. During these months, he said, he read Kafka's book every day to pass the time and ate cockroaches to stay alive, and he hallucinated. He thinks we'll all turn into cockroaches tomorrow."

"That's terrible."

Lola had a swig of beer and wiped her mouth. "These days, I can't stop thinking about Nietzsche. Have you heard of his famous quote, Grace? He said, 'You must be ready to burn yourself in your own flame; how could you rise anew if you have not first become ashes?'"

Nietzsche was not good for Lola. She had lost everything, everyone dear to her heart; living in the slum, a nebulous realm of insanity and isolation, was driving her to the brink of hallucination. I must find a way to get her out of the country.

CHAPTER 42

FENGSHAN

He was signing his name on a visa form when the phone rang. Ambassador Chen's voice came through the phone. "I'm calling you with grave news, Fengshan. The arms deal with Germany has fallen through."

He rubbed his face. Unfortunately, his suspicion about the Third Reich's commitment to the sale was confirmed. He had reported to his superior about Hitler crowning the Japanese the Honorary Aryans a few weeks ago, and Ambassador Chen had dismissed it as trivial. "It's most regrettable, Ambassador Chen. Perhaps we ought to look into weapons from another country—"

"We can't give up after one failed meeting. We must do all we can to continue cultivating our relationship with Germany and ensure that we will receive the weapons we need."

"But—"

"Have you halted the visa issuance as I've instructed?"

He paused. "With all due respect, Ambassador Chen, the telegram from the Ministry of Foreign Affairs indicated a lenient policy—"

"Leave the Ministry to me! I'll speak to the vice minister personally. You do what I say! Stop the visa issuance! Is that clear?" The ambassador hung up.

Fengshan's heart raced faster. His superior had given him an ulti-matum. If he continued to issue visas, neglecting his order, the ambas-sador could take it as an affront, and he would face potential censure or demotion. Would he risk his career for the visas?

He looked at the stacks of application forms on the desk, each sorted and marked by dates. He riffled through them, his fingertips smudged from the fountain pen, making a faint trail on the corners of the forms. He was used to these German names: Grebenschikoff, Girone, Goldstaub, Raubvogel, Reismann, Schultzman. These applica-tions were not simply papers; they were people's lives. Each name was a life, each life with history, each life pleading for a future.

He opened his cigar box, lit a cigar, and looked out. Outside, as usual, there was a queue of people, rubbing their hands, hunching their backs, their feet stamping the snow.

He walked out of his office. In the lobby, the vice consul was col-lecting the fees and writing the receipts in his sluggish motion. As part of his duty, the vice consul also collected the remittances and submit-ted them to the embassy at the end of each month. If he followed the ambassador's order now, the remittances to the embassy would stop, but if he didn't relay the order to his subordinate, the remittances would continue to be submitted to the embassy, and the ambassador would know Fengshan had disobeyed his order.

Fengshan passed Vice Consul Zhou, said nothing, and went into the elevator.

Grace was in the dining room, setting the table.

"Look what I made for you." She placed a bowl of sliced pork in brown sauce and garlic before him, which she had never attempted since their arrival in Vienna.

"Hunan garlic pork." Holding a pair of chopsticks, Fengshan took a bite. The result was surprisingly palatable. He had not had decent Chinese food, sautéed with savory soy sauce and garlic in the style of his hometown cooking, for ages. But sadly, he could hardly stomach anything.

"Is something wrong, my love?"

"I had a conversation with Ambassador Chen." He spread the rice to soak up the sauce and ate. Food would keep him focused, and he should not waste any. His countrymen were starving.

"Any good news from China?"

"No." His friends from China had sent telegrams about the war a few days ago. Despite the fact that Chongqing, the new capital of his government, had been bombed into a pile of rubble, to his greatest relief, his government had not surrendered.

"Something is bothering you, my love."

He wouldn't have continued with an explanation in the past, but Grace had changed. "The ambassador ordered me to halt the visa issuance."

She sat across from him. "Halt the visas? Why? I heard people in the slum were trying to apply to our consulate. If you stop, where will they get a visa? Do you remember Lola is in a slum? I wish you could see it. It's horrifying."

Grace had just confirmed what he needed to know.

"I asked Frau Maxa to find a boat ticket to Shanghai for Lola, my love. I'm afraid Lola's mental condition has declined. She might be hallucinating. She must leave Vienna."

"What did Frau Maxa say?"

"She said many people were looking for ocean-liner tickets. The prices are ridiculously high and there are few tickets available."

"I'll tell her to keep looking."

"There are many people confined in the slum, my love, sleeping on the floor. It's freezing out there! If you stop issuing visas . . ." Her beautiful eyes stared at him, anticipating.

"This is delicious."

She kissed his forehead. "I'll leave you alone. You think about it."

He nodded, grateful for Grace's understanding. Holding chopsticks, he slowly chewed his food, thinking about the ambassador's order.

When he went down to the crowded lobby, he heard a man in a black coat recounting his nightmarish experience in the Mauthausen camp to the applicants around him. Fengshan stopped to listen. The man, apparently named Herr Eisner, seemed to have been released from the camp a few days ago. He said he was tasked with transporting blocks of stones from the top of the quarry to the foot of the hill. Each day he carried on his shoulder a large block of stone that weighed about one hundred pounds and trudged down the 186 crumbling steps made of clay, ice, and rocks, the Stairs of Death, with his fellow prisoners following close behind and the whip from the kapos nearby. He had to take absolute care not to stumble on the frozen stairs or fall off the cliff or knock into people ahead of him. Once a man behind him dropped his block, and the huge rock rolled over his foot and crushed five men ahead of him. Herr Eisner lost two toes—he took off his boot to show them—but he said he was more fortunate than the man who dropped the rock, who became a "parachutist."

"Parachutist?" someone asked.

"One of the kapos grew angry and hurtled him down the cliff. The poor man flew over like a parachutist and fell to his death in a pond filled with huge rocks."

Herr Eisner's lips trembled, his eyes haunted by the memory. He had believed he was in a death trap until his wife found him a visa from the Chinese consulate—the ticket that granted him his release. And now, he came to the consulate to save his brother-in-law, who toiled in the camp.

Fengshan walked into his office, his back straight. He couldn't believe he had wasted time agonizing over his superior's order. His decision was already made and he intended to carry it out. There were thousands of Jews in Vienna; if he needed to issue thousands of visas to keep them out of labor camps, then so be it.

CHAPTER 43

GRACE

Two weeks later, after much waiting, I obtained a boat ticket to Shanghai with the help of Frau Maxa. The boat was to depart in September, in six months. I was disappointed. Lola couldn't wait for six months in the slum. At my insistence, Frau Maxa inquired at a law office and purchased, at a steep price, a boat ticket to Shanghai, set to sail in two weeks. Thrilled, I bought a train ticket at the station and folded both tickets in my handbag. Lola would be able to leave the slum and sail to Shanghai!

When I went to the district of Leopoldstadt, there were routine inspections and interrogations, but again, the Chinese flag saved me.

In the slum, Lola was talking to a young man outside the building. She introduced him as Theo. He had blue eyes, a face with prominent cheekbones and thick eyebrows, brown hair parted in the middle. He was attractive, and his eyes flowed with a certain intensity as if he had a hidden dagger in his sleeve and he was ready to use it. He was the old friend she had mentioned, and he had brought another bottle of Styrian beer.

He looked familiar, and then I remembered he was the man we'd met while waiting in line for exit permits at the Central Office for

Jewish Emigration. There had been something peculiar about him that I couldn't remember. Lola was not romantically involved with him, I could tell.

Theo had been in Linz, then shown up here, Lola said after he left. "He said we'd be transported to Mauthausen camp next month."

"Mauthausen." It sounded familiar.

"Let's go for a walk. I'll tell you more," Lola said, glancing at the people near the window.

I followed her, trudging in the knee-deep snow; the chilly air made my eyes water even though I had on the thick astrakhan coat, my gloves lined with fur, and high leather boots. Lola only wore a black jacket, a scarf around her head, and old boots. She shook her head when I offered her my gloves. She was not cold, she said.

When we passed a one-story tavern, I heard the pulsating beats of music coming from inside. Through the window, I could see a group of musicians playing fiddles and cowbells, swinging their arms. Lola stopped to watch, too, then sniffed, pulled the scarf to cover her face, and looked away. Since last summer, she had stopped talking about Strauss, Mozart, and her favorite song, "The Lark Ascending."

Then, suddenly, someone shouted inside the tavern. The door smashed open. A man without a hat stumbled out. He glanced at us, dashed toward the fence's gate, and disappeared. One moment later, two uniformed policemen burst inside the tavern, blasting German. A gunshot was fired.

Lola gripped my arm, swerving us into an alley. "Theo said the Gestapo arrested all the men in the block yesterday and sent them to Mauthausen."

"How did he know?"

The icy wind blew over me. I shivered. It was so cold that I felt my lips were frozen and my nose was hard like ice. In front of me was the canal, a vast strip of ice with white rocky mounds and frosty bushes. In the distance, the roller coasters were frozen; beneath them hung long, sharp icicles, and the great Ferris wheel was laden with snow, a white wreath like a diaphanous portal.

"Theo works for an organization that smuggles people out to Switzerland. They use false papers to help them escape—writers, composers, artists, and university professors who are branded subversive for their 'degenerate works' or for spreading subversive messages that endanger society, all dissidents wanted by the government."

That sounded dangerous. If they were caught smuggling, they would be shot. "I bought you tickets, Lola! A boat ticket and a train ticket. You're all set. Now you can leave."

She spun around so fast that she almost tripped over the thick ice. "You have a boat ticket? How did you get it?"

"Fengshan's secretary helped me." I dug into my handbag and handed her the tickets.

Lola stared at them, her breath swelling in the chilly air, an island in a mirage. She looked like she was going to cry, but, as she always did, she pushed her tears back. "Thank you, Grace."

"Leave Vienna and go to Shanghai, Lola. Here's my Dickinson." I gave her my poetry book that I had brought. "It's a long and tedious journey to Shanghai. You'll have something to read."

"Your favorite poet." She remembered.

"I never thought to part with it. Perhaps one day you'll give it back to me." This book was a light in my childhood, a token of Mother's love after her repeated slaps. Mother had received it from her friend Mrs. Maher, a maid of the Dickinson family.

Lola held it with two hands—she knew what the book meant to me; what she meant to me.

"I'll see you off, Lola. Remember, the train departs in three days. I'll pick you up and take you to the train station. And from Italy, you'll sail to Shanghai."

She shook her head. "You shouldn't come here so frequently, Grace. You're a diplomat's wife. This slum is not safe for you. You can meet me at the train station, what do you say?"

And I didn't argue—I could never argue with my friend. "See you at the train station, Lola."

On the day of Lola's departure, I went to the train station and waited. But the train came and left, and she never showed up.

Rudolf, at my insistence, took me to the slum. Lola was not outside the building. I knocked on the door; no one answered.

I peered through the window. The building was empty. All the families with suitcases, the hallucinating Kafka man with a beard like a winter bush, and Lola had disappeared.

CHAPTER 44

FENGSHAN

"She's not arrested; I don't believe she was arrested." Grace was pacing his office, biting her lips. "Do you think she was arrested by the Gestapo officers?"

"Well—" He was jotting down the visa number on a form. He wished there were something he could say to comfort Grace. Disappearances, in today's Vienna, only meant one thing. He had heard too many stories from the visa applicants and Captain Heine.

"There were many people inside the building, hundreds of them, and they all disappeared, including Lola. How could they all disappear?"

He frowned.

"In a few days, she'll show up. Right, my love?"

Where? In the slum? In the consulate? "Yes."

"Do you think she'll show up?" Grace took off her gloves and then put them back. She wasn't wearing her hat, looking distraught.

"She will."

"Still! All the people inside the building! How could they all disappear?"

One thing he was sure of: if hundreds of people in a building managed to escape together, with guards nearby, it was a fairy tale.

"I don't know what's going on . . . She's alive. I can feel her. Do you think she's alive?"

He had written the number wrong. "She's alive."

Poor Grace. He didn't have the heart to puncture the bubble of her dream—there was a good chance that she'd never see her friend again.

The vice consul reported to him that a few Chinese peddlers, who had heeded his warning to stay at home last year, had been beaten on the street. Fengshan went to visit them, and the small Chinese community gathered around him. They said they had not needed to apply for new passports for months since the police officers didn't seem to care about their business, but they were concerned about the violence in Vienna and planning to go to Italy to be safe. The students indicated they'd graduate soon and were preparing for their departure.

Fengshan wished them well, but his heart was heavy. Once his people departed Vienna, his consulate could offer them little help.

Captain Heine called, asking him to turn on the radio.

A man's voice, full of excitement, blathered that after months of anticipation, the Führer had fulfilled his promise to protect the ethnic German people in Prague and the Czech provinces of Bohemia and Moravia: "No longer will the German people be forced to take lessons from the corrupt Jewish teachers! No longer will the German children be brainwashed in Jewish theology and fabricated social justice stories, and forced to sit with Jews!" In the background rumbled the noises of tanks, cars, and soldiers marching. The German Wehrmacht had poured into Prague, and Czechoslovakia was declared a protectorate of Germany.

After months of coercion by Hitler, months of speculation and rumor, the unthinkable absorption of Czechoslovakia by Germany had finally happened. Czechoslovakia ceased to exist.

"You won't hear it on the radio, but Eichmann was among the parade that entered Bohemia and Moravia," Captain Heine said.

Wherever that man went, a disaster for the Jews followed. Fengshan hoped with all his heart that he would never see Eichmann again. And he hoped that the invasion of Czechoslovakia would serve as a warning to his superior and the leaders of the world. Hitler had rescinded the promise he made at the Munich Conference; the Third Reich had revealed its dangerous ambition and who they really were—an army of insatiable invaders, just like his country's enemy, the Japanese.

Had Ambassador Chen analyzed the situation with rationality and logic, he would have understood it was futile to pursue the friendship that had long ceased to exist.

One day, Fengshan was on his way to church when he came across Mr. Lord dressed in his casual double-breasted gray suit. In a serious tone, he said that the American consulate was planning on suspending the visa process for the Jews in Greater Germany in April. They had reached their immigration quota for the year 1939.

Fengshan was devastated. Czechoslovakia was dissolving, and borders to other countries such as Poland and Switzerland were closed. More and more Jews were driven to the brink of destruction, and yet countries such as the United States, which had provided one of the most coveted visas, were officially shutting their doors to the Jews. And only a few days ago, he had read in an English newspaper that the British government had issued a white paper to limit the number of immigrants to Palestine to five thousand a year. Five thousand would be permitted to live while millions were left homeless!

In the morning, Fengshan made sure to put an *Open* sign outside the consulate's gate. The lobby in the consulate was overcrowded, and the applicants lined up on the streets outside, heaped with mounds of snow.

❦

"Herr Consul General, there is a package for you," Frau Maxa said outside his office.

"Leave it. I'll open it later." He didn't lift his head, writing *Shanghai* in Chinese characters on a visa form. The applicant's last name, unlike the previous one, was short, as if saving his time: Baum.

"He said it was from Mr. Rosenburg."

Fengshan looked up. Mr. Rosenburg had left for Shanghai last year, and he had seen him off at the train station. His friend had a habit of gift-giving, but he had not mentioned a package sent to him from overseas. He looked down at the form again. He had to finish this visa first. It was not his character to leave something unfinished. "I'll open it later."

Frau Maxa came in a moment later. "The carrier of the box is waiting to speak to you, Herr Consul General."

"Bring him in."

He waited for a while, but Frau Maxa didn't appear. He went out to the lobby. "Where's the carrier?"

"I can't find him, Herr Consul General. Rudolf said the carrier just left."

He frowned. "Where's the package?"

It was a small box. Inside was a cup, an ordinary cup that anyone could purchase in a store. He looked inside the box again; there was nothing else except the wrapping, a newspaper from last November with the headline of the dreadful night when many shops were destroyed and many Jews were arrested and beaten—the *Kristallnacht*.

He held the newspaper. It was evident that the cup and the name of Mr. Rosenburg were only used as an excuse. Whoever had sent the package wanted to speak to him. But if the sender had come for help, then why so secretive?

A few days later, another package appeared on his desk. Inside was the same type of cup he had seen before, wrapped in newspapers in German.

Fengshan took his coat and hat from the coatrack and went to the lobby. A man, tall, wearing a black knit scarf and a black overcoat, was watching him at the entrance. But the moment Fengshan saw him, he slipped out of the consulate.

Whoever the stranger was, he desired a private meeting. Fengshan locked the office behind him, passed the crowd in the hallway, and came to the entrance. It was snowing outside; the man was standing near the statue of Beethoven opposite the consulate. Fengshan pulled his black coat tight and crossed the street covered with knee-deep snow.

"Herr Consul General?"

The young man looked to be in his midtwenties, with thick eyebrows and intelligent black eyes peering above the scarf wound around his neck. By instinct, Fengshan could tell he was a Viennese Jew.

"Yes, I'm the consul general of the consulate of the Republic of China."

Fengshan extended his hand and saw with sadness that the man hesitated. The Nazis had made it criminal for the Germans to shake a Jew's hand. But he was not German, and he still believed in courtesy.

The young man's grip was firm. "My name is William Galili. My apologies for the unconventional meeting in this horrid weather. I heard of your consulate through our mutual friend Mr. Rosenburg. There's an urgent matter regarding visas, and I'm afraid I need your help."

It was freezing; Fengshan had forgotten to wear his gloves. "Mr. Galili, the consulate of the Republic of China has a liberal policy regarding visas for the Jews in Vienna. If this is what you need help with, I advise you to fill out an application form in the lobby."

"Indeed, Herr Consul General, I've heard about the generous policy of your consulate, but I'm afraid I request more than one visa."

"How many are you requesting?"

"Seven hundred seventy-five."

He gave the man a good look. "You're applying for visas on behalf of seven hundred seventy-five people."

"Herr Consul General, it is most unusual, but I beg you to hear me out. All these unfortunate people have asked for my help; they're from Berlin, Vienna, Czechoslovakia, Hungary, and other countries in Eastern Europe. They are sleeping in a train, unheated, in Czechoslovakia, in this freezing weather, waiting to be transported to a ship that'll sail to Bulgaria and then China. However, they were refused passage through Rumania, and ordered to turn back to Germany, which must not happen. They have little provisions left, no fresh water, waiting for visas to go to China that would grant them a passage from the port police."

He was an eloquent speaker, appealing to his empathy, but the more Fengshan heard, the more suspicious this whole business appeared. "Are you saying that they're en route to China by train and then by boat and yet none of them have a Chinese visa?"

"That's correct, Herr Consul General."

He had an instinct that this man was not a friend of Mr. Rosenburg. "You have seven hundred seventy-five people's lives in your hands, Mr. Galili; if you're as serious as I think you are, you'll tell me the truth."

The young man glanced at the line of visa applicants near the entrance of the consulate. "Herr Consul General, perhaps I have started the conversation on the wrong foot. Seven hundred seventy-five visas certainly require some work, and I'd be glad to compensate you for your trouble. I'd like to give you two thousand marks for your trouble, or five hundred American dollars if you prefer. I hear you have a son. It'll come in handy for his education."

Fengshan turned around.

"One thousand American dollars, Herr Consul General!"

He stopped. "Mr. Galili, I believe your money will be more useful somewhere else. The consulate of the Republic of China does not accept bribes. You have demeaned me and my consulate by offering your bribe. I wish you a good day."

"Herr Consul General, wait! I apologize if I've offended you. Please give me one more chance to explain. As you know, many consulates in Vienna are unreachable for various reasons. I've spoken to representatives from Liberia, Argentina, and Greece in Berlin and Prague. They said they must report to their officials at home regarding the visas, which would take months. I'm afraid I don't have time. These people are waiting on the train and will be turned away in days if they do not have visas."

The flakes of snow plastered the man's face and melted. He was perspiring; his eyes glowed with urgency and fear. Fengshan relented. "Herr Galili, as I've stated earlier, the consulate of the Republic of China has a liberal policy regarding the Jews in Greater Germany. All applicants will receive their visas, provided they have proper documents. But bribery is not the path to visas."

The young man pulled his coat tighter. "My deepest apologies, Herr Consul General. This is a just cause, I assure you, and I'll be happy to tell you the details. The seven hundred seventy-five people, as you suspected, do not intend to go to China. They have their own destination in mind. They have been given a pass-through in Rumania by a local official, yet the official was unwilling to take a risk to accept them for fear they would linger in his country. He asks to see the evidence of their departure. So I have reached an agreement with him. Suppose each of them owns a visa to China, a faraway country, proving that they are en route to China. In that case, the official will let the train pass through his country, and they'll board the ship in Varna in Bulgaria and reach their destination."

"What's their intended destination?"

"Palestine."

The visas to China, it appeared, would be used as a device for the Jews to escape Vienna. If he were to follow Ambassador Chen's order to halt the issuance of visas, it would be for this type of visa—visas to smugglers and illegal transporters.

"Herr Consul General, I beg you. You must hear me. Palestine is the country confirmed to us by the League of Nations. We have the right to live there, but Palestine, a British mandate, is beyond our reach. Britain restricts the immigration of German Jews on a large scale, believing a Jewish majority in Palestine will pose a threat and complicate their ruling in Palestine."

This delicate situation of controlling the territory was nothing new. Fengshan knew too well that the Suez Canal, a corridor to India and other colonies, was vital for the British empire, and the British wanted absolute control in that region. What the young man didn't say was that the Rumanian official feared he would antagonize the British, since his approval of the passage would violate the British order. As a diplomat, Fengshan was aware of the risk of antagonizing the British as well, and for the interest of his country, it was best to avoid rocking the boat.

"I'm sorry; this qualifies you as a smuggler, Mr. Galili. You're conducting the illegal immigration of seven hundred seventy-five people."

"Herr Consul General, I wouldn't refer to it as illegal immigration; I would say it's free immigration."

Fengshan waved his hand.

"Herr Consul General, people will die if they turn back to Germany. Seven hundred seventy-five people."

Fengshan's heart grew heavy. "Is this the first time you're transporting people to Palestine?"

Those black eyes locked on him. "We've been transporting Jews to Palestine since 1930."

"Which organization do you work for, Mr. Galili?"

"It doesn't matter what organization it is, does it, Herr Consul General? We have a crisis in this country, and we are doing all we can to save people's lives."

This was an audacious man. "You're playing a dangerous game, Mr. Galili."

The young man wrapped his loosened scarf tighter around his neck. "If it's about saving people's lives, Herr Consul General, we don't have a choice."

Fengshan sighed. "Do you have the passports with you?"

"They're in four bags. I couldn't bring them all."

"Bring them to the consulate tomorrow and fill out the forms, Mr. Galili. I shall have the visas ready in two days."

The young man let out a long breath. "Thank you, Herr Consul General."

Fengshan's hands were freezing. He rubbed them to keep warm, turning to leave. "May I have your real name, Mr. Galili?"

The young man smiled, and there in his intelligent eyes flashed the light of admiration and gratitude. "My name is William Perl. I'm the founder of Die Aktion, Af-Al-Pi, an underground organization that helps Jews leave Vienna. The members of Af-Al-Pi owe you eternal gratitude, Herr Consul General."

Fengshan smiled and walked back to the consulate. His loyalty would always be to China, but when it came to saving people's lives, a man's obligation to his superior was no longer critical.

The next day, Vice Consul Zhou carried the package that contained seven hundred seventy-five forged passports to his desk. He looked anxious, scratching his head with his long nail. "Mr. Consul General, these passports, if I may say this, need further investigation. They look authentic, but none of the applicants could be contacted for interviews."

"Do not worry. Once the visas are approved, someone will come to pick up the package." He waved his hand.

The vice consul gasped. He was perhaps lazy, but not dim-witted. "Should we report to the ambassador . . ."

Fengshan had not relayed the ambassador's cessation order to the vice consul. "There's no need. I'll explain it to him."

He took out the cross on his necklace, kissed it, and laid out the passports on his desk. There were consequences he must consider—he, the consul general of his consulate, was knowingly issuing visas to those who were immigrating to Palestine, not China. There was no turning back after this. Not only had he defied his superior's order to suspend visas, but he was also supporting the illegal transportation of the Jews. His career would forever bear the stamp of defiance, and it was possible that he could face a brutal check from his superior or even suffer a permanent career setback. But the time to win the superior's approval and care for personal glory had passed; this was the time to save lives.

Holding his pen, he signed, in his steady strokes, his name on the visas.

CHAPTER 45

GRACE

For weeks, the roads were blanketed with knee-deep snow, the prancing equestrian statues in the plaza were a shapeless white, and on the streets, the Viennese, in their brown and black loden outfits, hunched their backs, hurrying along.

I agonized over Lola's disappearance every day. Sometimes, I believed firmly that she had escaped with all the people in the building; sometimes, a depressing thought sat in my mind like a rock deposited in a lake—she had been taken to Mauthausen and would be worked to death.

I couldn't bear it. I went to see Monto. He was sitting by the fireplace, reading a German book with pictures. He looked lonely, a twelve-year-old boy with bony shoulders and round eyes. The tuft of hair that often stuck out was lamely drooping near his ear—he needed a haircut.

"Could you still predict someone's future by reading their signature, Monto?"

"Of course I can."

"Wait here. I have something to show you." I went to the vice consul and asked to see Lola's visa application forms. He was reluctant, saying he was busy, but I insisted and offered to find them myself. Finally, he gave in. I took out the application page that bore Lola's signature and put it in front of Monto. "Tell me. Is she alive?"

He scrutinized it, his black eyes intense like his father's when he was contemplating something serious. "She's alive."

I let out my breath. "Thank you."

"Who's Lola? Is she the girl you were hiding in the storage room?"

"How did you know?"

"Of course I knew."

"Don't tell anyone, all right? She's a good friend. Like Willi to you. How's Willi?"

Monto burst into tears. "Willi is missing."

"What do you mean?"

"He hasn't come to school this year. It's been months! He missed many days last year too. I've been looking for him everywhere."

The absences on the transcript. "Monto, your grades have been low. What's going on?"

"Don't tell Father!"

"I won't, but how about we make a deal. I'll help you find your friend, but you promise me you'll focus on school and get your grades up. What do you say?"

"How will you find him?"

"I'll go visit him at home. Do you know his address?"

"I do. But Father wouldn't allow it. He said we needed an invitation."

"I'll tell Willi's parents I'm in the neighborhood. You can come with me too, and once you see him, we'll leave. How's that?"

"You won't tell Father?"

"Pinkie promise." I stuck out my pinkie.

The next day, I told Fengshan I'd take Monto to school; then Monto led our way to Willi's apartment, located on the third floor of a complex on the Kärntnerstrasse. When I knocked on the door, an elderly German woman, wearing a black dress with lace around her neck, opened it. Monto shrank behind me. I would have hidden as well, but this was for him. So in English and with gestures, I explained, as calmly as I could, that we were looking for Willi, Monto's friend.

The older woman's eyes misted, and, covering her mouth, she said something in heavily accented English that I finally made out. She was Willi's grandmother, and Willi, who had poor eyesight, had gone to the hospital one day but never returned. The hospital said he'd had surgery and was recovering in an undisclosed area but wouldn't allow visitors. Willi's mother had passed away two years ago, and his father had long disappeared, so Willi had been under her care.

I looked at Monto, waiting to see if he had anything to ask. He shook his head and turned around. We left the building and walked out to the street, passing the closed shops—many were tailors and dress-makers and retail shops selling stockings and knitwear.

I asked, "Is Willi Jewish?"

"I don't know."

"His grandmother said his vision was poor."

Monto nodded. "He got worse. He was almost blind. He loved to sing 'Dein ist mein ganzes Herz.'"

"What's that?"

"An aria from *The Land of Smiles.*"

That explained why Monto was good friends with Willi. Monto loved to sing too. "I'm sorry we couldn't see him."

He stared at the tram clunking on the Ringstrasse. The misery that had been etched on his face was replaced by something calm. This trip had helped him reach an understanding, it seemed. "I think he's dead."

"What are you talking about?"

He kicked the cobblestones. "Then why can't we see him?"

"He's in a very special place with good care, a special place for blind people, his grandmother said that."

"When I grow up, I'll be a doctor, so I can cure Willi's blindness, so he'll be able to see."

"Good idea, Monto."

A fleet of trucks loaded with golden Baroque chairs and sofas, rugs, lamps, and paintings passed us. Monto reached out to hold my hand.

This was the first time since I became his stepmother that he had held my hand. I did my best not to take special notice, did my best to pretend this was nothing out of the ordinary. But my heart fluttered. It was as if it was confirmed by this intelligent boy that I was worthy and that I was not the Grace who didn't know what to do with him.

And Monto wouldn't know this either—I had never held Mother's hand when growing up. Between cleaning people's houses and baking and doing laundry and digging clams and peeling potatoes, she was exhausted at home. And when we were in public, I toddled behind her while she walked ahead to distance herself from me.

"You have a small hand," Monto said.

I felt my eyes grow misty. I remembered—I was about seven—when my mother was in a good mood, her face pretty with her freckles, a shining constellation, and she had held me on her lap. She counted my fingers—*this little piggy went to market, this little piggy stayed home, this little piggy had roast beef*—and made the same comment. A small hand of a small child, she had said. A simple statement, without the color of rage or disappointment or distaste, a rare moment, like the sight of a rainbow, glittering after years of violent storms.

What if Mother had held my hand? What if she had said something like "You have small hands, but they're just as strong"? What if she had fought her own demons and stayed away from alcohol?

I turned Monto toward me—he was almost my height. "And you have a big heart, Monto. You remember this, will you? You'll grow up to be a great man, a man who achieves great things, a man with friends and family who love you. You'll be strong."

My boy smiled.

CHAPTER 46

FENGSHAN

He was in the middle of reading the visa application forms when he heard Frau Maxa's heavy footfalls.

"Herr Consul General." She knocked on the door. "You have a visitor from Berlin. He called himself Counselor Ding. He said he was dispatched by Ambassador Chen."

For a brief moment, Fengshan panicked. His superior had taken offense at his disobedience, as he had feared. He put down his fountain pen. Counselor Ding, the assistant to Ambassador Chen in the embassy, was an acquaintance he'd met a few times, but he had not been involved in specific missions with him. "Please bring him in."

A few minutes later, Counselor Ding, a man in his forties, wearing a pair of glasses with black rims, strode into his office.

"Counselor Ding." Fengshan went around to shake hands with him. "What a surprise. I didn't know you were coming. Did I miss the telegram?"

"I didn't send a telegram, Consul General. At the ambassador's behest, I'm here to investigate a few urgent matters that include visa issuance. Thus I hereby request you order the suspension of the visa activities at this moment." His face looked as severe as a grandfather ready to punish an unruly child.

The ambassador had intended to prove that he was guilty of insubordination and misconduct through the investigation, he realized, and if the ambassador got his way, he could censure or remove him.

"Of course, Counselor Ding."

Remaining absolutely collected, Fengshan went out to Vice Consul Zhou's desk and relayed the order. Zhou got up, made the announcement, and put the *Closed* sign near the door. A wave of sighs and groans rose from the applicants near the entrance, and Fengshan refrained from telling them to wait, to come back.

He went back to his office. "Counselor Ding, the visa issuance has been halted, as you have instructed, although I must bring to your attention that an order from the Ministry of Foreign Affairs was sent to me, and it has indicated we pursue a lenient policy regarding the Jews' immigration. I'm simply following the policy from the Ministry."

The order from the Ministry was irrefutable proof that he was indeed following an order coming from above the ambassador, and subsequently, the ambassador could not charge him with defiance.

Counselor Ding carelessly put his briefcase on top of the application forms on his desk—the pile of papers that held the key to people's lives—and took off his leather gloves. "The order from the Ministry of Foreign Affairs is also part of my investigation. Ambassador Chen would like me to examine it. May I take a look at it?"

The ambassador wanted to see his proof.

"Of course. I have the telegram. I shall retrieve it this instant." Fengshan opened the cabinet drawer that kept all the important communications between him, the embassy, and the Ministry of Foreign Affairs. He took out a large white envelope and searched among the letters and telegrams, all sorted by date, found the telegram, and placed it in front of Counselor Ding. "Here."

Counselor Ding pushed up his glasses and held up the sheet, which contained only two simple Chinese sentences, but he scrutinized it as if they were enigmatic hieroglyphs. "I've seen the instruction with my own eyes. Very well, thank you so much, Consul General."

Had he misplaced the telegram or lost it, the ambassador would have concluded the order didn't exist and accused him of misconduct. "How else may I assist you, Counselor Ding?"

"Consul General, it was brought to the ambassador's attention that there was bribery regarding the visa issuance in the consulate."

This was a serious accusation, and unexpected. And for a brief moment, Fengshan wondered if the ambassador was referring to the visas he'd issued to Mr. Perl. "I assure you, I'm not aware of any illicit behavior, and certainly, to the best of my knowledge, there is no bribery."

"Who is in charge of the visa application process?"

"Vice Consul Zhou."

"I'll need to speak to him."

Vice Consul Zhou was his subordinate; if he were found guilty of bribery, then, as his superior, Fengshan would be liable for being negligent. "Of course."

The interrogation of Vice Consul Zhou stretched for hours. There were questions about the friends and acquaintances with whom he associated, the venues he patronized, and the shops he visited. The vice consul answered them all, and to Fengshan's relief, he claimed he had not sold any visas to individual applicants, nor made contact with any suspicious middlemen buying visas. Finally, he was sent away.

Fengshan looked at the counselor, sitting in his chair, holding his pen that he used to sign visas, willing him to get up and return to Berlin with a report of his innocence so he could continue the consulate's business. But the counselor was not finished.

"Consul General, may I inspect the consulate's financial report and the receipts of the fees and the remittances to the Ministry?"

First the examination of the order, then the bribery accusation and now the review of the finances. The ambassador certainly seemed determined to prove his mismanagement. "I shall be glad to present them to you, Counselor Ding."

"Thank you, Consul General. You may take a seat."

Fengshan nodded, sat in a chair across from the counselor as he went over every line in the financial report, and listened to each scratch of the pen. It was unsettling and demeaning to have his integrity and capability evaluated this way. Still, the high stakes here were the fates of all the applicants. If he were found guilty of any misconduct, the visa issuance would end.

His financial report of the consulate expenses was, as far as he knew, immaculate; however, with the ongoing war in China, the remittances to the embassy had been delayed, which the counselor could misinterpret.

"I've prepared some homemade Chinese food. Would you like to have a taste, Counselor Ding?" Grace, who had been hovering outside the door, appeared at his side with a tray of sliced pork and a bowl of rice. She had that flushed look she got when she conversed with strangers, though she seemed determined.

He wanted to smile at her ingenuity in distracting Counselor Ding. If there was one thing a Chinese man living abroad craved every day, it was authentic Chinese food; Fengshan could attest to that.

The counselor glanced at Grace's tray, looking tempted, and finally put down his pen. He said in English, "Thank you, Mrs. Consul General, for your hospitality. You've come at the right time. I haven't had a chance to stop for food since I left Berlin."

Grace set the tray on the desk. "I just love this smell. Garlic pork with soy sauce. Help yourself."

It appeared Counselor Ding was starving, wolfing down the slices of pork. "This is delicious."

"I don't understand the workings of the consulate, Counselor Ding, especially the visas. In your opinion, why would a consulate accept bribes?" Grace asked.

"Visas are very much sought after these days, and many people are willing to pay high prices for them."

Grace looked at him; Fengshan cleared his throat. "If I may, Counselor Ding. It is true that people pay high prices for visas to America, but Shanghai is not as desirable as America. And the policy we have is to approve every visa for every applicant. If a visa is so easy to obtain, then there's no reason why people should bribe the consulate staff."

Counselor Ding dabbed his mouth with a napkin from the tray, looking thoughtful.

"How did the ambassador learn about the bribery of the consulate?" Grace asked.

That was the question Fengshan would like to know as well. He looked at the counselor.

"Well, there was a report filed by the police that the vice consul of the consulate has taken bribery for visas."

This was the first time Fengshan had heard that the Viennese police were watching his consulate.

The following day, Fengshan, with Grace by his side, walked out with the counselor to the consulate's car parked near the street, where some visa applicants had already started to line up. Counselor Ding would be taken to the train station and report to Ambassador Chen in Berlin about his discovery in the consulate, but he didn't indicate what would appear in the report or whether the ambassador would censure him.

"Safe travels, Counselor Ding." Fengshan opened the door for him.

The counselor gave the visa applicants a look of annoyance. "This is a big crowd."

"I'm only following the Ministry's order, Counselor Ding. I hope Ambassador Chen will understand."

"Ambassador Chen understands this too well, Consul General. He is under tremendous pressure. He is warned if China intends to maintain diplomatic relations with Germany, then China must stop accepting a large number of refugees who hate Germany. Our German friends have made it clear."

"Of course, Counselor Ding, I wasn't aware that our German friends were watching our consulate. Who filed the police report about the possible bribery, may I ask?"

"The chief officer of the Central Office for Jewish Emigration in Vienna notified the ambassador." The counselor closed the door, and the car rolled away.

Eichmann. This was a most extraordinary move indeed. When they'd met a few months ago, the man had kept up a pretense of thanking him for help in expelling Jews.

"Why would the ambassador believe Eichmann?" Grace asked, her face pale in the snow.

"That doesn't matter anymore." He went to the board with the *Closed* sign and flipped it to *Open*.

He had survived his superior's investigation, and now he was fully prepared to continue implementing the lenient visa policy for the Jews. With the telegram from the Ministry of Foreign Affairs, he could do so without repercussions. However, he had no illusions that his already tenuous tie with Ambassador Chen would be strengthened soon.

And he had made a powerful enemy—Eichmann, the new elite of the Nazis, who had set out to obstruct his work tied to the fate of the Viennese Jews.

CHAPTER 47

GRACE

Later, Fengshan called his friend Captain Heine and asked whether he was aware of Eichmann's involvement in the visa-bribery accusation. The captain had no knowledge of that, and he sounded annoyed at Eichmann and promised to keep an eye on the consulate.

That evening I didn't sleep well, dreaming of the investigation and the Nazi officer Eichmann.

A few days later, I made a bittersweet discovery—I was pregnant. Counting days, I could tell I was about two months in. After so many years of trying and hoping, after many lonely months, I could finally fulfill my wish to be a mother.

I nearly flew downstairs to whisper in Fengshan's ear.

He was pleased.

When Fengshan was buried in the applications again, I, alone, went shopping for baby clothes on the Kärntnerstrasse.

This was the second time in two years that I had gone out shopping on the street, nearly a year since I'd met Lola. I almost lost my way again among the boutiques with glittery glass windows, the neat kiosks selling newspapers in German and French and English, and the bakeries and flower shops, but I had kept a slip with the consulate's address, as Lola had advised. There was so much to see: patterned brown leather shoes, prim Tyrolean hats with feathers, stylish ladies' fur hats, long, shimmering gowns, and stockings. The area was a shopping paradise, a show of ultimate Viennese decadence.

Near the nursery shop, two German women in red and white dirndl passed by, their laughter a joyous overture under the April sun. The taller woman had a plump, youthful face like Lola's before the scar. Had Lola been here, she would have been overjoyed for me, and she would have come shopping with me, and we could have discussed which stroller to purchase and which bassinet was the warmest.

It had been over a month since her disappearance. Where was she? Was she safe? Was she alive?

CHAPTER 48

FENGSHAN

A few days after Counselor Ding's visit, he was deep in his work when Frau Maxa galumphed into his office again. Fengshan raised his head—the unflappable Austrian who rarely appeared excited or frightened looked pale. Adolf Eichmann, clad in his full SS *Obersturmführer* black uniform with a cap emblazoned with the skull and crossbones, had just entered the consulate.

Calmly, Fengshan put down his pen and walked to the lobby, where his staff suddenly appeared to be busy with their drawers and the applicants gazed at the floor. Eichmann was studying the paintings on the wall, his legs spread wide, his hands on his waist, still as a scarecrow.

"Greetings, Herr Eichmann." Fengshan gave the man a bow as a courtesy. The man had utterly disregarded the protocol, an officer barging into a consulate of another country without first sending a card or making an appointment.

"Herr Consul General, greetings. Quite a place you have here. Prime location. Superb paintings of the Empress Joséphine. I just saw two policemen pass by. Who sent them here?"

"The good police of Vienna."

There appeared that sly smile. "*Hauptsturmführer* Heine is a good man, although it's concerning that he'd ignore our Führer's instruction and use our resources to support the foreigners."

"He's only doing his duty. Sir, how may I help you today?"

"Herr Consul General, I'm doing my duty as well. The good German people have complained about the scum seeking visas from your consulate. The boisterous crowd has blocked the street, created traffic problems, and engaged in riotous activities that have threatened good Germans' lives and endangered the safety of drivers and passersby. Such gatherings must cease for the residents' safety, for the normal traffic flow, and for the neighborhood's peace. I want to ask you a favor: to consider halting the visa issuance at the consulate."

He had not expected such an insolent request from this man. "With respect, the activity of the consulate is important for my country and must not be interrupted unless by order of my superiors. The visa seekers do not block the street; if I may clarify, they wait in an orderly queue, and they do not engage in boisterous or disruptive activities that threaten the safety of the residents."

"Herr Consul General, are you deliberately ignoring the complaint of the good Germans?" The man's voice was laced with threat.

The Devil's Deputy—he recalled Mr. Rosenburg's words, and he could only imagine the fear and devastation that paralyzed the helpless men when they faced his gun in the dungeon. "I'm only fulfilling my duty as the consul general of the consulate of the Republic of China."

Eichmann's eyes narrowed, and he put a cigarette in his mouth, dug out a gold-plated cigarette lighter, and lit it. In the corner of his lips appeared a calculating sneer. "Herr Consul General, given our friendship, I feel obliged to inform you that your duty has come in conflict with the plan of our Führer. All Jews in Vienna are now banned from leaving. They must stay. They will live here, work here, and die here. It is my new mission, and I don't expect any challenges."

Fengshan felt his heart ablaze with the wildfire of rage. "I beg you to enlighten me. For months, I had the impression that your government encouraged the Jews to leave the country, and they're following the order to go through every legal step. Why this reversal?"

"I don't believe I owe you an explanation. This is our country's policy. It's adjusting as we speak, but if you really wish to know, I have received permission from my superior to operate some camps in Doppl and Sandhof. The Jews are excellent labor and cheap. They'll be trained for the technical and agricultural jobs in those camps and contribute to our country's success. To let them leave is a waste of resources."

Fengshan suppressed the urge to punch the man's face. "Allow me to reiterate, the main function of a consulate is to issue visas, and the order I received is to grant visas to every single person who applies. It is my duty, and my privilege, to carry out the order. May I walk you out?"

The man's gray eyes looked frozen. "How long have you been in Vienna, Herr Consul General?"

"Almost two years."

"I certainly hope you've enjoyed your life in Vienna so far."

"I have enjoyed the hospitality of many Viennese, and if I may add, China and Germany have also enjoyed decades of friendship. I think your car is waiting outside." He walked to the consulate's entrance and extended his hand, urging the man to exit.

But Eichmann remained where he was. "Who's the owner of the consulate?"

"Herr Goodman is my landlord."

There appeared that sickening, sly smile again. "Hendrich Goodman? That Jew? Where is that coward? I'd like to speak to him."

"I believe he lives in Switzerland."

"Hiding in Switzerland. Of course. Or he would be sent to a camp already. But he has left this building behind." The Nazi rogue looked as though he was enjoying the funniest joke.

Fengshan's heart skipped a few beats. What Eichmann didn't say was known to every Jew, and to him too: that the property of the Jews now belonged to the government. "You must forgive me. Herr Goodman and the consulate have signed a lease for ten years. This is our fourth year. It's a contract between a state and an individual, bound by legal terms."

Eichmann was smiling his oily smile again. "I beg to differ. This is Germany, and we have the right to revise the law and terminate a contract if we wish. As one of your old friends, I'd like to offer your consulate one last chance. Cease issuing visas. Take the *Closed* sign out and tell the ragtag and bobtail to disperse. Or it is assumed that the consulate will no longer be in existence."

The sanctuary of the consulate was only honored and protected by a decent state, which Germany had ceased to be. Should he bargain for more time so he could report the threat to the ambassador? There would be no rescue from Berlin after that vindictive investigation, he knew.

Or he could take a tactful approach—the approach his superior would prefer: bow out and stop the visa process.

Fengshan turned around to look at the men in shirts and hats, holding application forms, who were lined up outside the consulate. Their heads turned to Eichmann; they flinched, their eyes glancing away with trepidation. No one spoke. The boisterous crowd that had threatened the safety of the good Germans? It was a lie. These visa seekers were so concerned with propriety and obedience to the law that they could hardly step on others' toes.

Fengshan looked at them: a gaunt face, a wrinkled face, a face with a bruise, a face with hungry eyes, a face that was someone's brother, someone's parent, someone's son. They had come to him, their last resort, for salvation; how could he deny them?

"This way, Herr Eichmann."

Eichmann stiffened, stepped outside, and walked to his black Mercedes parked near a bench. He shouted at two of his henchmen near the car, and in unison, the two men opened the car door and carried out two long black rifles. Eichmann grabbed a rifle and marched toward the applicants.

"The illegal gathering on the street is disruptive to the residents' peace. I hereby order you all to disperse or face the consequences." Eichmann held his rifle.

Fengshan's heart stopped. Eichmann would shoot people in front of a consulate! "Herr Eichmann!"

"Herr Consul General, I've made it clear. Your assistance to the Reich is no longer required. Cease visa issuance or bear the blood on your hands."

Sweat ran down Fengshan's forehead. If he obeyed Eichmann's order, many people's hope to leave Vienna would die; if he refused, many people would die on the street, in front of his consulate. Fengshan turned to the applicants, who appeared stupefied. And then in an instant, the crowd seemed to awaken; they covered their heads and scattered in all directions.

Eichmann lifted his rifle.

A black Adler, which Fengshan had not noticed before, pulled right in front of Eichmann; from inside stepped Captain Heine. He must have come directly from a bar or a party, his face pink with alcohol.

Eichmann lowered his rifle and raised his arm, giving a *Heil* Hitler salute. The sly smile had appeared.

"*Hauptsturmführer* Heine, where have you been? A party with some actresses? Where was it held? I didn't get the invitation."

Captain Heine took out a small bottle of cognac from his pocket and had a sip. "*Obersturmführer* Eichmann, it was a fine party. A pity I had to leave because it was reported an urgent matter has arisen in the consulate. And I, as the captain of the police in this district, am obliged to resolve the dispute."

"Of course, except there is no dispute. You see, this is a government building in a prime location. But there have been some concerning noises that disturb the residents. I'm here to address their concerns, and I assure you that I'll have this problem taken care of."

"Well said, *Obersturmführer* Eichmann. I shall take this over and look into the issue myself. The first district is under my supervision."

"Of course, *Hauptsturmführer* Heine, I trust you will solve this problem promptly and wisely. Surely, it is on everyone's mind to keep distance from foreigners who intend to sabotage our Führer's order." Eichmann's eyes were hard and calculating.

His friend looked as though he were utterly bored at a disappointing opera. "*Obersturmführer* Eichmann, have you had too much drink?"

"Well, well, well. *Auf Wiedersehen, Hauptsturmführer* Heine." Eichmann, carrying his rifle, slid into his car and drove away.

"That clown." Captain Heine passed his bottle.

Fengshan gulped down the drink. The cold alcohol raced down his hot throat; a bolt of fire seized him. If it weren't for Captain Heine, there would have been carnage.

CHAPTER 49

GRACE

Captain Heine added some security staff, gave them instructions, and left, but the consulate staff continued to whisper about Eichmann's visit. Anxious, I came into Fengshan's office. The chaos in front of the consulate had made me nauseated. I didn't feel well, a throbbing pain sitting in my stomach.

"What happened? Why was Eichmann here?"

Fengshan closed the door behind me. "He demanded that I cease issuing visas. I refused. You need to sit, Grace. You look pale."

I rubbed my stomach. I was getting closer to three months in, which was reassuring but frightening. I had lost two pregnancies at this stage. "But why?"

"Eichmann made it clear that Jews are prohibited from leaving Vienna."

"I don't understand. But you'll keep issuing visas, won't you?"

"Of course. I've talked about this with Captain Heine. He'll increase the security and take care of the bureaucracy."

"The staff says that Eichmann will cancel the consulate's lease or confiscate the building." If the consulate building was seized, then

Fengshan would be left without an office. Without an office, there would be no consulate.

"Captain Heine promised to look into it. He's aware that the government has claimed all Jews' properties as their own, but he insists that by legal terms, they have an obligation to honor the contract since it concerns a consulate, not an ordinary business enterprise."

That was good to hear.

"Heine assured me that he would wield his influence at the city's planning division to honor our lease. He doesn't believe Eichmann has power over that division."

As a diplomat, Fengshan would be safe, but I was still worried. "What if Eichmann orders your arrest for defying the government's order?"

"Now you're overly anxious. I'm a diplomat from China, protected by diplomatic immunity. They don't have the authority to issue an arrest warrant."

"But Eichmann managed to report the alleged bribery to the ambassador. He could do that again and force the ambassador to pressure you."

Fengshan raised his eyebrows. "Captain Heine would like me to keep this private, since this is premature, but he vows to have Eichmann reassigned to Prague. He thinks he'll succeed. Does this calm your nerves, Grace? We have Captain Heine on our side."

I felt better after talking to Fengshan, but when I left his office, walking through the empty lobby—the applicants had all dispersed after the threatened shooting—anxiety possessed me again. I had grown used to the sight of the bearded Viennese and their quiet manners, and now the entire lobby was eerily silent.

Could we rely on Captain Heine to protect us? Was he strong enough? The violence of Vienna was endless and unpredictable. There was simply no structure, no safety, no reliance on law and authority anymore.

Was Lola dead?

CHAPTER 50

FENGSHAN

A few days later, Captain Heine asked Fengshan to meet him at Café Central. He had good news, he said: he had successfully requested that Eichmann be reassigned to Prague and the upstart SS man was scheduled to leave Vienna soon. Fengshan was delighted. He put on his hat and was on his way out when Mr. Lord phoned to bid goodbye.

The American consulate staff had decided to take a vacation. The new consul general, Mr. Morris, had left for Hawaii, and Mr. Lord planned to go home to visit his relatives. It was to be expected, Fengshan knew. His friend had subtly warned him of the withdrawal of the American presence in Vienna since the US had stopped issuing visas, reminding him of the isolationist stance of the country.

"We must meet before you leave," Fengshan said. "Would you care to have some coffee at Café Central? I'm going to meet Captain Heine there." Mr. Lord was acquainted with the captain as well.

"Well, you two drink more of the fine Vienna coffee for me. I'm afraid there are other matters I need to tend to before my departure. I heard about the incident in front of your consulate the other day. It's fortunate that the captain arrived in time to avoid bloodshed."

"Perhaps you might also wish to know that the Third Reich's policy regarding the Jews has changed?" Fengshan gave a brief description of Eichmann's threat.

"If this is true, then woe to the Jews in Vienna! Many of them are professionals who have expertise with a scalpel rather than a shovel. Training them to be farmers? That's inhumane. You must be careful, Dr. Ho. Please do bring my regards to the captain when you see him."

"He's my guardian angel."

"I'm sure he is. Let's hope he'll stay sober when you see him!"

When Fengshan arrived at the coffeehouse, the captain was already there, sitting at a round table with a marble top, under the golden chandelier, his favorite spot. The entire coffeehouse was silent. The men, in tan jackets and peaked caps, hid their heads behind newspapers, and the red-lipped women sat on sofas stone-faced, forgetting their cigarettes.

The captain was not alone. Two Gestapo men were standing next to him; one held a pistol against his temple.

"Captain Heine!" Fengshan felt a chill run down his spine. This was unthinkable—he was a high-ranking officer. "What is the matter here?"

His friend looked drunk, his face red and his eyes glazed, but he put his hand out. "I respectfully ask you to keep your distance, Herr Consul General. This is a private matter."

"*Hauptsturmführer* Heine!" The man holding the pistol was growling in German. "As I've stated earlier, you've broken the law. This is your warrant. You're ordered to come with us."

"Allow me to finish reading the warrant." The captain held the sheet in front of him; then, looking bored, he placed it on the table's marble top. "I could use another drink."

"*Hauptsturmführer* Heine! You're arrested for aiding the foreigners and the Quakers to smuggle children out of Germany."

"Is this some kind of joke?" His voice was smooth, with the same flirtatious tone with which he had courted women in a ballroom or a bar. Fengshan wanted to shout at him to be more serious. He was being arrested! But the Quakers . . . Only one man could have overheard that.

"You may explain at the Headquarters."

"Allow me to finish my cognac."

"*Hauptsturmführer* Heine!"

"Very well." His friend stood and straightened his collar. "It's a beautiful day with sunshine. I shall be glad to take a walk."

Fengshan watched helplessly as his friend gave him a nod and passed by. Outside the coffeehouse, Captain Heine came to a jeep, the sunlight casting a long shadow behind him. He looked around, saying something, but the Gestapo men grasped his arms and shoved him into the jeep.

Fengshan desperately attempted to free the captain, making phone calls to the Headquarters, to Mr. Lord, who was about to embark on his train, and to his other Austrian friends from church. He delivered a care package to Heine, but it was denied; he went to visit him at the Headquarters and was denied again. Two weeks later, he was told that Captain Heine was held by the *Geheime Staatspolizei* under protective custody, a Nazi term that meant he was being held without the benefit of a trial. Charged with breaching the state's security to the foreigners and conspiring to subvert the Nazi regime, he was stripped of his rank and transported to the Mauthausen camp.

CHAPTER 51

GRACE

Fengshan went to the window. Outside, Vienna was a graveyard of darkness with streetlights flickering here and there and the spire of St. Stephen's Cathedral a lonely glowing star. He was grieving for his friend, even though he had not said a word. I knew this about my husband: his grief came and went like a wintry gust, invisible, but it was always felt in the bones.

I held his arm.

"He's a good man," he said.

"You're tired."

"I dragged him into this."

"It's not your fault."

"Eichmann did this. He's a calculating man."

And now that Captain Heine was gone, Eichmann could do whatever he pleased with the consulate. "Come to bed, my love."

I took off his coat and boots and gave him a pair of black loafers from the closet. Lit by the dim light in the bedroom, he looked tired, with dark rings around his eyes, and his hair was receding, graying at the temples. For the first time, I noticed my thirty-seven-year-old husband, a vigorous man, was aging. His friend's arrest, the consulate's future, and the visas had stressed him, and he had not been eating or sleeping well. I should cook him more homemade Hunan food. The meals I made, though strenuous on my part, had delighted him, a traditional Chinese man who believed cooking was one of the essential skills for a wife.

"I need to go check on Monto, Grace."

"I'll go. You get some sleep."

I went to Monto's room. His lights were on, but he was deep asleep. I tucked the blanket around him and turned off the lights.

The following day I felt on edge. I worried about the consulate—would we lose the consulate? I also worried about myself. Something was wrong with me. At times the waves of anxiety, unbidden, washed over me, and I was that fearful, introverted woman again.

I was very tired all day, and when I napped, I dreamed of rainbows, of pink dolls, of small feet, of an infant's soft hair. I ran my hands through it, those filaments of wonder. I had waited for so long. Sometimes I dreamed I was sitting on a lawn pinned by a great icy Ferris wheel, and the sky was turning red, the summer air frosty with the winds from New England, whipping a soup of shattered violets, lilacs, tulips, and roses from my poet's garden in Amherst.

Monto kept me company while I folded the sets of baby clothing I had bought—it was like a soothing sport that I couldn't get tired of. When I told Monto of my pregnancy, he grinned. I jotted down my name and asked him to predict how many children I'd have.

"Two," he declared. "You'll have two children, Grace."

I smiled. I had no objection to two children. But three would be ideal.

Fengshan spoke less and less, which was another worrying sign. Was he concerned about another visit from Eichmann? Or an order of eviction?

Then one morning, I was sound asleep when I heard Fengshan's voice next to me. "Grace, Grace. Wake up, you must wake up."

The dawn light filled the room, luminescent like a glass jar, and Fengshan, holding a sheet of paper in his hand, was standing by my bed.

"What's going on, my love?"

"Grace, we need to pack."

I sat up, a dream still vivid in my mind, a chain of littered images. There was a train, a suitcase, a hand, and a face—Lola. It was a message. She was alive. I felt brave, confident, and full of elation. "Why?"

He gave me the paper. It was written in German.

"What does it say?"

His voice hoarse, Fengshan said that Eichmann, who had tried to stop him from issuing visas to Jews, who had complained to his superior, had used his power to speak to the Nazi city-planning division, which had ordered the consulate building to be demolished.

CHAPTER 52

FENGSHAN

He had six hours to leave the building before the tank would arrive.

He raced downstairs. The consulate wasn't yet open, but as usual, a long line had formed outside. He opened the door. "My apologies. The consulate is to be closed temporarily due to an emergency. Please come tomorrow and look for a sign outside the building."

Then he dashed into his office. All the sensitive files must be destroyed. The furniture must be left behind. Their personal belongings would be packed by Grace. The books he'd collected must be carted out and stored at a safe place. What needed his special care was the backlog of visa applications waiting for his signature. He must pack every single one.

He removed all the filled-out application forms, his fountain pens, and the seal from his desk and set them inside the two suitcases he had brought from his bedroom. Then he emptied his drawers, pulled out all the manila folders that contained correspondence between him and the ambassador and the Ministry of Foreign Affairs, and carried them all to the fireplace.

For the entire morning, Fengshan went back and forth from his office to the fireplace, feeding the fire with the sensitive files. Growing hot, he loosened his tie and rolled up his sleeves. He instructed Frau Maxa, when she arrived, to purchase all the boxes she could find and pack the books. He ordered the vice consul, who was still half asleep, to save all the blank application forms and bundle them together. Grace, thank God, knew exactly what to pack. Even Monto was helping, tossing manila folders in the fireplace, making sure not a single application form was thrown into the fire by accident, then prying the consulate's plaque at the entrance.

When noon arrived, Fengshan looked at the empty shelves, bare and battered, and his office, a hollow, cold cave, and the floor, a battlefield with torn sheets of paper and muddy footprints. When he spoke, echoes of his voice bounced in the air, a sad tune—but no, he didn't have time to be sentimental.

An ominous sound, a low rumble, rolled over the cobblestones outside, and the consulate's walls trembled. He picked up the two suitcases of application forms and turned to Grace, one hand holding Monto, the other holding her leather suitcase, standing by the door. The shadow draped over her narrow shoulders, and she shivered. Had she packed all their important belongings? Had she packed the clay statues? Her tiaras and dresses, his suits and medals, Monto's pants and sweaters, and the baby's socks and hats? He was counting on her.

"Let's go." He nodded at them and walked out of the building where he had worked and lived for over two years. Across the street, Frau Maxa, Vice Consul Zhou, and Rudolf were waiting; near them, a crowd had gathered—the visa seekers, whispering among themselves, anxious, already possessed by a looming sense of disaster. This consulate, his consulate, as far as he could tell, was their last bridge to life.

Fengshan tore his gaze away, told Monto and Grace to stay at a safe distance, and walked to the metal monster that came to demolish his consulate.

It was huge, blocking the street, the gun motor an unholy finger that mocked everything he held dear—the moral rectitude that was the bedrock of civilization, the codes that he lived by: honor, compassion, duty, and loyalty. And standing by it was the spiteful man who had sent his friend to the Mauthausen camp, legs apart, flanked by his depraved minions holding rifles.

"Good afternoon, Herr Consul General." On Eichmann's face was that sickening, oily smile.

About ten steps away, Fengshan stopped. Despite the swelling rage in his stomach, he managed to stay unruffled. He couldn't stop them. He, a single man, standing in front of an armed mob that sought to destroy his building, was outnumbered, overpowered, and outmaneuvered.

"You look surprised to see me, Herr Consul General. Don't be surprised. *Hauptsturmführer* Heine can't get me out of the way yet. Of course I must finish my job before leaving for Prague. Prague! It wasn't my choice. Anyway, we are even now. I do wish him well in Mauthausen!"

"Herr Eichmann, is there still a possibility for a friendly discussion?"

"The time for our discussion has already expired."

Eichmann had won. His cunning, his ruthlessness, his vileness was as cataclysmic as a bomb, and his voice, Fengshan prayed, would one day be strangled in the roars of righteousness and justice. He turned to give one last look at the building.

"It's too late to regret, Herr Consul General. I warned you. This is a bad time to be Germany's enemy." Eichmann waved his hand, and the tank driver raised the gun motor.

It fired. The first shell, a thunderous howl, struck the front of the building. The ornate pediment engraved with grapes exploded; white marble fragments and glass windows and wooden frames splintered, shooting in all directions. The three-story building, the seat of his career, an image of China, almost a home, detonated before him.

A downpour of thoughts fell on him. Could he have managed the situation with more finesse and reached a compromise with Eichmann?

Might he be the only consul general who bore this incident on his résumé?

The second shell struck the windows of their bedroom on the third floor. From behind him, across the street, Grace whimpered. He turned to look. She didn't seem to complain or blame him, her beautiful eyes two prisms of sadness. He had not had the time to comfort her, explain to her, or talk to her since he'd received the demolition notice. He wished to hear her speak now.

Another shell.

The belly of the sky, stained gray, was split open by a storm of ashes and bricks and clods of plaster. The cobblestones beneath him rattled. How long did it take to pulverize a building? How long did it take to construct a building? How long did it take for a man to build his career?

The street had turned into a white dome; a cloud of dust and ashes descended; in the place where the elegant three-story building had been, a building leased by a generous friend, piled a mound of rubble.

His consulate. His office. The seat of his success. Was gone.

Gone, too, were the moments he'd held the telephone reporting to Ambassador Chen; gone, too, were the hours he'd sat at the desk signing his name on visas with a fountain pen; gone, too, were those desperate people waiting in the lobby hoping for a future.

It was all but certain that from this spot, another stately building would rise, another struggle would spawn, and another story would be created. Hardly anyone in the future would remember the loss of a consulate. No one would remember him, either, a foreign diplomat who had failed to shield his consulate from a Nazi. Was this his future, too, the rubble? He resented this thought.

"Let this serve as the reminder that anything, anyone standing in the way of the Third Reich will be eliminated," Eichmann said near the tank, his hands cupped around his mouth, forcing his greasy voice through the echoing rumble.

It struck Fengshan, the brazen core of a man's soul, the depth of a man's evil. If a malignant man like Eichmann would dare to declare his intention to annihilate many lives and demolish a consulate that provided a passage to safety, then men, men of able means, men of faith, men of righteousness, must rise to stop him. This was how it had to be, then. As long as he held the fountain pen, the seal, the power to save people, as long as he was the consul general of the Republic of China, he would sit at a desk and sign, one visa at a time, fighting for other people's lives.

"Father?" Monto grabbed his hand.

His son had turned into a white creature, white-haired, white-faced, white-eyelashed, and the same with Grace, her purple dress now a dusty gray. The crowd seeking visas, also bathed in dust, sobbed, tears trickling down their faces.

He picked up the two suitcases that contained the application forms. "Let's go, Monto, Grace. We'll find an apartment for the office."

CHAPTER 53

GRACE

We were followed by an anxious crowd, and Fengshan spoke to them, assuring them in his confident lecturer's voice. I understood what this meant then—these Viennese, these sheer strangers, who were not his friends, nor his kinsmen, nor his fellow countrymen, were people my husband had given his heart to protect.

Walking down Beethovenplatz, though, with the luggage in our hands, Fengshan realized we needed to find a hotel for the night. He booked a room on the ground floor at a hotel near Schillerpark. Meticulous as always, he returned to place a sign on the street near the demolished consulate indicating the changed location so the visa seekers would find their way to the hotel.

Then he reported to Ambassador Chen, using the telephone from the hotel. I sat on a sofa near the wall to keep my husband company, remembering the look on his face as the shells struck. He was a reserved man, but at that moment I had seen how vulnerable he was; it was only a fleeting moment, for he managed to keep his emotions bottled otherwise—no remorse, no anger, only resolution.

The ambassador was devastated, and he lambasted Fengshan for his failure to mollify Eichmann for a good ten minutes. Fengshan held the phone, staring at the ceiling with the ubiquitous crown molding while the ambassador lashed out, his voice thrumming in the receiver.

Eventually, Fengshan indicated that the urgent matter for the moment was to find an apartment for the office to resume the consulate routine. "With all due respect, Ambassador, the consulate needs additional funds to rent a new office space, purchase new office equipment and furniture, and pay for the staff—"

The ambassador hung up.

I stood, worried. "What did he say?"

"The ambassador said the country was in the throes of the worst battle with the Japanese. The Ministry of Foreign Affairs is short on funds."

There would be no budget for the consulate, and Fengshan would need to pay for the new apartment from his own pocket. He had savings, but they were limited; if he rented a decent apartment in Vienna, they wouldn't last long.

In our hotel room, I took out our toiletries, my dresses and nightgowns, Fengshan's suits and shoes, and Monto's pajamas and slippers. I had not had time to pack everything I treasured, only my book, the radio—Fengshan's favorite—the gramophone, some discs, jewelry, shoes, and underwear. I had also brought baby clothing—so small and light, it could fit in the suitcase's side pockets.

It was a small hotel room. Fengshan and I slept on the bed, and Monto took the sofa without complaint.

For a few days, Fengshan went out looking for apartments to rent. But finding an apartment on short notice was a challenge. Many buildings owned by wealthy Jews had been appropriated by the Gestapo. The buildings near the Ringstrasse were outrageously expensive. There were apartments behind hotels, coffeehouses, and shops around the

Stadtpark, where Fengshan intended to rent, since it was within the close vicinity of the demolished consulate and thus easier for the applicants to find, but few rooms were large enough for an office and living quarters. The buildings south of the park had some vacant rooms, but the landlords shook their heads when they saw Fengshan. They had all heard of the demolition of the consulate, which seemed to give them the impression that they would face a potential risk if their buildings were rented to Fengshan.

Every day, people congregated outside the hotel, inquiring when the consulate would open and where the new location would be. It was May, the weather was pleasant, but they looked anxious, perspiring. The tension in Vienna was escalating and many of their relatives had been threatened and imprisoned, they said, and they'd be doomed if they stayed.

Two weeks had passed when Fengshan said a Viennese lady was willing to lease her apartment to him at a low price. The apartment, a block from the Stadtpark and the demolished consulate, was squeezed between a butcher's shop and a Laundromat where immense washing machines operated day and night. It had two rooms. Fengshan was delighted and paid the deposit immediately. He said that one room would be used as the office, the other as our living quarters.

Once again, I packed up our belongings and moved in. The building had a modest art deco front—not a grand mansion fit for a consulate—and it smelled of mildew.

Fengshan placed the cardboard sign that said *The Temporary Office of the Consulate of the Republic of China* outside the apartment and turned to me, glancing at my stomach, looking apologetic. I didn't mind.

The consulate still existed, and he would continue to issue visas to those in need; that was all that mattered.

꧁꧂

It was pleasant in the Schillerpark; the August air had the silky transparency of a veil; the rays of sunlight were mild, delicate like a silver needle. There was no lively music of an accordion, a pity, and many people and families, in their particular manner that reminded me that they were Germans, kept a distance from us—the foreigners. But Monto and I played; he ran around the fountain, and I chased him. Oh, that pleasure, to hear a child giggling, to imagine that one day I could have two children and many days of mothering them.

It had been three peaceful, fulfilling months since we moved to the new apartment. Monto and I spent each day together. He read his German books, and I read my magazines and poetry. When we were bored, we went to the park; when we were hungry, we treated ourselves with curd-cheese pancakes and Bundt cakes. In July, the canoe summer camp Fengshan had registered Monto for was canceled, so Monto whiled away his time kicking a weighted shuttlecock, a sport called *ti jianzi*, he said. I failed after one kick, but he maintained a good balance keeping the shuttlecock in the air.

Fengshan had been busy working and issuing visas, for the entire summer. For hours, he was glued to his desk, signing and stamping the visa forms, with little sleep. When he listened to the radio, he appeared anxious. Hitler had mocked the independence of European nations and vowed to attack Poland at the earliest opportunity.

In the park, I sat on the bench designated for people like Lola and thought of her. I missed her. It had been about six months since her disappearance, and I had not received any word from her. I wondered if I had been delusional. In reality, she had likely been sent to a labor camp like Mauthausen, where she would toil until her last breath, or she was perhaps already dead, murdered.

"Grace, Grace." Monto was shaking me.

"Yes." I had grown drowsy, almost falling asleep.

"A man is watching us," he whispered in my ear.

I looked around. Near a trimmed bush shaped like an egg, a man in a navy jacket smoked a cigarette. He stubbed his cigarette out with his foot and pulled his jacket aside to reveal a pistol in his holster.

I sprang to my feet. "What did he do? Did he touch you?"

"No."

"Let's go, let's go now." I took Monto's hand and rushed to the park's exit.

"Grace, he said to tell Father not to issue visas to Jews."

Eichmann's man! He had demolished the consulate, and now he was threatening us.

⚜

In our apartment, I waved at Fengshan, working at his desk. He put down his pen and walked to the bedroom with Monto and me. When he heard about the man in the park, his face turned pale, his hand gripping Monto's shoulder. "Are you all right?"

The seedy business of Eichmann had rattled Fengshan, who had never imagined that his job would pose a threat to his son's life, and we were unprotected, with Captain Heine gone—the only help we could seek was from the corrupt Viennese police, who had little sympathy for us.

"I'm fine, Father. Grace was there for me." The brave boy gave his father a cup of water to drink.

Fengshan finished it in one gulp. "This is beyond my comprehension. The newspapers said Eichmann departed in May after the consulate's demolition, reassigned to Prague, as Captain Heine had said."

Who else would want Fengshan to stop issuing visas? It had to be someone who worked for Eichmann. He had said Prague was not his choice. He must be resentful of Fengshan.

He looked pensive, pacing our bedroom. "Will you be careful?"

I glanced at Monto by the window. "Don't worry, I'll look after him."

Fengshan looked relieved and went to work. Feeling tired again, I took a long nap.

In my sleep, I thought I heard men's rough voices speaking German in Fengshan's office. It occurred to me that it was the radio broadcasting German. But then it was followed by a man's voice speaking English with a British accent: "Hitler claims that in Poland, gallows after gallows have been erected to hang the good German people, many Germans are persecuted in a bloody frenzy of terror, and innocent German blood is flowing on the streets of Warsaw. Hitler vows that as a protector of the German people, he'll take necessary steps to ensure their safety in Poland."

Germans? In Poland? It was all so confusing, and Fengshan murmured something and switched to another station: another man's voice, speaking French, followed by English again. "Breaking news. It is reported that German Foreign Affairs Minister Ribbentrop has signed a nonaggression pact with Molotov, the minister of foreign affairs of the Soviet Union. They have consented to avoid military action against each other for the next ten years. This is the second part of the pact after the two parties have agreed on economic development for both countries."

What was this rubbish? Germany and Soviet Union? I longed for some sonatas, some symphonies, or Bach played on violin. Or Lola's favorite piece. Last year, music was like the air people breathed in Vienna, and now the air was devoid of music. Was Lola listening to her favorite music?

CHAPTER 54

FENGSHAN

He had trouble sleeping ever since Eichmann's man threatened Monto in the park. For days, after work, despite his exhaustion, he lay in bed at night, his mind racing with fear. Sometimes he would go check on Monto when he slept. In the dark, sitting on the sofa, he listened to his son's soft breathing. He had been a good father, he hoped, encouraging his son to have hobbies to broaden his horizon, giving him a good education that was essential for his future, and teaching him to be a good man—that was what he valued most: a boy must become a man of good character. Monto had been mature for his age, resilient, and intelligent; all the moves, from China to Istanbul and to Vienna, had not dampened his spirits. Monto had learned to speak English and German and expressed great interest in music and math. He would have a bright future.

Had he neglected his son because of his work? Admittedly so—visa issuance had occupied his mind and soul, and he hardly had time to take a walk to free his mind. He should care for Monto more, his son, his legacy.

What if Eichmann's man hurt his son?

He could ask for more policemen, but without Captain Heine, it was doubtful that he could find reliable security from the Vienna police.

Grace had promised to protect Monto. He could count on her. She had been an absentminded girl, a dreamer, but pregnancy and the growing bond between her and Monto had turned her into a single-minded dragon mother.

The first day of September began with a great storm. Rain pummeled the rows of neoclassical buildings and blew through the apartment building's front entrance, sending the sign that said *The Temporary Office of the Consulate of the Republic of China* flying in the air and blank envelopes and sheets of forms to the floor. For the entire day, the sky turned dark like midnight, the wintry chill that used to arrive in October blasting through the hallway to his office.

In the evening, he had just put down his pen when he heard Grace switching the radio channels, from a French station to a German station and then a Czech station, searching for music. She didn't have success—all the stations were deep in discussions about something related to the military.

The Führer had decided to free the innocent Germans from the ruthless hands of the Polish, he heard, and the invincible German Wehrmacht had crossed the border.

"Stop, Grace. Turn it up."

He had heard correctly. Hitler had invaded Poland.

He rushed out of the bedroom and phoned Ambassador Chen from the office. The line was busy.

Fengshan had a difficult time concentrating on the visas for the next few days. The radio was turned on; everything he heard irritated him—the exhilarated declaration of a broadcaster speaking German, the orotund voice of a man shouting over the heavy footfalls of the marching army, the bombastic military songs—yet he couldn't keep himself from listening to it. He rubbed his eyes and switched to another channel; instantly, his ears were attacked by the threatening rumble of the tanks, the drone of the Luftwaffe, the chaotic shouts, the ridiculous chants, and the salvo of gunfire.

Britain and France had declared war on Germany, a man's voice heavy with force announced. And what would Chamberlain and Daladier do, after having fooled themselves for months? They had been overly confident in their power and ultimately outmaneuvered.

Ambassador Chen should have heard the news by now, and Fengshan prayed this would motivate the ambassador to reevaluate the situation and distance them from the Third Reich.

But perhaps the most urgent question he had was regarding the Jews in Poland, who now fell within the range of the Nazis' tanks. Where would they go?

He put down his pen and looked up. About ten people wearing bowler hats were crammed into his office; all were listening to the radio; none made a noise. Their fear, the sense of doom, was palpable.

A young, joyous voice erupted in front of him.

"I got it, I got it! Visas! Visas! I'm going to Shanghai! My family is going to Shanghai! Thank you, thank you!" It was a young man shouting, one button missing from his coat, his expression one of pure euphoria.

Fengshan was incredibly moved; he had to look away to collect himself.

"Do you honestly believe that saving Jews is a path to China's salvation?" Ambassador Chen had taunted him over the phone when he explained the consulate needed a new venue after the demolition in order to continue issuing visas to the Viennese.

He had held his tongue. His Nationalist government was still fighting in Chongqing; the sophisticated weapons they had dreamed of were still out of reach; the Japanese were still bombing Chongqing and setting fire to one town after another in China. It was clear to him that the salvation of China, his country that had battled with the Japanese for so many years, his homeland that many brave people had defended for so many years, was now in God's hands. But the salvation of the Jews, displaced, devalued, dehumanized in a world that was crushing down on them, was up to men.

No matter how fast he approved the visas, he was too slow. The pile of applications was stacked up as he pored over each one. Meticulously, he tracked the visa numbers, jotted down the date and destination in German and Chinese, and verified the applicants' information. This was not the moment for mistakes; every detail must be verified, confirmed, and copied with absolute accuracy.

The drums of the washing machines rang in his ears, his back ached from sitting for too long, and his hand grew sore from writing, but each time he raised his head, he was greeted by the eager faces of the people in front of him; he lowered his head and continued to write. He had no time to rest—these people's survival depended on him. Every visa he approved was a life saved.

And each day, devastating news continued to come through the radio.

The Soviet Union invaded Poland.

The Luftwaffe bombed Warsaw; Hitler captured Warsaw.

More than two hundred thousand Poles perished. Poland surrendered, divided by the Soviet Union and Germany, and hundreds of thousands of Polish troops became prisoners of war. And in front of his small apartment were men and women, the young and old who arrived at dawn. All day, they waited.

CHAPTER 55

GRACE

It was the man in the navy jacket who had threatened us in the park; he had appeared out of nowhere. I stopped midstep, holding a box of pastries; Monto was skipping ahead of me, walking backward, so he didn't know what was going on. We had just left the bakery with treats. Monto had selected his favorite apple strudel, and I had opted for *Topfenstrudel* and some fritters with cheese fillings. Fengshan was working in his office and said he didn't want anything—he had refused to eat pastries since the nightmarish evening when the server was thrown off the balcony.

The trip to the bakery had been a celebration, for the day before, I had felt something—a flutter inside my stomach, the drum of a new life, a most thrilling experience I thought I would never have the fortune to feel. I was ecstatic. The life inside me was growing and I would be a mother.

"Monto—" I was just about to warn him when the man in the navy jacket grabbed his shoulders.

"Get your hands off my boy!" I shouted, lunging forward, and struck the man with the box of pastries. Since the encounter in the park, I had been cautious, observing the people outside the window; every

German man in a navy jacket gave me pause. And now, my nightmare was unfolding in front of me.

The man let go of Monto, cocked his head, and, in a threatening voice, unleashed a string of German.

"Go away, go away!" I put my arms around Monto, stepped over the crumbled apple strudel, the shattered crust of *Topfenstrudel*, and hurried off. I was short and small, and with my jacket and a long skirt, I still looked slim, but my stomach was growing round, impeding my speed.

With a violent barrage of German chasing me, I walked as fast as I could, holding Monto's hand. One more turn and we would reach our apartment. I could see the visa seekers who had gathered outside the apartment and the German sign that Fengshan put out every day—*The Temporary Office of the Consulate of the Republic of China*.

The force on my back came so suddenly that I lost my footing, pitched forward, and crashed onto the cobblestones. A sharp, paralyzing pain stabbed my abdomen. My vision blurred.

"Grace! Are you all right, Grace? Grace?"

I'm fine, I wanted to say, but the pain. It was hot and vicious, shooting inside my stomach like a gun, and I sweated, soaked in a pool of stickiness. I tried to get up but couldn't, and Monto's voice, childish, innocent, flew in my ears like a bird's cry.

"Grace! Grace! Father! Father! Help, someone help!"

On the ceiling, a white sun burned; sharp rays spread, ferociously. There was a deafening silence, a black seed of venom. Then suddenly, tendrils of flames flared, then congealed and flickered.

There were wheels squeaking, glasses clinking, people smacking their lips; the radio was playing the accordion. Or was it a violin? I wished it would stop. *Let it stop, let it stop.* But it went on and on. I wanted to cover my ears but couldn't lift my hands. I dozed off again.

When I awoke, I saw Fengshan, a black shadow with a white face, slipping through the door. He quietly closed the door behind him and put his hands on the wall. For a long moment, he rested his head there, as if he had been shattered into pieces and must gather all of them before he could talk to me again.

"My love?"

"Grace. You're awake. It's so dark in here. Do you want me to open the curtain?"

His voice sounded strange, shattered, like glass. But what was he talking about? It wasn't that dark at all. And what did it matter? There was something important I wanted to know. But I was frightened.

"The baby, my love . . ."

He turned to the window.

All these years of hope, all these months of happiness.

A woman in a white gown appeared beside him. "Herr Consul General, your wife needs rest. She's agitated. She's too weak. I'll increase the dose."

Fengshan's voice, faint: "Let me speak to her about one more thing, please. It's important, Grace. Grace? Can you look at me? Can I tell you something important? I know this is devastating. You always wanted to have a child. But we'll get through this. We have Monto. He loves you. We're a family."

Poor Fengshan. After five years of marriage, he still didn't understand how much I wanted to have children. Monto was a good child, and I had grown to love him and treasure him. But one more child of ours. That was all I wanted. And now, after so many months of conceiving, hoping, dreaming, my unborn child had perished at the hands of a despicable man.

How long had Eichmann's man been targeting us, lurking outside the building to pounce on us, in order to threaten Fengshan to stop issuing visas?

Visas.

It was all because of visas. A ticket to freedom to some, a passage to the future for many, but a push on my back to me. It had taken me so long to conceive, to carry the life this far.

"Grace, Grace, what did you say?" Fengshan was asking.

"I don't know, I don't know, I don't know . . . if I get pregnant again . . . Even if I get pregnant again . . ."

He came to sit beside me, the gold cross on his necklace suspended below his chin. He closed his eyes for a moment and then said, "There is something else you need to know, and I want you to hear it from me. You had an infection, Grace. The doctor had no choice. Believe me. I didn't have a choice either; I can't lose you."

His voice was placid, his hands warm like gloves lined with fur, but my heart was chilled like a stone at the bottom of a lake.

In order to save my life, they had removed my reproductive organs, including my uterus.

Snow appeared out of nowhere, a thick curtain of white flakes, a thousand feathers from heaven, pouring down and vanishing at the edge of the windowsill outside, into the bottomless world of the unknown.

Then there was no snow, no wind, no sound. The silhouettes of the trees crept up to the pale sky like dark veins, with a wilderness of bristles and bones sprawling in the distance. So distant, desolate, and cold the void looked. One could wander in that blank space and walk forever without encountering anyone; if one screamed, the voice would perhaps fade and vanish, heard by no one.

Days came and went; darkness came and went. My eyes stung from staring at the blade of light thrust through the curtains' gap, piercing my head, an endless wheel spinning with spokes of darkness.

Sometimes I fell asleep, only to be awakened by a violent string of German from the man wearing a navy jacket, the boom of shells shot from a tank, and my own scream. Lola, poor Lola. Now I knew what she had to live through. Where was she now? Why couldn't she be here for me?

I wanted to see her, her scarred face, her steadfast green eyes. Perhaps she would hold my hand and say something, or nothing. Her presence would be enough. But maybe I was delusional. She was gone. She would never be here for me. Friendship was only a cold pall, a silver-ringed tale.

Monto, sweet Monto, came to see me every day after school.

"School has started, Grace. Did you know? Father sent me to a private school," he said, and he did his homework near my bed, munching on *Apfelstrudel*. He brought some for me, too, but I told him he could have them all. A precocious boy, he didn't say a word about the baby to avoid upsetting me.

"I've studied my own signature, Grace. Do you want to know what I'll do when I grow up? I'll be a doctor, a renowned doctor who will save many people's lives, as you said. Will you like that?"

I nodded but couldn't speak. Oh, my boy. He loved me. Children, when they were nurtured with the love of the world, would nurture the world in return. If I had to protect him again, I would. But why was this happening to me? Children were supposed to be my salvation, my redemption.

Sometimes I woke to see Fengshan sleeping in the chair near the window. His breathing was heavy, as though he were sighing in his sleep, his mouth in a sad droop. When he spoke, his voice hoarse, he talked about the visa seekers and the devastating stories of war, how the

German Luftwaffe was unbeatable, and how many people had become homeless and stateless.

He might as well have been talking about the weather in Boston. Boston. How strange I'd thought of that, as if it were a bag of candies hidden in a backyard that waited for my return. But what was there left for me? What would Mother say? *Told you so*?

"Do you still have headaches? Do you still have Tiger Balm?" he asked.

It took me a few tries to finally squeeze out these words. "Monto said I would have two children."

He sighed. "You've been through a most excruciating ordeal, Grace. Are you cold? Do you need clothes?"

"I believed him," I said.

He lowered his head. "Could I bring you anything from our apartment? Would you like to have your own nightgown?"

I turned my head to the window.

"I'll bring you the red nightgown; it's your favorite." He patted my hand.

"My love?"

"Yes?"

I wanted to take his hand and put it on my heart, but instead, my tears slid. "What have we done?"

There was a long silence. Then he said, "Get some rest, Grace."

CHAPTER 56

FENGSHAN

He walked out of Grace's room and headed straight into the untidy hallway with straggling trays and wheelchairs. The nurses and doctors in white gowns, who had rarely visited Grace since the surgery, were congregating around a radio in an office—the Soviet Union had invaded Helsinki, the capital of Finland; the Red Air Force was bombing the capital, and thousands of Red Army soldiers had stormed across the border. He hardly paused, still thinking about what Grace had said. *What have we done?* It sounded like an accusation, or a misgiving from the stalwart wife he had counted on, or, worse, a plea to turn away from the cause he had held dear to his heart.

Didn't she remember how the Nazis had destroyed Poland? Didn't she hear how many Poles were driven out of their homes? Some had fled across the border, climbed over the mountains, and managed to find him, begging for visas. He had told her all these things, and he had never imagined hearing this bitterness from Grace. Issuing life-saving visas had been their shared mission; questioning herself and what he was doing was inexcusable.

But he couldn't bring himself to chastise her. A hysterectomy would be devastating to any twenty-six-year-old expectant mother. Had he known the danger, had he known Eichmann's man was lurking behind her, he would have taken preventive measures before she left the apartment. Even with all his heart on visas, he had not thought of sacrificing her or their child. No. This was never supposed to be a sacrifice.

He had tried all he could to discover the culprit. He reported the incident to the police, but as he expected, no investigation took place. The vicious attack was brushed aside as a regrettable incident. Even though Monto had given a clear description of the attacker, he had no proof that Eichmann had sent the man.

And Eichmann, he had heard, had been promoted to be an SS *Hauptsturmführer*, the same rank held by Captain Heine before his arrest, yet another indication of the success of the self-titled genius's expulsion model for Jews, now hailed, sickeningly, as the Reich paradigm. It was said that he reported directly to Himmler. The vengeful man's retaliation and the devastating loss he had inflicted on Grace and their family were overlooked and would probably be conveniently erased.

Fengshan stepped out of the hospital. It was snowing now, the flakes of snow fighting in the gusts of wind, lashing at the windows of the closed shops, flaying the pedestrians and the swastika flags on a black Mercedes. A chill swooped on him, taking his breath away. The great velocity and the merciless violence felt like a proper punishment. The life of his unborn child had been aborted; Grace had suffered a life-changing wound.

Captain Heine, the consulate, and now their impossible losses.

What had he done?

Oh, God. Grace had the right to ask.

He arrived at his apartment building and walked into the quiet emptiness of his office. It was late; the visa seekers had left the building. He sat in his chair, stewing in a rare moment of solitude, looking at the pile of visa forms in front of him.

He reached out but withdrew his hand. For the first time in two years, he felt weak. Had he gone too far? The visas had cost his unborn child's life, his superior had not contacted him for months, and consul general though he was, he was a lone soldier, a solitary man with a pen. How long could he keep holding his pen and signing the visas?

The tolling from St. Stephen's Cathedral's bell echoed outside. He listened. The bell, he had heard, was Vienna's pride. It had been forged in 1711, weighing approximately forty-nine thousand pounds; its extraordinary material was melted from cannons left by the retreating Turkish soldiers during the second siege of Vienna in 1683. Such exceptional material had produced a notable bell that continued to toll after two hundred years, the token of Vienna's unyielding spirit.

The unique "Pummerin" sound, deep and solemn, filled the room; he prayed for a voice that would steady him and strengthen him and prayed for the child he had lost. He was a man, a father, a husband, after all, and this was a loss he grieved and must atone for. And sadly, in a world where the earth cracked open, where the countries disintegrated, where the families were torn apart, he was not the only man with grief. If he stopped now, there would be hundreds more men with broken hearts.

He leaned over the visa forms and carefully arranged them in a stack.

A man's heart was a church; its site might not be seen at the darkest hour of the frostiest night but must be fought for.

The next morning, he was working at his desk when Vice Consul Zhou handed him a slip with the Chinese characters for *love* and *peace* on it and said that a boy in line had asked to deliver this to him. A clever tactic to get his attention—Fengshan smiled and asked the boy to come in.

He was thirteen years old, wearing a wool cap, applying for his family of eight members. He had been waiting patiently outside for a week but lost hope, so he thought of this trick. His father had been sent to a camp three times, each time he was released on the visas Fengshan had issued, but now had been arrested again. The visa must be received in two days, or his father, who was too sick to walk, would be sent to a camp again. Speaking in formal German, the teenager was full of youthful gumption but had the manners of an adult.

Fengshan told him to come back tomorrow for the visas. Hardship and tragedy could rob a boy of his childhood; he knew that well, having grown up fatherless.

The next day, he gathered the visas he had approved and gave them to the vice consul to distribute. But a few minutes later, the vice consul returned with the papers.

The boy hadn't shown up.

Frowning, Fengshan put on his coat and gloves and went out of the apartment building. Under the leaden sky of December, flocks of snowflakes cartwheeled down on the empty street. There was not a single visa seeker outside.

CHAPTER 57

GRACE

On a late afternoon in December, I was discharged. The previous morning Fengshan had come to complete the paperwork, paid the fees, and helped me pack. He had also rented a wheelchair for my convenience. But after a two-hour wait on the day of discharge, it still hadn't been delivered—it seemed that with the war going on, a wheelchair was the last thing the nurses and doctors cared about. Fengshan looked at his watch and said he needed to return to the office to wrap up for the year before it would close for three weeks. He would return later to help me.

When my wheelchair arrived, Vice Consul Zhou came to assist me instead. The consul general was busy with work, he said, and wheeled me out of the hospital while I, wrapped in a blanket, held the bag filled with my gowns, toiletries, and medicine, my mind sedated with morphine.

"Could we wait for him?" This felt like abandonment—me, a mutilated woman, helpless in a wheelchair, and my husband unwilling to miss an hour of work.

"He's working, Mrs. Consul General," he said again.

"Is he so busy that he couldn't leave his desk?"

"On the contrary, he's not busy at all."

"What do you mean?"

"For some reason, the visa applicants have stopped coming. The consul general believes something disastrous is holding them back, a mass arrest or something similar. But to be sure, he wants to wait in the office so he won't miss anyone."

Outside, the wind was bone-chilling, the sky the tone of iron, and black snow piled on the side of the street. This was not the weather to venture out, or ride in a car alone, or weep in a wheelchair holding a bag of toiletries.

I held the blanket around me, hunching my back to avoid tearing the tender muscles of my stomach, and inched forward into the consulate's car, a slow, joyless movement. And when I sat in the back seat, I was exhausted, out of breath.

When the car turned toward the Stadtpark and the familiar cardboard sign of the consulate appeared, I could see the bend where I'd fallen, and I could feel the wet trickle down my thighs. My hand went to my soft stomach. But how foolish I was. My body was hollow now.

In front of the apartment building, the car stopped. There were no queues of visa seekers holding folders and briefcases, the butcher's shop was closed, and at the front step of the Laundromat, a woman, her head covered by a black cloth, was carrying a basket of laundry. With the noise of the washing machines drumming in my ears, I struggled to get out of the car and into the wheelchair; then I entered my apartment building.

Fengshan, his fountain pen in hand, was sitting at his desk. He explained that he had been ready to pick me up at the hospital, but then a man, desperate, had knocked on his car's window and thrown the application forms into the car. So he had decided to take care of them.

Nothing could stop him. Not Eichmann's intimidation, not the demolition of his consulate, not the loss of his unborn child or the mutilation of his wife.

"There you are. How are you feeling, Grace?"

"I'm still alive, for better or for worse." And he was still signing visas. The world hadn't changed, but it would never be the same.

"Look." He paced the room. "I believe people still need visas, but for some reason, they were prevented from getting close to the building. I wondered if they were intimidated, so I've been watching the street. I haven't seen anyone suspicious."

By that, I assumed that he meant the man who had attacked me. "They've ruined my life. What else do they want?"

His look was sympathetic, and his eyes grew brighter. He felt my pain, of course he did—it was our child that we had lost, but that was not enough. Why couldn't he come to help me get discharged? Did his visa application forms matter more than I did?

I wheeled to my bedroom.

Such a small room. Empty. And cold. Nothing belonged to me, the comforter, the curtains, the bed. Just as in all the places I had stayed in before. In a slow and agonizing motion that I wished never to repeat, I got out of the wheelchair and sat on the edge of the bed. To the right was the solitary bay window to the street, and to the left, a small court-yard embedded with dead nettles and ice. Outside, the snow fell, piling on the cobblestones and crumbly earth, reaching the windowsill, a sea of shadows.

It was December, the month I liked the least, the end of the year, a time of family, of friendship, of warmth.

A few days later, Fengshan sent Monto to stay with a friend of his for Christmas, so I wouldn't be burdened with caring for him during my recovery. But I would have liked to take care of him; Fengshan should have known that. But what was the point of arguing?

I was such an invalid, unable to get up for a cup of water, or go to the bathroom, or even fetch a handkerchief. A single cough racked my body; a slight push tore the severed muscles in my lower abdomen. To alleviate the pain, I was hooked on morphine.

All day, I floated in the painless void, sleepless and dreamless. When I awoke, I stared at the baby clothes I had salvaged before the building was demolished. Rose pink. Warm yellow. Powder blue. All colorful, crumpled, discarded, meaningless. Like all my efforts. Saving Lola's family, saving Lola, getting pregnant.

Yet it didn't have to be this way. In another world, I could have been a mother, I could have been the strong woman I had hoped to be, and I could have been a beloved wife and a good friend.

CHAPTER 58

FENGSHAN

The year 1940 began with a blizzard. In mid-January, on a cold morning, Fengshan went out of the apartment and staked the consulate's sign in the snow. Pulling his fur hood up with his gloved hand, he paced in front of the building, peering at the street. It had been two months; not a single visa applicant had appeared.

He scoured the news for possible clues. The newspapers printed victories of the German U-boats in Scotland and extolled the successes of the German Wehrmacht and the Luftwaffe. The radio, broadcasting endless debates and fierce criticism of the leadership in France and England, often lapsed into bitterness and recriminations. Daladier's authority was impugned, and Chamberlain's war secretary was dismissed.

No one said a word about the Jews in Vienna.

❧

Fengshan called Ambassador Chen, with whom he hadn't spoken for several months, and reported to him the current situation in Vienna. It was a short report. The American consulate had remained closed. The news from other countries had been nonexistent.

Out of abundant caution, Fengshan inquired about the Jewish policy.

The ambassador said, "I've spoken to Mr. Xu Shumo, the vice minister of the Ministry of Foreign Affairs. He has agreed that given the current situation, with Germany at war with Britain and France, it is in our best interest to stay neutral. Additionally, Shumo has ordered that we close our doors to Viennese refugees. You may discard the telegram from the Ministry."

There were few visa applicants these days, so the Ministry's new no-visa policy hardly exerted any pressure. However, the neutrality stance signaled his government's intention to break away from the aggressive Third Reich, which Fengshan deemed sensible, but he could also see a withdrawal from Greater Germany would inevitably diminish the importance of his consulate.

Fengshan requested funding for the consulate again since he had paid the rent out of his own pocket. His superior was noncommittal. The war in China appeared to be at a stalemate, he said. While the Japanese had a sophisticated air force and had seized the seaports and railroads in the east, the Nationalists' relocation to Chongqing, near the Yangtze gorges, had proved advantageous in terms of geographical location. The resistance was prolonged, and no one could predict how or when the war would end. It could take months or years.

No funding for the consulate, and the rent he'd paid wouldn't be reimbursed.

"One more thing," the ambassador said, his voice full of formality. "As part of the bureaucratic process, the Ministry of Foreign Affairs has requested an evaluation of diplomats in Greater Germany. You may start the process at your earliest convenience."

The annual evaluation included a comprehensive assessment of a diplomat's character, disposition, and capability, as well as the superior's appraisal of the subordinate's job performance; it was standard procedure, inspired by the American Foreign Service's practice. Last year, due to the capital's relocation, the Ministry of Foreign Affairs had been understaffed and decided to skip the evaluation. The annual evaluation was thought to determine a diplomat's career, but not entirely, since a diplomat's promotion also relied intricately on alliances within the Ministry of Foreign Affairs and the government. After years of service, Fengshan had learned that for a Chinese career diplomat, personal and familial connections were always the prime indicators of his career.

"As you wish, Ambassador Chen."

Fengshan put the phone back in the receiver; his stomach flip-flopped in anxiety. It was a routine process; he would assess the vice consul's job performance, providing accounts of merits and demerits. But it also meant his superior, Ambassador Chen, would evaluate him for the Ministry. He had great confidence that he would receive a high mark in many aspects; however, his implementation of the Jewish policy had caused a rift between the ambassador and him.

Fengshan predicted that the ambassador's evaluation would include a report of Counselor Ding's investigation and the rumored bribery and perhaps even a hint of his defiance, even though Fengshan had presented the telegram from the Ministry and proved there were no cases of misconduct or bribery. But how Ambassador Chen felt about his conduct was another matter.

To keep the consulate running, it was time to curtail the costs, reducing staffing to preserve the cash flow. That afternoon Fengshan spoke to Frau Maxa about the consulate's financial difficulty. Frau Maxa took it well. She didn't lapse into sentimental weeping or fly into a fit of explosive rage. In the reserved manner typical of the Viennese, she expressed her gratitude for working for the consulate and packed up.

He should speak to Rudolf, too, but his movements would be restricted without a chauffeur. He didn't know how to drive a car. So, in the end, he requested the manservant take an extended leave.

In February, a letter arrived on his desk.

It was from the Shanghai Municipal Council, the governing body of the Shanghai International Settlement. He opened it. The council indicated that the influx of penniless Austrian Jewish refugees who arrived at the city with the visas he issued was placing an enormous financial burden on the established, wealthy Jewish community in Shanghai. They requested that he enact a financial requirement on the applicants to weed out the poor. In a similar effort to stanch the flow of Jewish refugees entering Shanghai, the port had established an admission program requiring a specific fee for the refugees before they entered customs.

Fengshan threw the letter into a trash basket. The council in Shanghai didn't understand that even the wealthiest Viennese Jews were now beggars on the streets. And with the war, many displaced Jews were homeless and destitute. They were lucky to be alive.

But who cared to listen to him? He was alone, with his pen, fighting every opposition. First Ambassador Chen's order, then Eichmann's threat, and now the council. And Grace, but maybe not Grace.

Poor Grace. For the past few months, the hysterectomy surgery had robbed her of her energy, her youthfulness, and the tenuous will she had forged. The pain was so excruciating that she could only get through the day with multiple doses of morphine. After the injections, she'd slide into a pitiful stupor. She became more capricious than she used to be. At times she appeared peaceful, sitting by the window, watching the snow drift, listening to the washing machines pounding on the other side of the wall, her mind somewhere else; at other times she grew mournful, sobbing uncontrollably, and refused to get out of bed. On good days, she longed for company, lingering around the fireplace, commenting on the dreadful weather, and asking to go to the park but then changing her mind at the last minute.

She had not dressed up for months, lounging around in her red nightgown, her hair messy. She drew dark eyeliner on one eye but forgot the other. Her former self, forgetful, diffident, had returned with a vengeance.

Someone was knocking on the door. Monto, who had returned home from his friend's care, went to open it. "Father! You have a visitor. I'm going to school."

At the door, almost like an apparition that defied logic, stood a woman wearing a black corduroy coat that was too big on her, half of her face covered with a scarf. Those green eyes were startlingly bright, like a pair of gaslights.

"Miss Schnitzler!"

She was alive! He could hardly believe it. It had been nearly a year since her disappearance, and he had lost all his hope. Grace, though, had believed she was alive.

"Herr Consul General, it is such a pleasure to see you again," she said in English. Her voice was surprisingly loud. Perhaps it was because of the thrumming of the machines from the Laundromat, which had annoyed him initially but which he had grown used to.

"May I come in?"

"Of course!"

She slid in, wearing a pair of tall black galoshes and carrying with her a particular odor. And she glanced behind her as if to ensure no one was following her.

"Where have you been? Grace was so worried about you. She'll be pleased to see you. Come, take a seat." He took her to a chair near his desk.

She went to the window instead and peered out. Then she pulled the curtains across the windows. Her caution alerted him. For months, he had been watching the street piled with snow and the nearby shops, but he had not spotted the attacker in the navy jacket. He hoped that the consulate was no longer a target.

He said softly, "Are you in danger?"

"Those bloodhounds. They are everywhere." The volume of her voice didn't lower in pitch. "It took me a while to find this apartment. I went to the consulate's old building. It's a pile of rubble—*rubble!* What happened? Where's Grace?"

The machines from the Laundromat were winding down. "Eichmann demolished it. I'm glad you found us. Grace is sleeping; she just had some morphine. Something tragic happened. She's in pain. I'm sure seeing you will cheer her up."

"Pardon?"

"It's a long story. Maybe Grace will tell you herself. She's sleeping. Where have you been, Miss Schnitzler?" he asked again.

"Where's Grace? How is she?"

She was woozy with morphine, he wanted to say, but didn't; instead, he watched Miss Schnitzler, alarmed by her eccentricity. She was asking questions, but it almost seemed she was ignoring him. "You must be eager to see her. Perhaps you can wait until she awakes. But I'm warning you. Grace has been relying on morphine for a few months, and it's taken a toll on her. She made an effort to withdraw from it, but it hasn't been successful. Perhaps you could persuade her to wean off it."

Miss Schnitzler nodded but appeared preoccupied with something, leaning over to read the newspaper on the desk. She picked it up, mumbling something in German.

He studied her. Miss Schnitzler carried an air of indifference, almost akin to disinterest, even as she appeared ardent. It was contradictory and baffling. She was Grace's friend, and a good friend, whose friendship had nurtured his wife and strengthened her mind, but he didn't know her very well. "This may sound personal, but I believe Grace would like to know as well. Why did you disappear, Miss Schnitzler?"

She didn't reply, reading the newspaper, ignoring him.

"Grace said that all the people in your building disappeared. What happened to them? What have you been doing these months?"

Miss Schnitzler didn't speak until he put a hand on the newspaper. "Herr Consul General, are you still issuing visas to Jews? Is this your office?"

"It is. I haven't seen any applicants since December."

"Pardon?"

With great patience, he repeated himself.

"I heard you were recommended by many desperate Jews. Many people are talking about visas to Shanghai. How many visas do you approve every day?"

"I've lost count."

She appeared to be thoughtful. "Have you heard that Eichmann has arrested eighteen hundred Viennese men without visas and sent them to Nisko to drain a swamp?"

"Nisko?" This was not the camp Eichmann mentioned last year.

"Near the eastern Galician border. Nine hundred Jews from the protectorate of Bohemia and Moravia were sent first." She dug into her coat pocket and produced a crumpled piece of a newspaper with the headline in bold: *Under Hauptsturmführer Eichmann's command, Jews are ordered to be deported to the Nisko camp.*

That explained why no one had come to the consulate for visas.

The thrumming cycle of the machines in the Laundromat stopped temporarily; the room grew mercifully quiet, and there from their bedroom came Grace's hoarse voice, asking whom he was talking to.

"Miss Schnitzler, I think Grace is awake."

But Miss Schnitzler, standing right next to him, didn't seem to hear him, or Grace. Suddenly, he understood—it was the only explanation to her eccentricity and indifference. He gave the newspaper back and told her again that Grace was awake, and just as he thought, Miss Schnitzler appeared oblivious to his words. He gestured toward the bedroom, and finally, she turned around.

How had it happened?

Grace could use a warning; he was ready to follow Miss Schnitzler into the bedroom when the squeak of a car came outside from the street. Fengshan went to the window, pulled aside the curtain, and looked out. At the intersection where few cars and pedestrians had passed, a black Mercedes stopped, and out stepped two Gestapo officers.

His heart raced faster. The Gestapo had made routine arrests of Jews on this street last year but stopped coming, since many Jews had either fled or been arrested. They couldn't possibly come here to visit empty apartments.

CHAPTER 59
GRACE

"Grace?"

That voice. Loud and clear. A light piercing the fog of my mind. I snapped upright, struggling to rise—the dagger of pain, ever-present, seesawing in my abdomen. My recovery had been slow and painful. For two months, I could not ingest any solids, suffered spells of headaches, cramps, and constant bleeding, and remained bedridden. To ease the pain, I relied on morphine, and I had become addicted to it.

Tearing my gaze away from the bottle, I could see at the door, where only Fengshan and Monto came, a figure, shadowy, feminine, and familiar. But I could be imagining it. It had been almost a year since her disappearance. In all likelihood, Lola was gone.

She sprinted toward me, a shadow of speed and surprise, and then that face with the seam of a scar, with those placid green eyes, was beside me.

"Lola? Lola? Is that you? Oh my God. It is you. I can't believe it. Where have you been?"

She tossed away something in her hand and embraced me. Almost violently. Engulfing me with tears and groans and a firmness that almost hurt. Oh, how stiff I was, how awkward I was. I wished I had grown stronger, for every tremor from her body shook my body, the body that I was no longer in control of, but how I wanted to embrace her, to grip her with power and earnestness so she would know she had been missed. Fengshan had said she must have become a victim of the Nazis, but except during my darkest days, I had held the steadfast belief that she was alive.

"Lola! I was worried about you. What happened to you? What have you been doing?" I stammered, my voice hoarse, my throat rusty after months of disuse.

She straightened, laughing, dabbing at her eyes. "You're so thin. Your face. Your arms. So thin," she said.

Her voice. So loud. Intimidating. Confusing. Had I been in isolation for so long, sick for so long, that I was too weak to accept a human's voice? "I've been sick."

"I can't hear you, Grace."

"I don't have much strength. I can't raise my voice that much. Can you hear me now—?"

"I'm almost deaf. I lost my hearing."

"How?" I had cramps again and the awful sensation that my blood was draining from my insides. My hands trembled; I couldn't focus.

"What happened, Grace? Do you have paper and a pen? Could you write it down?"

I could certainly write it all down. How I had missed her, and how I longed for her company. I scrambled for something on the nightstand but stopped as a sharp pain stabbed my lower abdomen. Each twist of muscles, each stab of pain, was a sharp retort to my will.

Lola spun around and went out, and a moment later, she returned with a pen and a piece of writing paper. From the door, Fengshan peered at me, sighed, and went back to his room.

I held the pen. Suddenly, I didn't feel like doing anything. Writing down the incident word by word. Explaining what happened sentence by sentence. What was the point? My body had been destroyed, and my future as well. But Lola. This was for Lola. I wrote slowly. *I had a terrible accident and had a miscarriage. They removed my uterus.*

Had I told her about my dream to be a mother? I was sure I had.

"You'll recover, and you'll grow strong, Grace," she said.

I can never have children again, I wrote.

She took the pen, dipped her head and wrote, *But you're still alive. I've watched so many shot or beaten to death. Many lost their children and their families. Many Jews were driven apart and cruelly murdered.*

I let the pen slip from my grip. Was this all she could say to me? Was my loss anything less because of the losses of others? By the light coming through the windows, I saw my friend had changed after a year. Her plump face sharpened, her green eyes were huge; there was a flinty look and a steely intensity in her that belonged to those who had been caged and trapped.

"What happened last year? I went to the building in the slum, but you were gone," I asked, forgetting her hearing problem. So I wrote the words down.

"I lost the tickets you gave me. So I was ordered to get on a train to the Mauthausen camp with the others in the building. The train ran into cattle and flipped. We were rescued by Theo. Since then I've joined him to complete missions."

Who's Theo? What missions?

"Smuggling. Living on the edge of death and horror and betrayal, in and out of the country."

For almost a year, she had been saving people's lives. While I had been worried that she'd been arrested or killed.

Why did you come back now? Holding the pen, I scribbled on the paper, each word untidy, childish, squiggles of shadows. How exhausting this form of conversation was, spelling out the letters.

"I was severely injured during a mission and my hearing was impaired. I'm no longer useful. It's time to start a new life. I wanted to see you. Here's your Dickinson. I kept her with me all these months."

The book felt heavy in my hand and warm with her touch. *Do you like her poetry?*

It was an easy question, but Lola didn't pay attention. She picked up the bottle of morphine on my nightstand and mumbled something in German.

"Lola?"

She didn't answer, immersed in her silent world. Perhaps she didn't realize she was speaking German; perhaps it was no longer important for her to include me; perhaps this was all that we had come to be, creatures of aloofness, apart from others, adrift from the world.

I put down the pen, tired, my body numb from bedsores. How had it happened? All these months, I had thought of her, but somehow I wished she hadn't returned. Or had I been poisoned by morphine? I only wanted someone to commiserate with, cry with, and wipe tears with. But the person was not Lola.

She had changed, but she was still agile, still young, and she looked strong, healthy, with her baggy outfit, her boots, and her scar. She had lost her hearing during a mission, but she could still be a mother, start a family and live a blissful family life; she was unlike me, a useless, pathetic thing.

What was happening to me? Where did those unhealthy, bitter thoughts come from?

Fengshan came in. "Grace, I'm afraid Miss Schnitzler has to go. The Gestapo officers are coming."

"Gestapo?"

"It looks like they are searching for her."

He handed Lola a note, and she raced to the window, looked out, returned to Fengshan, and jotted something on the paper—she was too adroit, too swift—and he nodded. *Eichmann*—I caught the word in something she said, and Fengshan wrote something quickly down. They were debating, discussing something.

Their silent communication was not well coordinated, but they were compatible enough. Fengshan appeared urgent and Lola alert; it was like watching a silent movie.

I was thirsty. I should ask for water—Lola couldn't hear, but Fengshan would undoubtedly get it for me. Yet I didn't feel like asking. It all seemed irrelevant: quenching thirst, or asking what they were talking about, or getting away from the Gestapo, or even Lola.

"Grace, I need to go, but I'll see you again," she said at the door.

I didn't say anything. She couldn't hear anyway.

Fengshan left with her. The bedroom, once again, sank into an empty socket of dimness; the thrumming of the machines began to drone from the adjacent building, mixed with the creaking of Fengshan's office door. And then the door was shut.

There was silence, and then from somewhere came the clatter of doors and the harsh commands in German.

I looked outside. The sky looked like a damp handkerchief, and the trees were bare like bones. I needed more morphine.

CHAPTER 60

FENGSHAN

He could hear what Lola wasn't able to: the boots outside the window and the Gestapo's questions to the apartment's doorman, and he urged Lola to leave. But all she wanted to know about was Grace's accident and how it had happened. When. Who. When she saw Eichmann's name, Lola unleashed a string of curses in German and swore, "I'll kill him, I'll kill him!"

Fengshan had to be brief and forceful in order to lead her to the back door of the apartment building. Thank God she trusted him, following him out of the hallway. By the time he returned to his room, the two officers had entered the hallway, imposing a lockdown on the entire building.

They were looking for a female smuggler with a scar on her face, they declared, and they would search from door to door.

Fengshan locked the room behind him and looked out the window. The snow was storming outside, bending the thin limbs of sycamores and chestnut trees; the black Mercedes was parked near a pile of white snow. There was no sign of Miss Schnitzler in her oversized black coat. He held the cross in his hand, praying that she would be safe.

⁓

The next day, the snowstorm gathered force, turning into a blinding blizzard. The vicious wind whipped the windows; heaps of snow reached the windowsills. The fire in the fireplace wouldn't ignite; all the logs appeared to be damp. The temperature in the apartment plunged below five degrees Celsius. His feet freezing, he paced the room, wearing layers of coats. Monto's school wouldn't close, so Monto had gone to school as usual; Grace was shivering on her bed. He piled on her all the blankets they had in the apartment.

Still, not a single Viennese came to apply for visas.

If what Miss Schnitzler said was true, that many Viennese Jews, confined in camps, were unable to come to apply for visas, then he should be accustomed to resting his pen on the desk from now on. And in fact, without visa issuance, with few staff and little news to report, his consulate was playing a negligible role for his country. For the first time in his five-year career as a diplomat, he wondered if the Ministry, or the ambassador, had laid out a design he wasn't aware of. It was likely that he would be reassigned.

There was nothing else to do, so he spent his entire day reading newspapers in German and listening to the radio.

The conflicts between the countries intensified. The German newspaper declared that Germany would torpedo enemy British merchant ships they encountered on the sea; all British ships, which had aided the transfer of British soldiers, would now be regarded as warships. The British radio avowed that the government supported the merchant ships and armed them with weapons. A few radio channels also broadcast the French people's displeasure at the Daladier administration. If this continued to escalate, Fengshan predicted a revolt against the president was on the horizon. But to his disappointment, there didn't appear to be a strong voice or the emergence of a pivotal force to counter the growing power of Hitler.

The phone rang.

Fengshan put down the pair of long metal tongs he was using to stir the fire—the logs in the fireplace wouldn't ignite. In his hurry, his tongs knocked on the fender and overturned it, spilling a tray of soot and ash. Frau Maxa was the one who took care of the fire. Had she been here, she would know what the problem was. Maybe the chimney was leaking.

Fengshan answered the phone. It was Ambassador Chen, who called to inquire about the annual evaluation process.

Yes, it was ready and would be mailed soon, Fengshan replied. It was likely that the ambassador's evaluation of him was ready, too, but Fengshan held his tongue. He didn't know what conclusion Counselor Ding had reached in his investigation—if the conclusion were unfavorable, then he would earn a demerit that would tarnish his entire diplomatic career.

He wasn't an optimistic man, but he hoped that his superior, despite his personal feelings, would still give an accurate description of his job performance. After all, it was at his suggestion that his country was able to receive the twenty-five-million-dollar loan.

"I reckon you're concerned about my evaluation of your job performance, Fengshan, and I shall be frank with you. I'm drafting it at the moment. Would you care to explain your relationship with a female fugitive?"

"A female fugitive?"

Grace, in her wheelchair, appeared at the door. She looked sluggish, her long hair draping across her face, her lips purple. She had been wearing two coats, covered with two blankets, but was still cold. Slowly, inch by inch, she wheeled toward the unlit fireplace.

"A Viennese Jewess. She has a scar on her face. She smuggled two hundred Jews across the border, and the German police are searching for her," the ambassador said.

He hadn't known this.

"It was reported that she came to your apartment and had interactions with you."

As a diplomat, he knew this too well: inappropriate involvement with a woman, any acts of malfeasance, or any appearance of impropriety reflected poorly on his career and portrayed him in a negative light. And to be involved with a fugitive wanted by the Gestapo was a grave accusation indeed. His entire body tensed. "She's Grace's friend."

"May I have a word with your wife?"

"Of course." He held the phone up and beckoned Grace over. She looked puzzled, pulling the blankets tight around her, and slowly, she inched forward to the receiver. The thought that he should warn her about the grave consequences of this conversation crossed his mind.

"Greetings, Ambassador Chen," she said in English, shivering, holding the receiver with her small hand.

Their conversation was brief, and Grace responded with a terse *Yes* or *No* a few times and then hung up. "The ambassador wanted to know if you were having a relationship with Lola."

One wrong word from Grace and his reputation would be tarnished. "It's for the annual job evaluation, Grace."

"I told him that Lola was my friend."

Thank you, he wanted to say, but she was already wheeling back to their bedroom.

Did she know her friend was a fugitive? Did she know Miss Schnitzler was in danger? He didn't have a chance to ask.

Two days later, while he was again trying to start the fire in the fireplace, Miss Schnitzler returned, carrying a black bag, snow dusting her hat and coat. Her green eyes looked intense, her lips pursed. If what the ambassador said was true, he would like to help her.

"It's good to see you, Miss Schnitzler. How can I help you?" Then, realizing she couldn't hear, he jotted his question on a notebook from the desk.

Miss Schnitzler glanced at his note and walked to the fireplace, lit a match, and threw it under the logs. A spark leaped. Smoke smoldered. Expertly, she stirred with the tongs until a steady blaze of fire burned.

"Oh, this is wonderful. You started the fire!" he said.

"May I speak to Grace?" she said in her loud voice.

Of course, she'll be happy to see you. But she's asleep at the moment. Would you mind waiting for a while? he wrote.

She nodded, and then, looking around in her vigilant manner, she wrote, *May I borrow twenty reichsmarks from you? I'll pay you back one day.*

She did not need the money for a meal, he could tell. With the Gestapo searching for her, he hoped she was putting the money to good use. *Are you buying a boat ticket to Shanghai?*

Nein, she wrote. *I need some clothes.*

Fengshan fetched his wallet from the desk. Had his superior known that he was giving a Jewish fugitive money, this would certainly ensure a demerit. *The situation is quite dangerous for you. Are you planning to go to Shanghai?*

Not yet.

Then where are you going?

To the Hotel Sacher.

He frowned. All Jews had been banned from entering the hotel since the Anschluss.

Miss Schnitzler took the money and began to scribble. *He's in Vienna.*

Who?

Eichmann.

He was not aware of that. A Spanish newspaper had been talking about Eichmann's promotion in Prague and his purchase of a home for his wife, which had previously been owned by a well-known Spanish artist. It hadn't mentioned Eichmann's return to Vienna.

He's now reporting to Himmler directly. He's been given the job of eliminating the Jews in the entire protectorate.

Fengshan shivered. That was unthinkable.

She wrote, *He's staying at the Hotel Sacher with his mistress.*

It was a fashionable thing, Captain Heine had said, for elite Nazi officers to keep mistresses.

She took another piece of paper. *Room 1004.*

How do you know this?

I must go now. She put down her pen and went to their bedroom.

"I've come to say goodbye, Grace." There came her booming voice.

Grace said something, her voice sleepy, weak. Then a long silence.

Fengshan scrutinized the words in the notebook. He would like to ask how Miss Schnitzler learned so much about Eichmann and why she would go to the hotel when the Gestapo officers hunted for her. He was moving toward the bedroom when Miss Schnitzler appeared at the doorway with her bag. She raised her hand and wiped at her eyes.

Something fell out of her bag. A black object. She hastened to pick it up and stuff it back in her bag. It was smoky in the room with the fire, but he was certain what he had glimpsed: a revolver.

Before he could ask, she was at the door. "Goodbye, Herr Consul General."

The door closed behind her.

Fengshan sprang into their bedroom. "Grace! What did Miss Schnitzler tell you? What is she planning to do?"

Grace was sitting in her wheelchair, looking out the window. "She didn't tell me."

"I think she intends to mortally wound Eichmann in the hotel, Grace. She knows too much about him. And she has a revolver."

Grace leaned back in her wheelchair, the look in her eyes—devoid of interest, fear, or despair—shocking him. He remembered that she'd once had the dreamy look of a girl who had yet to grow up, as if she were lost in another world. She had outgrown it, but with the miscarriage and the surgery, she had lapsed into something more frightening, a state of carelessness, utter indifference to the people around her or even herself.

"Grace?"

"I heard you, but she won't do that. Where's Monto? I haven't seen him for a few days."

"He's at a private school, I told you. Could you write a note to her? I'll bring it to her. She must abort this insane mission. Now. Here. You write it, tell her to abort before it's too late." He handed her the notebook and a pen.

Grace took the pen, and her tiny hand, bony and pale, trembled. She had been debilitated, frail, lacking energy and clear thought, and now simply gripping a pen seemed like lifting something heavy. It fell through her grip and hit the floor.

Fengshan picked it up and put it in her hands. His wife, who had been with him for almost six years, gazed at the pen, the fountain pen that he had used to sign the visas, and those small hands disappeared under the blanket. "Where is she? Is she still here?"

"She's gone. But I'll run after her. I'll find her. She's going to the hotel."

"What's the point? She won't listen to me."

"You're friends!"

"It's freezing here. Can you try to light the fire again?"

"She's doing this for you!"

He had never lost his temper before, not in front of her, but for the first time in their marriage, he felt anger shooting in his stomach. For months he had thought he understood her pain, her loss, her trauma, and he had remained hopeful, refrained from commenting on her insouciance, her indulgence—she was young. The wound was hard for her to bear, and she would get through it, and she would heal. But how could she express such apathy about a friend? Who had he married?

"Write a note to Miss Schnitzler, Grace, I implore you. She trusts you; she'll listen to you. The hotel is full of SS officers. She'll get killed!"

CHAPTER 61

GRACE

All I could think of was the crumpled note in my hand, the note Lola had written for me, the note with those black lines, quick strokes, twisty curves, careless, ungainly, daring me to face them—*Stay strong, start anew. You can still create your legacy beyond progeny, Grace.* What was that supposed to mean? Had she ever known what I wanted? For all these months, I had thought of her, worried about her safety; had she ever thought of me?

Did she really dare to assassinate Eichmann? Eichmann deserved to die, for the man's depravity had no bottom; he would continue to plot the destruction of humans, and he wouldn't stop. But Lola had changed; she wouldn't risk her own life to avenge me. Fengshan was wrong about that.

"Don't you care about her, Grace?"

I looked at my hands. I had cared about Lola, and I still did, but maybe not as much as before. And even if I could summon all my strength to write a lengthy letter, it would not get into Lola's heart. I wished Fengshan could understand.

He looked angry, his eyes piercing. The frown, the disapproval, the disappointment, the intensity. It astounded me. We shouldn't have come to Vienna. This city was doomed; people here were doomed. I had thought that this city was just another Istanbul, but I was wrong. It was worse than Istanbul or China.

He turned on his heels and rushed to the coatrack for his coat and hat.

"Where are you going?" I wheeled out of the bedroom to his office.

"I must find Miss Schnitzler and talk her out of this before it's too late."

"You said the hotel has many SS men. They could arrest you. You're risking your own life."

"I'm a diplomat. The Nazis won't dare do me harm."

Suddenly, my head burned with fury. "You've done so much. For two years, you've been issuing visas to people in this country. You've put your life, your family, your country in danger, you have lost the consulate building, you've rented the apartment with your own money. You've lost your unborn child! Don't you think that's enough?"

"There are simply no other options."

I trembled. "What about me?"

He froze, holding his bowler hat, but didn't turn to me.

"What about your job evaluation? The ambassador had many questions about your involvement with Lola."

"She'll get killed." He put on his hat, opened the door, and walked out of the room.

The room was quiet. On his desk were stacks of blank visa forms, his pen, his seal, and several torn pages with scribbles in German. Fengshan's writing was recognizable, neat, grand, with sweeping curves; the other handwriting was hurried, with round corners, Lola's, I supposed. I wheeled to his desk, and with one single swipe, I swept them all to the floor.

I wept.

For months while I had been mourning, mired in a hazy agony, I had seen mild sorrow in his eyes—some care, some sympathy, but not grief over our unborn child, no mourning of our childless future. I had longed for a moment of tenderness, longed for company, wishing he could sit down and have some coffee with me, or perhaps spend a few hours in the park, where he would give me his assistance as I ventured to take a slow walk. But those moments never happened.

From the very beginning of our marriage, I was aware of what was in the forefront of his mind—his country, his job, not me. I had been fine with that, but I understood now—I was not in his mind at all. We had been living in the same apartment, breathing the same air, but rarely sharing the same thoughts. We had looked at each other, but we only saw a reflection of our minds.

The washing machines started to spin again, and the floor seemed to quiver, the burgundy carpet with those golden diamonds crested, a marbled, slippery tide of shadows.

Later, Vice Consul Zhou came. He looked glum, sniffling, his eyes watery. He picked up the scattered pieces of paper from the floor and glanced at me. He must have thought I was sloppy, but only those who had gone under the surgery blade knew the challenge of bending over, squishing the abdomen muscles. He collected the papers and set them on the desk, seeming bored, yawning. Then he went to the fireplace, which I had just noticed was lit.

I went to my bedroom and closed the door. I wished Monto were here. I missed his childish voice and his face. He was busy at school these days. When he was up early in the morning, I was usually deep in sleep. When he was around, I hardly had the energy or mental power to engage in conversation. A considerate boy, he trod lightly in the room to avoid disturbing me.

The phone rang, a trail of hollow alarms, annoying, persistent.

I wheeled out. Vice Consul Zhou had fallen asleep near the fireplace. The phone, in the corner near the window, was out of my reach. I turned to the other side of the desk, but Fengshan's chair was in my way. This was my life now, a constant test of frustration, as a disabled woman in a wheelchair, unable to accomplish the simple task of standing up and reaching for the phone.

Vice Consul Zhou grumbled, rubbing his eyes, and as he reached out, the phone stopped ringing.

It could be Fengshan, calling from the hotel. Had he been arrested by the Nazis? Or it could be Lola. Although, with her impaired hearing, that was unlikely. What had led Fengshan to conclude that Lola would assassinate Eichmann?

I wheeled back to my room. On the nightstand sat my Dickinson book, constant as it always was. I picked it up—I had not opened it since Lola returned it to me, and it felt heavy. Lola had said she kept the book with her all these months, but she never said whether she liked it. I turned the pages—they looked different. In the center of the page was the garden of thoughts that my poet had sprouted, but on the margin were streaks of shadows. I leaned over—the shadows were words in a minuscule script.

> *Dear Grace, my apologies for defacing your book. Can't write you letters. Hope this will do. I've been thinking of you and I want to write to you so you'll know I'm still alive. It looks like I won't be able to leave Vienna. One of the guards trampled over the boat ticket you bought for me and now I'm on a train . . .*
>
> *Dear Grace, this train reeks. People are frightened. We don't know where we're going. Some think we're going to the Mauthausen camp . . .*
>
> *Dear Grace, there's no room to stand straight, no room to rest my hands, so I'm writing this on my lap. Someone*

*behind me keeps hitting my head and apologizing. Well,
I'd like to apologize to you—I never had a chance to say
goodbye. I wish I could go back to Vienna so I could tell
you in person . . . Look—the rays of the sun are spinning
through the cracks of the windows. A golden clef, radiant,
blooming like a fruit tree. It's beautiful. Do you recall those
places I mentioned when we first met? There were so many
places I could have shown you, the Schloss Schönbrunn, the
Danube, the Wienerwald, the Eisriesenwelt cave. Vienna
is beautiful, Grace, the world is beautiful.*

There were about ten pages' worth of margins filled with Lola's
handwriting, her journey through the mossy terrain, the emerald fields,
the craggy mountains, each letter neat, all addressed to me with care
and diligence. It hit me that in the crammed train, even though she was
going to a camp, Lola had kept me in her mind and written me letters;
she had not forgotten about me.

There was a note about the train hitting a cow on the track, a note
about her rescuing people caught in a swamp, a note about her being
beaten to senselessness that had impaired her hearing, and the last note
from her:

*I can never listen to the music again, the music I
played, the music I was born to play. It was a shock. For
days, I sat on a rock near a cliff, engulfed in a terrifying
silence, and I wanted to cry. But what was crying good
for? I still had my arms, my legs, my heart, my sight, my
taste, my life, and you, Grace. I might never hear your
soft voice again, but at least I could still see you. Yes, that's
what I should do. It's been long enough. I'm coming now.
Not for the last time, of course. Between us, there should
never be THE last time.*

I'm coming, she said, despite the danger in Vienna. Time, terror, and distance had not changed her. And it dawned on me, her rage, her devastation, her anguish when she learned of my grief. Of course she knew the depth of my loss, Lola, of all people, but I had failed to see.

Oh no. She was going to assassinate Eichmann for me.

I dropped the book and called for a taxi to the hotel. It took forever to arrive, and when the apartment door opened, I wheeled out. It was March, I realized; the late afternoon sky looked bleak; the wind growled, the air a sharp claw on my naked face. I wrapped the scarf around me; it felt thin like threads, the chill drilling in my bones. Near the car, enormous and towering, I put my feet on the ground and rose. All the disused muscles in my abdomen stretched tautly and screamed, but I edged, inch by inch, to the back seat.

Lola, Lola, Lola.

CHAPTER 62

FENGSHAN

The car was of no use without Rudolf. So Fengshan walked to the hotel as fast as he could, pulling his coat around him, his nose in his thick scarf.

He was furious at Grace. He had been wrong about her. She had shared his ideals once, shared his goal once, but she had changed. Her heart was no longer with him, and she had forgotten his belief: *Fu Chang Fu Sui*—the husband sings, and the wife accompanies. The key to a healthy, balanced marriage.

What about your career? she had asked. If the ambassador heard of his potential confrontation with Eichmann, he could well expect an entry of demerit on his profile. He hoped it wouldn't get to that, but if that was what it took to save a life, then it was inevitable.

He passed jewelry stores with glittery glass windows, a fashion boutique, and a small shop selling furs and stockings, all with new shop names and fluttering swastika flags. Near the snowy slopes of a park, people were sledding, children playing on their toboggans. A child, his face red, crashed near his feet. He was about to help when the boy sprang up and spat at him. "Foreigner!" he shouted, and ran away.

Fengshan would never have dreamed of hostility from a child in Vienna three years ago. Vienna, a city of culture, decorum, and tradition, had changed.

He arrived at the Hotel Sacher, the majestic building that he had visited several times with Captain Heine and other diplomats. Snow was plowed and piled on the sidewalk, where many Mercedes and Adlers were parked, and there were no signs of turmoil inside the hotel. He showed the guard at the hotel his identification card and entered the lobby.

Miss Schnitzler was not in the lobby.

He had arrived on time.

He thought to go to the room that she had written. 1004. But the hallway was crowded with cleaning maids. He went to the lounge near the lobby to sort out his thoughts. How would Miss Schnitzler, a Jewess, banned from the hotel, approach Eichmann in this place? The moment she appeared, she would be identified, and he would like to intercept her before she got caught.

The lounge was crowded with SS officials and their female companions dressed in tasseled golden dresses, their wrists flashing gold and silver. A soft Italian overture was playing, the same type of elegant tune he had heard each time he came here. But he couldn't help thinking the hotel, with the same rich red drapery, wood paneling, and golden chandelier, looked severe and joyless, like a military club for Nazi officials.

He went to a table on the right and sat; a few officers nearby turned in his direction and smoked furiously.

Fengshan took the newspaper from the rack behind him and tried to read. Before the Anschluss, the Hotel Sacher had been a haunt for aristocrats and diplomats, but now he felt outnumbered.

"Herr Consul General."

He looked up.

That sly smile. Here he was, the murderer of a Jewish waiter, the self-proclaimed genius who designed the plan to rob the wealth of many

Jews and expel them from their homes, the enemy of his dear friend Captain Heine, the ruthless plotter of the Nisko camp, the relentless lout who had demolished his consulate and sought to destroy his career, the Nazi who had caused Grace's miscarriage and their incalculable loss.

And he was alive, standing, a blonde woman on his arm. "Herr Eichmann."

The Nazi looked decorated, with golden pins and medals of *Hauptsturmführer* on his uniform, his eyes probing, calculating; it seemed to Fengshan that he was always seeking innovative ideas to torment people.

"Such a pleasure to see you in the hotel, Herr Consul General. Are you here to meet someone?"

The man spoke with a degree of triumph, clearly remembering what he had inflicted on Grace. Miss Schnitzler was right. Eichmann was evil to the core; he deserved to die.

"A female friend?" the brute pressed.

"A good friend." It was maddening, but Fengshan managed to remain polite. He spread the newspaper in front of him, while Eichmann circled him, a cigar in his hand.

"Do I happen to know her?"

"I doubt it."

There were three SS officers decorated with medals following Eichmann in an obsequious manner. It sickened Fengshan. How fast the death-scheme peddler had ascended. He used to be one of those low-ranking men looking to climb the greasy ladder of power.

"How's your wife, Herr Consul General?"

He looked into those despicable gray eyes. "She has changed. The miscarriage has infected her heart and soul. May the criminal who caused her pain have his due."

"I've warned you, Herr Consul General, we all need friends in Vienna." He laughed and took his companion out of the lounge; his laughter, shrill, a violent jangle eclipsing the Italian overture.

Eichmann would get his due, too, but not today. Fengshan stood, left the lounge, and came into the lobby. In the corner near the marble staircase, a team of maids, wearing their white uniforms and caps, were dusting the banisters. A maid with golden hair turned, her gaze following Eichmann, laughing with his mistress, heading to the hallway.

That face with a scar.

Miss Schnitzler had disguised herself, perhaps with the money she borrowed from him, and infiltrated the hotel despite its security. This was reckless. Most reckless indeed! Fengshan picked up his pace, crossing the lobby as Miss Schnitzler, pushing a cart stacked with towels, trod steadfastly toward the hallway Eichmann and his mistress had entered. By the time Fengshan made his way to the hallway, she was knocking on a door some distance away. Room 1004.

Fengshan stopped, his heart jumping to his throat. *Don't do it,* he prayed. If she dared to shoot, even if she killed Eichmann, she would not be able to get out alive.

The door opened.

"Herr Eichmann!" That loud voice.

A shot.

Eichmann's body tumbled out and thumped to the ground in the hallway. Blood sprayed from his chest, and his mistress shrieked near the door. Lola pushed the cart aside and stepped closer to Eichmann, ready to give him another shot. But she didn't see, or hear, that the SS men from the lounge, drawing guns, were rushing into the hallway. Someone fired.

"Go, go! Get out of here!" Fengshan shouted, waving his hand, and realized that she couldn't hear him or the gunshot. He picked up his pace and dove to the hallway, but a force behind him threw him against a round table with a marble top. He lost his balance and stumbled.

But Miss Schnitzler finally saw him and the swarm of SS men surging in the hallway. She pivoted, sprinted to the other end of the hallway, turned to the right, and magically disappeared. There must be a staircase leading to the basement or the back door. She must know the layout of the hotel very well; Fengshan prayed that she had escaped.

He turned to Eichmann, surrounded by his men holding guns near room 1004. It was rather chaotic there, with the officers, hotel staff, and women in golden dresses, and in a shocking moment, the Nazi rose and stood, his hand over his bleeding shoulder.

Words could not describe Fengshan's disappointment. Miss Schnitzler had risked her life for this scoundrel.

Another gunshot came from somewhere in the hallway, startling him, but he couldn't see through the crowd.

Then the people parted around Eichmann, and Fengshan felt his knees weaken—Miss Schnitzler had appeared, clutched by two SS officers, a gun under her chin. When she came closer to Eichmann, she cursed. A fist was thrust into her stomach, and she doubled over, her golden wig falling on the floor.

"A Jew!"

The hallway boiled with profanities, threats, and curses, and Miss Schnitzler's screams—"I'll kill you, I'll kill you!"

"How dare you, you Jewish whore." Eichmann grabbed a revolver from one of his men and fired.

Blood spurted on her shoulder. She dropped to the ground.

"Stop!" Fengshan pushed through the crowd. She had lost her entire family; she had disappeared but returned; she had risked her own life in exchange for a scoundrel's.

Eichmann threw his head toward him, his eyes murderous. "Herr Consul General, do you know this woman? She tried to kill me!"

"Stop. That's enough," Fengshan said. There was a splash of blood on her scarred face, but she was pleading with him to leave her alone. But Miss Schnitzler. It was not worth it.

"This whore is trying to kill me! No, no. This is hardly enough. This will not stop. She must be eliminated, and all of her kind will be eliminated! I swear I will squeeze every single ounce of strength from their bodies and extract the last drop of blood from their veins; after that is done, I'll incinerate them, and the earth won't show a trace of their existence. I'll kill them all, all of them." He thrust his head at his minions. "Kill her."

A salvo of gunshots exploded in the hallway.

CHAPTER 63

GRACE

The sound of gunshots continued in the hotel.

I froze in the taxi, fear surging through me. That could be Lola; no, that couldn't be Lola. I willed the taxi to go faster; the hotel, a giant broken tooth, glaring, right in front of me. When the taxi stopped, I almost rolled out, threw myself into my wheelchair, and flew to the entrance lined with black Mercedes and carriages and motorcycles.

But the guard, shouting nonsensical German, thrust his rifle to my face and barred me from entering. Back and forth, back and forth, I wheeled in front of the building. Those gunshots had nothing to do with Lola. She would come out, and in her loud voice, she would cry out to me, "Grace!"

For an endless moment, the chilly Viennese air was devoid of her voice, and inside the lobby there was no violin concerto, no human voices, no gunshots, only the globes of lights, the bulbous eyes of a beast, threatening, gnawing at my heart. I saw who I was, a weakling, miles away from Fengshan, from his faith and his beliefs. And he had been right; I should have listened to him.

A pandemonium, suddenly. Armies of officers in uniforms, men in black suits and bow ties, and women in long tasseled dresses and velvet gowns swarmed behind the glass doors, surging past me. None of them was Lola.

Still, I wheeled back and forth, back and forth, craning my neck. When the tide of human bodies slowed, thinned, and then stopped, through the dizzy light behind the glass door, I saw that uniformed hotel workers were carelessly scrubbing at a trail of red, flowing from the hallway to the stairs in the lobby.

Fengshan appeared in his black overcoat, his movements slow, his head lowered, as if he were saying a prayer.

"Fengshan?"

He looked up, and for a moment it seemed he was having a hard time comprehending. Then he came to me, his face a mask of darkness. "It's cold here. Let's go back to the consulate."

"I . . . I . . . Lola . . . Did you . . ."

The look in his eyes made me wince, and I rubbed my hands on the handle of my wheelchair. He was going to tell me something, but I wished he wouldn't say it.

He said, "You're too late."

CHAPTER 64

FENGSHAN

In his dark office, he sat on the sofa, without taking off his coat or hat. It was good to be encapsulated in the space of silence, of darkness, of grief. A light, a life, had been extinguished in front of him, and he had been unable to stop it.

The phone rang. It must be Ambassador Chen.

He got up but went to the bathroom. In front of the sink, he took off his coat and hat, splashed water on his face, and stared at himself in the mirror. His nose was red, his eyes bloodshot, a red speck wedged in the corner of his eye. His face was that of a scarred old man.

The phone stopped ringing, but then it rang again. He went out and picked up the receiver. Ambassador Chen's voice burst in his ear like thunder.

"Where have you been, Fengshan?"

He was about to speak when the ambassador's voice burst again. "I've been trying to get in touch with you regarding your evaluation. But a devastating report of your involvement in an attempt to assassinate a high-ranking SS official reached my table. What on earth were you doing in the hotel?"

"Ambassador Chen, you can't honestly believe—"

"What else do you expect me to believe when the secretary of the Ministry of Foreign Affairs in Berlin called me up! It's a disgrace, Fengshan! I thought better of you. You've jeopardized the reputation of your country, and you've greatly damaged the friendship between our two countries! You've willfully disregarded my order and obstinately enforced a dated instruction from the Ministry of Foreign Affairs. I've tolerated your behavior this far. And I strove to be objective with regard to your great contribution to the twenty-five-million-dollar loan. But assassinating a high-ranking SS official?"

"Ambassador—".

"The evaluation of your job performance has been completed, and I'll submit it to the Ministry of Foreign Affairs for review. In light of the recent event, I've also had a serious discussion with the Ministry."

He swore, despite the formality of the ambassador's tone, that there was a hint of relief in his voice. It was all too evident what the discussion entailed. He must pay the price for defying the ambassador's order.

"I'd like to inform you that the Ministry of Foreign Affairs and I have reached an agreement that with your talent and skill, you'll prove to be a great asset at home. I've requested you return home in May."

Return home, a term all diplomats dreaded to hear, was a euphemism for discharge.

CHAPTER 65

GRACE

The night was a blur, the bedroom a shadow in guttering light. For hours I didn't know what to do, sitting in the wheelchair, stiff, drowsy with morphine. When I managed to keep my eyes open, I tried to read Lola's letters in my poetry book. But all I could see were musical notes and words like leaves, golden like autumn, flying around me.

Lola was truly gone now. Never would she reappear out of thin air to speak in her thunderous voice; never would she ask me to write something down. Had I listened to Fengshan, would she still be alive?

How was it decided—who must live, who must die?

I wondered what had gone through her mind when she envisioned killing Eichmann. I wondered what her thoughts were when she had the evil man within her reach—rage, fear, peace, or triumph? There had been a chance for me to understand her, to prevent that moment. Instead, all I could do now was imagine, through the wall of life and death.

I imagined the days when we first met: her pride at being part of Vienna, her belief in her people, her fight for her family; I imagined her decisions of not letting her tears roll, fighting for her brother's freedom, for Eva's life; I imagined how she became the name of suffering, of loss, of injustice, of silence. Lola—the sound of vivacity, the voice of life that we aspired to live by.

Stay strong, start anew. You can still create your legacy beyond progeny, Grace.

I wheeled to the nightstand and held my poetry book. Did I understand? I could try.

I stopped taking morphine the next day.

I made an effort to stand up and walk. I nearly fell, nearly injured myself. So weak I was. It didn't matter. I would keep trying.

I would start anew. For Lola and myself.

CHAPTER 66

FENGSHAN

He started the transfer of the consulate to Vice Consul Zhou, now the consul-general-in-waiting, the next day. He gave detailed instructions regarding the protocol, the businesses, and the handful of Chinese citizens left in Greater Germany and their professions, and, finally, handed over the consulate's seal that was essential to the visas. In a tone that he hoped was indifferent, he asked Zhou if he had thoughts about the immigration policy for the Jews.

"It is up to the ambassador," Vice Consul Zhou replied.

Ambassador Chen had gotten what he wished, an obedient subordinate who would carry out his orders. As for the Jews who were still desperate to flee—if they were still coming—there was nothing he could do now.

Five days later, he completed the transfer process, loaded all his belongings and Grace's and Monto's in a taxi, and moved out of the apartment.

In the garden of the Hotel Imperial, he took a walk with Grace and Monto. His diplomat's term would end in May, and he had a month to leave Vienna. It was time to plan for his future. The return-home order was just as it sounded, returning without official assignments or being appointed to a post. He could return to his hometown, where his family home had been bombed by the Japanese and which was now under Japanese occupation, or he could return to his government, hiding in the hinterland, and hope for another job.

"I don't want to go to China," Grace said from her wheelchair.

She was gazing at a blackbird flitting on the bare horse chestnut tree. The sunlight showered on her face, a blanket draping over her shoulder. She seemed to be drifting in her own world again, but her eyes were etched with the edge of clarity. It seemed that she was looking at something at the end of the street, a sight at the furthest distance.

"Where would you like to go, Grace?"

"Is it up to me?"

He smiled wryly. Since when did she speak to him in that tone? "Your decision. Wherever you decide to go, we'll go. We'll start a new life."

But where else could he start his career, if not in China?

Her eyes flickered. "I'd love to go home."

He couldn't blame her; if China was a compass in his heart, then America was hers. He should take her home; he owed her that, after years of relocating for his career. Now that his career had ended, it was her turn to choose where they'd live. The United States was reachable with his diplomatic status, though that would expire soon. "We'll go to the US."

The next morning, he purchased three boat tickets to the US with a departure date of May 10. They would embark on a liner from the Italian seaport of Trieste and sail to New York. He also sent a telegram to a friend in China, Mr. Wang Pengsheng, the director of the Institute of International Relations of the National Military Commission, indicating his travel to the US—his friends, he was certain, had heard of his discharge by now.

⚜

Two days before their departure, he received a telegram from his friend, Mr. Wang, asking him to write reports about President Roosevelt when he arrived there. A minor assignment, with a paltry compensation, nothing like an official post with salary and dignity. Fengshan gladly took it. This would keep him occupied while Grace recuperated.

The day of his departure arrived. On the radio, a British announcer said in a sober voice that Prime Minister Chamberlain had been replaced by Winston Churchill, a pugnacious politician. The tide of the war, it seemed, had taken another turn.

Fengshan turned off the radio and went downstairs to pay the hotel fees, and then the three of them, Grace, Monto, and himself, took a taxi to the train station.

In the car, he turned to the window. Outside, the grand art deco buildings, the Baroque apartments, the stately monuments, the cathedrals, the theaters, the coffeehouses, the palaces, and the parks passed by, all looking so real yet like a dream. For three years, he had lived in Vienna. He was familiar with the buildings, had studied their architecture and their history, and admired them. He loved Vienna, but he loved its people the most, their refined manners, their keen interest in culture, their delightful conversations, and their heart-throbbing music. With the Viennese, he had drunk coffee at coffeehouses, danced the waltz in chambers, and attended balls in palaces. Sadly, the era of Austria that he had admired was the past, and the people he had conversed with were either dead or gone, Mr. Rosenburg, Captain Heine, Miss Schnitzler, whom he barely knew, and other fine men, audacious women, the very people a country should feel pride in.

For them and many people who had been born here, grown up with its language, its culture, its customs, and its history, this city had been a cruel execution ground, a quagmire of death; they had been persecuted by a country they called home, had loved a country that denounced them, and had been driven to death by the people they called country-men. Their faces, their names, and their struggles would fade into the unknown. The grand buildings, their former residences, now the homes of the persecutors, would not bear a trace of their blood or tears.

What was a country without its people?

It would merely be a landmark on a map without a heart and a soul.

How many visas had he issued? How many people found new lives with those visas? He would never know. His only regret was that he could no longer help them.

The Vienna train station appeared in the twilight, the brass signs, the poles with gaslights, and the platform full of people holding suit-cases. He couldn't help thinking that when he had stepped out of the sta-tion three years ago, greeted by the grand buildings on the Ringstrasse, the teeming cars, and the well-dressed pedestrians, his chest had swelled with optimism and confidence—this city would be the springboard for his diplomatic career. But he had been mistaken. Vienna was a trap for the honorable men and women in this city; it was a trap for him too. He had arrived at Vienna as a rising diplomat with a promising career, and now he was leaving Vienna as a disgraced official. Like the very people he had tried to protect, he was driven out, jobless, and denounced by his own country.

CHAPTER 67

GRACE

Finally, the train began to move, the floor quivering. I held on to the table's edge and looked out the window. When I had first arrived in Vienna, I had been fearful and lonely; now, looking at the shadowy platform in the night's darkness, the desultory figures of the passengers, and the solemn-faced men in uniforms, I still felt lonely but no longer fearful.

I had seen off Eva at this exact spot in the winter of 1938, and now Eva was out of my reach. Poor Lola never made it to this platform, but she would still be with me. Her words, at least. She was part of my Dickinson book now, safely tucked in the bottom of my suitcase, and she would be with me wherever I went.

On the train, Fengshan was deep in his thoughts. He would talk to me when he felt like it—his style, which I had grown accustomed to. And when he did decide to talk to me, I wondered if he would lash out at me. For my refusal to stop my friend. For my ineptitude. I would have welcomed it, but knowing him, there would be only silence, disappointment, bubbling and distant.

But who wouldn't say that the disappointment wasn't mutual?

We arrived in Trieste in the early morning and embarked on the ship, *Saturnia*, in the late afternoon. On the distant horizon, the

Mediterranean sun shed brilliant strands of gold, the air fresh with the scent of the sea, and the water a pristine shade of blue. Had Lola been able to leave for Shanghai, she would have seen this sight.

On the ship crowded with many Americans going home, Monto was excited, asking about this and that, and Fengshan had answers for everything; I had none. Once again, I was the irrelevant parent, a stepmother, but Monto was happy; that was all that mattered.

The cabin was small, and there was limited access for people in wheelchairs. So for a good amount of time during the day, I stayed inside the cabin with a porthole the size of my hand, learning the sway of the boat, avoiding the risk of falling and tearing my muscles. Fengshan and Monto took daily walks on the deck, where they mused, read, and played.

When we stopped at the ports, we went sightseeing. Greece, Naples, Genoa and Gibraltar, and then Portugal. Always a father intent on education, Fengshan took the opportunity to teach Monto about everything, the volcano Mount Vesuvius, the Gibraltar sea lane under the watch of the British warships, and Lisbon with terraces and hills just like the Nationalist capital Chongqing.

Fengshan was polite to me, sometimes pushing my wheelchair on the gangway and assisting me with sitting in a chair at dinner. Other than that, we talked about the food on the liner, the heat in the cabin, and the spiffy Chinese man who was engaged to an heiress of the du Pont family and awaiting a visa to the US.

We didn't talk about the last argument we had; we never talked about Lola.

༺ஐ༻

We landed in New York on a quiet, foggy morning. It had been almost six years since I left my home country; everything, the one and only Statue of Liberty, the towering skyscrapers, the Pepsi-Cola sign in neon light, and even the giant toothpaste on the billboard, was a sight of pleasure. New York, America. English. Home.

I wheeled down the gangway, beaming at Monto, pointing at the skyscrapers here and there. I did not need to look at Fengshan to know how he felt. He had appeared to be in a somber mood since we'd docked, frowning. Before our disembarkation, he had heard the war in Europe had taken another turn. It seemed that France had been fighting with Germany when we left Vienna, and by our arrival, Paris had been lost to the Nazis.

At the pier, Fengshan complained about the mist and the bleak weather and the loud traffic noise in New York, but, capable as he was, and strategic, he booked a room at the Hotel Victoria in Brooklyn and went to rent an apartment. When he found an apartment with a *For Rent* sign, he called to express his interest. But when he went to put down the deposit the next day, the landlord rejected him on the grounds that colored people couldn't be his tenants. Fengshan was stunned— this was the first time he had encountered racism. This encounter was repeated until he met a custodian who had visited Hong Kong and Shanghai and believed that he, a Chinese, was not a man of color and agreed to lease to him. The rent was expensive, sixty dollars a month for a one-bedroom apartment; for my convenience, Fengshan asked for the ground floor. We moved in the next day.

It felt like we were in Vienna again with the moving and packing, except I was happier, and Fengshan was disinterested. What mattered now, he said, was that I would regain my health.

Always concerned about education, Fengshan enrolled Monto in a public school in the neighborhood near the apartment, and then Fengshan spent his days in the library researching whether President Roosevelt would join the war in Europe—his topic. As he had agreed with his friend, he would write a report about the president and the public opinion in the US every two weeks. So each day, he perused the newspapers and listened to the radio. He was to be financed by his friend's institute, which would be our only income. His salary as a diplomat had ended in May.

Brooklyn, with many redbrick buildings, felt different from Vienna. There were no policemen in Nazi uniforms or street signs in long, indiscernible German. Each morning, listening to the chatter from the neighbors' radios, all in easy, familiar English, I freed myself of my wheelchair, held on to the wall, and took small steps.

The day I edged away from the bedroom, entered the small kitchen, and reached for the door's handle was the first day of July in 1940. I opened the door and gazed at a wooden fence on top of which sat a pot of colorful zinnias in an explosion of red, yellow, and orange, their slim stems straight toward the sun. I took a step, a small step to the street, but a giant leap in my life. *Start anew.*

CHAPTER 68

FENGSHAN

A year after his arrival in America, on a cool afternoon in May 1941, Fengshan walked out of Prospect Park, perspiring. He had just jogged in the park for hours to clear his mind. This morning he had read a telegram from his friend in China; it had indicated that the consulate of the Republic of China in Vienna had been abolished and relations between China and Germany were officially severed. And Ambassador Chen, who had so doggedly pursued ties with Germany, had been reassigned.

Out of the park, on the pavement, Fengshan stared at the busy street teeming with taxis and pedestrians. When he had heard the news that Japan had signed the Tripartite Pact with Germany and Italy in September last year, forming the Axis alliance, he had predicted the inevitable fate of the consulate in Vienna. But still, to hear of the abolition of the consulate was a shock. For three years, his Nationalist government had resisted the unrelenting Japanese assault in Chongqing, depleting the twenty-five-million-dollar loan received from the US, but he had remained hopeful that his country would reemerge on the world diplomatic stage. This sad retreat was a hopeless setback, a heartbreaking defeat, and, to him, a reminder that a chapter of his life had been forever closed.

What would happen to China's diplomatic future?

For almost a year in Brooklyn, he had thought of his country and dreamed of China. Now his analysis of whether Roosevelt would join the war in Europe had been submitted with a foregone conclusion. His work in this country was nearing completion, and he was only making ends meet with the small fees he earned by writing the biweekly reports about American history and economy for the Institute.

"Dr. Ho?"

A man's voice came from somewhere. Fengshan was not certain if he had heard right. These days, people called him Mr. Ho, rarely Dr. Ho. In and out of the public library, passing little shops with greasy glass windows, he conversed with custodians, librarians, fellow Chinese laborers, and Chinese cooks in cheap Chinese restaurants. They were all decent human beings, but he found his attention drifting elsewhere. In this borough crowded with people of different races, he was no longer a distinguished diplomat following protocol; he was just another Chinese man, approaching forty, unshaven, with a balding head, clad in his sweat-stained white shirt and a rumpled black tie with white dots, puttering around in his cloth athletic shoes.

It frightened him. That after years of studying, learning, cultivating himself to be a knowledgeable man, he would live the rest of his life like this, anonymously, unfruitfully. That he would struggle like many people in Brooklyn, as a civilian, as an impoverished immigrant, as a man who would make a living with his hands rather than his mind. That his dream to serve his country, to represent his country, was simply a dream.

"Dr. Ho!"

He turned around and gave the man walking toward him from under a ginkgo tree a good look. "Mr. Wiley!"

What a surprise to see an old friend from the past—although strictly speaking, they were only acquaintances. But still. Mr. Wiley's smile looked genuine, and God knew how the memory of the American diplomat had warmed his heart.

"I thought that was you, Dr. Ho." He was dressed in a white suit, with a pale-blue tie and a bowler. His eyes flashed behind the black-rimmed glasses, friendly, beaming with a warm glow. "How have you been? What brought you to Brooklyn?"

"Well, I was going to ask you the same thing. How wonderful to see you! Would you like to grab a drink and chat?"

Mr. Wiley looked at his watch. "I have about an hour. When did you come to America? How's Mrs. Ho?"

"Grace is doing well. I've been here for about a year. I recall you were dispatched to Latvia and Estonia. How wonderful to see you here!" They walked to a neighborhood convenience store and sat at a small iron table outside. It was not what he would have imagined as a proper place for a diplomat, but Mr. Wiley didn't seem to mind. He asked for a bottle of Coca-Cola; Fengshan ordered the same thing.

"Coca-Cola. It's my sin. I've been craving it in Latvia. Did you know there was an illegal trade in Coca-Cola in Europe? These bottles were hard to come by."

He smiled. "Of course. So what brought you to Brooklyn, Mr. Wiley?"

"Visiting family. My mission as envoy extraordinaire and minister in Estonia and Latvia has been terminated. Irena and I decided to come home to handle some family business before my next assignment."

Mr. Wiley's manner was impeccable, but, knowing his background and his enviable posts to Russia and Antwerp and then Vienna, Fengshan could tell the American was holding back on his next post. Perhaps it was an ambassadorship. Would he dare to dream of such a position? His government was embroiled in war, and its own survival was in question.

"How are affairs in Vienna, Dr. Ho?"

He didn't know. Fengshan grimaced. "Ah, I'm not sure if this has come to your attention. I was dismissed from my consul general's duty in 1940. Since then, I've been in Brooklyn for Grace. And I just heard the consulate of the Republic of China in Vienna has been abolished."

Mr. Wiley sighed. "The Department of State has also decided to suspend its involvement in Greater Germany temporarily. The American consulate in Vienna was closed last week due to the escalating tension in Europe."

He had not been aware of that. "This is truly devastating."

What was happening to the Jews in Vienna? Where did they immigrate to? Although it had been almost a year since his departure, Vienna and the fate of the persecuted Jews never left his heart. Even in the library during his research, when he encountered a mention of immigration, or an argument about the refugees in Europe, he would stop and peruse the entire article. However, with the intensifying tension in Europe, there was little news about the Viennese Jews. As far as he could tell, the German Jews were left in limbo, and those who lived in Poland, in the neighboring countries, and in warring France had receded into the unknown.

"May I inquire, Dr. Ho, where is your next post?"

He was not a sentimental man, but he almost felt tears sting his eyes. "Regretfully, I'm no longer involved in diplomacy."

Mr. Wiley put down his bottle, looking thoughtful. "It was Vienna, wasn't it?"

Of course, Mr. Wiley understood politics well. Arranging a path out of Vienna for Dr. Freud had cost Mr. Wiley the consul general job, and his own effort to issue visas to Jews had dissolved his career. They had something in common at least. Holding his Coca-Cola, Fengshan recounted his visa issuance to Jews in Vienna from 1938 to his departure, his superior's anger, and ultimately the order to send him home. He tried to sound as unflappable as he once had been in the bar in Vienna.

Mr. Wiley pushed up his glasses and gazed at the dark drink in the bottle. "You continued to issue them visas for two years after I left. How many visas did you issue?"

"Thousands."

"How did you withstand the pressure?"

"There was no other option. Each visa was a life."

"Do you have regrets, Dr. Ho?"

Fengshan thought about this. "You know this well, Mr. Wiley—as diplomats, we do what is right for our country, and as men, we do what is right to our hearts."

Mr. Wiley nodded. "Did you know Dr. Freud was euthanized a year after his arrival in England? His cancer was too painful to bear. He was eighty-three. His family let me know."

None of his visa holders would think of contacting him, understandably. Most had not met him, and few even knew how to pronounce his name. That was just as well. He had never sought friendship or recognition. He had accomplished what he wanted to accomplish and rescued the lives that he needed to rescue, and as a result, he came to Brooklyn as a civilian Chinese. There was nothing heroic about it, and therefore there was nothing more to be said and nothing more to discuss.

Mr. Wiley raised the bottle in a toast. "You're an indomitable man, Dr. Ho. It's China's loss that you're no longer advocating for its welfare. I do hope we will sit in a conference room in the future."

"I shall only wish the same. Please." He stopped Mr. Wiley as he reached for his suit pocket. Americans. They took pride in paying for their own drinks and meals, but he still believed in his Hunan hospitality—that you never allowed your friends to pay for their drinks. "It'll be my treat."

Fengshan dug into his wallet but only found seven cents. All he had left for this month's expenses. His face grew hot. He was short three cents.

Mr. Wiley put a dime on the table and patted his shoulder. "Take care, Dr. Ho."

Fengshan sat there long after Mr. Wiley left, mortified. Never had he thought this would happen to him—too broke to pay for his friend's drink. And all these months of worry and Grace's complaints about money came to haunt him. The monthly rent of sixty dollars was draining his savings, and for months he'd had nothing but his paltry income from the Institute. In two weeks, the reporting would end too, and he would need to find a job.

Another job. What would he do other than be a diplomat who fought for his country? But in Brooklyn, he could never work for his country. Brooklyn might be a haven for many immigrants and people of color, but it was not for him. He was the son of China and the warrior of China. His future lay in China—even if it was wreckage, a dangerous battleground.

In their small apartment, Fengshan sat at the dining table with a wobbly leg wedged with a stack of newspapers. Monto was still at school; it was just Grace and him.

She was washing dishes at the sink, wearing a flowery cotton dress reaching her calves. At twenty-eight, she was still beautiful and graceful, still had a body like a girl's. She had fully recovered from the hysterectomy and was now active and involved with housework and Monto's school. Frequently, she cooked Chinese dishes—sliced pork stir-fried with green onion and garlic or pork belly stewed in sugar and soy sauce; sometimes she hummed the popular tunes she heard on the TV and radio.

But life had not been as peaceful as he had hoped. They had disagreements about Monto's schooling, arguments about money, quibbles about food, and even quarrels over the choice of soap. Their relationship would have been improved, he believed, if he could make her happy in bed. So he went to bed early, put down whatever book he was reading, and turned to her when she entered the bedroom, but she turned off the lights and moved to her side. When he initiated, Grace appeared to be uncomfortable. Their moment of intimacy, of healing rapture, of spiritual union that once had captivated her and invigorated him became a confusing chore. Until finally, he stopped trying. Had the hysterectomy changed her body and affected her mood? He searched for an answer.

They were still husband and wife, though, and he would like to have her opinion.

He cleared his throat. "Grace, I ran into Mr. Wiley today."

"Who?" She set the dishes down on the counter and wiped her hands on her apron but didn't turn around.

"Consul General Wiley from Vienna, remember him?"

She nodded, her back still facing him, the red strings of her apron a tight, inscrutable knot. Since when did she turn her back on him? Since when did they turn their backs on each other?

He cleared his throat again. "I've been thinking, Grace, and this is a difficult decision, but I think I'd like to return to China."

She finally turned around, her beautiful eyes wide with dismay. "China."

It still irked him that China was like a footnote that she skipped when reading, but for him, China was his entire thesis. Writing the reports for the Institute had been an integral exercise for his patriotism, but she had shown little enthusiasm.

"Why?"

"My assignments will complete soon. There's no more work left for me to do."

"But you can find a job here. You speak three foreign languages."

"I can't work here."

"But . . ." She put her hand on the edge of the table and scratched a dot of dried ketchup stuck on the surface. "But I don't want to go to China."

His heart dropped. This was precisely the response he had predicted. She was happy, healthy, and here in America she never lost her way home. In China, she would need to start over again, learning the language, learning how to make friends, how to catch chickens and cook, just like what she had gone through years ago, and that was China before the war with Japan started. Now, with the Japanese bombers hovering in the sky, China wouldn't be a safe home for her. Asking her to go to China with him would be asking her to go to a war zone.

But her reply also confirmed the thought that had haunted him for the past year. They had come to America together, but they had gone separate ways in Brooklyn. "Then you may stay here. I'll give you half of what is left of my savings, not much, so you can have something to start your life."

Her face turned pale. "Are you divorcing me? After all these years together?"

Helplessly, he stared at her. He didn't want to part with bitterness, with acrimony, with hatred. "Grace . . ."

She stood up and went into their bedroom.

He looked around the kitchen, cleanly swept, spotless. Grace had become a capable housekeeper, sweeping, dusting, keeping the apartment tidy. The life of a housekeeper was a major departure from that of a diplomat's wife, yet she had not complained. She had cleaned, shopped, and cooked. She had been a good wife. What should he do?

"I'm sorry I lost my temper. I don't know what happened. Please forgive me." Grace appeared at the bedroom door.

He looked at her. She was crying. Oh, she had not changed, still a little girl, a capricious mind. How he had loved her, showing her off in China, in Istanbul, in Vienna.

"But . . . but . . . must we part ways? Can't we do something, my dear?"

"Of course we can." He squeezed out a smile, looking at her, searching for a clue on her face, a clue to the real, meaningful question that could have made them whole again—would she like to?

She looked at her feet.

He was choked. Seven years of marriage.

How had it fallen apart?

Vienna had something to do with it. Those days of him issuing visas, Grace's accident, the loss of their unborn child, the loss of his job, and maybe even Miss Schnitzler. Yes, her friend. Even today, he still believed that her death was preventable, had Grace tried harder. And he had told himself countless times that it was all in the past and he must forgive his wife, a young, vulnerable woman with a fragile mind. But it was difficult. It was as though a perfect silk strip of their relationship had been rent in the center, and when he looked at her, he could always detect the fissure, the emptiness, the disappointment, and the discontent.

What were her thoughts about Vienna? He had never asked her, but now it was confirmed. Vienna never left her mind.

He had never foreseen this: Vienna had upended many aspects of people's lives while he was there, and now, hundreds of miles away, years later, after the losses of everything, his unborn child, his career, the memory of Vienna had dissolved his marriage.

He stood up, put his hand on Grace's shoulder, and turned away as tears rolled down his cheeks.

CHAPTER 69

GRACE

I supposed I knew it was coming. The past year had been challenging for Fengshan as a civilian in Brooklyn. No German, no polite conversations with dignitaries, no phone calls with his superior, no visas to issue, and, worst of all, no friends. He spent most of his days in the library, researching President Roosevelt, and analyzing the country's racism, and when he came home, he checked Monto's homework; on Sundays, he went to church. He laughed less, became more reserved, and jogged often.

I had changed as well. My body had fully recovered, and I was healthy again. But strangely, the body that I was in became a shell, a burden; it no longer belonged to me. I began my menopause at twenty-seven; I no longer had menstruation, felt no sexual desire, and was repelled by the thought of intimacy. When Fengshan touched me in his way that had once melted me, I stiffened, even panicked—the discomfort, the pain. His look made me ashamed, and I had avoided him since.

Sleep also became troublesome, with unexpected hot flashes during the days and nights. Many nights I lay awake, drenched in excessive sweat, tormented by insomnia.

Did Fengshan know? He might; he might not.

We seldom talked, living in a tacit agreement of silence, and when we did talk, I was not interested in his opinions. He looked surprised at my lack of interest. And then we raised our voices a notch too high, and then we scoffed at each other unknowingly, but then knowingly. Lying in bed in the dark, listening to his breathing, I thought of those drugged, lonely days in Vienna as he buried his head in visas, so busy that he never thought to push my wheelchair or walk in the park with me. But visa issuance was not the salt on our marriage, I could see, for even before the issuance, I was that forgettable aide in his life. The husband must sing the melody and the wife must play the accompaniment, he had said, but why must it be so? Shouldn't the wife carry the melody once in a while, now and then?

If the seed of our disharmony had been sown in Vienna, then in Brooklyn, it had grown to be a giant, malignant tree.

Life was still tolerable, however, with poetry and Monto, my sweet Monto. He was the most intelligent boy in the entire school; after years of taking courses in German, he now read and studied lessons in English, and all the classes, math, science, and history, were easy for him. I packed peanut-butter-and-jelly sandwiches for him, which he grew to like, and walked him to school every day. When a bully at school taunted him about his looks and his German-accented English, I reported it to the principal. During the winter break, I took him to the movie theaters and Broadway shows. He was my American boy.

"What about Monto? Will he leave with you?" I asked, wiping my eyes.

"Of course." Fengshan was looking out the window.

I said carefully, "China is warring with the Japanese. It's not suitable for a child to grow up there. How would he receive his education?"

Fengshan was always concerned about education.

He rubbed his face, looking tormented. He had only thought of his future, not Monto's needs. He knew Monto would be much better off in bustling Brooklyn, not war-torn China.

"If he stays here with me, he'll still be able to attend school. And I'll take care of him."

"He's my son, Grace."

"But I love him too. He's only fourteen. He needs a home, a mother, and a future. In China, how can you keep him safe? Where will he go to school?"

Fengshan rubbed his face again. He knew I was right.

"Perhaps you might want to ask him? He has the right to decide."

"I'll ask him," he said.

That evening we sat at the table, Monto in the middle. He listened, looking distressed, weighing his father and China on one side and me and America and a good education on the other. In the end, Monto gave me a firm hug and said he would go to China with his father. I stood on tiptoe and kissed his forehead—he was taller than me. How fast he had grown.

A few days later, Fengshan and Monto sailed to Hong Kong, since the port of Shanghai was closed, and I waved them goodbye. After a year of seeing it coming, I still couldn't believe that our marriage had indeed ended. Maybe my reluctance to stop Lola from carrying out her mission had made Fengshan see me in a different light, or maybe his devotion to visas and his mission had made me see him in a different light—I had been so lonely and depressed after the surgery. It didn't matter anymore. We had lost the belief in each other, in marriage. It was impossible to move forward in Brooklyn.

Start anew.

I called my mother in Chicago, hoping to visit her. A man answered and said she had moved back to Boston after she'd divorced again, and he gave me her address. So I went to Boston and discovered she was in the hospital for a slipped disk. She was not a cooperative patient, complaining and yelling as she crawled on the floor under the doctor's order to strengthen her joints; she also refused the nurses' care. So I brushed her teeth, changed her bedpans, gave her a bath, and kept her company while she napped. When she was awake, she frowned at me, saying I was all skin and bones and looked like a woman in my fifties. I didn't take offense. Mother hadn't changed.

To take better care of her, I rented an apartment with the money Fengshan gave me and found a waitressing job at a café nearby. During the day, I worked; after work, I went to see Mother. Life was quiet. I took the cues of my body, grew accustomed to rising early, watched the sunrise at four o'clock in the morning, and indulged in freshly brewed coffee and fresh seafood at the market. Sometimes I chatted with the fishermen.

Boston was different from the city I remembered. It was beautiful, with the quiet brilliance of summer where the air was clear like a diamond, with alluring tall red poppies and yellow colonial buildings that stood like a revolution. I was glad I had returned.

Dickinson was still my companion, and now that Lola was part of my poet, I read Lola's messages at the margin and then Dickinson's. They calmed me. And sometimes, when thoughts infused my mind like the summer sun, I jotted them down to compose something here and there.

Sometimes I went to the library and bookstores, looking for information on Viennese Jews, Eichmann, the Nazis, and the war in Europe. There were few mentions of Jews or Eichmann, but the war in Europe was all over the papers.

When my mother was discharged, I invited her to stay with me. All day long, she talked about the pains that plagued her, the confinement after the surgery, and the cold weather that made her bones stiff. I did my best to soothe her. She still drank, and when she passed out on the sofa, I put a blanket on her. One day, she wanted to go visit my father's grave. We took a bus, me drinking a thermos of tea and her a bottle of gin. When we reached our stop, she appeared to be sleeping. But I was wrong. She had stopped breathing.

She had a simple burial, without the presence of her beloved priest or Irish clam-digger or domestic-helper friends. She left me fifteen dollars, all her hard-earned money.

I wrote a letter to Fengshan in his hometown in the Hunan province, informing him of my mother's passing—he had said to keep in touch. He never replied.

It was possible that with the Japanese controlling the majority of China, the letter never reached him. But it was also likely that keeping in touch with me was no longer in Fengshan's mind, and he didn't have the desire to remember our marriage or me.

I still thought of him, sitting at his desk, a ray of sunlight scribbling on his shoulder like a silver pen, how he had rushed to his friend on that night of shattered glass, and how he had watched the shells strike the consulate. And I knew that even though our love had been buried in the dust of Vienna, my admiration for him would always remain. He was stronger than me, indeed a man destined to carry his melody. He had been a man who was wed to an idea, to a dangerous hope, to the soul of a future for thousands of men. In the hour of a violent storm, he had held on to his idea, carrying a torch of faith, trudged on, and delivered it to those in need.

The memories. His ideals. The gift he had instilled in me.

Lola, in some ways, was just like him, a true fighter. *Start anew. You can still create your legacy beyond progeny.*

She might be gone, but she had always known what I needed.

I enrolled in the state's nursing program and started my training as a nurse; meanwhile, I began to write.

In 1948, on my thirty-fifth birthday, the year Lola would have been thirty, I published my first poem, "Vienna," in a literary journal, and for the first time, I was called a poet.

Months later, a card was delivered to me by a young nurse at the front desk at Massachusetts General Hospital, where I worked. It had a red peony printed on the front, and inside was the neat handwriting of an educated man. He proposed to meet at the Foot Bridge in the Public Garden on the coming Saturday.

He had not forgotten me.

CHAPTER 70

GRACE

When Saturday came, I took off my nurse's uniform and hat and changed into a pair of long straight pants, a red blouse, and a sweater. I walked all the way from the hospital to the park—it wasn't that far. When I came to the Public Garden, I was reminded again how much it resembled the parks in Vienna: the fountains, the neatly spruced bushes, the towering beeches and horse chestnut trees, even the statue—although this was General Washington, of course, not Emperor Franz or Beethoven.

I arrived half an hour before our meeting and stood by the Foot Bridge. The early fall air was nippy; groups of people meandered through a grove of crab apple trees; some families were riding the pedal-operated swan boats on the lagoon. On my right, two horses were plowing in a vast victory garden, harnessed by two men wearing black suits and bowler hats. Fall. The season of harvest.

Here he came, holding a bouquet of flowers, walking from the other end of the bridge. It had been seven years since we parted, and he had changed, but I would always be able to recognize him. He was handsome and energetic, with a broad forehead, perceptive eyes, and faint eyebrows, the spitting image of Fengshan.

"It's so good to see you, Grace." Monto opened his arms to hug me.

His voice had changed, too, a man's voice, deep and intense, but something, thank goodness, remained the same. "You came to Boston. I'm so surprised. When did you come to the States? I thought you were in China with your father."

For seven years, I had been sending him birthday gifts, comic books, and math workbooks—math was his favorite subject—but he had only replied once. I couldn't complain. He was only a child; he didn't have the persistence to write to me regularly.

"A few months ago. I read your poem. It was very touching. I'm honored to meet the poet."

"Vienna" had received some lukewarm comments from mainstay critics but rapturous acclaim by many readers, to my surprise. It had been reprinted by several publications overseas, and I was invited to do readings here and there in Boston. In my plain shirt and pants, I read to a small audience. Always a small audience, but that was fine. A poet, after all, was meant to be read, not to be seen.

"I'm pleased you like it. Why are you in Boston?"

"I was admitted to Harvard College." He gave me the flowers: hibiscus, roses, and asters.

"Harvard. Of course. And you'll be a doctor?"

"You remember."

"Do you still read people's signatures and predict their futures?"

He laughed—he had his father's laugh. "It was a silly game. I played it out of boredom. What else could I do, a kid, alone in the consulate? No one believed me; no one except you."

"You were knowledgeable. Why should I not believe you? How's your father?" I went to sit on a bench.

Two years after I sent him the letter notifying him of my mother's passing, Fengshan had replied to me. He explained that the mail delivery had been interrupted because of the ongoing war with Japan, and it took him two years to receive the letter I sent. He informed me that he had remarried. His new wife was Chinese, and he was a happy man.

Since then, we had kept up our sporadic correspondence. Overall, his letters had been cordial and diplomatic, with little personal information or emotion, addressing me as Miss Lee.

The latest letter I received from him brimmed with his anxiety over the escalating tension between the Nationalists and the Communists in China. A civil war, he had said, seemed inevitable, another blow to the Chinese people who had just survived the Japanese invasion.

"Father has received an assignment to Egypt as an ambassador. He sends you his regards."

"Congratulations to your father." So he was once again a diplomat, and an ambassador. I was happy for him. He was, as always, a public servant through and through, a warrior for his country, a fighter for humanity. I was glad the Vienna episode had not tarnished his reputation. The past seven years had been a long dip in his career, a waste of his talent.

"Is he coming to America by any chance?" I asked, hopeful, though I knew well Fengshan, a husband, a father, and a diplomat with a second chance, would likely avoid meeting me, which was just as well. In order for the mirror of the present to shine, the dust of old memories must be wiped off.

"I wouldn't say no. As the ambassador to Egypt, he's destined to travel across the globe."

I smiled. Monto was good to me.

"How about you, Grace?"

I knew what he wanted to know. Seven years since my divorce, I had not dated anyone. It was not for lack of men around me—there were male nurses, too, who had been working as medics in the war. But the family life, which had once been my only thought, was no longer my pursuit. Besides my love for poetry, my career as a nurse was my focus now. I injected penicillin into patients' arms and cured boys' tubercular meningitis with a giant syringe containing streptomycin. It gave me great satisfaction to see them healthy and walking again.

"Oh, I'm fine by myself. Work keeps me busy. There are many patients and war heroes who need constant care and attention. Just what I need."

"Are you happy?"

"I am."

I meant it. I had people who needed me at the hospital, and when I came home, I read poetry and listened to classical violin music on the radio. Lola, of course, was always on my mind, and sometimes, her executioner Eichmann. I had sought to find any news about him whenever I could. During the war, I had heard from the patients in the hospital about the Nazis, and after the war, many gruesome details from Europe also emerged. I had compiled the crimes committed by Eichmann.

In the summer of 1941, Eichmann announced the deportation of fifteen thousand Berlin Jews and forty-five thousand Viennese Jews to Poland; in the winter of 1941, Eichmann, newly promoted to *Sturmbannführer* for his devil's work, directed five thousand Berlin Jews, all aged between fifty to eighty, to drain the Rokitno marshes during the freezing winter, who were later joined by women and children, in a deliberate business to murder them all.

At the beginning of 1942, when the Jews were banned from leaving their countries, Eichmann was actively involved in eliminating them, arranging transportation to camps, and recruiting criminals to torture Jewish prisoners. He proposed the Final Solution for the Jews in Germany, Poland, Prague, Bohemia, and Moravia. When Himmler began the mass extermination of the Jews in gas chambers, Eichmann was responsible for arranging the arrests, driving the prisoners in cattle cars to the gas chambers. After the Jews were murdered, he was the head of the team that disposed of thousands of bodies.

Had Lola been alive, she would have tried to assassinate the mass murderer again.

I had learned, too, with great fury, that he had escaped after the war, carrying gold bullion, together with other criminal Nazi officials, and had vanished in Germany, leaving no trace. Maybe one day he would be hunted down and tried in the court of justice. When that day came, Lola's soul would be at peace.

Monto said, "I came here with an important message, Grace. Someone from London reached out to my father a few months ago. She said that she knew you and asked to get in touch with you. My father is busy with his work in Egypt, so he asked me to meet you."

"Where's she from again?"

"London."

I didn't know anyone overseas.

"I've talked to her over the phone. She flew in yesterday. I told her to come here to meet you. I hope you don't mind. Look, there she is."

Near the tall arborvitae, a young woman, about eighteen, walked toward me; she wore a green ankle-length dress and a necklace with a six-pointed silver star. Her face was plump, her eyes green.

"There you are. I've been searching for you since the war ended. Do you remember me, Tante Grace?" Her voice was familiar; her English had a sweet accent.

I dropped my flowers. Of course I remembered her, her small frame tucked close to my body as I smuggled her out of her family's apartment, her lonely figure stumbling toward the carriage, carrying a suitcase half her size, and her favorite toy, a music box that had been left behind and lost, like her aunt. She had wanted to stay, but I couldn't keep her.

"Eva," I said. *She is here! Eva—whose life Lola and I had fought for.*

Eva hugged me, her face fitting in the nook between my neck and shoulder, just as it had when she was nine years old. "I'm so happy I found you."

"Ten years, Eva! It's almost ten years, isn't it? How was life in London? How did you get through the war? Tell me. Oh, tell me. I have so many questions. Is this real? I can't believe it." I was laughing and I was crying too.

And Monto was smiling. *You'll have two children,* he had said.

AUTHOR'S NOTE

Though this story features historical events and figures, this is a work of fiction. Some names, characters, organizations, events, dates, and incidents are products of my imagination or used fictitiously.

Dr. Ho Fengshan, who rescued thousands of Jews between 1938 and 1940 by issuing them life-saving visas to China, is lauded and admired by many people worldwide. It is my honor and privilege to reimagine his life in Vienna. Any errors or failures in this novel are my own.

Dr. Ho Fengshan had a distinguished diplomatic career after Vienna. He later served as ambassador in Egypt, Mexico, and other countries, representing the Republic of China. After his retirement, he lived in San Francisco with his family. It is said that during his lifetime, he didn't speak to his family about his heroic efforts to rescue Jews in Vienna. He described his tenure in Vienna briefly in his memoir, written in Chinese, published in 1990. His heroic deeds were only discovered after his death in 1997. He was posthumously recognized with the title Righteous Among the Nations.

Grace Lee is loosely inspired by Dr. Ho's second wife, although little is known about her. The story of Grace and Lola Schnitzler is completely fictional.

ACKNOWLEDGMENTS

This book would not have been possible without the studious care and attention of my agent, Rachel Ekstrom Courage, and the entire team at Lake Union: Danielle Marshall, Melissa Valentine, Nicole Burns-Ascue, Jen Bentham, Tegan Tigani, Gabriella Dumpit, the copyeditors, the proofreader, the cover designer, and the marketing team. My profound gratitude also goes to Jodi Warshaw, who acquired this project when it was only a seed of an idea.

I'm indebted to my dear friend Andrea Peskind Katz, the founder of Great Thoughts' Great Readers, once again, for brainstorming and informing me of Dr. Ho Fengshan's story. Thank you for your suggestions and support along the way.

Thank you to "the" Mike Leibling, the wise man across the pond, for many delightful talks, counseling, and the proposal of the angel in a previous title.

Thank you to Cathie Ghorbani and Helen Lui for your warm embrace and generosity, and my deep gratitude to the diligent librarians for supplying me with all the books I requested. Among them, the memoir by Irena Wiley, last checked out in 1967! Imagine my thrill!

Boundless thanks to Timothy Hummel, for researching tirelessly the information on Dr. Ho Fengshan's family. And to Andrea Abrams, for your enthusiasm, for your steadfast support, and for introducing me to Mr. Hummel.

Many, many thanks to Maria Totniou for examining the German passages in this novel.

I'm extremely grateful to my writer friends, the gracious souls who have lifted me on my publishing journey: Dianna Rostad, Kate Quinn, Kathryn Craft, Carrie Callaghan, Pam Jenoff, Patti Callahan Henry, Kristin Harmel, Lisa Barr, Chanel Cleeton, Sally Koslow, Erica Rubock, Diana Giovinazzo Tierney; my new friends in Boston: Kimberly Hansle-Lowrance, Anjali Mitter Duva, Yelena Lembersky, Helen Fremont, Kerri Maher, Crystal King, and Jessie Chen; and all of my Tall Poppy Writer friends.

My heartfelt thanks also go to the intelligent, loving women whom I've met since the publication of my first novel: Susan Blumberg-Kason, Jocelyn Eikenburg, Sarah Johnson, and Cathie Coyne. Thank you for your support and friendship.

To my friends and family who have read all my books and will hopefully keep reading my books: Marcy, Judy, Lisa, Sue, and Gail. To my family in China: yet again, you'll need to wait for the Chinese translation.

To Rabbi Geoffery Dennis at the CKA, for your meticulous reading and support. To my friends and neighbors who have read my books and recommended them to their friends and family, thank you.

To you, reader. Thank you for reading this novel!

FURTHER READING

This is a pandemic book. I'm indebted to the following authors, whose memoirs, research, and scholarship helped me visualize Vienna and walk through the painful period of history.

Around the Globe in Twenty Years, by Irena Wiley, illustrated with drawings by the author

Broken Threads: The Destruction of the Jewish Fashion Industry in Germany and Austria, edited by Roberta S. Kremer

Diplomat Rescuers and the Story of Feng Shan Ho, produced by the Vancouver Holocaust Education Center in partnership with Visas for Life: The Righteous Diplomats and Manli Ho

Eichmann Before Jerusalem: The Unexamined Life of a Mass Murderer, by Bettina Stangneth

Holocaust and Human Behavior, published by Facing History and Ourselves

My Forty Years as a Diplomat, by Feng-Shan Ho, translated and edited by Dr. Monto Ho

The Four-Front War: The Most Daring Rescue Operation of the Century, by William R. Perl

The Green Bottle: The True Story of One Family's Journey from War-Torn Austria to the Ghettos of Shanghai, by Vivian Jeanette Kaplan

Night Games: And Other Stories and Novellas, by Arthur Schnitzler, translated by Margret Schaefer

Schindler's List, by Thomas Keneally

The Tobacconist, by Robert Seethaler, translated by Charlotte Collins

We Shall Not Forget! Memories of the Holocaust, edited by Carole Garbuny Vogel

The World Must Know: The History of the Holocaust as Told in the United States Holocaust Memorial Museum, by Michael Berenbaum

The World of Yesterday, by Stefan Zweig, translated by Anthea Bell

外交生涯四十年 *(Forty Years of a Diplomatic Career)*, by Dr. Ho Fengshan, published in Chinese

ABOUT THE AUTHOR

Weina Dai Randel is the award-winning author of *The Last Rose of Shanghai* as well as *The Moon in the Palace* and *The Empress of Bright Moon*, a historical duology about Wu Zetian, China's only female emperor. Weina is the winner of the RWA RITA Award, a National Jewish Book Award finalist, a Goodreads Choice Award semifinalist, and an RT Reviewers' Choice Award nominee. Her books have been translated into twelve languages and sold worldwide. Born in China, Weina came to the United States at twenty-four. She holds an MA in English from Texas Woman's University in Denton, Texas. Interviews with Weina have appeared on WFAA's *Good Morning Texas* and in such publications as *China Daily*, *World Literature Today*, the *Wall Street Journal*, *Huffington Post*, and *Los Angeles Review of Books*. After living in Texas for years, Weina now resides in Boston with her loving husband, two children, and a family of chipmunks in the backyard. For information, visit www.weinarandel.com.